To Gracie,
Megan, Matthew
and Emma
Come back & see us again!
love
Mary

The Escape Plan

Mary Weston
The Escape Plan

Quartet Books

First published by Quartet Books in 2001
A member of the Namara Group
27 Goodge Street
London W1P 2LD

Copyright © Mary Weston 2001

The moral right of Mary Weston to be identified as author of this work has been asserted by her in accordancewith the Copyright, Designs and Patents Act 1988

All rights reserved. No part of this book may be reproduced in any form or by any means without the prior written permission of the publisher

A catalogue entry for this book is available from the British Library

ISBN 0 7043 8154 0

Phototypeset by FiSH Books, London WC1
Printed and bound in Finland by WS Bookwell

Part One

September 1953

A concert was being held at Tripler Hospital. Major McKenna was forced to park halfway down the hill, and had to fight his way through the building. Crowds of patients and visitors were blocking the corridors and lobbies around the courtyard, pushing to get a look at the stage. Some Waikiki entertainer was giving a medley of patriotic songs the tropical treatment, backed up by steel guitars, a double bass and falsetto harmonies from the Palama Glee Club. McKenna screwed up his eyes, as if compressing facial muscles would close the channels of his ears. He was sick of Hawaiian music and even sicker of Welcome Home parties and End of War celebrations.

Eventually he gained a clear run to the main stairwell in the west wing. A new returnee, one of the last, had arrived yesterday, and this morning the medics had passed him for debriefing. He was in the ward on the top floor, Special Psychiatric, where they secured the brainwashing cases – and Lieutenant-Colonel Phyllis Randell. McKenna ran up three flights, found the entrance unlocked and unguarded, and made it to the ward desk unchallenged.

There she was, catching up on her paperwork. Lt-Col Randell was a World War Two 'vet' and probably over forty, but her gypsy eyes made frequent guest appearances in McKenna's dreams. 'Where is everyone?' he asked.

She tipped her chin so that she could regard him from underneath a wing of auburn hair and explained that the others had all snuck downstairs for the concert.

'Leaving you all on your lonesome?'

'I prefer jazz.' She sighed and stretched. 'If you're looking for the latest from Korea, he's just there.' The 'just there' she tilted her head at was a private room directly in front of the ward desk, the one you could keep an eye on. The upper half of its door was glass, reinforced with a fine wire grid.

The room was as simple as a cell: a bed, a cabinet on wheels beside it, a transom window with two vertical bars and a view over Red Hill to Pearl Harbor. An old-fashioned ceiling fan circled uneasily. The new patient was half-sitting on top of the bedclothes, tall and underfed, with a big nose and a grown-out yellow crew cut. He had kept his beard, too, as if sticking to his identity as a prisoner of war. Most of the others shaved the first chance they got, in Red Cross camps or on ship.

McKenna let himself in. The patient ignored him, apparently concentrating, staring at the wall. He was so completely absorbed in whatever it was he was thinking or doing, that the major's trained dignity gave way to a more natural shyness. He transferred his weight to his toes, leaned forward a little, cleared his throat. Then, remembering his rank and entitlement, 'Are you waiting for me to salute, lieutenant?'

Lieutenant Sterling lowered his head, spent twenty seconds disengaging himself from the state of concentration before looking up again. 'Sir?' The voice was light, Western and serious enough to acquit him of intentional insubordination.

Phyllis brought in a folding chair and set it up by the side of the bed, a friendly three feet from Sterling's right hand. McKenna pulled it a yard further back before sitting down and launching into his list of questions. The patient blinked and stared at his knees with wide eyes, as if it was overwhelming and perhaps rather offensive that he should be asked for an account of his capture.

'You don't need to go into too much detail,' McKenna said dryly. He swung his briefcase onto the foot of the bed, unlocked it and found a copy of a transcript. 'Try it this way.

Corporal Wilson told me you were captured by a party of Chinese on 26 November 1950, just south of Hyesanjin near the Yalu river. The surviving members of the platoon were eventually taken to Camp Number 13 at Changhung and interned there. Is that correct?'

'Why are you asking me if you know the answers already?'

'I take that as an assent and register the insolence.' The major made a couple of business-like notations. 'Moving right along... During the time you were held was there any attempt made to indoctrinate you or any of your men?'

He seemed to be genuinely considering this, with a thoughtful hand pressed against his mouth. The major leaned forward to reward and encourage him with a gentle prompt. Sterling hit him.

The intelligence officer had gone out. He could be seen through the glass, talking to the red-headed nurse with some energy, waving an arm. There was a lizard on the wall, in the corner above the sink. About three inches long, khaki-coloured, just slightly translucent-looking. It let out a series of resonant tongue-clicking noises, as if it was disgusted by someone's behaviour.

McKenna's anger meant no more than the lizard's. That was the way you did it, and if you did it right it worked. But it was trickier here than it had been overseas to focus on sensations rather than meanings.

The four propeller blades of the fan, moving too slowly to blur, stirred up the faintest possible stream of air. Space and light and warm air, yes, that's how it is now, but space and light and cleanness cannot be rated more highly than the dark and cold of the hole in Changhung – not if there is no subject to prefer it. And there wasn't one. There was nothing but a will to emptiness. The thing that had once been self was utterly torn up, chewed, spat out, walked into the dirt. Maybe in some sense it was still there, tied into the body, but it didn't matter, it had no voice.

A pleasurable wave of hatred for that shred washed over, like the wake of a distant powerboat lapping onto a lake shore. But that was also no more than a sensation: the pleasure and the hatred were nervous reverberations from the remains of the soul. If you pinched the lizard's tail off, it would wiggle on its own for a quarter of an hour or so.

For an hour the fan turned, making a full rotation every two seconds. For an hour the room was full of light, and the lizard scuttled around the upper walls, sometimes venturing onto the ceiling, sticking upside down on its padded fingers. He studied the crack in the plaster, a jaggy curve like the course of a river or a natural boundary. After that there was still an unknown continent to chart, as big as the ceiling, but darker and more complex: the linoleum. On the other hand, staying with what was simple often triggered floods of interior stimuli: the visions, the voices, powers of understanding other minds or strange languages or of shifting awareness outside the body. Back to the ceiling then.

The angle of light coming in through the window had changed slightly, its source sinking just enough to give it a harder, more defining quality. A faint shadow of the fan had appeared on the opposite wall, a near perfect profile, so that the movement of the blades showed up as a cloudy flicker. It was as subtle and indefinite as colour and light, but precise in time, with that rusty marching rhythm. Observing it took consciousness into its clearest state. First, as usual, a tingle between the eyes, a little swizzle of euphoria in the brain, and then a light was switched on in the universe and it was emptied of everything.

Lt-Col Randell came in before going off shift. She looked in vain for a displacement activity, something to tidy or check or click her tongue over, but there was nothing, so she pulled up the chair and gave the patient a piece of her mind. 'You're getting yourself a reputation as a bad actor.'

He regarded her peacefully.

'It's no good smiling at me! Major McKenna is the one you've got to impress. What he writes about you goes to the repatriation panel, and believe me, honey, they are your future. Your pension, your medals, your pineapple upside-down cake if you eat all your dinner. It's time to straighten up and fly right!'

It was time to start work on the linoleum.

She was there again in the morning. 'Well, don't say I didn't warn you. They're bringing in Dr Connelly. Major McKenna just phoned to say.'

'Who's Dr Connelly?'

'A bad influence.'

'Huh.'

She shook her head and went out. The linoleum was dark green, with a black and white marble effect. Along the walls and in the corners where layers of polish had built up it had turned brown; it faded through a dark pine colour to the bluish olive of the worn paths between door, sink and window. There were many scratches and dents to be studied and catalogued, but for some reason consciousness was being tugged away to a speculation about light.

Ordinary light, the stuff that came through the window, made lizards and intelligence officers visible. But the light he had seen last night revealed the emptiness of those phenomena, illuminated them out of existence. Compared to that, ordinary light was darkness, more blinding than darkness.

What if there was a higher order of light again? The heart was racing...

There were voices in the hall. McKenna came in, holding the door for Randell. Behind her, the bad influence. There was a flame and turquoise aloha shirt beneath his unbuttoned lab coat, an assault of colour after a morning spent on the fine gradations between pine green and olive. But even more disturbing was the blinding air of personal engagement that radiated from his grinning face. Dr Connelly's mission on earth was to have a good time, and he was determined to recruit you onto his project. 'Lt Sterling! At last!' He bumped past Randell and grabbed the patient's hand with a freckled paw. Then, laughing at the confused expression, 'Well, of course I know all about you, from Corporal Wilson and the others. You're my negative case!'

'This is Dr Connelly. A psychologist, not a medical doctor. He's doing research on – er – coercive persuasion for the Rushmore Foundation.'

But Sterling had latched onto what Connelly had said. There probably wasn't a better description of this empty state than 'negative case'. It was kind of unnerving, being seen with X-ray vision like that.

Connelly was short, sunburned and brown-eyed. He looked eight to ten years younger than a PhD could possibly have been, and his explanation of his theory about brainwashing compounded the impression. 'Isn't it just an intense form of social pressure? The same thing as having to be a regular guy in high school, except that instead of winning first prize for being the varsity first-string quarterback you have to be the number one progressive thinker?'

The patient shrugged. 'If he's that susceptible, your all-American boy is going to be the first to... straighten up and fly left.'

Randell shook her head. Connelly said eagerly, 'That's right. That's why I'm trying to find out what's different about the guy who does hold out against it, the negative case. Is it a technique you can teach, or a personality trait you can select for?'

There was a long pause – the major leaned forward onto the balls of his feet, intending to break in, but losing his nerve at the last minute. Finally Sterling sighed, 'The Chinese talk about having a "mind of jade" that breaks before it bends. You want to select for breaking?'

'So it's bend, or break? No other option?'

'In the long run? No. There are ways and ways of breaking, that's all.'

Dr Connelly parked a hip on the lower bedstead and looked

at the patient with his head tilted. 'Tell me your way.'

There was something about the sculptural balance of diagonals in this posture that had an inviting effect. 'It's a kind of subtractive process. Things just seeping away gradually...'

'Things, yeah, what kind of things?'

A stern look. 'The kind of things you can't know about until they're gone.'

Connelly folded his arms, as if he heard this as a challenge. 'You're not talking about the obvious things here, not patriotism or loyalty or your democratic ideals. Am I right?'

There was not exactly a nod, but a dip of the head and an allowing expression.

'Mm, it was something closer to home, these were things that had something to do with having, what, an identity, a self?'

'Things!' This was scornful, though the word had been his own. 'There aren't any things and selves! Things are just tricks of the light. Optical illusions, and when you've seen through them you can't get them back.'

'Like spitting in soup,' suggested Connelly. McKenna let out a little whimper of pain – there was a lady present – but the vulgarity won an optical illusion of a smile from the trick of the light on the bed, who topped it, 'Or virginity.'

'Does it make the pain go away?'

'You wouldn't say that if you knew.'

'Feelings, emotions, memories? All still there?'

'They're just sensations. Sensations without all the stuff that makes them matter. Pain, it's just like "pain, pain, pain, so what?" There's a reflex to avoid it, that's all.'

Randell stepped in. 'That may be so, but you can't keep avoiding things for ever. That's enough for today, doctor.' And she was herding them out – Connelly twisted to hang onto eye contact for as long as he could – and up the corridor to her office. Sterling stared at the door for several minutes, as if he couldn't understand what had been happening, and so had no chance of assimilating the fact that it had, abruptly, ended.

★

The wave of hysteria that swept the country when the pictures of brainwashed American prisoners hit the news had been a gift to the Rushmore Foundation for Applied Psychological Research. It happened just at a time when the director's connections with the state department were becoming more of a liability than a shelter. And the foundation, founded after the war to provide useful work for displaced academics, did need sheltering. It was right there in the middle of Georgetown, full of Central European intellectuals; there was certainly something perversely *non*-American about it and, likely enough, *anti*-American or downright communistical.

But Oss Pointdexter, the director, was a contriver, and he promoted the sleepy little college as the Los Alamos of the Human Brain, there in the nick of time to avert the threat of communist world domination through mind control. Of course, a charitable foundation could not afford the hardware to compete with the CIA and their experiments with robotry and chemicals, nor could they get hold of disposable foreigners, defectors or criminals for the experiments with electricity and brain surgery. But Pointdexter had a hunch that the Chinese couldn't afford these things any more than he could (the Russians maybe, but not the Chinese), and that their very own Dr Bronsky's Structural Social Analysis was going to be the key that unlocked the mystery. And lo and behold, Bronsky's study of the first returnees coming back in the 1952 'Little Switch' supported the Rushmore thesis: plenty of haranguing, social pressure, inversion of previous hierarchies and of course the simple need to survive had done for all but a die-hard 28 per cent of American prisoners.

The follow-up study (and trip to Hawaii) had been given to Bronsky's protégé as a reward for not taking up a post at Princeton. Connelly was based at Fort Shafter, under McKenna's aegis, and he had made himself useful: returnees spoke more freely to him than they would to an officer. Sometimes the major suspected he was a little too inclined to be sympathetic to his cases, to make excuses for them, but he had to admit that Connelly had got more out of Sterling than he and Randell put together.

'What do you think?' the major asked him, as the three of them assembled in the ward office after the interview.

'I'd really like to work with him. If that's OK,' he added, with a deferential glance at Lt-Col Randell.

She shrugged. 'We have to put national security before the good of the patient, so I can hardly object.'

'Whaddaya mean? Why wouldn't I be good for him?' Connelly queried.

'If you pay too much attention to his symptoms, they'll stick. We should be rewarding him for getting back to normal, not malingering.'

'Getting back to normal, or getting back to his unit? I'm never sure if it's the patient's good or the army's we're talking about in this place!'

'Hey, we don't want any of them back! Not if they're cowards, even less if they're communists,' McKenna objected.

Connelly laughed but she still wanted to argue. 'As a matter of fact I do happen to care about this individual. He's a career soldier, and there's more respect in helping him stand up and fight his problems than in encouraging him to run away.'

'Maybe he's not running away. Maybe he's just advancing in another direction.'

'Well, he's not advancing anywhere until the panel's cleared him,' the major pointed out. 'Take a week, Connelly, and see what you can do.'

Connelly left the hospital as soon as he could, spinning his rented Chevrolet swiftly down the hill and through the late afternoon downtown heat to Fort de Russy, the army's R&R foothold in Waikiki. It was too late to be worthwhile renting a surfboard, so he had a swim, then started walking the length of the beach, mentally coasting along on the unsubjective surfaces of sensation. Deep dry sand underfoot, sun and wind playing seductively on wet skin, flirting between shiver and sizzle. It was the time of day when the tourists began to realize the extent of their sunburn, when terrace bars up and down the strip started dispensing mai-tais. Connelly kept going towards Diamond Head, but it wasn't until he reached the far end, the grassy park known as Queen's Surf, that he at last began to feel he had left the tourists and the military behind. The people in the park were locals. The waves were better, too, out over the reef.

He squinted out to sea to watch the boys on the breakers. How did they get the board to turn and scoot across the face of the wave like that without losing balance? Every time Connelly tried a ski turn he just got slammed over sideways for his presumption. But these guys seemed to know what they were doing. He overheard the comments of a small gang of beach boys seated higher up on the grass. 'Eh, Leong, spark da guy. Get hot *okole* or what?'

'He OK. Too *haole*, but.'

Connelly edged his way backwards in the hope of picking up a few tips – rather a forlorn hope, given the incomprehensibility of their dialect.

'Eh, Hoku, wake up. Get hot stuff kind action on the right.'
'What? Eh? Ho, da sweet!'
'Redondo going ask him for do stick hula next.'
'Shut up, Leong.'
'Da buggah is mines.'

The critical commentary continued, although there was a lull in the sets. Connelly took the opportunity to glance back at the speakers: three of them, brown bodies, black hair. Immediately they started whooping and shouting, and Connelly's eyes shot back to the water, expecting to see the action hotting up again.

'Ah-whoop! Whoo-whoo-whoo!'
'Da cute!'
'Chee, movie star face.'
'Eh, sweetheart boy, you like good time?'

There were no waves. The surfers were all sitting astride their boards contemplating the horizon. There was absolutely nothing happening on the beach or in the sea. Slowly Connelly realized that the only possible action the beach boys could be talking about was... himself. Sweetheart boy, eh? He felt the blood go to his face. When it had cooled he turned around and smiled.

He trotted over to join them, feeling like a kid again, not sure of the rules, too terrified and too excited to do anything but keep on smiling foolishly. They lay on the stretch of grass between a big kamani tree and the beach, sunlight flickering over them as the land breeze stirred the branches. At first Connelly had taken them all for Hawaiians, but as he sat down and looked around him he realized only one was, the big guy with the lazy muscles and pure expression of a Sistine nude, the one they called Hoku. He welcomed Connelly with the air of an old Hawaiian king, authority concealed under gentleness, and introduced his courtiers. Sam Leong was a taut, sardonic person, and Robbie Redondo wore a large crucifix, an emaciated saviour setting off bare pectorals.

Leong made a brief effort to place Connelly – he one

tourist? Military? Oh, *kinda* military? They let you do it like that, just *kind of*?

'They let *me* do it like that, anyway,' Connelly said, winning a little laughter for his determination not to explain himself.

Hoku spoke quietly, and touched the back of Connelly's neck, just under the hairline. 'This one knows how to get what he wants.'

Connelly looked at him, wondering what had made him say that. Hoku went on, softly, 'Something so special going happen for us...' His voice faded into a deep breath, as if he was inhaling the scent of sandalwood. Then narrowing his eyes at the grinning Leong and Redondo, 'So just ignore these rice and these altar boys. Try come here.' Hoku manœuvred the stunned and unresistant Connelly until he was lying alongside, then obliged him to lean back against his chest. 'Eh, relax already!'

If I relax I'll faint, Connelly thought, but he shut his eyes and tried not to pant too obviously. Hoku smelled of salt: sweat with a note of fish. Resting against his chest as it rose and fell was like lying on a float in a sheltered bay. Suddenly he wanted to faint, to dissolve in the euphoria that was seeping into him. He felt a stronger, more explicit thrill when it belatedly came home to him that he was lying with another man in the middle of a public park, in broad daylight. He opened his eyes. Redondo and Leong had returned to their talent spotting, sitting up and watching the beach.

One by one the surfers began to paddle in as the sun grew weaker and the breeze cooler. Some of them passed close by, dripping, boards under arms, apparently oblivious to their embrace. 'Eh, Hoku.' 'How's it going, brother?' Connelly just couldn't get over it! Who would have expected to find this kind of openness in a cultural backwater like Honolulu? Was it like this everywhere, and if so, how had he managed to miss it? Perhaps this was just the local hotspot. He could almost imagine it was generated by the power of Hoku's personality, radiating a freedom and warmth that showed up the stylized salacity of Greenwich Village for what it was: scared, guilty, essentially Victorian.

The sun was going down beyond the reef, bronzing the water, shadowing the waves into little black crescents. When there were no male bodies to admire they lay there in untroubled silence. And then Leong began to feel the cold, jumping about and complaining. This prompted Hoku to warn Connelly about the Night Marchers, and the souls of the dead who made their way along the coast at night to the place where they left the island to cross the sea to whatever afterlife awaited.

'Let's go, eh?' suggested Redondo, fingering his crucifix. Connelly volunteered his car, and they trooped up Kalakaua Avenue to the Fort de Russy end to get it. Hoku directed Connelly across the canal and up into the mountains, to a vantage point where they could park and look down at the red lights of Iwilei and Chinatown, the torches lit on the terraces of Waikiki hotels.

Behind them, the heights were forested, dark and spooky in the twilight. They could hear the wind in the pines. 'Can we go in there?' Connelly wanted to know, and Hoku said they could. The paths were soft and bouncy, covered in the pine needles and always wide, but somehow Leong and Redondo got themselves lost. Hoku let them go, leading Connelly past the pines onto rockier paths, hedged by bamboo and guava trees. Finally they stopped in a grove scented with ginger and fern and dampness. There was a stream somewhere nearby, running over rocks.

'This is a place I wanted to show you,' Hoku announced as if he had known or at least been expecting Connelly for a long time. Maybe it was a regal courtesy, smoothing away the briefness of their acquaintance.

At five in the morning, when it was still dark, Redondo and Leong came stumbling over them, looking for Hoku to show them the way to some waterfall. It was barely light. They had to make their own trail through ohia trees smothered in passion fruit vines or trample over beds of ferns in order to keep within sight or at least hearing of the stream. Connelly thought it was bad enough in shoes, but the local boys managed it in rubber Japanese slippers. At last they came upon the regular trail, like poached mud in standing water on the flat, lethally slick up or downhill. But it led to a delightful little waterfall, just twenty feet high, plunging into a pool broad and deep enough to swim in. Here it was Connelly's turn to show off: it was 'icy' to the others, who jumped out a few minutes after they had jumped in. They stood around on boulders marvelling at his stoicism, then hopped around hugging themselves to build up some body heat.

Suddenly it was seven o'clock and they had to be reconstituted into their daytime selves: Leong to his parents' general store in Kaka'ako, Redondo to St Patrick's Cathedral for 8 a.m. mass, and Hoku to Kewalo Basin where he hoped to net a day's work on a fishing charter. 'You find us guys there, Queen's Surf, most days, pau-hana time, yeah? Goodbye, sweetheart.'

After a shower and a sleep on the couch, Connelly got out his most conservative shirt and tie and forced himself back into the form of a white-coated smartass on a government research project. There was kind of self-disgusted, nauseous feeling lurking on the edge of his awareness, not a hangover, but something like seasickness. It came from lurching too violently from one world to another and back again.

For a couple of years now there had been a truce between the official and the unofficial sides of his character, a sort of a 38th parallel. He did what was necessary to keep people looking at him in the right way, did what he wanted when nobody was looking. As a policy, it was working well. He believed himself to be psychologically healthy, for what he was, and before yesterday, would have called himself happy.

Yesterday a 'mind of jade' had captured Seoul and last night Hoku had blazed all the way up to the Yalu river, and was it going to be three more years locked in a pointless conflict before he could get back to the ante-bellum status quo?

★

He met Phyllis Randell on his way in to Special Psych. and they flirted their way down the corridors. Not knowing how much he had to compensate for, she assumed he was just trying to re-establish diplomatic relations after yesterday's argument. Her responses were so friendly Connelly was moved to squander his best line on her, and pausing in the doorway of Lt Sterling's room he gave it his all. 'I'd ask you out but I make it a principle never to date unmarried women.'

'Mamma always told me never to talk to familiar men.'

The prisoner was taking all this in, standing at the window and gazing at him. Connelly hadn't realized quite how tall he was, yesterday. The face had also been designed by someone with no embarrassment about working on a heroic scale: high-boned and roman-nosed, the crew cut overgrown but refusing to lie down, though someone had persuaded him to shave at last. Sterling stared at Connelly without speaking. Looking into his eyes was like seeing into a pale grey emotionless world: bleak dry hills and wintry skies, as if the pupils had indelibly retained the images of North Korea impressed on them for so long. It slowly dawned on Connelly that he had been staring into them and they into him for several minutes; a very long time.

'Take a seat,' said Sterling, pointing his chin at the end of the bed.

'Thanks.' Self-consciousness made him clumsy as he tried to hitch himself up backwards, and unable to balance on the cold steel tube once he was perched up there, he had to sneak a toe under the mattress to steady himself. To camouflage his awkwardness he said, 'I've been thinking about what you said yesterday. You know what it keeps reminding me of? That expression "dying unto self". I don't know if you're a religious man or not, but what do you think? That cover it?'

'Maybe.' This was accompanied by an apathetic single shoulder shrug.

'Like I noticed you very carefully don't say "I" or "me" or anything.'

'Who's there to say it?'

'Mm. But how did it happen? The obvious answer would be just snapping, breaking when it all got too much. But you said it was a gradual process. So I thought, did it go something like this: "I'm not a traitor, I absolutely refuse to betray my country or give in or compromise in any way" – being the strong-willed type that you are, or were. And therefore, any contradictory "I" that showed its head over the parapet – even if it's saying nothing more than "Ouch" – gets eradicated. So the worse it gets, the more of you that can't exist.'

'Yes,' breathed the patient. Everything had to go. He thought of certain Japanese rooms, wood grain and clean right angles, space itself the only furniture. He turned his face into the sunshine. If thine eye be single, thy body shall be full of light.

Connelly was still unbalanced by the furniture. 'So the big philosophical question *that* raises is whether that is actually more accurate than the ordinary human state? I *feel* like I have a self, but is that just an illusion?'

'Looked at your way you have a self, and it matters, and looked at from the opposite angle it's a temporary effect, and so what?'

'Try it like this. To get to your way of being a lot of stuff had to get lost. So does that mean it's a limited or damaged or – excuse me – pathological state? Or was the missing stuff so deceptive or indulgent or just plain unnecessary that without it you're actually seeing things more clearly, facing the truth more ruthlessly than the rest of us are?'

'That's a better question but the answer's still the same. Both.'

'They're logically exclusive.'

'They're not, but if you insist, *neither*.'

Sterling was leaning forward with his chin sticking out, looking like someone right up at the net in a game of tennis. Connelly suddenly realized he probably didn't look all that different, crouched up there with every muscle ready to pounce on a logical flaw. He chose to relax and laugh, disarmingly. 'Obviously I'm not going to be able to *argue* you out of this. But if it's all just a temporary effect and so what, then what's the point of winning an argument? Why are you talking to me, for Chrissake?'

'Talking to you is a cross between a pastime and a pain in the butt.'

'Thanks.'

'Hey, everyone else is a total pain in the butt.'

Not allowing himself to be mollified, Connelly hopped off the bed and made for the door. 'You want me to come back tomorrow, or is the pain in the ass outweighing the pastime?'

'Come back.'

'OK, I'll come back, if you will tell me why you want me to come back.'

Sterling swallowed and seemed to make an effort to meet his eye. He had to look down again before he could speak though. 'You remind...you're reminiscent of someone. Someone back there behind the bamboo curtain.'

'Someone who chose to stay?' asked Connelly, alive to the possibility that this someone was Sterling himself.

'No. Someone who didn't have the option to come. Political Re-education Specialist Chang Wo. One of the officers at Changhung.'

Connelly had heard of him from the other returnees. He stared at the patient, too shocked to be offended. 'I remind you of *him*? Jesus!'

Sterling gave a single-shouldered shrug. 'He was the one who also wasn't a 100 per cent pain in the ass.'

Connelly had known he must not go to Queen's Surf that evening. He had gone straight to the green little house in Fort Shafter that McKenna had organized for him and worked on his project. But a night of hot, tropically coloured dreams told him the tension between the two halves of himself was still rising. The next morning he contemplated it fatalistically, as if it was a source of grim satisfaction. 'If it gets any higher I'll crack. I'll go around staring at people with crazy Sterling eyes believing I'm an optical illusion.' Well, maybe that was the only moral way out of the impasse. What would Sterling have done in his place? Eliminate the contradiction. A very final solution. But which half of him was he supposed to eliminate? Both? Neither?

Leaving the house that morning he tried to do life without saying 'I'. This is happening. That is happening. Locking the front door is taking place. A body bounces itself down the steps and across the lawn. There is a cool cleanness in the air from the early morning rain, and the sun was trickling down in dancing streams through the big old monkey pod tree that made his little house an oasis of coolness. The Hoku-shaped curves of the ground and the slouching tropical vegetation resisted the army's best efforts to regiment the streets and houses on the base, though a mynah bird was marching around like a sergeant-major, bawling out anyone who would listen. Whoops, anthropomorphic, and he was not even trying to be anthropomorphic about himself. Something tells me I'm not very good at this, Connelly decided. It was probably a good thing. He wouldn't exactly be a whole lot of use to Sterling in that state. They'd just sit there agreeing, like two drunks in a bar. And anyway, it was such an effort. Saying to yourself 'Car door is opened' when the alternative wasn't so much saying 'I open the car door,' as just opening the damn thing, getting in and driving away without even having to think about it. The fact was, this schtick of Sterling's was a luxury only a prisoner or a patient could afford. Once he was back in the real world he'd have to change his tune!

Rejoicing in the illusion of selfhood that allowed him to coast unconsciously through the rush of sensation a morning trip up a Hawaiian hill hurled at him, he hairpinned past the great trees and summer palaces of the Moanalua Estate gardens to the point above, which reduced the panorama to a Military–Industrial complex: canneries, warehouses, Hickam Airfield, and behind Red Hill, the great Harbor.

Then, as he rounded the last bend and turned his face upwards, the pink geometry of the hospital buildings above recalled a speaking image from his trip out here: that morning in San Francisco, looking across to Alcatraz, long square blocks perched on green crags and lit champagne pink by a fog-tinged shaft of the sunrise, just like Tripler up there. He shivered, and thought about the political education officer who was also not a pain in Sterling's ass. Maybe he'd been wrong to take that remark as a simple personal dig.

When he came into Sterling's room he said directly, 'Is this place still a kind of prison?'

Sterling looked at him expressionlessly, then turned and made his way to the bed, lowering himself onto it to sit bolt upright with one foot tucked up under his knee. Connelly took his usual place, hitching like a cowboy on a fence on the rail at the end of the bed, and pressed, 'Well, is it?'

'*Why are you back?*' This was said with such contemptuous energy that Connelly suffered total amnesia of the fact that yesterday Sterling had said he wanted him to come. Instead he could only stammer, 'Because you're important...'

'For your project.'

Stung into courage, 'For maybe something more than that.'
'Like what?'
'Like... like how's a person going to live? Sticking up for your principles or playing safe; break or bend?'
'Oh *God*,' breathed Sterling, as if this was the last thing he wanted to hear.
'*Is* this place also a prison? A political re-education camp?'
Sterling leaned back, twisting away and drawing his knees up towards his chest, as if defending himself against whatever crazy angle Connelly was going to start firing from next.
'Is that why I remind you of Chang?'
'At least Chang was honest about his motives. You keep coming back but it's not at all clear what you want.' He sat up again and faced Connelly, back on the offensive again.
'But – ' Connelly began and then broke off to wonder what it was he did want. To find the anti-brainwashing vaccine and save his country? To be the hero who made the patient better or caught the communist infiltrator? Well, he had to admit they were attractive pictures, but there was something else that mattered more. To vindicate Sterling's way? Maybe that was it. Or to vindicate himself? But these couldn't coexist, not peacefully. Either Sterling was a fool or Connelly was a hypocrite.
Sterling had been watching him think, and from the cynical expression on his face, it was hard not to feel that he had been reading his mind pretty accurately. Connelly swallowed and said, 'Anyway, it doesn't matter what I want. The point is, what's going to happen to you? You can't keep this up, just being an optical illusion who never says "I". Sooner or later you're going to have to shape up and act happy to be home and give McKenna a straightforward report in normal English grammar.'
'Or else?' Sterling demanded, dragging himself up.
'Or else he's going to start calling in the heavy counter intelligence guns and/or else you're going to spend the rest of your days as a pathological exhibit of atypical symptomatology on the psyche ward of some veterans' hospital.'

'Who cares?'

'I do. I don't want either of those things to happen to you.' Sterling looked down at his dried-up hands. 'Bull.'

'No.' Connelly's throat was tight, his heart was going fast, and it probably sounded like he was lying.

'The original story was you wanted a negative case. Now you want normal.'

'No, I . . . I . . .' Hell, what a mess. And from the way Sterling was looking at him, only the truth was going to do. Connelly's face was hot. 'Look, the fact is, I admire, um, it. What you're doing. And I know I couldn't do it myself. If I had your strength of mind I'd be rooting for you to hold out, but as it is I'm hoping you'll play safe in the end.' He forced himself to meet Sterling's gaze, saw an expression of shock, and lost his nerve. He made the lamest of excuses and got out of the room fast.

Sterling jumped up and went to the window. In that corner of the room he couldn't be observed from the desk. How stupid could you get? You would have thought Connelly would have more self-respect than that! There was a shaky nervy anger running up and down his arms, and a strong craving for a cigarette. He went to the end of the bed and delivered a barefooted kick at Connelly's luminous corner of the chromium-plated frame. This converted the nervy feeling into a sharp pain across his toes but it didn't get rid of his anger.

'If I had your strength of mind . . . OK, maybe he didn't, not everyone did. But he didn't have to *talk* about it shamelessly like that! The beginning of toughness is pride, but admiring a virtue you have no intention of cultivating is just despicable. He stood at the window despising Connelly, gripping the lower edge of the window frame.

He didn't have the stamina to keep that level of hate going for more than a few minutes. The shaky feeling returned, almost a faintness. Lunch was late. He went back to the bed and lay down. The fan wasn't on today.

Resting, heart slowing down, shoulders beginning to come out of spasm. Slowly, the recognition that there was something unbalanced about that hatred rose. Anger was a sensation, like any other, but why be angry with Connelly? He was on a par with McKenna, with the lizard. More than that, *despising* didn't exactly accord with the will to emptiness that was supposed to be there. There was a dropping sensation in the stomach, the slight shock that goes with one of those dreams where the sidewalk suddenly falls out from under you, combined with a twist of dread, as if this was an ominous sign.

Well, it was. It meant stuff was beginning to matter again.

But it didn't matter. It didn't matter what kind of a fool Connelly chose to make of himself. And so what if some remnant of the Sterling personality reacted against this? Elevating emptiness to some kind of moral or even religious position was Connelly's interpretation, and so was the notion that falling away from it would be a betrayal. But these ideas just led back to the illusion of selfhood. And what did it matter if a particular carcase rotted in a psychiatric hospital or got shot for treason? One method was slow, another fast.

But it had to go and matter to Connelly. Stupid little prick. What business was it of his anyway? Before he knew what was happening, Sterling was up at the window again, heart pounding. Whoa. What the hell was going on?

Oh, Jesus. The twist of dread returned, grew into nausea. Oh, not that! That susceptibility, the stupid dangerous weakness of letting people matter more than lizards. How had *that* come back?

He thought he'd got rid of it for good last winter. He'd been in solitary, and Chang was his only visitor. It probably wasn't strange that loneliness and desperation had softened him up to the point that he was starting to find the intense, idealistic little Maoist good company. But when he'd caught himself thinking 'God, I like this man, in other circumstances we could have been such friends...', he knew that this susceptibility had to go.

Out with the trash, out with the corpses. And later, when he heard that Wilson had ratted on him, the subtractive process famined itself down to absolute zero.

Better to be free of people you can't trust.

Connelly did his best to put down the nauseating sense that he'd made a fool of himself, trying to drown it in fantasies and images of Hoku as he raced down to Waikiki. He parked under the line of shaggy ironwood trees near Queen's Surf, scanning the grassy area for evidence of the threesome. The beach park was busier tonight, family parties picnicking, kids playing football. Was that a bad sign? Because he couldn't see Hoku anywhere. He jumped out of the car, hurrying towards the far corner, but before he was even halfway to the kamani tree it was clear they weren't there. He walked around it twice, and they really weren't. Something like panic assailed him. Having just found a freedom like that, you couldn't lose it again! Could you? You couldn't lose Hoku! And yet he didn't even have a phone number or know where he lived. Hoku couldn't get lost, but Connelly could.

Maybe he was just a little early. The other evening he'd walked here all the way from de Russy. *Pau-hana* time, Hoku had said. According to the glossary at the end of his guide that meant after work, happy hour. 'Try relax,' he instructed himself, borrowing Hoku's vocabulary. He perched on the crest of the rise; there the sand met the grass, like a mirror image of the waves out there, but with the colours reversed, green sloping up to white. The swell looked big today; good surf always happened on work days. He was annoyed, but he was also glad he wasn't honour bound to be out there, pushing the edge of his competence in front of all the hotshots skidding around, at double the speed of the big fellow riding out in front, tall and stately and arrogantly slow, shoulders arched backwards, on an old-fashioned board as long as a boat. Oh!

Hoku rode the wave until it dissolved into froth, then dropped to his hands and dismounted. A kid came wading through the shallows and reclaimed the borrowed board.

Hoku strolled up the beach, making straight for Connelly, but not yet seeing him. When he did he stopped, boggled in disbelief, pointed, laughed hysterically, covered his eyes, dropped to his knees. 'What's so funny?' Connelly called, going over to him.

'Eh, get back. I not with you – some tourist I never met before,' he explained to an imaginary audience. He sprang to his feet with a surfer's push up, to caress Connelly's tie and try to coax it into life. 'Aw. What's the matter? Hard day at work? Not in the mood?' Then he slung a sandy arm over Connelly's broadcloth shoulders and propelled him inland. 'Tchah! Going around the place with the *uliuli* hanging out! I'm going to get you out of this place before anybody see you, for your own good.'

In the car Hoku directed him to the road that wrapped around the arid slopes of Diamond Head, covered in thorny mesquite. There were several scenic lookouts clustered around the old lighthouse, where tourists could squint across the sapphire and turquoise and indigo-charted sea, and on a clear day make out the islands of Molokai and Lanai, and maybe even the slow symmetrical dome of Haleakala, the great mountain of Maui, its *mana* potent even at such a distance.

Hoku had been pretending to discover that there was more to Connelly than a tie, and as they approached the last lookout point, the car suddenly swerved into it, screeching to a halt just before smashing into the brown turdlike rock of the Amelia Earhart Memorial.

'Cheez, cannot hold onto um or what? We can go my house, get relaxed, take our time. What's the hurry?'

'I have to hurry; I'm from New York.'

'Ho-kay, show me New Yahk style...Like dat, huh?' Not long afterwards: 'Eh! Try wait, we go my house, eh? Leave um! Whoa...! I kinda big for your car, everyone going see um *shaking...auwe...*' But if anyone saw the car shaking, they must have figured the person in there was too big to be safely disturbed.

When they were back on it, the road brought them down and inland gently. It passed big spread-out beachfront houses, then a bulldozed plain of rich red volcanic dirt on which a new suburb was being planted. But Hoku showed him the way towards the inner mountains of Waialae, up a valley fenced into little homesteads. There was an air of lonely dereliction, rusting cars and sagging shacks, livened only by the sassy chestnut caped fowl strutting about the road. The scent of pigshit invaded the car. They turned down a dirt road that wound deeper and damper into the upland jungle. Cleaner, sweeter scents summoned them, and they came to another clearing. Rusty chickens scattered at their approach. A strand of barbed wire made a corral for a spavined half-blood horse and two small bantangus ponies, above it was a shack with a rusty corrugated roof. Connelly didn't know whether to be charmed or appalled. Everything the earth made was so rich, every human artefact decaying in an apathy beyond mere poverty.

At the sound of the car's approach a girl came out of the house and stood on the porch, tilting her head to study them, pushing her hair back around an ear with a finger, in thoughtful repetition. 'Ho! Momi still here!' Hoku exclaimed, in something like dismay.

Connelly looked at him sidelong. She was a beautiful girl, though solidly built to match Hoku himself. Arched, scowling eyebrows, flaring nostrils, full lips curling contemptuously suggested Hoku was in big trouble with his woman.

'Do your best for make her like you,' Hoku implored him, jumping out of the car. 'Eh, Momi, how come you no at Auntie Lydia's luau?'

'Cause no one never come for me, that's why. Who dat?'

'Huh? Who? Oh! That's my friend Connelly. Connelly, come out, meet my sister Leimomi.'

Scornful eyes, light golden brown, looked him over up and down, and, he guessed, knew exactly what kind of friend he was. He wondered if she was really his sister, but decided she was not the kind of person to put up with that title if 'wife' or 'girlfriend' was more accurate. She turned on her heel and marched into the house, creating angry slapping reports by flicking her rubber sandals up against the soles of her feet with each step. She came out again with two brown paper bags, overstuffed with flowers, and a handmade conical parcel of ti leaves. 'Perhaps you *gentlemen*,' the word accompanied a scornful glance at Connelly's abused tie, 'would get the rest.'

She placed herself in the back seat of the Chevy. Before Connelly understood what was happening he had loaded cases of beer, gallon jugs of Malolo syrup, boxes of food and more flower leis into the trunk, and set off to chauffeur her to the family party on the other side of the Island. 'Always better *kokua* Leimomi,' was the way Hoku expressed their spineless acquiescence.

Connelly sang most of New York, New York, it's a helluva town under his breath.

'Eh, Hoku,' said Leimomi sharply. 'How come you not at Auntie's party already?'

'Oh, things come up,' he said vaguely. Even before he had found Connelly on the beach he had planned to miss the luau, as part of his policy of avoiding his mother. The more you avoided her, the worse it would be next time, and now, with a three-month backlog of scoldings, he felt he had reached the point where it was better never to see her again.

The long coast road wound beneath the Ko'olau mountain range that formed the spine behind Honolulu, and they rounded the far southeastern corner of Oahu, through wild places of lava boulder, prickly pear cacti, and throbbing chaotic currents dashing against the black frothy rock shore. Now they were on the other side of the mountains, and the sun had already set behind them, though it was still shining obliquely on the surfers back at Waikiki.

They came to an inland plain populated by small wooden houses set in big yards of dry grass, flatness broken only by the plumeria trees with their rubbery trunks and plain flowers. One of these, set back from the main road, was the obvious site of the party. A crowd of cars parked on the grass, a bunch of kids was playing circular volleyball in the front yard, fragrant smoke rising from the back. Momi got out, carrying her leis. Hoku whispered, 'If I go back there we never get loose again tonight.' So it was Connelly who followed her with armloads of drink and food and flowers. When everything was delivered to the outdoor kitchen at the back of the house, Momi suddenly noticed that Hoku wasn't there and that Connelly was retreating as fast as he could. 'Come back!' she bellowed after him.

His shoulders hunched with the instantaneous humility of a dog whipping its tail between its legs and he returned, trying not to take up space. 'Tell Hoku, how Auntie Lydia going *feel*? And if I find out he never came back on account of you...'

She was interrupted by the arrival of a tiny figure in a crimson dress of late Victorian design, though its high neck and leg-of-mutton sleeves were concealed under a great heap of waxy stephanotis flowers, white ginger and *maile* leaves. A circlet of pink and red rosebuds crowned Auntie Lydia's iron-grey head. Everything that was tough and big-mouthed about Leimomi vanished instantly. She greeted her aunt in courtly Hawaiian and kissed her in a minimalistic embrace that respected the fragility of the flowers. Then she presented Connelly with an air of conscious mannerliness, covertly ripping open the conical ti-leaf package and putting its contents, a string of yellow ginger, into his hands. She tilted her head in her aunt's direction, until he realized he was supposed to put the lei around her neck. It was all terribly disorienting, Momi's sudden change in manner and expression, in the very way she stood, as straight and gracious as the Victorian figure herself. It was only later, on reflection, that her singular courtesy in passing him her best lei became salient.

Auntie Lydia exclaimed over the latest addition to her flowers, directing her thanks through Connelly to her niece. 'You are very welcome to our family party.' Her accent, Hawaiian in its rhythms, nevertheless made such a point of pronouncing all the final consonants everyone else was leaving out that it sounded more English than American.

'Thank you very much.'

'And where is Hoku?'

'I'll go find him,' Momi said quickly. 'I was with him a minute ago, but he disappeared.'

'I should say he is avoiding Dolores Esposito,' Auntie Lydia said, more to herself than anyone else. There was a certain hawklike humour to her eyes, which she veiled when she turned again to her guest. 'You are new to the islands?'

'Yes, ma'am. I've only been here about a month.'

'Ah! And you are enjoying yourself?'

'I don't think I've ever been happier in my life.'

There was just the slightest sense of an inclination, as if she was accepting the tribute on behalf of the island. 'I'm glad. We who live here try to show our gratitude for the beauty that surrounds us by trying to extend the most hospitable welcome we can to our visitors.' There was the faintest touch of lemon in her voice, an emphasis on the word 'visitor' that made Connelly feel like a gatecrasher to the island, as well as to the luau.

Hoku came running around the corner of the house, skidded to a halt and seized his Auntie in an embrace that released a heady drench of sweetness and spice into the air from a thousand bruised flowers. She scolded him for his lateness, for arriving in his board shorts. 'Leimomi's young man found time to make himself presentable.' At his blank look she gestured at the *haole* in the rumpled shirt and detumescent tie. Hoku raised an eyebrow, and at second squint she decided not to argue the point. 'I wanted you to sing with your father. Don't refuse. Why are you young people so afraid of your talents, your achievements?'

The regal apparition turned and made her way through the crowds to where a string quartet of two guitars, a ukulele and a double bass were trying to tune up. Hoku allowed himself to lose sight of her, grabbed Connelly for a quick escape, but was diverted by the sight of the refreshment table. 'Oh well, now we here we might as well eat, eh?' He heaped two plates with *poki* and *laulau* and *haupia*. Connelly learned later that he'd eaten a considerable amount of raw fish.

'A very impressive old lady,' he ventured to remark.

'Very old school, yeah? She grew up in Hana, brought up on the big Calhoun Estate as part of the family, and on the Hawaiian side she comes from the line of Maui kings. She's my father's Auntie really, but she brought me up, Leimomi too; she's also Leimomi's Auntie on the other side. So Leimomi's half my sister, half my cousin...somekind like that. One complicated family. E, try the *laulau*, delicious. That one. No, open um up, here...' He set his own plate down and extracted the steamed pork from the parcel of leaves (like Momi's lei carrier in miniature). He fed it to Connelly with the watchful air of a parent introducing solid food, and did not notice the family complication approaching on his right until it had overtaken him: a hunched, aggressively drab creature, all over olive brown in colour, hair, eyes and skin. 'Oh, hello, Mama,' said Hoku weakly. Up and down his entire body muscles contracted, as if he was trying to make himself smaller, or ideally invisible. 'How are you?'

'*Considering*,' she quavered. 'After all, you cannot expect much, my age, and the life I had. You cannot complain. I was in Castle Hospital two weeks for tests, and they never found nothing at all, these people who don't know what they're doing. They get ahold of Esposito, those doctors, they tell him, "You got to leave her alone" but he never leave me alone, it's disgusting. Plus the tow truck break down next week and the bank will not lend, so the business going be ruin. And nobody never came near me the whole time, not my own son, but the life I had, what can you expect? I bear the Cross and all the tribulations, the only peace I get going be the Grave.'

'E, you had anything to eat yet?' Hoku inserted quickly, and led her by the arm to the refreshment table. Her voice drifted back to Connelly, fading like a ghost, 'Never going be any different. I used to it now.'

The musicians were getting started, with a great energetic strumming and a lot of private laughter. Maybe he and Hoku were here for the duration. Perhaps he should have been grateful for this unexpected chance to visit the real Hawaii that tourists never saw, but he could only feel dislocated and lonely there, wondering how to put the contradictions together, aristocratic Auntie Lydia, drab Dolores Esposito, Hoku himself suddenly more than a beach boy... but what more? The introductory slack key fanfare was over, and by popular acclaim Auntie Lydia herself stepped forwards and danced for them all. She moved with an arthritic grace that distilled rather than lost physical expressiveness, giving them a hula from the twenties, racy but regal, a glimpse of the high-living Hana of her youth.

Leimomi appeared at his side and said softly, 'Hoku said to tell you he's out front.'

He thanked her and slipped away, only to discover that Hoku's escape had been delayed by another distraction, this time an injured child. He was sitting on the porch, rubbing a little girl's twisted ankle, scolding away the tears, 'No cry, eh? No make A,' and then distracting her with the story of Kaahu-Pahau, the queen of the sharks of Oahu. Other children gathered to listen, sitting on the porch railings or at the storyteller's feet. When he did the royal voice it was high and tongue-splittingly correct; many, including Connelly, recognized the parody of Auntie Lydia.

'She lived at Pu'uloa, Pearl Harbor, and she protected the people of the island from the Man-eating Sharks that came from the harbour of New York. These terrible creatures can unlock their jaws at the hinges and swallow you all the way down, even a big fellow like me.

'Anyway, Kaahu-Pahau got caught by some of them and they put her in a coral prison, with a big ugly guard night and day, waiting just outside the only crack in the reef big enough for her to get out. There's other smaller holes, and the other fish, the little flat yellow ones and the long skinny silver ones, they can get in and out, but she cannot. Then she gets an idea. A green parrot fish, about so big,' Hoku gestured a foot in length, 'he swims past the guard right into the reef cave. So she transforms half her spirit into it, and leaves the other half in her body, to keep it there. The parrot fish swims out of the prison, and blam! the guard jumps on it and eats it. Kaahu-Pahau quickly transforms her spirit back into herself.

'Still, it was a good idea. "I mustt be more disccreett," she thinks, and this time selects a kumu, a smaller fish, able to get through the holes in the coral. She does the same with her spirit, and makes it past the guard, but not past the other big shark guy who's just coming along to take over the watch. He grabs the kumu for a snack, and she transforms her spirit back into herself.

'The queen sits there thinking, and while she thinks her eyes rest on a little floating piece of *limu*. That's seaweed,' Hoku translated, for Connelly's benefit. 'The waves going in towards the shore carry it a little this way... the current coming back out carries it a little that way. It's just drifting along. But Kaahu notices that the tide is going out, and slowly but surely the limu is making its way out to sea. So she transforms half her spirit...

'Ho, it took a long time! Few inches forwards, few inches back. Even once she's outside the prison, she wants to get clear away from the guards before they raise the alarm. The limu floats this way a little, the limu floats that way a little more, and then at last the riptide picks it up and speeds it out for the blue water. And Kaahu-Pahau transforms her whole spirit together and the limu becomes a shark, and she hulas her tail, whoo, whoo! and shoots to freedom in the depths of the ocean.

'And now my story is done, and I got to take New York boy away before he eats anyone.' Hoku jumped to his feet, slinging his hips left then right in imitation of the shark queen's tail action, 'Whoo, whoo!' and powered his way to the freedom of the car, with the man-eater from New York in pursuit.

Darkness was falling as they travelled back along the coast road, and Connelly was silent, feeling as if he had been shown too much, too suddenly. He realized that he'd never actually been allowed to meet anyone's family before, and maybe that was what was bothering him as much as all the cultural and sociological confusion. The picture of Hoku camping it up before an appreciative audience of very small children was something that would stay with him for a long time. Presently he said, a little shyly, 'I liked the story. I've been doing the same thing all my life.'

'What you mean?'

'I mean, only putting half my heart into anything. Never giving anything or anyone my all.'

Hoku was startled by the unreserved, and disturbed or possibly hurt by the reserve it described. 'You supposed to put the halves together when you get past the guard,' he pointed out sternly.

'When are you ever really past?'

'So that... that on Waikiki, that time...' Hoku's voice shook, as the memory or the compound image that had overtaken the memory flooded his mind: the angles of Connelly's shoulders and backside, soaking up attention like a wet body soaking up the sun, of the seductive innocent smile that said 'I was sent from Heaven to show you a good time.' '...that was just *half*? You were walking around with your spirit in pieces?' He sounded scandalized, as if Connelly had been walking around with his flies open, or maybe with a ruptured appendix; as if to him your spirit was as concrete as your heart or your guts.

'It's just a metaphor,' Connelly tried to laugh it off.

Hoku looked out of the window, as the dark rock walls of the coastal cliffs loomed jaggedly against the phosphorescence and faint reflected starshine of the sea. They came around the points, and were coasting downhill toward the lights of the Honolulu suburbs before he found his voice again. The hurt had not gone from it. 'What you want me to give you? Only half?'

A stabbed noise, like a throat being opened. 'Hoku... I'm going away. I've got maybe a couple of weeks here, at most.'

'So? I'm willing to give, for that time.'
'I don't want anyone to get hurt.'
'I'm willing to get hurt, but not to cut myself apart.'

He spent the night at Hoku's little shack, but driving to work the next morning he told himself he'd better not go back there. That almost wilful vulnerability, that poverty made more poignant by the picture of the aristocratic past, no, he couldn't live with all that on his conscience. But he kept having visions, so real they were almost hallucinations, of those deep-set, arched, heavy-lidded eyes, and hearing that voice still resonating, '...only half?' All those things that had seemed contradictions in Hoku, turning out to be facets of a wholeness, and wholeness wilfully vulnerable to pain; no, he couldn't take it. Sterling's way was better.

It would be a good idea to concentrate on the project itself for a while, spend more time with the academic stuff and less with the patient. He sat at the desk in his living room and unlocked the filing cabinet beside it, pulling out Sterling's file and a transcript of his interview with Corporal Wilson. Get back to the data, back to the facts.

He re-read the dossier on Sterling that McKenna had given him, various pieces of army paperwork assembled for the use of the repatriation panel, lines to read between. Sterling had come into the world via New England, but seemed to have done all his growing up out west, in and around Reno, Nevada. Not much you could deduce from that. He read on. The Ironwood Academy: was that a classy prep school or one of those military boarding schools for wealthy delinquents? A single year at Stanford University, suddenly abandoned in order to join the army. Now what connection did that have with the wedding that happened at about the same time, and the kid that arrived not quite long enough afterwards? And Sterling, who looked so dried up and blown away, was the same age he was, only twenty-seven. Chilling.

Then there was the military career to follow, from its peaceful beginnings as information and education officer at Fort Wynkoop, Nevada, through the increasingly frantic series of transfers to new units in Japan and Korea, with all kinds of confusing ordinal numbers, places and battles. The Pusan Perimeter, the Naktong Bulge; the names invoked no historical specifics for Connelly, but summoned a powerful sense of what it had been like then for himself, finishing college, caught in a pincer attack between his terror of being drafted and the guilty memory of his adolescent vow 'First Hitler, then Stalin (as soon as I finish high school)' and the crazy, paradoxical temptation to escape the pressure by volunteering as a medical corpsman.

Jesus, what was wrong with him today? OK, forget about Sterling; concentrate on the bare historical facts. He picked up the transcript of the Wilson interview.

Corporal Kirby Wilson, a man like an autumn leaf, mealy and brown, crinkled up and shaking in the wind. He had to keep his cigarettes wedged deeply between his knuckles, or the tremor in his hands made them fly all over the place. There was something Connelly had liked instantly about his bleak honesty, his stoical single-shouldered shrug: it was something like Sterling's 'so what?' but still human. As informants went, he did more than anyone to back up Bronsky's structural thesis that it was what went on in the group that mattered.

14 September 1953
Dr Connelly: So how'd it all happen, in the first place?

Cpl Wilson: Don't know where to start. We were trapped inside a disused mine, me and the rest of the platoon, what was left of us. There were Chinese outside, plenty of them, though they seemed to have run out of grenades to throw in at us. Our commander wanted to make a sortie. This was going to be suicidal, because the Chinese out there were battalion strength, at least. I told him I didn't think the men were going to follow. They were talking more along the lines of surrendering. Lieutenant Sterling didn't want to surrender because of the way the Japanese had treated prisoners in the last war, how in the samurai code if you lost your honour you were nothing. I personally thought it was a damn stupid time to be thinking about the samurai code, and I told him straight that he had fu – excuse me, he had made the mistake of getting us in this mess, and we had done our best for him and now he owed it to the men not to force them into mutiny. Sterling just waved an arm at me, go away and do it.

There were a lot of times afterwards I wished I had listened to him and finished it then and there.

Anyway, they shot two of us right away, just to let us know, and then a couple of guards started marching us north, for two days, until we came to a little town or village... (laughing) I'm just remembering how the villagers came out and threw rocks at us, and Delahunty saying that it was durned unwelcoming of them. I never found out the name of the place, but the name we gave it was Hara Kiri, because we all got dysentery through the conditions there. The Chinese had commandeered the schoolhouse and we were housed in that through the winter. Fifty or sixty more prisoners arrived, so it was very cramped. A lot of them were captured from the Chosin Reservoir area.

It was a terrible winter and there were a lot of frostbite casualties. They lost fingers, toes, pieces off their ears and noses and everything. The medical corpsmen told them if they didn't get rid of all the dead flesh they'd get gangrene and die. They were snapping them off themselves, even joking about it. The whole place was filthy. Dozens of people died.

Dr Connelly: Jesus.

Cpl Wilson: Yeah. Well. We were moved in February, another long march, to Changhung. The place was hardly built when we arrived, 'durned unwelcoming'. It was just a plateau with snowy mountains all around, windy and freezing, and we were living in lean-tos. If you wanted four walls you had to scavenge and build them yourself, shanty-town style. The NKs and Chinese built a compound for themselves, plus cells and stuff. Eventually there were concrete blocks for us, but that took longer, especially if you were a reactionary. That was their name for the people who wouldn't play ball with the brainwashing.

Dr Connelly: So how did the brainwashing work? Was it just like, if you accepted communism you were rewarded with better housing?

Cpl Wilson: Better everything. To be fair about it you didn't actually have to accept communism. There was a path of least resistance, and most men walked it.

Dr Connelly: But you didn't?

Cpl Wilson: No, sir, I did not.

Dr Connelly: I'd sure appreciate it if you'd tell me what it was like, what happened to you when you resisted.

Cpl Wilson: Well, at first it was just lectures and pep talks. This started in about late March, when the political officer arrived, Chang Wo, or Wo Chang as we'd say. He seemed different from the other Chinese, I don't know why, maybe it was just that he was the first one I met who really spoke English. He told me he'd learned it when he was growing up in Hong Kong. He claimed he'd actually crossed the bamboo curtain to join the Long March because of his love of communism. The love of communism part was sincere anyway, because he could talk about it for hours. Hours and hours and hours, about Mao's ideas and his poetry and how wonderful it was for the Chinese people, how much he'd loved the commitment and comradeship of the Long March, how privileged he was to be able to bring us the message of communism. How we were not his enemies, it was only that we'd been tricked and oppressed into fighting for imperialist capitalism, he was on our side and going to help us. It was like a tent revival, except nobody got converted.

Then there was phase two where we were put in groups to discuss it all. Chang or one of the others who understood English would sit in, and I guess they were figuring out which ones of us were going to be pushovers and which ones were going to be troublemakers. And then there were bribes. Some supplies would arrive, and it would be, fifteen blankets for the fifteen most progressive souls in the camp. Or jobs in the kitchen or the garden. But hardly anybody bought it at that stage. Only the guys who were maybe kind of communistically inclined already, or had a grudge against their commanders and this was a way of getting on top of them, plus the usual number who were just plain bastards. If we caught any of them when the Chinese weren't there to protect them they got it.

But Chang was just turning the heat up, slowly and gradually. He was smart. There was always some little thing you were being asked to do. Maybe it was sign a petition saying you wanted the war to end. Sure you did. But then the next petition would be you wanted the UN to withdraw. And then, it would be the aggressive forces of American imperialism... And there was always some little thing – a pack of real Meiguo yan, American cigarettes, or five slices of pork or dog on your rice that evening – for the ones who went along. Until after a while it was not so much the progressives being rewarded as the reactionaries being punished. 'Wing Sun bu chow!'

The balance was shifting, just very quietly. It wasn't a question of two hundred decent Americans against twenty rats, it was getting to be more like thirty or forty reactionaries on one end of the scale and thirty or forty collaborators, and the rest of the camp somewhere in the middle all doing their own private calculations between pride and survival. 'Why can't you play it cool, man, then they'll leave you alone,' someone told me; I guess that's the way he saw what he was doing.

So from there all Chang had to do was just turn the middle of the roaders against us and then automatically he's got the scale tipped on the progressive side. I remember the night I caught on that this was going to happen. We were in a discussion group, about twenty people, sitting in a circle in the middle of the parade ground, and it was raining. Chang was telling us that the Americans had dropped rats infected with typhoid on Hagaru-ri and Hyesanjin and a few other places not far from Changhung. Sterling whispered to me, 'Aw, that's cute. Do you think they each had their own little parachute?' I was snickering, and Chang said, 'Please have respect to share joke with group.' He could be a real schoolmarm, old Chang. So I said it out. Chang said, 'If capitalist tycoons so rich each Meiguo rat even has own helicopter still should not make typhoid on Korea people.' I don't know if he realized it was funny, but it cracked me up. Then Sterling said, 'Let's hear it for Chairman Mao, who gives his rats a bed in the concrete block and dog meat once a week!' So Chang announced that this group was going to sit in the rain until Sterling and I apologized for our disruptive behaviour.

So we all sat there getting wetter and wetter and colder and colder, and from time to time Chang would ask the others what they thought of us. And of course at first no one would say anything, but after an hour or two they were asking us to just get it over with, and by the early hours of the morning we were feeling pretty unpopular. In the end Chang said he was going to bed and got a guard who didn't speak much English to take over the group. So when he was gone, Sterling and I apologized for cheering for Chairman Mao, and the guard was dumb enough to let us all go.

Anyway, we talked it over, me and Sterling, and decided

what Chang was doing was like a judo tactic: using the enemy's strength against him. The more the reactionaries held out, the more the middlemen would resent them, and the more progressive they'd become. And maybe, in terms of the whole camp, there wasn't much we could do about it, but we could at least try to keep our own unit together. There were seven of us left from the First Platoon, and the thing of being in it together had kept us alive.

Dr Connelly: I bet that was really important.

Cpl Wilson: Well, I know for myself I wouldn't have made it through the early days alone. I felt like if our unit split like all the others there wouldn't be anything to live for. So I came up with a system that every time we were faced with a decision, like whether to fill in the confession and self-criticism forms with bad language or just to rip them up, we would vote and always follow the majority will as a group, even if we personally didn't agree with the outcome. We invented signals, like scratching the right side of your face for 'stick' and the left for 'fold', so that we could do this in front of the Chinese without their knowing what was going on. And the fact that there were always the seven of you together made it a whole lot easier when it felt like the whole rest of the camp was shouting you down for bucking for a hero.

Chang figured there was something going on, and he upped the ante. He knew who the big troublemakers were – basically, by now it was whittled down to the First Platoon, and about ten or twenty others. I'm not saying that we were the only loyal Americans, we were just the ones who were prepared to stick our necks out, and we were the ones that got hammered. I got put in the cells I don't know how many times, sometimes for making smart remarks, sometimes for nothing at all, or on the say-so of some rat who's denounced me. I got beat up. Sometimes they'd blindfold you first, that was bad. I tell you, we walked a whole lot more carefully now. We still wouldn't compromise, but we sure as hell gave up provoking them. Not that it made a difference any more. There didn't have to be a reason. For example, none of the First had done the confession form, but it was me they picked on. I was locked up in this interrogation room, chained by my arms so if I tried to sit down I had to hang by my hands, left standing there overnight. I practically slipped a disc trying to get my pants down for a crap. And they just kept me there until they'd extracted enough answers to call it a confession. When I finally came out, the guys in the platoon had all done theirs, so it wouldn't look like I'd broken down. I don't know, maybe that's dumb, but it meant a lot.

Well, it was good while it lasted. The first thing that started it all going wrong was when Chang had all the colored folks moved to the new progressives block. We had two Negroes in the First, which I didn't agree with, but no one could say they were progressives. But Chang saw to it that they had all the privileges and comforts the camp had to offer, just to try to divide us. We swore we wouldn't let it make a difference, and it didn't, but the plain fact was that we just saw less and less of them because their days were scheduled different, and finally one of them, Eugene, came to Sterling and me and told us it was more important for him to concentrate on organizing a resistors' movement among the Negroes. I said to Sterling, 'He means we're fine people and he has a lot of respect for us personally, but he just doesn't want us in his neighbourhood.'

So we were down to five and then Suarez died in November. One night he said, 'I don't want to live through another winter,' and the next morning he was stiff.

Dr Connelly: Useful talent to have.

Cpl Wilson: You bet. Anyway, what actually wrecked the platoon in the end was the arrival of some new prisoners transferred from another camp called Happy Valley. One of them was a one-legged man. I guess I need to explain that there had been some friction between us and the other main resistance outfit. They were mostly marines and when Chang started his line about Negroes being the progressive race he also used to say that the reactionary thing was organized by the Ku Klux Klan, so they took on that name as a badge of pride, I guess. They'd invited me and Delahunty to join them. I knew the two leaders, Farrell and Chapman, back from Hara Kiri. They were Chosin Reservoir vets and had had the frostbit bad. Chapman had lost all the fingers of his left hand and Farrell had this raggedy open-nostrilled face from when the corpsman had to cut off all the gangrene with an old razor blade and no anaesthetic. To be honest I admired him but there was a... I don't know what you'd call it, rivalry, I guess, between him and Sterling. They had this elitist marine thing, they were the tough guys, and Sterling had the charisma and for awhile it was like a contest for who was going to be the leader of the resistance in Changhung... until one way or another the post of camp hero wasn't something anybody wanted any more. Well, to get back to the story, the new contingent arrived and there was something fishy about them, we thought, but they were marines, so the KKK gave them the benefit of the doubt. I was actually in the cells the day when Sterling heard this one-legged man, this amputee, spreading the story that he'd been abandoned by his platoon when they were retreating: they knew he was injured but they bugged out and it was only when the NKs found him that he received any treatment. Well, that part anyway was bullshit. Any medical attention anyone got after being captured came from our own people, and hell, I knew of corpsmen who had treated Koreans and Chinese who were just being left to rot by their own. So anyway, I guess what Sterling did was just give him the usual rat treatment, but because he was an amputee some people thought it looked bad, and because he was a marine Farrell ordered the guys from the KKK in on Sterling. And then the beef caught the attention of the guards and Chang was in on it and Sterling was arrested and tried in a kangaroo court and they chained him up in the parade ground, and by the time I was released the other two members of the platoon had ratted on us. They had written out denunciations of me and Sterling and told Chang the voting signals and disappeared into the ranks of the collaborators. In the January of the cholera epidemic they died and serve them right.

So it was 'Wing Sun' and 'Tser Ling' against the Chinks, the rats and the Klan. We spent the winter in the same old shanty town shack, missing the body heat from the other five. When the epidemic took we were given the honour of being camp grave-diggers. Ground was frozen so hard we had to light fires to get the spades to bite. We buried them under the vegetable patch because that was the only place there was any depth of soil.

Dr Connelly: Did they plant in it, the next year?

Cpl Wilson: Yup.

Dr Connelly: Sorry I asked. Go on.

Cpl Wilson: Well, on account of carrying out the bodies we got to know the Limey padre who was there at the time, and Eugene used to give him food and once even a blanket to smuggle out to us, until he got the cholera and died too – the chaplain, I mean. It was a low-key time, everyone just trying to survive, Chinese too.

Funny thing was that Chang used to come in and visit us. There might be a pretext but mostly he'd just sit there and talk. I guess he was curious about America.

Then in the spring, this is '52 now, one morning we were woken up by a dozen guards busting in and dragging us off to the cells. There was a lot of noise, coming from a bunch of Chinese gathered in a knot in the middle of the parade ground, others arresting Farrell and Chapman, everyone shouting. I was put in the interrogation room. The noise from outside was getting louder and louder, American voices joining in, it sounded like a riot. After awhile Chang came in, looking upset. 'Why? Why you kill?' he kept asking me, and after awhile I figured out that it was Eugene had been killed, beaten to death, and the four of us were the suspects.

He was after a confession or at least a denunciation of someone else. As the hours and days wore on he'd come in with things purported to be signed by the others. Hell, I wasn't going to sign! Soon as I did I'd either be hung by the Chinese or lynched by the Nigras.

Then I got moved to a small cell, just a cupboard, no window, no bed. No way of telling the time, except that at some point a guard would hand in a bowl of rice soup and a bottle of water, and I guess this must have happened once a day. Well, I couldn't stand it. I used to just sit there and cry. Once they came and got me to take me back for another interrogation and I heard Sterling's voice from another cell and I tried to talk to him but the guards pounded me flat and shoved me back in the cell. After that I tried raising Cain whenever I felt I couldn't take the aloneness any more, so at least they'd come and beat me up and that would be some kind of human contact. Only they must have figured my game and ignored me. And finally Chang visited and I was so happy to see him I cried and he said if I confessed I could share a cell with Chapman who had also broken, so I did.

Chapman was being kept in another building, the block where the guards lived. He told me there was a room in there with a hangman's noose dangling from the beam and he had been made to stand on a plank balanced on boxes, kinda shaky, with his head in the knot and his eyes blindfolded for hours at a stretch. He said Farrell had hanged himself and he didn't know whether it was by accident or not; the Chinese had just brought him in to see Farrell swinging and he caved in after that. Chapman and I spent four months in the cell together. Then suddenly they just turned us out without an explanation.

We were scared of getting lynched but nobody seemed to care or remember. There were a lot of new prisoners and the blocks had been desegregated and our old shacks demolished and nobody stopped us from moving into the big block. I got the feeling nobody even knew who we were any more.

They turned Sterling loose the next day. I ran up to him, but he just said 'Rat' and walked away. That hurt bad but after awhile it was clear he was out of his mind, solitary had driven him crazy and he was just walking around in a world of his own.

Another winter hit. Everyone was just tired of the war, and even Chang was almost too disheartened to push communism. It was a blank, frozen, hard time. Rumors came in the spring, about it being all over, going home, but you couldn't find any hope to put in them. Even when it was really happening and the soldiers from India came to take us out, I couldn't believe it in my heart. Even now...

Chang's last shot was to tell the Hindus that a number of us had been so impressed by communism that we wanted to stay. He gave them a list of a hundred names. They must have known it was bullshit, but they had us line up according to who wanted to go home and who didn't. Only half a dozen didn't, but one of them was Sterling, standing there like a zombie, staring into the distance. I started yelling and screaming at him, but he wouldn't even look my way. I begged the Indians and the Red Cross medics to get him, explained the whole story. I don't know whether they could have done anything. When they loaded us on the Red Cross trucks he still wasn't with us. I couldn't believe it. Sterling staying in Korea! Later on on the ship back some officer told me the commissioners were sure to have private interviews with the ones who stayed behind. I sure hope they got him out.

Connelly with his elbows on the desk, resting his chin in his hands, pressing his fingers in his eyes, for almost ten minutes after he had finished reading. There was no sense of having arrived at anything, no new understandings or decisions or resolve, but when he stood up his feet took him out to the car, and the car took him up the hill to Tripler.

★

He found the patient at large, pacing the pea-green hall outside his room. He moved slowly and stiffly, but Connelly imagined he saw something of the physical presence he must have had, the impact he must have made on his platoon and the whole camp. He carried his head high, and his eyes went right over Connelly, deliberately focused on something loftier than any mere person or physical object that accidentally shared the world his body did. Connelly laughed aloud at him, or at the part of himself that fell for it. 'You talking today?' He stopped by the door of Sterling's room, inviting him to go back in.

'What's it matter?' Sterling shrugged. He chose to enter, ducking into the room and wrapping his arms around his chest as if he was cold, sitting on the edge of the bed. But he resisted all attempts to be drawn into conversation. Even the prime bait of 'I've been rereading what Kirby Wilson said about you', was refused.

Connelly went over to stand by the window, to study him covertly. What had gone wrong? He was farther away than ever, a hundred times farther away than he had been, even that very first day. He worried over it – had he said something wrong?

It was a sudden piece of self-knowledge that allowed him to figure it out. Distance was what you grabbed for when someone wants too much of you, and doesn't seem to care how much it's going to hurt. 'You're running away from me,' he accused.

Sterling twisted round to face him, meeting his eyes for the first time with a look of angry shock. 'Fuck you.'

'I don't blame you,' he said mildly. 'Someone you never met before, only going to be here a week or two, why should you trust him? Plus I'm not even a real doctor, I'm here for my project, not to help you . . .'

This admission pleased the patient, who smiled coldly. 'Chang did things for Our Own Good and it made him absolutely ruthless. At least there's no chance of me falling for the idea that you're going to help me.'

For some reason Connelly was looking at him in a strange way, tilting his head and squeezing his eyes into unreadable oriental slits as if he was trying to twist and compress himself into a fine point. 'Hey, stop looking so funny about it! I don't want your help!'

Connelly kept on looking. 'Do you realize what you've just said?'

'Huh? I said, "I don't want your help".'

'That makes two in the same sentence.'

Sterling caught on at last. His face lost colour as the full force of the irony struck him: his attempts to defend himself against Chang and Connelly had betrayed him to them in the end. 'It's not important. It's just grammatical; it doesn't mean anything's different inside.'

'Sterling,' said Connelly. 'You can't get the spit out of the soup, you know?'

This was not exactly accurate, because even as it went on, there was still a higher layer that was aware that none of it mattered. It was like standing at the top of a mountain looking down with a masterly knowledge at the mists and clouds that shrouded the flatlands below. He had the choice of remaining up there at the top of the mountain for as long as he wanted, but he knew that sooner or later he was going to pick up his pack and walk down into the mist. The decision had already been taken. One last look around, a sigh of farewell.

'Welcome back,' said Dr Connelly.

The sun had gone down with its usual tropical fruit palette, pulping shades of guava, mango and passion fruit and sloshing them into a sweet, sticky mess all over the sky. Now it was starting to get dark, and Connelly was still sitting in Sterling's room. The chow wagon had already been and gone, and Connelly had raided the staff canteen for coffee and its last four stale doughnuts. He'd bought a pack of Lucky Strikes from the vending machine for Sterling, who was now standing at the window shooing smoke out of the transom so that its smell would not sneak under the door and give him away to the staff. There was a look of sleepy euphoria in his eyes, probably only the result of nicotine narcosis, but it was an expression which Connelly associated with late nights or next mornings in Manhattan studio apartments. Perhaps this was what prompted Connelly to say, 'So what happens next?'

'I'd like to get out of this place.'

'Think you can give McKenna what he wants? The report, and the reason you nearly got left behind in Korea?'

Sterling frowned. 'Why?'

'Until you get your clearance from him you won't be going much of anywhere.'

'When I get my clearance from him I'll be back on the army conveyor belt. I was thinking of a different way out.'

Connelly's heart missed a beat. 'Not suicide?' he demanded, fear making him tactless.

Sterling laughed high-heartedly. 'Nah. You've managed to spit in that bowl of soup too, I don't know how. No, I was thinking more along the lines of an escape plan. I was wondering if I could trust you enough to ask you to bring me some street clothes or if I should just knock you on the head and steal your white coat and stuff.'

'You want me to smuggle in clothes for you?'

'A topographical map of the island would be a help, too, and a camping knife if you could manage it. I wouldn't expect you to find me a firearm.'

'Sterling, are you crazy? This island's about 90 per cent occupied by US Armed Forces.'

'I know, I've been here before, a couple of days' break on my way out to Japan. I'm going to find a way over the mountains and get to where the native settlements are, and hide out there, living off the land, beachcombing, fishing, until they get tired of looking for me. Then maybe find a job on the docks in Honolulu, or maybe work my passage on a ship back to the coast, or head out to Japan and see my girl there, or get on a tramp steamer (do they still have tramp steamers?) and just bum around the world...'

It was funny how what was probably nothing more than the enthusiasm of a romantic twelve-year-old, when combined with the heroic presence of a crew-cut Sigurd, could produce such a dangerous inspirational intensity. Suddenly he could really imagine Sterling winning past the hungry, frozen apathy of a captive platoon to sell them his boys' secret society, complete with team spirit, cobbled-together clubhouse apart from the concrete block, and private code designed to fox nosy sisters, pesky little brothers and evil Chinese indoctrinators. Repressing the knowledge that *falling for it* had kept Kirby Wilson alive, and the others (for a time) more honest than he had ever been, Connelly stomped hard on everything susceptible in himself and sighed, 'God knows, Sterling, I'd give anything to be able to jump ship and never mind tramp steamers and passports, just spend the rest of my life on a little Hawaiian homestead watching the bananas grow. But –'

Sterling bounced knees first onto the bed beside him and grabbed his arm. 'Then this is your *chance*, isn't it? Together, it'll be a cinch. Maybe we could even hitch a lift on a sampan to one of the outer islands, somewhere totally beyond military civilization... live off the land... take native women as wives... or, in your case, take the natives' wives.'

Connelly knew that he could not allow the notion of jumping ship with Sterling to gain any kind of toehold in his imagination. A memory of a retreat with the Brothers in his senior year at high school came back very clearly: his tearful (but ambiguous) confession to impure fantasies, and Father John Chrysostom's three-stage delineation of the temptation process:

1 *Provocation:* An image-free stimulation in the heart, coming at you from outside your own free will. If it was not swiftly met with virtuous *rebuttal* it proceeded to...

2 *Coupling:* Not what it sounds like, but the way the

provocation gets connected up with an image that you allow your mind to dwell on. Moral responsibility began here, and if you didn't watch your ass this was likely to lead to...

3 *Assent:* Ohh...

Fortunately Sterling's misguided attempt at temptation provided the exact image he needed to rebut the provocation. 'Hang on. Haven't you already got a wife? Not to mention kids?'

The light died out of Sterling's eyes instantly, and a miasma of bleakness and exhaustion swamped the room. 'Aw, hell, yeah but... Hell, they've survived three years without me, or I guess they've survived, I haven't had one single letter, not even since I was released...' His head drooped. He's just a *kid*, Connelly realized.

'Hey,' he said, punching his shoulder. 'Hey, Sterling, I'll make a deal with you. You get back on the army conveyor belt. Give McKenna what he wants. Go back and see your wife and children again. And then, if you're still not happy and you're still not free, OK, then divorce your wife and give me a call and we'll escape back here together.' This was out of his mouth before he knew what he was saying, and his face must have shown how horrified he was to hear himself saying it.

Sterling looked at him and shook his head.

The rec room where you could smoke had a view out onto the mountain ridge behind the hospital and a map of the island of Oahu. He'd been brought under escort when he was caught lighting up after breakfast the next morning, but they apparently trusted him enough to leave him there on his own. That must mean Connelly hadn't ratted to McKenna about the escape plan. Maybe there was still a chance of talking him into it.

The slope of the ridge went vertical at a hyperbolic rate. You'd probably need climbing equipment to tackle it. The map was more decorative than topographical, but at least it enabled him to select the place farthest from any military bases: an unnamed coastal stretch east of the northernmost point of the island. The nearest town or anything was called Laie. Out to sea beyond it was a cutely stylized picture of a bulbous sperm whale, spouting. Its knowing eye and fatuous smile depressed him with one of those sweeping sadnesses that used to overcome him, frequently when he was a child, often enough since. He felt too weak to smoke now, and dropped his cigarette, still burning, into the Bakelite ashtray.

Back in his room he curled up sideways on top of the made-up bed. Maybe the whale had depressed him because his own enthusiasm for escaping was every bit as falsely drawn and pathetic. No, it was deeper, younger than that. There was something so unwanted about the map. It was a tacky piece of rubbish. Nobody had bothered to take it down because the patients on this ward didn't merit anything better. But someday they'd come and clear the whole place out, maps and people and ashtrays, and bulldoze them to some dump in a dust bowl in the middle of nowhere, stacked with old tyres and broken plastic dolls.

He tried to pull his mind out from there but lost hold of it, and it dropped in a dizzying plummet through self-hatred to self-deadness, landing at last in an unlit, gravityless unconscious place. When he came to he was standing at the sink, reaching for his razor in its soapy puddle on the frosted glass shelf.

Whoa!

Sterling pulled his hand back quickly: there was someone in the corridor outside.

'Hi! How are you this morning?' He didn't even knock on the door any more.

'Suicidal.'

'Oh, for... Come on, Sterling! Why?'

'Just am.' He locked his hands behind his back and went over to the window, pretending to look out.

Connelly knew an act when he saw one: he narrowed his eyes, figured it out, and darted to the sink to pocket the weapon. Sterling declined to react. Connelly came over and put his arm around his shoulder. 'Don't get so down about it. Nobody's asking you to go back to Changhung. It's only your old life. OK, so maybe I'm picking up the message that it wasn't all that great. But, hell, neither is mine. The thing about being free is now you can start doing stuff to change it, you know?'

Sterling jerked free of him and spun around. He stood, rearing his head back for a minute, as if his whole body was filling fast with an unbearable pressure. Then it all exploded, as blue overpowering light, as a fist aiming into Connelly's face, only just parried, and another coming into his solar plexus. Connelly staggered back, more knocked by the light in his eyes than by the anticlimactic weight of the punch. Sterling, overextended, one hand and one knee on the ground, was twisting his head up to keep his eye on his adversary. Connelly could only stand hunched there, mouthing obscenities he couldn't give breath to. When he was finally able to straighten up, the only word that came out was, 'Why?' Sterling shook his head. Connelly inhaled at last, was out, down the hall, in his office phoning Fort Shafter.

'I'm sorry, major. I can't work with this guy any more.'

'Really? Randell said you were really getting somewhere with him.'

'Yeah, I thought so too, but I'm not.'

'So what am I supposed to do now? Because he's a serviceman you know. He can't keep putting his nose in the air and saying he doesn't feel like being debriefed today. The longer it all goes on, the more it looks like we're being given the runaround.'

'I know. All I can suggest, sir, is that you put it to him straight like that.'

'Yep, if the velvet glove isn't working...' McKenna sighed. 'Well, I'll be over just as soon as I can put on the iron fist.'

By the time the major had fitted his disciplinary prosthesis, Connelly was sitting with his head on his desk, repenting his act of revenge. Why did he have to be so goddamned petulant?

Why couldn't he just have hit back, like a man? God, Sterling would despise him, as soon as he realized what he'd done.

And what had he done? Sterling had confessed to being suicidal, and he'd arranged for McKenna to be going in there with an iron fist. If it sent him over the edge completely, Connelly would be the one to blame. His hand found Sterling's razor in the pocket of his lab coat. He drew it out, contemplating it, contemplating its use. Until then a suicidal thought had never entered his head, but now that one was there it seemed strange for its familiarity, like a half-brother you have never met before. And not frightening at all.

No, not yet. Better hand the razor in to Phyllis, explain why he'd taken it from Sterling, so she could at least keep a close watch on him.

McKenna found him at the station, and urged him to come with him to give Sterling 'moral support'. Connelly shrugged and followed, unable to explain how unlikely that was.

They discovered Sterling sitting in bed. He had his arms twisted around each other and himself in a way that renewed and deepened Connelly's remorse. McKenna glanced back at him in doubt whether he ought to proceed. All Connelly could manage in reply was a miserable shrug.

'Well, lieutenant, time's getting on and we're not getting any farther with your case.'

'Could Dr Connelly go out please.' His words were low, quick and expressionless.

'Why, of course, but I thought...' McKenna looked back again, but Connelly was already gone.

'What do you need to know, sir?'

'Would you be able to start at the beginning, with the circumstances of your capture?'

'I'll try, sir. I don't know what I can remember.' With his arms still twisted together and his head down, Sterling shut his eyes and after a minute's thought said quietly, 'Thanksgiving.'

'Pardon?'

'It was Thanksgiving Day, sir, 1950. I remember that.' He

sighed, long and hard. It wasn't just the straightforward irony of being captured on Thanksgiving, it was the bad feeling in the platoon about being dragged away from their turkey dinner, their suspicion (correct) that he had volunteered them for the mission. But that memory led down a long dangerous enemy-watched road; he pulled himself up and retreated back to battalion. 'I was the commander of the First Platoon, F Company, of the 17th Regimental Combat Team. We – I mean, the RCT – were on the main road to Hyesanjin, we were nearly there, I'd say we weren't twenty or thirty miles from the Yalu. My platoon and I were on the ridge above the road. We'd cleared out a couple of NK machine-gunners who were overlooking the road ahead, where it bent around. So I decided to circle back around the other side of the ridge, because there was this quarry marked on the map, and I thought it might be the kind of place you'd put an army of Chinese, if you were bringing them south on the same road.

'I was right, or at least, we met a bunch of them, People's Army, and they chased us, and we were having to run north, and when we found an old mine tunnel we thought we'd just hide in there and hope they'd pass us by but of course they didn't. That's where we were eventually captured, sir.'

'Uh huh.'

'There were fifteen of us. As soon as we came out, the Chinese commander shot Corporal Stidham and Private Collins. For no reason, except I guess to improve our morale. Mickey Moranha was shot on the march the next day; he had frozen feet and had been lagging behind. Five more died in the temporary camp, of dysentery. They were, let's see, Corporal Black, Marcus Waters, um . . .'

McKenna said, 'I don't want to know where they died.' There was an abrupt note in his voice that made Sterling look at him, unable to tell whether this was just tactlessness, or the result of some bad memories of his own. The major took a deep breath, recovered his self-control (or his tact), and went on, 'You and the surviving members of your platoon were taken to Camp Number 13 on the Chinese border. That correct?'

'Yes, sir.'

'During the time you were held, was there any attempt made to indoctrinate you or your men?'

'Yes, sir. Ha.' A ghost of a sardonic laugh.

'What, precisely?' Sterling looked confused. McKenna prompted from a list, 'Propaganda, misinformation, haranguing, prolonged interrogations, threats, criticism sessions, mock trials, solitary confinement, manacles or leg shackles, public humiliation, or physical torture?'

'Yes. Sir.'

'Were you asked to sign peace petitions, anti-American statements, write communist propaganda in letters home, make pro-communist or anti-American radio broadcasts, deface patriotic symbols or show disrespect to the American flag?'

'We were asked.'

'And?'

'No one in the First Platoon did any of those things to my knowledge.'

'What about discrediting the American cause, offering passive assent to communist or anti-American statements, spreading despondency or anti-American feeling among your fellow prisoners, co-operating or collaborating with your captors in exchange for better food or conditions, or failing to make use of opportunities to harass the enemy?'

'Sir, I refuse to answer that question.'

'On what grounds?'

'On the grounds that it is an unfair question, sir.'

'I am aware that it is probably a painful question, lieutenant, but we have to know the exact extent of prisoners' co-operation with the enemy.' Sterling's face was still set. McKenna waited for a minute, then sighed and said, 'We already have Corporal Wilson's testimony. He says that on occasions he co-operated with the communists, when it was a question of physical or mental survival, and that he was aware other members of the platoon did too. Are you prepared to comment on that?'

'No, sir.'

'An outright refusal to answer will have a negative effect on your overall case. More so than an honest admission.'

'I'm sorry, sir.'

'This is making me pretty damned depressed about our American way of life, you know that, soldier? You people collaborated with the communists to save your butts, and you're too damned arrogant to answer a legitimate question from a superior officer in your own army because you know I'm not going to have you chained up in the parade ground or stuck in a four-foot box underground. God, it worries me!'

'I never collaborated!'

'Thank you,' said McKenna dryly, writing something on his form. 'It contradicts Corporal Wilson, but we'll let that stand for now. What's next? Let's see.' He consulted his list of questions, then looked up and said, 'You know, I think we'll call it a day there? There's some kind of jazz evening at Schofield I want to catch. We'll pick the rest of this up in the morning.'

Sterling recognized the strategy: quit while you're ahead. It was pretty damned depressing about the American way of life when staff officers in the US Army were sneakier interrogators than Peking's finest.

Connelly had fled to the peace of the Catholic chaplaincy to wrestle his conscience into submission. He even considered going to confession but was deterred by the two-year backlog of grave sexual sin. It wouldn't be fair to the padre to hand him the moral dilemma of choosing between the seal of the confessional and his patriotic duty to report a massive security risk operating in this very hospital. And anyway, confessing to Sterling was going to be a whole lot harder, so he should choose that option, by way of penance.

He went back to the ward late that afternoon, and conferred with Phyllis. 'Bill McKenna said he was fine, but I thought he was looking kind of blue, so I gave him the flowers Dr Patterson's bride donated after the wedding, and all the newest magazines. Plus I sent Helen MacPherson to take him for his smokes.' She winked at him.

'Is she the cute brunette with the – um – with the figure?'

'That's right, the figure that's restored the will to live to a dozen cases a whole lot worse than his. I think she's with him now.'

'Oh. Maybe I better not visit.'

'Well, let's just say knock before you go in.'

A feminine voice answered when he did. He stepped into a bridal bower filled with white chrysanthemums. Lt MacPherson sat by the door reading *Life Magazine*. Sterling was facing the opposite wall, huddled into an incommunicative crumple on the bed. His will to live was obviously down from this morning. A small, selfish corner of Connelly's soul was not displeased by this. 'Think you could excuse us, Lt MacPherson?'

'Sure!' she said, jumping up and getting out as fast as she could.

Connelly went round the bed and crouched down to face Sterling. 'I have a confession to make.'

'I don't want to hear it. You did what you did, nothing can be done about it now, forget about it.'

Forgetting was foreign to Connelly's soul 'I know, but getting *McKenna* in... it must have felt like I'd ratted you to Chang. I just wish there was some way –'

'I said, shut up. But if you want to know, it wasn't McKenna – he was coming sooner or later anyway, like you said. It was squealing about the escape plan that really hurt. That was *between us.*'

'Squealing...? But I didn't. Sterling, I swear I didn't.'

'Then how come all these nurses are following me around everywhere?'

'Oh. Oh. That was the razor. You know. But I only told the boss about it because I felt so guilty and I was afraid you were really going to try something. That's what all these crazy flowers are about. She's trying to cheer you up.'

'Christ,' Sterling groaned. Slowly and carefully he began unrolling and stretching himself out around his bedsores. His face was sunken and abraded-looking, as if McKenna had scraped something out from inside him.

'Oh, God, I'm sorry,' Connelly mourned.

'Please, please shut up. I need to think.' He shut his eyes and pressed his hands to his forehead, pressing the sockets of his eyes with the bend of his wrists as if this would help clear his brain. 'I don't know what's happening to me. I don't know if I'm the one who's been betrayed or the one whose fault it all was in the first place. I don't know if my stand in the camp came from being a loyal American or a conceited fool. And what happens to all this information McKenna gets? Is it passed on to their relatives or my court-martial?'

Connelly gave a little, incredulous exhalation. 'Since when are you being court-martialled? McKenna's just trying to screen out communists, and I mean real communist agents, not people who bent under pressure. He's not the recording angel saying, "Lt Sterling, I'm afraid there was a certain amount of egotism behind your resistance."' Connelly laughed a little (Sterling didn't) at the sound of sanity, remembering his own squirming that morning. Then he frowned, wondering if it had really been his own, all that complex around guilt, and betrayal, and confession. 'It's funny, you know, 'cause I'm as confused as you are. I feel like I'm in a play, and I'm not sure whether I'm method acting the loyal–disloyal sidekick, the evil Chinese mastermind, or the hero himself. You know?'

Sterling looked displeased. 'You're not tall enough to be the hero.'

'Gee, thanks.'

'You've got to be six feet and have a certain kind of chin, and the knack of saying corny things and really meaning them. If you can do that, and back it up with a little public life-risking or genuine suffering, why then everybody on your own side and the other will hate you so much they just keep kicking you until there's nothing left but a little heap of shit.' With this he rolled away from Connelly and pressed his face into the pillow. His shoulders were starting to shake, as if it was taking him all his strength to keep it all under control. Soon he was fighting sobs, and sweating with the effort of it: a heavy harsh smell that was painful to inhale filled the room. Breathing through his mouth, Connelly could still taste it, metallic and bitter, on his tongue. Eventually Sterling exhausted his power of resistance, and his body sank into a shaking chaos of breath and raw noises. Connelly suddenly couldn't stand it any more: he jumped up, opened the transom, went to the sink and splashed his face, trying to shut out those sounds. They were sounds no human being should be allowed to hear, let alone make. If he doesn't stop in a minute I'll have to get out of this room, he kept saying to himself.

It wasn't a minute, it was more like ten, he was somehow still there, back by the bed, squeezing Sterling's wrist, and at last the naked rhythms of pain were slowing down. 'Are you OK? Are you gonna be OK?'

A couple of sobs of assent.

'Don't try to talk, tonight. Go to sleep, now. I'll come in tomorrow early, and if McKenna comes back I'll stay by you.'

'Stay now.'

'Yeah. Yeah. I'll stay.'

Connelly stayed until after the shift changed on the ward, and came back at 8.30 the next morning. Any earlier would have looked distinctly peculiar, and he wasn't sure if he was imagining the curious (or was it interested?) look from the male nurse on the ward desk. Sterling's room was empty and he had to ask him for directions to the smoke room. Asking directions was a humiliation to his city-bred heart at the best of times and an occasion of special self-consciousness today. He lectured himself that if Sterling was still in a bad way, that was what counted, not these minor risks and embarrassments. Even if someone did begin to make surmises, it wasn't like he was actually employed here: he'd be gone in a week or two. But it was a relief to find Sterling and his chaperone in the smoke room, and not to have to go hunting any further up and down the ward.

The new nurse was of a different physical type, blonde and slender, but Sterling was ignoring her just as pointedly, turning his back to stare out of the window, not even looking round to acknowledge the person who had just entered the room until he heard Connelly's voice saying, 'Hiya!'

'Oh.' Sterling's face went a little pink. He indicated his cigarette. 'Just let me finish this, then we'll go back.'

'I'll be OK here if you've got other stuff to do,' Connelly told the nurse.

When she was gone, Sterling observed with an air of randomness, 'There weren't any fences around the camp at Changhung. Not even barbed wire or nothing. The commies didn't have the resources for that kind of thing. The only resource they had was people. So wherever you were going, these little bastards would follow you round to make sure you didn't escape.'

'I get it.'

'Chang himself used to stick by me, when he didn't have anything better to do. I don't know if it was because I was considered an extra high escape risk.'

'OK, OK, uncle, you don't have to rub it in.'

Sterling stubbed his cigarette out in the ashtray and went back down the hall with Connelly tagging along. When they were alone in the room he announced, 'I don't know what got into me last night –'

There was a choking sound from Connelly, who had heard this one before, in contexts very different. Or maybe not that different.

'What?' Defensively.

'Nothing. Sorry, tickle in my throat.'

'I must have been pretty confused. I can't remember much of what happened.'

'Don't worry about it,' said Connelly, in the careless voice that was most soothing to people who hadn't been themselves the night before. 'The thing we need to do now is concentrate on getting you past McKenna. That's the only serious way outa this camp, you know?'

Sterling frowned. 'What's with this "getting me past"? I don't have anything to hide. If being a loyal American qualifies me for the court-martial, then I guess that's what I want.'

'Oh, Sterling, you have to learn to be more of an *operator* than that!'

'Why?'

'Because...because that's what life is like. If you want people to leave you alone you have to tell them what they want to hear. And all McKenna wants to hear is that you were no different than the others. Claiming to be better than the rest makes him nervous. This is America, remember. It's undemocratic to be different.'

'America has changed, then. When I left it was the land of Walt Whitman and Henry David Thoreau.'

'Well, now it's the land of Joseph McCarthy.'

'Who's he?'

Connelly ignored this. 'Look, your story has to tally with Kirby Wilson's, or you both look bad. You've got to admit that when it was time to go home you stood in the wrong line.'

Sterling looked shaken. 'Kirby told him *that*?'

'He had to. It's one of the questions. Why? Is it a lie?'

'No.' Sterling looked away, raising his chin, sighing.

Voices and footsteps in the corridor warned of the major's arrival. Connelly whispered urgently, 'Then wipe that "Judased again" expression off your face and listen. He said you were crazy. McKenna thinks you're crazy anyway. Say you were crazy, but admit it happened!' He jumped off the bed and went to stand by the window.

McKenna knocked and let himself in. 'Good morning, lieutenant. Oh, hello there, doctor. Shall we pick up from where we were yesterday?'

'Good morning sir. Yes sir.'

'Now, let's see. Which question were we getting stuck on?' he said, with the patient air of a teacher helping a stupid pupil. 'Oh, yes. Co-operation and collaboration and failing to harass.'

'My answer from last night stands, sir.'

'You see, lieutenant, I know what went on in these places, I know the Chinese didn't exactly keep the letter of the Geneva Convention. I know that there were times when it was a question of survival and I'd be the last person to condemn an officer who had to make hard choices for the good of his men. I know you were in a situation where there just weren't any right answers. And quite frankly, when you tell me that you and your platoon absolutely never co-operated, well, I don't believe you.'

'Excuse me sir, but I didn't tell you that.'

'Well, did they?'

'Sir, if you remember, I refused to answer that question. I can't answer on behalf of the platoon.'

On an inspiration, Connelly said, 'Hey, Sterling, did you actually personally eyewitness any member of the First going along with the communists or discrediting the American cause or any of that?'

'No.'

'Can you accept that as an answer?' Connelly asked the major.

'Looks like I'll have to,' he muttered, and went on to the next question. 'Do you know of any surviving American servicemen who converted to communism or became communist sympathizers?'

'Yes, sir,' said Sterling promptly and gave him nearly a dozen names. Connelly was shocked, and McKenna looked as if he couldn't believe his luck. He just stood there with his eyes wide open, and had to ask Sterling to repeat them all when he remembered he was supposed to be writing them down.

It was a long time before Connelly reflected that these were people Sterling knew as enemies, that with this question he didn't feel he was being asked to act as an informer on his friends but as a law-abiding citizen alerting the authorities to a genuine threat. He had to remind himself that the naming of names had resonances for him that it wouldn't have for a man who had never even heard of McCarthy. The referent Sterling was comparing it to was probably Nuremberg, not a senate hearing. Still, his stomach felt uneasy. He prayed that the people Sterling was naming were real traitors and not scared nineteen-year-old boys.

He was so upset that he only realized Sterling was on the next, potentially the most dangerous question when he heard Sterling saying, 'I can only say, sir, that I was completely out of my mind.' When McKenna asked him to name the other men who had stayed behind he couldn't.

'That wraps it up, then,' said McKenna. 'Coming, Dr Connelly?'

Connelly went out after him, without looking at Sterling. Several yards down the hall, McKenna remarked, without particular feeling, 'Insubordinate type there.'

'Yes. But then I guess that's what it takes to resist brainwashing.'

'You probably got a point,' the major yawned. Connelly wondered how anyone could be so unmoved after such a session. Or was that only the effect of his own loss of objectivity?

McKenna was saying, 'Anyway, that's it for you, isn't it? You want me to see if I can get a place for you on a flight, or are you going to make the most of the beach for as long as you can?'

Connelly was shaken again. 'Oh! The beach, I guess.'

'Ha ha. Why not? Well, I'll catch you later.'

He felt too wobbly to check in with Sterling just yet. He needed to step back, regain some objectivity. He went back to his little square house in Fort Shafter and read a torrid Polynesian novel about a white man who jumped ship and took a native woman as a wife. He fell asleep in the late afternoon heat and only woke up when the sun was going down.

Connelly decided to buy his own surfboard. It was maybe a funny time to buy one when he was being threatened with having to go back to the mainland. Or maybe that was why. Somewhere, somewhere on the east coast there had to be a surfable break and he would search until he found it. Sure, it'd probably be freezing but he could wear a wetsuit like a frogman. If all else failed he'd just have to get a job in Southern California.

He found a marine store near the yacht harbour and chose an expensive piece of blue fibreglass, short and manœuvrable at ten feet. The streamlined cut of the rails did something sexual to his solar plexus. Protecting it with a couple of towels, he lashed it to the car roof and drove off in the direction of Hoku's Waialae homestead. So much for his noble resolutions. He had to show it, show it off to someone, and Hoku was the only someone he knew.

But only Leimomi was at home. She came out, stood

transfixed on the porch, at once repelled by Connelly's presence, yet fascinated by the board on the car roof. 'You surf?' she demanded presently.

'Kind of.'

She came down the steps slowly, her eyes fixed on the board, 'Da short,' she observed critically, but stroked the streamlined edges. 'I can try it?'

'Sure thing. Get your suit and let's go.' She disappeared into the house, came out wearing a pair of Hoku's shorts stretched low across her hips. She tied her sleeveless blouse under her bosom and jumped into the car.

'Where's a good place to go?' Connelly asked her.

'Kahala not far. Got to paddle out for miles for get past the reef but.'

Kahala was a shallow and unpromising beach with a lot of cross-wind chop. Leimomi pointed off to the left and squinting into the distance he made out long white lines, lazy comfortable looking three-footers he guessed, rolling along with placid regularity. Leimomi decided it would be best for them to paddle out together, in tandem, then one could swim around and relax while the other surfed.

The board rode rather low under their combined weight; it felt sulky and unstable. Connelly tried to stifle an ominous and growing sense that his new pride and joy might just be too much for him. What if he'd just made a big, expensive, dangerous mistake, like someone who has just learned to ride on a twenty-year-old carthorse, and has gone out and bought a half-trained thoroughbred.

The water was shallow over the reef and once, twice, he heard the sunken fin bump and grate against the coral. 'I'll swim,' he announced, and rolled off into the water. His feet and shins and hands would heal if he scratched them, his board would not. Leimomi lay flat to paddle more efficiently and shot ahead, then slowed and waited for him to catch up. In places he had eighteen inches or two feet of clearance and swam comfortably enough; in others he had to compress himself into a flat, inefficient breast stroke with most of his efforts going upwards rather than forwards. Once or twice it was easier to just stand up and wade, though the soles of his feet complained about this. The reef was matted over with drab-coloured seaweed. Schools of thin silvery fish scattered at his approach. In crevices of the coral he saw spiny sea urchins, fat sea cucumbers, starfish.

As they approached the end of the reef and the breaking waves Leimomi slid off the board and insisted he go first. Perhaps she was also a bit wary of its instability. 'OK, then, if you're sure,' he said, and scrambled aboard.

'No run into me, eh?' Leimomi called, then dived from the edge of the reef into the blue hole that opened so suddenly before them.

The water under the board went from turquoise to deep cobalt as he drove forward. He was farther out, and deeper than he'd ever been. The waves were particularly gentle, and he sailed over them, hung in the air for a fraction of a second until the board tipped nose down with a slap. He spent some time picking his spot – not easy out here all alone, when you are used to just tagging along after the other surfers in the line-up – finally selecting the patch where foam floated in quilted ripples, over a ridge of the reef that reasserted itself farther out. The sun was hot on his back. He'd be peeling like anything tomorrow morning.

Here came the set. He checked Momi's position, let the first one go, the second, no, yes, go for broke! Lashing his arms into the water until the board slid silkily forward, stalling a little as the hunger of the wave sucked it back. Connelly slung himself to his knees to get his weight forward and the thoroughbred beneath him sprang ahead – he was on his feet – for a minute – then the board wallowed to the right and he wobbled and fell in beside it, grabbing hold of the side just before it cantered away.

He scrambled back on board, glanced self-consciously at Momi, who stood on the coral watching. She was grinning but anyway not bent double killing herself with laughter.

The next sets were disappointing. He sat astride with his feet dangling in the water, rocking gently, listening to the wavelets resonate against fibreglass. Leimomi's head appeared here and there, like a seal's, but she spent most of her time underwater.

A change in the voice of the sea out there heralded a bigger set on the way. He waited for the third wave this time, swung up onto his feet straight away, found himself executing a totally unintentional swivel, but recovered to balance for about twenty yards across the face of the wave before falling back into it on his butt. He came up, shook the water out of his eyes and saw Leimomi's arms flashing as she sprinted to catch the board. 'Your turn now!' he called to her, and whether or not she heard him, she took it.

She was a better surfer than he was: cautious but dignified, slower to get to her feet, but smarter about getting down again before the worst happened. She took her time getting used to the board's nervy instability, and once she had got its number was in no hurry to give it back. Connelly figured he might as well give up hope of surfing again today, and decided to make what he could of the afternoon exploring the holes in the reef.

He stood up on the side of the nearest shelf, and flipped himself in a semi-jack-knife to plunge as fast and as far down the blue gap as he could. Down, down, past a flickering school of yellow tang, God, it was so deep. If the bottom didn't come soon he'd have to give up and go back up for air. But if he didn't get to the bottom, he wasn't going to be able to bounce off it for the speed to get back up to the surface in time. His ears were going to burst in a second. Oh, thank God! His hand hit rock, he threw his feet down and shot up through the horrified golden fish, up, up, with his chest exploding. Involuntarily he exhaled – sunshine cutting through the water above, the ripples on the surface like lines of brown and green – he couldn't hold his lungs empty another second – mind and reflex, throat and diaphragm at war – air! His whole body shook, his heart pounded, his ribs pumped massively in and out.

Leimomi's voice, alarmed, almost a scream. He opened his eyes: the water was wrong, brown, cut open, swirling. Something rough dragged against his waist. For a moment he thought he'd drifted back into the coral, but it wasn't like that, and then he saw the brown fin cross in front of him, not four feet away. He was shaking for real now, and trying to fight it, frightened of stirring the water. The shark came close again, brushed his side with its sandpaper skin, coiled round the small of his back like a cat

Leimomi was paddling like hell for him. 'Get back!' she bellowed. 'Get back over the reef!' But Connelly was too frightened to move. The shark came round and buzzed him again; through his raw skin he could feel its aliveness, faintly warm, the ripple of its muscles long and lazy as it hula-ed its tail this way, that way. Then it seemed to notice the board and made its way over to investigate that. Leimomi stopped paddling and slapped her palms on the surface of the water, hoping to frighten it away. She coasted to Connelly on the remnants of the waves, using her weight rather than her arms to angle the board. Suddenly his paralysis gave way and he swam like crazy for it, dragging himself out of the sea. The two of them knelt there, facing each other with huge eyes, Connelly shaking with such extravagance they nearly capsized. The shark went back and forth, circled; once it came close, angling its chestnut brown body to look up at them. Its eye stared deeply into Connelly's: alien-looking, utterly cold, beautiful. In the sunlight its skin was red and rich-looking. It came near again, then suddenly swished its tail with an exasperated air and swam slashingly back out to sea.

'Ho,' said Leimomi, with a great heaving sigh. 'Good thing for you he's not hungry, eh?' Connelly nodded, unable to speak. He pivoted on his knees and they began paddling back to shore. 'He went shred your back,' Momi observed.

'He k-k-kept brushing me,' Connelly managed to say, through clattering teeth. Slowly, as he bent to paddle, the sensation of stinging began to break through the numbness of shock. Stinging, then pulling tight, then burning until he couldn't bear to move for stretching the skin. They weren't far from the beach, and he got off the board, to pad and plash his way on top of the reef.

On land, Leimomi took charge of the board, slinging it along like a stevedore, as well as the car. Connelly sat twisted forwards in the passenger seat while she cruised home at a stately 20 miles per hour, never taking it out of second gear. When they reached the dirt road down to the homestead they came upon Hoku, carrying a spear with two red snapper impaled on it. Momi put her head out of the window and capped his fish story, 'Wop your jaw, we went catch one eight-foot shark!'

It was raining. Down on the plain the sun was shining, but up here on the edge of the mountain it was raining big fat extra wet-sounding streams of water. Sterling had grown up in a desert state, and so it was the wetness that made him conscious of being in the tropics, rather than the standard-issue sunshine. The rain looked like it should be richer and thicker than water, and taste slightly sweet, and slightly alcoholic. He opened the transom window and managed to angle a forearm out, but couldn't reach past the shelter of the eaves. He could feel how much warmer and damper again it was outside, and he sighed. Maybe he'd never make an escape.

He walked around the room a couple of times, restless, but not feeling strong enough for real exercise. God, Connelly was late. He left his room and found Lt MacPherson at the desk. 'Where's Doctor Connelly today?'

'Was he supposed to be coming in? I thought I heard him telling that intelligence major that he was going to spend the rest of his time before he had to go home at the beach.'

'What?'

'I don't know, that's just what I heard and it was none of my business anyway. You have an appointment with him or something?'

Sterling turned without answering and went back to his room. At all costs he must not allow himself to imagine that Connelly had just been playing him along until he produced the goods for McKenna. That was just another variant of confusing him with Chang and Kirby. He sat down on the bed and tried to remind himself of all the little things that proved Connelly was sincere. The trouble was, they were just memories, abstract. His absence was right there, concrete.

He couldn't go for a cigarette, because he needed to save the last one for after lunch. The room, which had once seemed so light and spacy, felt now cramped and dull and ugly. Why couldn't Connelly just come, and bring some Meiguo smokes while he was at it? He fell onto the bed, face first. He could have yelled or cried with frustration, if only he'd had the energy. He was too angry to sleep and too tired to lose his temper.

The minutes went slowly, endured. Nothing got better, or different. Lunch came around at seven minutes past twelve. The guy on the chow trolley looked at him with a diagnostician's eye. 'Fed up?'

'Damn right.'

'Why doncha get something else wrong with you, so they have to move you to a better ward? Fall out of bed and break an arm, they gotta hot poker table going in orthopaedics. Not but what you loons ain't got the best nurses.'

Lunch was Red Flannel Hash, corned beef stained fuchsia-coloured with beet juice. Sterling ate it with the same swift amazed non-discrimination with which he ate everything that had come his way since he'd been in American hands. The cigarette afterwards was what he was really thinking about. Somehow it had got magically attached to Connelly's arrival. As soon as it was gone Connelly would have to come, because then he wouldn't have any more smokes at all. Maybe there was a bit of confusion in a detail of that logic, but overall it was compelling. He used his bread to clean his plate, stuffed it into his mouth and loped down the hall with his packet and matches.

The return trip was much slower, ten minutes later. Connelly was not waiting in the room for him. Well, he hadn't expected it. It was absolutely in the scheme of things that he should be there alone, with no source of tobacco. He sat on the bed and hugged his knees for a while. He tried looking at the magazines, but that only underscored the already intolerable sense of waiting, killing time. He got up and went to the mirror.

In it was the reflection of an ugly old man, the features of a crazy hobo who used to pass through the neighbourhood when he was a little kid. Oh Jesus, he'd lost himself again! He jumped away, then had to go back and have another look. What was he, John L 'Tiger' Sterling, supposed to look like? Because for sure it wasn't that hideous article. If that was anyone it was the tramp. He used to come around regularly in marbles season. He exposed himself to the little girls, and all the kids used to come running out to see the spectacle. They knew how to keep a good thing secret, and it was several years before Mom found out. When she did she had given Tiger the responsibility of scaring him away. It was the kind of thing he was good at. He looked forward to the hobo's annual return more eagerly than ever, as a licensed spree of violence, but after the second experience the old fellow had apparently decided not to chance his luck any further in northeast Reno.

But what was he doing in the mirror? No matter how far you got separated from your own self, you couldn't accidentally land back in somebody else's, could you? Or what if the old hobo hadn't been a real person but a prognostication, a ghost in reverse of what that kid was going to decay into? This thought scared him so badly he shot out of the room and found himself gasping for human company at the ward desk like a drunk in a bar that's just opened for the day.

Randell looked up and said, 'What's happened to Dr C.?'

'I – don't – know,' he choked, unable to conceal the fact that he was panting with fear.

'Someone's husband's probably shot him,' she said, smiling at the pleasing image of Connelly lying lifeless in his blood-soaked aloha shirt. Sterling looked appalled and sprinted back to the room.

He shut the door and stood with his back to it. If you don't get a hold of yourself, how long is this going to go on? The empty afternoon ahead of him seemed to fill itself with all the crazy horror of the solitary months in the cell at Changhung. But even back then there had been a way out. Why couldn't he find it now?

He couldn't find it now because this was it. The empty state of being that had looked like an escape route then just landed up in this dead end he was stuck in now. As the full import of this was slowly sinking in, something in his brain just decided to quit in disgust. A nauseous but welcome dizziness arrived to dissolve terror. Very total blackness that promised dreamless anaesthesia airlifted him out of the dead end. And then he was landing again, hard, forehead first on the floor.

There was a long paralysed time in which he kept checking in and out of consciousness. It was the chuck wagon medic who found him and summoned help. 'Careful! He may have broken an arm!'

The night was in and out too. It seemed like every time he was just drifting off to sleep, someone came in and took his blood pressure. At least it stopped him from dreaming. The healthy solid headache was keeping his waking self rooted, and the farther shores of terror were impossible in the face of physical pain. After breakfast a wheelchair came to take him down for his skull X-ray.

On the way back up there was a commotion at the ward entrance. All the nurses, male and female, were gathered in a huddle watching someone taking their clothes off. Hm. He had been blaming his mental state for all the surreal things that had been happening to him, but maybe the hospital itself was partly at fault. He could almost hear the chuck wagon man advising orthopaedic patients to feign insanity. 'They gotta hot striptease upstairs every Saturday morning.'

'Lieutenant!' called Randell. 'Come and see what the shark did to Dr Connelly!'

'No, thank you,' he said, looking away fastidiously as the chair rolled past the exhibition.

When Connelly came in, Sterling was tucked up in bed reading the *Saturday Evening Post*. 'Wow! What happened? Some egg on your head!'

Without looking up: 'Fell.'

'You'll never guess what happened to me! Look! This shark – '

'Spare me.'

'OK.' Connelly shrugged and made to leave.

Imperiously: 'I didn't say to go.'

'I need permission or what?'

Sterling put down his magazine and just looked at him. Connelly sighed. 'Sterling, you're hard work. I really needed a break yesterday morning. I was going to come in the afternoon, but then this shark –'

'Forget it.'

'Anyway, I'm sorry.' He lowered himself onto the bed, carefully, as if every muscle was stiff. Sterling applied the silent treatment for another minute and a half, then asked, 'What was the major's verdict?'

'Insubordination. But he doesn't sound like he's in a hurry to order the firing squad. I think he's recommending the panel to clear you. Never mind. You did your best to wreck your life, but it just didn't work.'

'Jesus.'

Connelly observed him. 'Come on, spit it out.'

'What?'

'Whatever it is. You don't want to go home. That's been the

real problem all along, hasn't it? How come?'

Sterling twisted his jaw with his hand. He was hunting for a way of saying 'Because I need you to keep my whole personality from falling apart,' in a way that would sound tough and aggressive rather than desperate. It was a tall order, but he knew it was not beyond him, given time.

Before he found the words, Connelly got impatient and prompted, 'I guess most of the men that come through here are a little scared. "Has my wife been faithful, will the kids remember me?" But the pull to get back usually outweighs the fear. I don't get the impression there's any pull at all, for you.'

Sterling got out of bed and went back to the mirror. There was a pale face, a yellow crew cut, blue eyes with a stretched wary look. Not a winning sight, but not the old tramp either. With his back to Connelly he said, 'The day before they were coming to take us back Chang made me go with him into the guards' quarters, where there was a large mirror. Probably not any bigger than this one, but it must have been the biggest in the camp. I had to take my shirt off. He just said, "Much kinder your relatives you stay here. You bring terrible shame to family."'

Connelly whistled. 'Oh, so it was all your fault?'

'I don't know. Chinese thinking, but he was right. The shame sticks, no matter whose the blame was. And it's not just the physical thing, it's all these mental states I have no control of. I'm sicker in the head now than I was then. And what if they think it's because I was brainwashed?'

'You are brainwashed, if you believe every stupid thing Chang said.'

He looked stubborn. 'So that's the reason I don't want to go home. That's the real reason I stood in the line with the commies who wanted to stay.'

Connelly said nothing. No doubt he should have been saying something, dishing out a common-sense view, but it was suddenly as if a weight was pressing all the words and energy out of him. For some reason he'd always felt confident that Sterling was more tough-minded than this, that because he was A Hero he was immune to shame on this scale.

Maybe something of disillusionment was showing on his face, because Sterling said, rather aggressively, 'Well, you told me to spit it out.' He went over to the window and leaned to look out, forearms resting on the sill.

Connelly still didn't have any words to offer. After about ten minutes' silence, Sterling pulled himself up straight and heaved a big sigh. 'You know, it's not even my family I can't face. They're good people, they're not gonna... It's this invisible enemy who's going to make my life hell when I get home. He thinks he's so wonderful, he's going to ride in triumph in MacArthur's jeep through Seoul and Pyongyang and Peking and probably Moscow too. He's got nothing but contempt for a failure like me.'

'So who is he? Your brother?'

'No, stupid, me. Tiger Sterling, circa 1949.'

'Oh, I get it. Sorry. I'm not on the ball today... What did you just call yourself?'

'Tiger.' He turned a little red. 'Dumb family nickname. Beats "John" but that's about all you can say for it. You can use it, though, if you want.'

'OK.'

Tiger looked at him, waiting for something. But Connelly would have endured the worst of Changhung rather than reveal his own family nickname, which was Sasha. To move the conversation ahead, he said, 'Well, if it's only your old self, you've got nothing to lose but your pride.'

Sterling's eyes went wide with shock, then he swiftly turned away to look out of the window again. 'That doesn't help,' he said, in a voice only partially mastered.

'Oh, God, sorry. I don't know what's wrong with me today.'

'Go get yourself a coffee and wake up. And get me some more cigarettes while you're at it.'

'Jeez, don't they pay you people in the army?' Connelly complained. But he went, and once he was out of the room it occurred to him forcibly that a person who had been attacked by a shark yesterday had every right not to be on the ball today. He didn't bother with the coffee, but bought the Lucky Strikes and went straight back, to say, 'Look, St—Tiger, I'm only screwing up here. It's better for both of us if I get a good night's sleep and come back tomorrow with a brain that functions, yeah?'

'No, wait.' There was a sharp note of panic in his voice.

Connelly waited. Sterling was looking at him, but saying nothing. 'What is it?'

'I'm only OK when you're here. When you leave my mind starts exploding. Yesterday afternoon . . .'

A tremendous weariness sank into Connelly. He couldn't hear the story of yesterday afternoon as it was confessed. He was going to run out of air, he was going to drown, he had to fight for the surface and interrupt, 'Sterling, stop it! I can't do anything for you. If you're crazy, you're just crazy and there's nothing another person can do about it.'

Sterling shut up and looked at his hands. Connelly pulled himself together — if he'd allowed himself to go on he'd have started off counting up the hours he had spent in this room and ended up bursting into hysterical tears or something. He swallowed and said, 'See? Another screw-up. I'm doing more harm than good. Goodbye, Tiger.'

Sterling shrugged and refused to say goodbye.

Connelly had gone back to get his good night's sleep at Hoku's place, and it was past ten when he got back to the hospital the next morning. Phyllis told him that Sterling had gone to chapel. 'When's he likely to be back?'

'The Protestant service usually finishes after eleven.'

'Oh.' He wrinkled his nose. He was supposed to be meeting Hoku and Leimomi for the lunchtime show at the Pikake Terrace. Turning up for his show was the only way they could be sure of catching their father, and Leimomi wanted to consult him before they did anything about Connelly's shark. 'No, I can't wait,' Connelly decided. 'I've got a date for lunch.

Would you tell him from me I'm sorry and I'll look in later this afternoon?'

She winked. 'Sure thing.'

The Pikake Terrace backed onto the beach just a few hotels up from Queen's Surf. It was raised a little, and partially screened by trellises of stephanotis and jasmine, but freeloading tourists could gather at the edge of the sand and listen to Abraham Manono, or even get a glimpse of him through the vegetation, if they were shameless enough. Hoku was shameless enough to give a little performance of his own, a very graphic hula of *Kaua i ka Huahua'i* that made the original meaning (You and me in the spray) perfectly clear, despite his father's attempt to button the number up as the Hawaiian War Chant.

'You going get yourself arrested, Prince Leleiohoku,' Momi warned.

Hoku bowed to his stunned audience, put his arm around Connelly. The Hawaiian warrior behind the microphone inside was winding up his show with the big 'Alo-o-oha!' that was his signature. As the tables slowly cleared, Momi pushed through a gap between two trellises and gestured to them to follow. Hoku cracked several of the slats as he forced his way through.

Abraham Manono was still on the stage, flirting with a party of grey-haired ladies from Oregon. He was an impressive sight, barefoot, in pure white trousers and an open-necked, cavalier-looking shirt, with a red sash around his waist and a matching carnation lei around his neck. He seemed to radiate warmth and friendliness, actual genuine love, Connelly thought, from the way he stood, the way he moved his arms. But his children hung back, unsmiling, until the last tourist was gone, and even Leimomi seemed to have to nerve herself up to approach him.

'*Aloha ka kou!*' The greeting was grand, physical and inclusive. He called to the other artists and the backstage people to come and meet his wonderful keikis, the beautiful princess of his heart, Leimomi, his son who played football for

Kam School. He insisted on taking them down the beach to the Halekulani bar and buying lots and lots of brightly coloured cocktails for them all. Every time he met someone he knew – every few minutes – he told them about his wonderful beautiful children. Three times Hoku tried to tell him it was five years since he had graduated, but the football story kept being repeated. It had to be; it was the only interesting thing his father knew about him.

They were getting pretty drunk by the time Leimomi finally managed to make him listen to her. 'Do you know where we can get an *ilima* lei?'

'*Ilima?*'

'Yeah. Real *ilima* flower, not paper or anything.'

He frowned, shook his head. 'Hard to find, nowadays. If you want a really good lei, I could get you some *maile*, you can still get *maile*. Or beautiful orchid, double carnation lei? What you need *ilima* for?'

Leimomi had spent the day before doing more oral research among all her oldest relatives, and Hoku had been at Kahala beach all morning, fishing in the concrete canal, but thinking and feeling about it, and independently they had arrived at the sense that a lei of pale orange *ilima* blossom, sacred to Kaahu-Pahau, would be the best offering Connelly could make to the shark who had declined to eat him. Hoku had been reluctant to involve his father, but Momi had insisted. If the shark was a family *aumakua*, they needed the blessing and advice of the head of the family. 'It's for this offering,' said Hoku, deliberately vague.

'An offering!' he exclaimed. 'Now let your father tell you the best kind of offering. Listen to this. Get a ti leaf, trim the edges, and put upon it a glass of Tanqueray gin. Never fails. For the big things in your life, maybe the whole bottle. Why not? Come on!' He finished his drink and jumped up and took them to a liquor store and bought the gin for them, and then to a little lei stand, where the lady knew him, and strange to say, today she did have a *maile* lei, she never usually, tourists never bought da kine, but today yes, something told her bring *maile*. She lifted a strand of vines twisted together, scrappy to look at, but scented of the uplands, ferny and damp. 'I must have known you coming,' she smiled, and insisted on giving it to them for free.

'You see? Meant!' beamed Manono.

A rum punch-drunk threesome made its way back down Kalakaua Avenue to where the Chevy was parked. Connelly felt hot and sore. An uncharacteristic depression seemed to have settled on Momi, which the meantness of the *maile* lei did nothing to soothe. 'Oh, let's just forget it!'

'We going feel better in the water,' Hoku said. 'Come on, finish um.' He took the wheel and hula-ed around the curves of Diamond Head, through the heat and glare, down to the little beach park. He swam out with Leimomi. Connelly, despite the heat, increased by the *maile* lei wound three times around his neck for secure keeping, had no intention of getting into those shark-infested waters. He paddled the board, keeping the bottle trapped under his chin, nestled in the aromatic leaves.

They came to the same place. Connelly got to his knees, but the unstable board rocked anxiously with every passing wavelet. 'Sit on your butt,' Leimomi instructed. 'The shark not going want your skinny legs when it can get Hoku first.'

Connelly tried to laugh and lowered his calves into the water. 'What do we do now? Am I supposed to say something?'

Leimomi winced. 'Better not, unless you got something to say.'

'Eh,' said Hoku in a calming voice. He swam over and put his arm across the board to touch her hand. 'We're doing our best, you know, Momi. Dad too.'

She tossed her head, then suddenly dived under the water and swam forty feet out to sea before coming up for air. Salt water from her eyes, into the salt water all around her. A weight of pain inside so great she didn't know how the sea could hold her up. She didn't even know who it belonged to, herself, her father, or this island whose sacred flower tourists never bought. 'I don't want to be his beautiful princess. I just wanted him to give me an *ilima* lei!' she said aloud.

When she rejoined them, Hoku passed her the lei. She floated it, spreading it into a U-shape as if it were around an invisible neck. Connelly poured out the gin. They floated silently in the waves for a few minutes. She turned first and started swimming back.

Back at the homestead, Hoku whispered to Connelly, 'Let's leave her alone for awhile, eh? Come, I show you the stream.' He led him up past the corral and chicken shed, in towards the apex of the valley, where the spiny tangly jungle growth took over the slopes. A tiny creek, just a little spill of water, clearing a width of maybe a yard of bare black rock, ran concealed under greenness. Hoku had made a little clearing further up, where you could sit on a high, dryish stone and cool your feet. 'My secret place to get away from Momi,' he confided. 'Here, squeeze up, there's room.'

Connelly pressed in against him, but felt he had to balance this with the news, 'You know, Hoku, I'll be having to go soon.'

'Yeah, you told me.'

'I wish I could live here for ever, with you, but I can't.'

'Just enjoy,' Hoku advised, with a silencing gesture. Connelly felt scratchy inside, and it was hard to hold still, but he managed to keep his mouth shut. It was Hoku who broke the silence. 'I had a brother, you know. Alapa'i. He used to help on Uncle Nobu's sampan. Last year, one night out in the Molokai channel out there, he was lost.'

'I'm sorry.'

'Don't be sorry. He was my brother for a little while and now you're my brother for a little while.'

Sterling hadn't been to church since the death of the British padre who had briefly blessed Changhung. He wasn't exactly a believer, but he came back today feeling quieter inside, able to take Lt-Col Randell's news that Connelly wouldn't be in till later with composure. Somehow the service had shifted his focus on the moral universe, widened his sights just a little beyond the twinned prisons of camp and hospital. He found himself remembering his father, whose gentle nature mysticism had concealed itself under lip-service Episcopalianism. Maybe that was a clue to what was wrong with him now: he'd just been cooped up indoors for too long.

After lunch a corporal turned up to issue him with a uniform. The trousers were huge: Sterling had to knot the belt to force the waist band into enough accordion pleats to keep them up. The corporal refused to go back and exchange them for another pair. He had paperwork that proved Lt Sterling had been issued with a pair of 34-inch-waist trousers in 1948, and if he was going to turn up now with an unauthorized weight loss on that scale, he should just be glad they weren't getting him for destroying or mislaying army property.

Despite the fit, Sterling was so taken with this new state of being – he was a man, not a patient, and maybe even a soldier, not an inmate – that it never occurred to him to wonder why this transformation had suddenly taken place, or what it was for. This didn't prevent the answers to these unasked questions from arriving an hour later. MacPherson delivered written orders from McKenna to report at 1500 hours to Sgt Walcott who would drive him to Hickam Airfield, where a transport was taking off for California. Minutes later a consultant he had never met before arrived and discharged him. Around two it began to dawn on Sterling that he was leaving. Around 2.30 he forced himself to face the possibility that Connelly might not show before he had to go. He went out to consult with Randell. 'I doubt it,' she leered. 'He said he had a hot date for lunch.'

'Can I borrow a piece of paper?' he demanded. She gave him a sheet from her telephone message pad and a pen.

He went back to his room, but couldn't write. The paper was about two inches by three inches. Maybe if he'd had a nice big legal pad and a couple of hours he could have started in a relaxed, joky style and found his way slowly to whatever had to be said. His guts were starting to churn and he had to go out for a crap. As he came back into the room the thought struck him that he would never see it again, this place where so much had happened.

He was going to go away and live the rest of his life (whatever that added up to) and he was never going to see Connelly again. Leave your address, stupid, ask him to write! urged a voice in his head. He picked up his pen, then hesitated. No. If he was going to walk into a life like that he had to go looking straight forwards, not back at an escape plan that was never going to happen, not wasting time hankering after a letter from Connelly that might never come.

A sudden memory of that first day, Connelly coming in with that aloha shirt under his coat, the bewildered sense of wondering who he was. Or maybe it was a dim premonition about what he was going to be? Sterling left the pen and paper on the table and walked out.

'Hey, don't I even get a goodbye smile?' cried Randell as he passed the desk.

'Goodbye, um, thanks.'

'Good luck, lieutenant.'

Connelly turned up at 4.30. His hair was stiff with salt, his bare knees scratched and muddy from the hike up the streambed. Hoku had been initiating him into another one of Prince Leleiohoku's songs; that showed in his face and made Phyllis click her tongue. 'Must have been some date!'

'S'just the heat.'

'Of course. Afraid you've missed the patient though.'

'Huh?'

'He's gone home. Lt Sterling.'

'Home? But...why?'

'There was a plane out from Hickam Field. The next boat wasn't till Thursday or something crazy so the major pulled strings for him. No point in him stewing in here when he could be with his family, though I guess it's not such good news for you, huh? End of the vacation? Broken hearts all over Fort Shafter? Seventeen officers' wives found drowned in Lake Wilson?'

Connelly was shivering too hard to laugh. He felt sick, and hoped he wasn't going to faint. 'Did Sterling say anything... leave a message or anything for me?'

'Oh, yes, that might have been what he wanted the paper for. He didn't leave anything with me, but it might still be in his room, they haven't turned it over yet.'

Connelly went to look and came back shaking his head and bearing the empty sheet. 'Only this.'

'Isn't he awful, and all that time you spent talking to him! And you know, I think he would have walked right past me without even saying goodbye if I hadn't made him. Never mind. You made a difference, you know, even if he wasn't the type to show it.'

Part Two

Barbara Sterling sat with the children on the floor, cutting out accessories for paper dolls from McCall's magazine with a pair of blunt-nosed scissors. She was a delicate blonde with the wistful eyes of someone whose life had begun promisingly, but suddenly took a wrong turning and skidded out of control; brown eyes that were still wondering, helplessly, where she had gone wrong. But eyes that also had a sad bleak honesty about them, a child's eyes, that didn't know they weren't supposed to say how bad it all was.

Betsy McCall's' autumn wardrobe was particularly elaborate this year, and Barbara should have been able to predict from experience that the little tartan scarf and matching purse and gloves would be shredded or lost or vacuumed up before the end of the day. Caroline, the elder of the two children, did not really appreciate the neatness and completeness of these tiny paper outfits, and if the brown eyes had been even more honest than usual, they might have admitted that she was doing this for herself, as a distraction, a consolation. Little Henry had the same feeling about it she did, but you could just about guarantee that whenever she indulged him in it, one of the neighbours or the colonel's wife would drop in and feel sorry for him growing up without a father.

But today it was the phone that rang. 'Is... is this the right number for a Mrs Barbara, um Sterling?' A high-pitched, shaky, male voice.

'Speaking.'

'Mrs Sterling, you don't know me but, um, my name is Kirby Wilson and I was a friend... was in your husband's platoon, we were in the camp together. He's... he's not back yet, is he?'

'No, we haven't had any news, except that his name was on the list, that he was being released.' Her voice sounded calm, at least in comparison to his. Her heart was racing.

'Oh well, I was just phoning to let you know, I mean, I guess you know he's alive now.'

'We found out two weeks ago. I mean, they told us. It is a relief to know you've seen him... You have seen him? Recently?'

'The day we were handed over. What would that be? The second of September, yes, that's right.'

'The only other thing they told us was that he's still in a hospital somewhere. Do you know what's wrong with him?'

'I... there's not... he's um, he's um...'

'What?' her voice sounded harsh, abrupt.

'He's had a hard time. Well, we all have. But Sterling, he's had it harder than most.'

'Please,' said Barbara, speaking with a force that didn't feel like her own. 'It would help me to know the worst.'

'He's troubled in his mind.'

This sentence, flat, unerasable, hung in the air. In the end it was Kirby who backtracked, gulping, 'I mean, he was. Only towards the end. Probably it'll all go once he's home. Oh, look, Mrs Sterling, I didn't mean to say this. I'm awful sorry. I only wanted to set your mind at ease.'

'It's all right,' she said automatically. 'I asked for it, didn't I? Thank you for calling.' She put the phone down. Luckily the children were deep in their game and hadn't noticed anything wrong in her voice.

She stepped around them and into the kitchen. It was only ten days ago that she had reacquired a husband. Now she had one who was troubled in his mind. Whatever that meant. Crazy? Brainwashed? She poured a cup of coffee from the percolator, lit a cigarette. It occurred to her that she had never heard of this Private Kirby. Maybe there was no such person.

Maybe it was a hoax. Tiger had one or two enemies; there were one or two catty wives on the base.

What should she do? The first instinct was to pick up the phone and call his folks. But what good would that do? It would only make them feel as scared as she did. Worse: think how she would feel if it was Henry, instead of only Tiger. Virginia always said, 'Of course it's so much worse for you, dear.' But that was the kind of thing she said.

Anyway, there was no reason to even let herself feel scared until she had checked the caller's credentials. She took a deep breath and decided the thing to do was to go back through all the old papers and see if there was anyone by that name mentioned. She carried the coffee up the stairs, lifted a cardboard box down from the high shelf in her closet. It was not a box she opened very often, but it had undergone several different incarnations. First it had been a shoebox, holding a few letters, six of them personal, four of them official. Then a parcel of personal effects had arrived, and had gone with the letters into a bigger box. After that, memories were more painful than hopeful for the children, and all kinds of little items that spoke too clearly of Tiger were thrown in with it, until nothing remained but two photographs, displayed in the living room for the benefit of his parents and other visitors.

Because she looked at it so infrequently, it exerted a kind of painful fascination, especially the stuff they had sent back: two Japanese swords, a deflated football, a red satin bathrobe she couldn't for the life of her imagine him wearing, a typically atypical Tigeresque treasure hoard. Her letters to him were with the rest of the things, the older ones looking worn, much read, the ones that had arrived after he was gone were kept all together in a large manila envelope. She had continued to write for almost six months after they told her he was missing, and had only given up when the letters were sent back this way, like a slap in the face. Now she blew out an angry sigh, pushed these things aside, dug down to the bottom to extract the original shoe box, as if it was still the essence of the whole thing.

First she looked through the official letters, but they didn't mention anybody else's name. She sighed again, went downstairs, for another cigarette, wondered if it would be better just to call, maybe not his parents, maybe Colonel Sadlachek, maybe her brother. No, no, she would figure the Kirby mystery out by herself, she couldn't be leaning on other people all the time. She marched back upstairs and confronted his letters.

Sept. 9, 1949
Dear Barbara,
This is just to let you know I am here. I'll probably call you later if I can get the chance. I haven't got much of an impression about the place. I'm going to make a real effort to bust out of here and see the real Japan, this brainless thing of never getting out of the base etc. really ticks me off.

Write to me about the kids and stuff when you can. T.

Sept. 30
Dear Barbara,
No. I don't think I can apologize. I decided when I was about 12 that there was no point in it ever because it doesn't change what happened, and if you can't change what happens why should you be let off the hook? And if you aren't going to be let off the hook, why apologize? In this case it would be just insulting, at least I would see it that way if I was you. So I'm not doing this to add insult to injury. It's just that I respect you too much to ask you to pretend things are all right.

I won't bore you with news because it's so boring here, Yours, Tiger

Nov. 17
Dear Barbara,
I haven't written but I have been thinking a lot, I guess I can't write because I'm not sure what I want to say, I keep changing my mind.

On top of trying to think things through I'm also having to fight off the moral sickness of this place, I mean of the other officers and even some of the men. There's something corrupt and cynical in the air and half the time it's turning my stomach, the other half I feel like it's invading me, making me lazy, aw go to heck nobody else cares why should I? The thing that's keeping my head above water is the reading up I'm doing on Japan, a really interesting book about the Pearl Harbor pilots and the kamikazes. Say what you like, their attitude was a whole lot healthier than the guys here. I got a weekend's leave and went to Kyoto, which was beautiful. Unfortunately the Japanese people aren't very eager to discuss the war as I would like, and that's understandable too, in fact it's part of the same pride. Americans in that situation would be all too eager to run their country down, of course!

I enjoyed your letter with the description of the Sedlachek Cocktail Party. You should keep that kind of thing up, and get a book out of it, the Jane Austen of Fort Wynkoop

Yours, Tiger

Dec. 7
Dear Carol and Henry,
A very merry Christmas to my two dear children, I hope you like your presents. The kimono is just like traditional little Japanese girls wear, the birds on it are cranes which stand for good luck and long life. The carp is actually a kind of kite, which you tie to a pole and put up outside the house on Boys' Day, one fish for every son in the family. The cat is called Manekineko, he also brings good luck! I wonder what you think of the snacks, probably not much but the kids here love them. You can even eat the paper on the candy, because it's made of rice! Be good for your mommy, I hope we see each other again soon in the new year.

Love, Dad

Barbara, I always swore if I ever had kids I wouldn't give them expensive presents that they couldn't play rough with, nothing in the world is crueler, but I've 'went and did it' when I saw that beautiful little kimono, it's pure silk and authentic, not the trash they try and palm servicemen off with, but from this extraordinary little place I found in Tokyo, up two flights of stairs. The shopkeeper asked, through the interpreter, if my little girl also had yellow hair and when I said yes he brought it out; because of the colour he thought it would go and sold it to me for half its value (but still a lot) and made me promise to come back with a colour photo of her in it. So if you would oblige...

I hope you have a good Christmas. Don't feel like you need to spend it with my folks if it would make you happier to go back to Nebraska.
Tiger

January 23, 1950
Dear Barbara,
Well, I still don't know what I want to say to you. Actually I know what I want to say, but how can I?

The only thing I know for certain is it was a mistake to transfer out here. I have this feeling that if we were together just talking, I would have just said it all in the heat of the moment but once you are writing your conscience is there censoring everything. *How* can you ask her to take you back? If some other guy had done that to my sister, I would have shot him before letting him go back to her.

I hate it out here. I hate hate hate it. They've even had to stop the football teams because it ended up in too many fights. I hate every minute except when I can get leave. The only consolation is my platoon is slowly starting to shape themselves up and instead of resenting me for trying to impart a bit of spirit, learning to take some pride in trying to be the best even if it does mean more work. I get along best with the NCOs, Corporal Wilson is probably my best friend here. God, what an awful letter. Poor you. T.

Feb. 10
Happy birthday to me.
Barbara, what can I say?
The selfish part of me says Yes. In fact, the unselfish part of me would also say, OK, try it, you can't change things but maybe you can start again. I think I would certainly say that except for the fact that these past couple of weeks I've had a bad experience which has made me face up to the fact that there is a wrong streak in my character. Maybe it doesn't come out very often, but it's there underneath and I can't pretend it hasn't been there all along, not just when I hurt you, but a couple of incidents where I was a kid. It's not even always violent, just crazy. It actually has me quite scared at the moment.

Later Oh geez, I don't know. Maybe it's just because I'm so fed up and depressed here. I'm reaching a real low, maybe that's all it is. I can't decide.

Anyway there are the facts for you.
Maybe I should just say: I want to. Take me back at your own risk.
Love,
Tiger

Barbara put the letter down. She was shaking. Why had she forgotten that? The word crazy in that letter, way back then, and it had just disappeared from her memory. Why? Had she just put it down to Tigerish overstatement, his dramatic way with words? No, it was more than that, she remembered now. 'Crazy' had seemed like an excuse, and she had no intention of taking him back 'at her own risk'.

March 8
Point taken. I didn't mean it that way though. I just meant I can't promise anything, not honestly, if I'm to be certain of my own ability to control it. And just right now, I can't. So I guess that's it.
So probably what's best is to figure out some kind of unofficial separation for now. You have more of an idea of what's going to be socially difficult, so you tell me how you want to work it. The main thing for me is to get out of this place as soon as I can. At the moment I'm feeling really disillusioned with the army, but that might ease off if I was in some kind of halfway decent unit. I'm going to stick out my time, anyway, then see. Obviously the main thing is some kind of financial security for the children.
Yours, T.

It was Connelly's last day. He had an early flight out from Hickam Field the next morning. He came to Hoku's to give him the surfboard as a goodbye present. 'Shall we take it out one last time? Where shall we go?'

Hoku looked up into the mountains, considering. 'Kaena Point,' he decided at last.

'What's Kaena Point?'

'The far end of the island, I only been there one or two times, but I think it's the best place to go when you feel all like this inside. No, leave the board behind. I cannot surf today.'

Connelly didn't know what he meant, and wasn't sure he wanted to ask for clarification. They jumped in the car, without telling Momi where they were off to, and Hoku navigated him through Honolulu and the canneries and up through the centre of the island, past Wheeler Air Force Base and Schofield Barracks, the sentried and chain-fenced blank front they presented to the world. After this the plateau between two mountain ranges opened out, plains of crew-cut pineapples or shaggy sugar cane. They were far away from the coast: red dirt baked in the windless heat, wind whipped in through the windows, bare thighs stuck to the car seats. Hoku's voice went rippling through wordless melodies, drifting currents of arpeggios more like an imitation of a slack key guitar than a vocalist's exercises, and then occasionally coming around the corner into an unexpected song, like a break in the upland foliage that suddenly throws out a view of the island, or like coming to the end of the reef, to a dark blue depth full of yellow tang and parrotfish.

After an hour they reached the coast again, the North Shore. The mountains closed in, the Waianaes that ran up the western side of Oahu. The other range in the distance behind them had captured all the cloud cover, these looked rocky and baked, like a desert, not at all soothed by the nearby sea. The salt and the light glaring off the surface only added to the sense of heat. Perhaps it was something different in the landscape or the light that enabled Hoku to explain now, 'Out to sea, out there, one great big current is pouring down towards the island, and all the power from the winter storms is pumping the waves down from Alaska. Get twenty-, thirty-foot waves back that way, Waimea, Haleiwa.' He jerked his thumb backwards, towards the windward side, 'But anyway, Kaena, that's where the current opens and goes down either side of the island. And also something like that happens to the wind; so many different forces, lashing onto the island, torn apart, going crazy.'

'Sounds dangerous,' said Connelly.

'What? Oh, the water. Not just dangerous, nobody ever goes out, not even guys with big boats, nobody, nothing, the buggah is impossible, the shore is just rocks. But listen to me, sweetheart, all that with the ocean is *no ka* nothing compared to the end of the mountain there. It opens up a space, a way, a crack... Like the point of the island opens up the current, yeah? So the end of the mountain opens up something... tchah!' he clicked his tongue in frustration. 'You know the old-time Hawaiians before the missionaries, they tell us this was the place where the spirit come after it leave the body, the jumping-off place to go on the road to Po, the underworld. And maybe so, sweetheart; I don't know what you think, still yet, maybe so, eh?'

Connelly spoke carefully, as if Leimomi had her eye on him, 'And is that not also dangerous?'

'Very sacred, very dangerous. But you going away tomorrow, so we need one place like that for us.'

They passed a couple of farms, but as the dry mountain encroached on the sea, the road grew rougher, more deserted. Presently it abandoned its effort, sighed and slumped into a red dirt-track. 'Park the car,' Hoku directed. 'Better to walk the rest.'

Soon there was nothing so clear cut as a track, just a desert space between the mountain and the sea. Connelly wanted to rush up and down the splash zone of black rock, exploring the tide pools, stopping to gaze at the churning mountain ranges of water pounding in, steaming with spray, foam flying behind them like the tail of a comet. Not even a shark would survive that shorebreak, he thought, nothing alive at all, a lifeless place.

But Hoku's heart tugged him inland, towards the dry brown scrub, mesquite and manzanita and dry grasses, with sudden low-flowering greennesses held concealed. A stand of cactus-like century plants, thick sword leaves slashing up from the earth in a spiky crown, tall dry stalks of dead flowers soaring twenty feet above. They were surreal things, plants that might guard the entrance to a dead world.

Closer to the mountain, the endless pounding reverberation of the waves seemed filtered, and another low hum seemed to speak from the heights: an echo?, the voice of the wind in dry sticks and lava crags? or maybe the voices of wandering spirits who had failed to take the right road, cowardly souls, or leaderless. 'A world with endless darkness, the darkness of *Milu*; the deep darkness; the strata with the deep cleft; the cold underworld; the plane of the spirit protectors, the *aumakua*. Other worlds: a rolling heaven, a floating cloudland, worlds in the ocean depths or in the volcanoes fire...' was that what they were talking about? It was strange that he did not feel afraid.

There went Connelly, straying to the shore again. Hoku sighed and followed him until they came nearer the turning point of the island. Now they had to go inland: no good if one of them wandered onto the actual jumping-off place! Here the mountain came to its end, sliced off as if with a knife, so that if you stood facing it, looking up, it had the profile of a pyramid. Then, beyond it, the other side of the island, the leeward coast, looking blue with mist. As they approached it, coming towards the foot of the hill, stepping down into a little depression like the trough hollowing at the bows of a wave, they suddenly walked into a silence, a hot dry windless place. The sound of the waves was just unexplainably gone, the echoes or voices from above were transmuted into a feeling of hot pressure, as if two equal winds met, and stalemated. The pounding of the waves and the furious confusion of the torn open current seemed held back, visible, but standing off from them. It was a place at once dead, and sacred.

Was this the place he had come here for? Loss was just a weight here, a heavy burden in the unforgiving heat. Oh, this was the place, tears rose smoothly, swiftly up from his heart. Connelly was dashing about like a long-legged bird, testing the limits of the silent space, how on one side you heard the voice of the leeward waves on the other the northshore waves; the difference in their voices... "Ae, 'oe, 'ae, 'oe,' Hoku wept. Connelly looked up, his face suddenly, instinctively, reflected the pain, blinding as a mirror catching the sun.

This was it, goodbye? Connelly felt shocked, cheated. They had the rest of today and all of tonight, they didn't even have to think about it yet! Hoku's face was utterly final. 'No!'

Hoku pulled back the sobs as effortlessly as they had started. He took hold of Connelly's shoulders and explained, 'I have cousins live the Waianae side. I'm going to walk down that side, and you are going back to the car. Not yet, but. By and by.'

'No!' he protested again.

'I wait until you are ready.'

Connelly pushed against him with his forearms, hard, like an angry child. Hoku held him tight, in a circular grip, until he gave up, dropped his head and cried, not easily, fighting it. Grief outside of time, in an opened-up strata between worlds: he and Hoku could be here together for ever, for as long as he could stay there bearing the pain.

Huge spray-maned arcs of blue water opaque with dissolved foam and phosphorescence, the waves of the divided current throwing up cross sets, meeting at a wide angle, interfering, doubling up to brief ecstatic peaks. Connelly felt stripped, laid out bone by bone, as if he had already died and decomposed into the landscape. He was an early Sterling non-person, a trick of the light twisting and shaking in an immensity of pain. In the distance, the blue cliffs of the leeward side, the side of the island he had never seen now misted into a magical land beyond loss. Redoubling of the ache!

Hoku stood ten feet away, weeping out to sea, where the two currents parted against the burdened shore, one to travel along under the wind, along the sweet green-shaded eastern shore, the other visiting the unknown coast.

It was Monday evening and a party of five was being escorted along the broad bright corridors of the Fort Wynkoop Base Hospital. Colonel Sedlachek was leading them, and their progress was marked by salutes, deferrings, porters hurriedly wheeling their burdens out of the way. At the forefront, walking abreast with the colonel was a middle-aged lady, a striking, rather aristocratic-looking woman with a bony nose and thyrotoxic eyes. Mrs Virginia Sterling wore a fawn-coloured suit and hat and day-length pearls (she always dressed in descriptions for the local paper's social column). Everything about her from her matching shoes and purse to her confident East Coast voice was *consciously right*, even the exact amount of conscious rightness. It was the amount that was appropriate to an intelligent woman of some standing in the community, but never an amount that strayed beyond the bounds of good manners. She responded with judicious yeses and I sees to the colonel's explanation of her son's vicissitudes: how he had suffered blackouts on the trip from Hawaii and had been admitted for tests.

Her husband was altogether more diffident: lanky, lantern-jawed, with a leathery olive-grey complexion and hazel eyes. There was more than a hint of the rancher in the old-fashioned rather dandified tailoring of his suit. She was East and he was West, and people seeing them together always wondered how the twain had met. His words were characterized by tentativeness and the conditional mood: woulds, coulds and do you thinks?

Barbara Sterling was sickly pale and silent, walking behind

the others with the children. Even in her very best navy blue with touches of cream, she was not in her mother-in-law's league, though she did her best not to offend against her canon of rightness. The strange little gold and crimson Japanese brooch she wore was Tiger's last gift before he had been shipped into action.

Caroline, broad-faced and blonde, was obviously her mother's child, although the energy that fizzled from every bouncing step might have been the legacy of her paternal grandmother. She had a new pair of Mary Jane patent leathers for the occasion and if you thwacked the heel down hard enough with each step they could almost have been tap shoes.

Last of all, with an air of resistance, long-lashed eyes downcast, six-year-old Henry paced along. He disliked the clothes he had been forced into and disapproved of the fuss being made. His mother had been in a strange mood for a week about it. He had no clear memory of his father, and the pictures of him that were displayed in Grandma's house gave him a bad feeling. There didn't seem to Henry to be any real need for him to come back.

As they came to the room, Colonel Sedlachek stepped back to let the senior Sterlings in. He stood by Barbara, observed her pallor and gave her arm a kindly squeeze. 'I won't stay. The first day belongs to you folks. Don't worry, it'll all go fine.' And he set off down the hall. She looked back after him, then took a resolute breath, held both the children's hands, and stepped forward into the long six-bed room.

All of the other beds were occupied, but the first thing you noticed were the eyes at the far end of the room, powerful staring eyes, the effect of a Byzantine Christ, except that these eyes were pale, and as frightened as they were frightening. Slowly, gathering an awkward collection of limbs, an attempt was made to stand, but it was defeated by some sudden weakness or dizziness. A compressed, terribly human gasp and sob escaped Mrs Virginia Sterling's correct façade. 'Don't cry Mom, there's nothing much wrong,' said the man on the bed.

'Dad. Barbara...' – as if he was Adam, having to name them to make this new world real. 'Caroline? Is that... Henry?'

'No!' said Henry, and shot out of the room. Caroline followed his example, and Barbara had to go after them.

His mother had pulled herself together and forced herself to approach the bed. He looked too thin and breakable to touch and she stood about three feet away from him. Dad hovered behind her, perhaps wanting to come nearer, but respecting the maternal right to the first hug. 'Well, Tiger, you made it!' he said.

Barbara came back. The children were still outside, refusing to come in. 'They're shy,' she apologized. She looked formal, standing with her back very straight, clasping her gloved hands in front of her.

He looked down. 'I know I'm not exactly Dr Connelly,' he admitted. His family all looked blank and polite. Oh, yeah. Well, no point in explaining. Try again. 'I look like that old tramp that used to exp –' whoops, no not that one either. 'I can't blame them for being scared.' But why were all the adults scared as well? Why were they all standing there so stiffly, on the other side of an invisible wall?

'Mommy!' an urgent cry from outside. 'Henry's done something and it's falling out of his pants!'

Barbara shut her eyes and bent at the knees as if she was about to sink with humiliation. But Virginia, galvanized by a practical task, a displacement activity, announced that she would take care of it, and marched out, pulling off her white gloves and calling her husband, 'Give them a minute alone together, for goodness sakes, Michael. "Alone" – wouldn't you think they'd have found him a private room, as an officer? If Colonel Sedlachek is still around perhaps he could do something about it.'

'Mom,' said Tiger, shaking his head ruefully. All the other patients were gazing after her, in something like awe. But Barbara was still standing there, with her hands together like a child in church. He said softly, 'I guess it hasn't been easy for you either.' It was a cliché, but it was also an invitation to come to the other side of the invisible wall.

'Your folks have been just wonderful.' She said this precisely, as if it was a scripted speech. 'And everyone on the base.'

She had refused his invitation. Oh, naturally. The barrier here wasn't just self-consciousness or even what Chang would have called the shame of what he had done to himself. It was a massive construction of doubt and guilt and anger and a moment's violence and three years' separation and God knew what else. It was going to have to be taken down slowly and delicately, with an archaeologist's care...

Nah. He didn't have the tact, or the patience; he certainly did not have the mental stability for the task. He wasn't Dr Connelly. He was Tiger and if she didn't like it she shouldn't have married him. He stood up and launched himself at her. He could see her looking terrified as he staggered forwards, but he wasn't going to stop. And then, there she was, inside his arms, under his hands: it was like being in a totally different element, like diving off a high rock into an icy lake, and just suddenly being there with every cell in your body tingling to register the difference. And there was a different life there, under his hands, separate but connected, a different body, small and collected and seemingly boneless, just perfect, perfect. He could feel her tension melting, something inside her deciding it was all right for him to be holding her, maybe even all right to want it, and to hold him right back. Maybe he was going to pass out again with the too muchness of it all; he realized he was weeping but couldn't spare the attention to give a damn because it took the whole of his consciousness to just be there holding her. Her fingers were on his back, in awe of his skeleton, the ribs that jutted out through wasted muscle. 'That's right, just get inside me,' he told her, not aloud. She had started to cry too. Then things went blackish and he had to retreat to the bed and get his head down before he fainted. 'What's wrong?'

'I can't get over how perfect you are. You look like a store-bought cake.' He pulled her onto the bed next to him and tried to sneak a bite of the fancy fluted icing under her ear.

'Your Mom wouldn't approve,' she giggled. Suppressed noises from other corners of the room indicated that this romantic drama was being avidly followed. Barbara blushed and jumped six inches away from him.

'Christ,' he swore. 'Get me out of here. Tonight.'

'Ssh, Tiger. Here comes your Dad.'

He came in with the message that Henry was soiled beyond remedy, and that Mom had taken both children out to the car. There was an anxious, conflicted look in his eye, which Barbara read instantly: he had been given his marching orders. 'We'll have to go,' she said.

'What?' cried Tiger.

'We'll come back tomorrow,' she promised. Then Dad took his hand and squeezed it hard, with a long, profound look. And then they were gone.

Promptly at the first visiting session of the next morning, Barbara and the children appeared. Barbara had a suitcase and a little lady's dressing case, as if she was planning to move in with him. Henry carried a gift-wrapped box of candy and Caroline managed a beribboned package from the most effusive bakery in Reno. Seduced by the promise of See's chocolate and Store-Bought Cake, they climbed up on the bed trustingly and allowed the horrible old tramp to kiss them and believe he was their long-lost Daddy. Barbara had brought a knife and picnic plates and served out the cake and the children were sweet and charming for about ten minutes, until they became aware and resentful of their father's cake-eating capacity. He had eaten at least half of it by himself and was still going strong; he was almost as sticky as they were, from trying to talk and laugh with his mouth full. 'Look at you!' she exclaimed, pulling a damp washcloth out of the dressing case, and trying to clean his upper lip.

'I can't tell you how strange and ecstatic it seems to me. A kind of electric rejoicing in cake and bodies, and their little faces, more cake, your neck; it's not even eating, just wanting to wade in and dissolve in it all. Come on, pull up, sit down. If the rubbernecks want to stare at us, let 'em. I can't help it if my family's prettier and more interesting than theirs are.'

'Oh, Tiger,' she protested, but got on top of the bed beside him, pulling the little suitcase up onto her knees. 'Look, I brought you some things. Will they let you wear your own clothes? I hope so. Those pyjamas look like they ought to have a Star of David on the pocket.' She opened the case and gave him a faded Stanford sweatshirt, which he put on. 'And of course the books, you've got a heck of a lot to catch up on, but start with this one,' she handed him a novel called *The Catcher in the Rye*, 'I can't wait to hear what you think of it. Oh, and this is the picture album I've been making in case you... for when you got back, mostly just the kids. That was his third birthday, isn't he sweet? I think he's just the loveliest little boy, I know it's probably only because I'm his mother. That's Care's first day at kindergarten. She's doing well, you know. The teachers all say she's extremely bright and unusually imaginative. It's a shame they weren't at their best last night, but they'd been up and expecting you since half past five, just like Christmas' – this was true of Caroline, anyway – 'so of course by the time we got here they were emotionally exhausted. That's the Christmas play – she's the angel, casting by looks and not by character I guess.'

'Put that down,' Tiger kicked the cake box off the bed and pulled her back to lean on the pillows with him. The children had seized control of the candy box and were hiding under the high hospital bed with it. 'I don't want pictures when I've got the real you here.' His left hand went on a reconnaissance mission and discovered a gap in the defences, up and under her jacket to a slender, soft valley between her ribs and hip bones. 'You know what? I think I'm only just starting to be alive again.'

'What I can't get over is how... I don't know, you look like you've been to hell and back but the way you are is so... so all right, so like it all used to be, it's like nothing awful's happened, like maybe we're back at college,' she plucked at the Stanford sweatshirt, 'and we've just gone out for a soda or something.'

His heart started to race. 'Do you mean... are you saying... do you think maybe we could go back to something like that... I mean, what if we just got married too young? What if we needed something like these years away, I mean, what if *I* needed to just grow up and... deserve you?'

Her face looked as though he had just launched himself at her again; well, maybe he had. First she looked scared, then she tried to smile, but ended up crying again instead. She twisted around to press her face into his shoulder. His heart was full beyond tears. Everything awful was over.

Virginia and Barbara had been dividing the spoils of Tiger's return: Barbara and the kids got the afternoon visiting hour, when the children were less likely to get over-excited, and the Sterlings senior would have the evenings. Professor Sterling cancelled his last appointment so that he could stop at the grocery store on his way home. He bought supplies of beef jerky and sunflower seeds for Tiger, traditional offerings that dated back to all those hospital stays of Tiger's youth and childhood. Beef jerky, sunflower seeds roasted in their shells, and rattling good yarns, to distract a young daredevil from the frustrations of hospital routine and the pain of the usual multiple fractures. A sentimental impulse detoured Professor Sterling to the public library, where he picked out such yarns as might withstand reading again fifteen years later, *Ivanhoe* and *The Deerslayer*. Even if he didn't read them, Tiger would be touched by the allusion. They would remind him of that summer they had spent alone together. He still thought of it as The Year of the Tiger.

The boy was twelve that year, and having a bad time of it. Undersized, accident prone, behind at school, a nuisance at home and a terror in the neighbourhood: you couldn't even feel sorry for him as the defiance permanently smouldering in his eyes sizzled up any tender emotion that came his way. For several years he and his mother had been locked in a battle of wills, a colonial revolution of the spirit, she with all the big guns and red-coated battalions, he conducting an impudent and passionate guerrilla campaign. Michael had a guilty sense he should be acting the peace broker, but he felt powerless to intervene, and in truth, he didn't have the stomach to get between them in one of their big scenes.

Michael was spending the summer in the cabin up at Lake Tahoe on his own; he was prepared to concede most things to Virginia, but his need for communion with nature for two months out of every twelve was absolute, and for all her dominance, she seemed to know the one thing she must not challenge. In earlier years she had gritted her teeth and endured the great outdoors in the name of family togetherness, but the 1936 trip, in which Joe had communed with poison ivy and Tiger had started an avalanche, had been the last straw. Since then she kept the children in town over the summer, and had her own private trip back East in the spring. Michael Sterling felt there was a lot to be said for this flexible attitude to family togetherness. Tahoe was much better without the children, and even without Virginia. No doubt she felt something similar about her museum visits, luncheons and bridge parties in Boston.

But one day, in the middle of July...'38 it must have been, peace was shattered when Virginia motored up in the old black Wilys Knight with a face like fury. She didn't even get out of the car; it was Tiger who scrambled out of the back seat with his things in a dufflebag. 'I don't see why I should be the one who has to handle him all the time!' was Virginia's only explanation. 'He needs a father's discipline!'

Michael stood there, scratching his head. This did not make sense. Virginia's discipline was far more formidable than his, and she knew this as well or rather better than he did. But before he could respond, she had turned the car around and was pulling away. Woken to action, he dashed after her, grabbed the door – she kept on moving and he had to run alongside for the length of the drive, protesting that he didn't think he had the natural authority.

'Then find it,' she told him, and accelerated out of his grip, disappearing around a tree-edged bend. Michael only just saved himself from sprawling in the gravel.

Tiger had apparently been ignoring the drama, standing there staring at the ground and kicking his duffle bag from foot to foot. Recovering himself, his father suppressed the rising sense of doom and asked, as mildly as possible, 'What happened?'

He lifted a face wrung between resentment and humiliation. 'Nobody ever asks if Ralph did anything to me. It's always my fault because I'm faster in a fight than anyone else. Nobody ever asks who started it.'

'Who started it?'

'Ralph. He said I was playing Post Office with Louise Verdine.'

'Who threw the first punch?'

'But what was I supposed to do? He was going to tell everyone.'

Michael sighed. 'If you hit him it's a sign it touched a nerve. If you just laughed or ignored him...'

'That's what grown-ups always say and it doesn't work.'

'Well, hitting him hasn't exactly worked either.'

Tiger shrugged and slouched into the cabin.

The cabin wasn't a log cabin, but it came close, rough wood walls creosoted purplish black, open rafters and a tin roof that sang and drummed through rainstorms. It had an electric light now, but you had to use the wood-burning stove for heat and cooking and hot water. Overlooking the room like guardian spirits, Michael's collection of Indian artifacts were ranged on the high shelf that went along the four walls: pots and medicine bundles and quillwork and kachinas. Tiger had not been here for several years, and memory combined with a more sophisticated appreciation to knock the rebellious mood out of him. 'Wow! Those are real, huh? Not souvenirs?' He pulled a chair over to climb up and get a closer look, then was diverted by the sight of the pot-bellied stove. 'Are we gonna cook our dinner over a fire?' 'I guess so, if we want it hot.' 'Can I go fishing for it?' 'Not many fish in Tahoe, son. It's a dying lake.'

'A dying lake.' He savoured the concept. 'Can I go see it?' Before the assent was anything more than a considering look in his father's eyes, Tiger had shot out. The cabin was uphill and across the road from the shore; Michael decided he'd better run after him for safety's sake. A track led through the pines down to a scooped-out sloping beach, just about wide enough between two bluffs to launch a small boat or to wade out and swim yourself, if you didn't mind sharp pebbles underfoot and a disconcertingly sudden drop. 'Can I swim?' Tiger demanded: he already had his shoes off.

'It's too late in the day. It'll be too cold.'

Tiger accepted this, to his father's amazement, rolled up his jeans as far as they went and waded back and forth skimming stones. Michael scrambled up one of the yellow dusty bluffs to sit and gaze across the glassy water and sigh for his lost tranquillity.

This gently contemplative self-pity took him into an abstracted state, one of those timeless trances that drove Virginia mad. The ripples of thrown stones expanded, met and danced, died out. Further out, towards the centre of the lake, a breeze velveted the water. The sun came lower, silver light angled back down into bronze, and the lake wore a darker, more opaque face. A splash like a gunshot startled the little inlet into agitated life. Tiger had lunged into the lake, in all his clothes. When he emerged, treading water, having swum some thirty feet, he twisted round to wave at his dad and shout, 'I saw a fish! Big one!'

Michael stared, and said things that would have had Virginia racing back to rescue Tiger from his influence, had she heard them. Tiger twisted and dived and played for sixty seconds, realizing the freedom and weightlessness of swimming; then, suddenly realizing the temperature, he turned around and pelted for the shore in a furious crawl whose aim was as much raising body heat as speed. He'd stuffed his feet into his tennis shoes and sprinted for home before Michael had even slid down from the rise he'd occupied. 'Christ,' he said, picking up the forgotten crew socks and trudging up the hill.

'I'm sure it was a fish,' said the blanket-clad person huddled in front of an impromptu blaze of the whole week's supply of tinder and kindling. 'A rainbow trout or maybe even a salmon.'

The next day Tiger discovered the padlocked cupboard. 'What's in there?'

'Grandma Sterling's gun,' Michael answered unwisely.

'Grand*pa* Sterling,' Tiger corrected.

'No, Grandma. She was a widow running a silver mine and she had a shotgun and knew how to use it. If you think your Ma's a hard woman you should have met mine.'

But Tiger was not interested in hard women. 'Can we get it out?'

'Nope. I doubt it works any more.'

'Prob'ly just needs cleaning.'

'It probably just needs throwing away. It's not safe, Tiger, and neither of us knows anything about guns.'

'Well, what *are* we gonna do today?'

'I guess today we can go swimming.'

His face fell. Swimming was now doubly boring, as something he'd already done, and in comparison to cleaning Grandma's gun and going up the mountain to kill something. For a split second, Michael understood this. When the split second was over he thanked his manitou that the key to the old padlock had got lost a long time before. But he retained enough of this excursion into Tiger's frame of mind to ask, casually, 'Can you handle an axe? If we could get some more wood split we could build a campfire down by the water...'

After a week had passed, he was cautiously congratulating himself that he had cracked it. All you had to do was devote all your heart, all your imagination and all your energy to supplying Tiger with activities that were strenuous enough to keep him too tired for trouble, dressing them up to sound as dangerous as possible. A hike in the hills was disdained, but if you turned it into a pilgrimage to the valley where a bear had been spotted earlier that spring that was a different matter. They borrowed a neighbour's little boat to visit the sites of drownings, hiked to abandoned cabins Michael arbitrarily designated 'haunted' and hurriedly supplied with grisly histories, and to a number of saloons and beauty spots where Grandma Sterling was credited with an increasingly fanciful series of exploits. You had to pack a full complement of survival gear, in case an avalanche or a storm or an injury prevented you from getting home that night: bedrolls and tarps, hatchet and sheath knife, flints and a length of good rope, all carried on your own back. No edged tool was actually ever unpacked, because once they were out in the woods they had to be like Indians who didn't injure living things unnecessarily. Tiger accepted this: there was romance enough in the fact that he was trusted to carry the axe. He hadn't caught on that it was only being brought along as ballast, in order to tire him out more thoroughly.

The final proof of the way the wilderness was civilizing Tiger happened one Sunday morning, about two weeks after his arrival. He normally woke up around 5.30 and bounced in on his father before six, but on this day it was a quarter to seven when he came tiptoeing in, only waking him when he set a cup of coffee on the bedside chest. 'Sleep as long as you can,' he whispered, when Michael opened an eye. 'Don't worry about me.' He glided out, leaving only the coffee as proof that it wasn't a dream.

The coffee smelled good but sleep smelled better, and Michael was drifting off before he could rouse himself to taste it. Yesterday's seven-mile hike had left its mark; he must be getting old. Will was gone, and consciousness left, and around the cabin it was so silent and still that nothing disturbed him until his body had made up for its exhaustion, for so many early mornings. It added an extra half hour, against future early wakings, and then slowly started to stretch and stir. Michael twisted up on an elbow, to see if the coffee was still drinkable.

It was utterly cold. The alarm clock said that it was twenty past ten. My word the boy was outdoing himself! He'd have to come up with some kind of reward. He stretched, got up and started dressing very slowly. When he called 'Tiger?' there was no answer. Well, that explained the silence. He must have gone for a walk or down to the lake. Michael injected a little more energy into his getting ready. Of course Tiger knew better than to swim alone; it was just that you could never be sure how well knowing better would balance out the impulse to dive in after an imaginary rainbow trout. 'Tiger?' he called again, louder but in vain.

He was just heading out when a difference, a disturbance in the far corner of the room caught his eye. The door of the padlocked cupboard hung unevenly: its hinges had been unscrewed, and Grandma Sterling's gun was not there.

Tiger had been caught and returned by the proprietor of the store two miles down the road, where he had tried to buy ammunition. Old Mrs Shaw had not believed Tiger's story that his Dad had sent him for a minute. 'I knew you didn't keep a gun,' she said. And eyeing the boy with an air of detached and unmalicious assessment, she added calmly, 'If I was you I'd beat that one.'

Tiger had a bedroll and a tarp tied under the pack on his back, the axe and sheath knife strung on his belt. 'Where were you going?' Michael asked, with a calm that was not detached at all.

Tiger had been poised for sullen defiance, but found he could not sustain it. He felt suddenly scared, and summoned a rusty memory of wheedling charm. 'I just wanted to see if I could live for twenty-four hours on my own.'

Michael shrugged and went indoors. He would say nothing, there was nothing to say. Tiger came in a few minutes later, looking wary, half-frightened of the inevitable bawling out, half craving it. He crept around the room, putting things away in their places. Eventually he found the silence unendurable and asked, 'Are you going to send me home?'

'Is that what you want?'

'No.'

He shrugged again, and wouldn't be drawn to give any more answers. Tiger, trapped in a vacuum without punishment and without forgiveness, grew white and shaky and finally cried, 'What are you going to do to me?'

'Nothing.'

He made a breakfast which he shared out in silence, and afterwards went to the lake alone. The day was shaping up hot, the sun intense in the high altitude, a faint land breeze slowly stirring itself into action as the earth heated up. Michael sat until his insides were stiller than the surface of the lake. When he returned to the cabin, passing the newly restocked woodpile with a cynical snort, he discovered Tiger in the kitchen, trying to tie up a bleeding left hand in a triangle bandage. 'Here,' Michael said, taking over the operation with a face set against any sign of relenting pity. 'Have you washed it?'

'Yeah.'

He didn't have to ask how it had happened: peeled and partially chopped potatoes were marinating in blood on the kitchen table. Other signs of preternatural goodness kept jumping out at him all over the house: washed floors, a raked-out stove, split kindling lying beside it. Eventually he gave in and said, 'Hey, Tiger, being good isn't a coin you can use to bribe people.'

He sat up, straight and tense. 'What do you mean?'

'I mean, all this is no different from that cup of coffee this morning. I'm being asked to overlook something.'

Tiger howled, 'What am I supposed to do then?'

'Whatever you want. It's just that personally I'd rather see you stick by your decisions even if it means going to hell in a handbasket than trying to play me like this.'

'I don't understand. I'm trying to say I'm sorry, what's wrong with that?'

'You're sorry? Really? And not just afraid of the consequences?'

'No, I'm really really sorry,' Tiger said passionately.

'I don't think so. If you really cared about the consequences of what you did – I mean, what it made me feel like, well, you just wouldn't have done it.'

'I do. I do care now – I just wasn't thinking then.'

'No, it's different,' Michael frowned, trying to analyse for himself what was wrong. 'It's like you feel you have a right, or even a *duty* to get into trouble, because adults' ideas of good and bad are being imposed on you unfairly.'

Tiger froze, transfixed not by tension but by recognition. 'Well, they are, aren't they?'

'Not up here they ain't.' He looked at the boy hard. 'You haven't been punished. You can go and live twenty-four hours in the wilderness if that's what you really want.' This was not as rash as it might have sounded: Mrs Shaw had confiscated the gun and, he trusted, disposed of it safely. 'Do you see what I'm saying, Tiger? Morality has to come from the inside, or it's not worth shit. *Do what you want.*'

'But you can't do what you want!' he cried, scandalized. 'What about the consequences?'

'Har-hum!' said Michael, finally giving way to a smile.

He realized now that it had been a discovery for him as well as a lesson for Tiger. Since he had married he had come to believe that his live-and-let-live attitude was the result of character weakness and fear of conflict. 'I don't have the natural authority!' he had protested, not all that long ago. 'Then find it,' Virginia had said. And he had found it, in the last place he'd expected it to be, right down there at the bottom of his *laisser-faire* approach. He hadn't known himself what a fine moral philosophy he possessed, or how strong he could be in resisting the temptation to stray into either punishment or forgiveness.

Tiger had renounced the 24-hour survival test ('I can't even cut potatoes') and they spent the rest of the summer doing things together, albeit at a less frenetic pace, now that Michael was no longer having to alternately dodge and charm that rebellious itch for trouble. The boy's behaviour wasn't exactly self-regulated yet: he seemed to suffer from a congenital defect in the part of the brain that assessed personal safety; but he made it a policy to consult his father ('Will it worry you too bad if I swim around that point to the next cove?', 'Of course it will worry me, but if you need to prove yourself I guess I can understand that') and to pace up and down, audibly ledgering pros and cons, before embarking on his venture, or, once in a rare while, abandoning it.

It all worked beautifully in the rarefied atmosphere of the mountain lake. It was Tiger, rather than his father, who foresaw that it was not going to be so easy in town. 'What are the consequences of you and me just not going back?'

'In the long run, son, starvation.'

The house in town was five or six times bigger than the cabin they'd been inhabiting, and built in a prosperously spacious part of town. They felt it as cramped: there wasn't spirit room to swing a cat. Michael tried to live and let live himself out of it: Virginia liked discipline, order, routine, and she was entitled to have things the way she wanted. But Tiger had inherited some of her appetite for conflict, and used his embryonic ethical sophistication to go on the attack.

On Sunday morning he came downstairs in his usual playclothes, jeans and checkered shirt with a Tahoe summer's worth of wear and staining. 'I don't want to go to church.' Virginia ignored this: what children *wanted* had no effect on what they were going to do. Previously Michael would have fled at this point, but an uncomfortable sense of responsibility kept him there this day. 'Why don't you want to, son?' he asked.

'I just don't. We never did, up at the lake.'

'Well, that's because up there Wakan Tonka is so close all

around you there's no need to. Down here, we need church to remind ourselves –'

'Why are you arguing with him?' Virginia demanded. 'He's going and that's it.'

'I'm not and that's it. I don't pray better in church. I hate every minute of it. The others do too, they're just too scared to say so. The only reason for us kids to go is what the neighbours think, and that's hypocritical.'

'Well, not necessarily. It might be an expression of family togetherness . . .' Michael began.

'*Go upstairs. Get dressed for church. I'll deal with you later.*'

It was strange the way the ethic of doing what you wanted could end up forcing you to do something you didn't want to do at all, Michael reflected. Despite the distance of fifteen years he still had a very clear memory of the visceral belief in the doom he was bringing down on his head, he could still hear the shake in his voice, as he said, 'Well, honey, maybe the boy has a point . . .'

After that his memory for what actually happened was chaotic, condensed into an image: himself and Virginia being forced to stare into the abyss of their essential difference, the spiritual distance between them. Tiger had got a glimpse of it too, and it frightened him right upstairs and into his Sunday best. Perhaps the words that passed between them were no more than, 'For goodness sake, Michael, back me up! You have to be *consistent* with him!' and 'I am. That's the way I handled things up at the cabin and it worked.' But the unspoken stand-off was cataclysmic. The moral universe was reeling around him – there he was still, at the centre of the hurricane, looking her in the eye and realizing he wasn't going to back down whatever that meant. Things spun even more violently, because it seemed – impossible! and yet true, he somehow knew it – that Virginia couldn't say the same. And he realized with a start that her dominance up to then had not been her strength and his weakness, but at the bottom a sense of chivalry, because he knew that she needed him more than he needed her.

He only really registered it as a victory when he was upstairs in the chaos of the Boys' Bedroom, saying to a smartly dressed Tiger, 'You don't have to go.'

'It's OK,' he had gulped. 'Really. What you said about family togetherness.'

That afternoon, Tiger had gone out on his bike and had, apparently, played chicken with Ralph Lemke's father, who was driving a station wagon at the time. Eleven different bones were broken, but it had the undeniable effect of distracting his parents from the abyss between them and promoting family togetherness.

And now, fifteen years later, driving through the desert with Virginia to Fort Wynkoop, he wondered about that time, and about the undernourished person in the hospital bed, about bloody potatoes and also about certain hints or slips that Barbara had let out over the years, and he wondered, with a growing sense of discomfort, how they were all connected.

Tiger was lying with his hands behind his head, low and listless. The afternoon had gone badly downhill after Barbara and the kids had left. He'd tried to read the book she'd recommended, but the New York accent that jumped off its pages had triggered this awful feeling, like someone had *died* or something, for Chrissakes. It was stupid that when you were home with the wife who has stuck by you after all, your kids who had only got cuter over the years, and your parents who seemed to be glad to see you — it was really dumb to be lying there missing someone you hadn't even known for a week.

Of course it had to be more than that, as Connelly himself would have been the first to point out. It was probably the whole weight of all the shit from the past getting on top of him as it usually did, this time of day. *Were* they glad to see him? Would they still be, when they heard what had happened? If he'd been in a private room he might have had the luxury of sinking into one of those surreal despairs or weeping fits, but out here in the open ward he was fighting it, not only out of pride, but out of a sense of responsibility for the morale of others.

Because there was something about him and his family that was noisy and unembarrassed, he'd been silently elected as the one who was going to dramatize Homecoming for the rest of them, and according to the script it was a happy occasion.

Mom had got hold of a copy of the play too: she came in a few minutes early with two cake boxes, and her celebrated Lady Baltimore cake was Lady Bountifulled up and down the ward. Dad couldn't act, and dodged her attempt to press him as a cake server, coming up close to the bedside and tucking a rolled-up paper bag into the bedside stand, muttering, 'Open this when you've got a minute on your own.'

'Well,' said Mom, when the cake was served and the visit proper began. 'How are you? Have the results of the tests come back yet?'

'No, or they haven't told me. But I'm fine, really.'

'Were the children any less shy today?'

'Maybe a little. You can't blame them. It's so strange, the way you can't help expecting time to stand still but it hasn't and they've had half their little lives without me...' He had to stop himself abruptly and shut his eyes.

'Is something wrong?' Dad asked.

'No, I'm just always kinda low this time of day.' He made an effort to drag himself up to sitting and inject a note of energy into his voice. 'So what about Mary? And Joe? And everything that's been happening since time stopped standing still?'

Well! Mom was in charge of the relating of Family Achievement, and she had evolved a judicious matter-of-fact air which made it not boasting, even when broadcasting outside the family. Well! Mary was a freshman at the University of Colorado and had pledged Kappa Kappa Gamma. If you knew these things, you knew that was one of the *social* sororities. And Harold Goode had proposed to her, but she had very sensibly decided to finish college before getting engaged.

'God,' said Tiger. Proposals, sororities... when he'd gone overseas Mary had been a Grandma Sterling in the making, rivalling his own reputation for risky exploits. It sounded like she was different now.

As for Joseph, he was at Oxford. Oxford, England. He'd got a Rhodes. Mother was straightforward: this was the truth, there was nothing she could do about it, though her audience might marvel, doubt her word or grit their teeth with envy. She was only facing facts. Dad looked uncomfortable. He always felt that if God had gifted you with brains or anything else you ought to show your gratitude by concealing it all under a bushel. Tiger said, 'Wow.' While there was no clink or crunch of gritted teeth, there was a weak, unstable quality to his voice and an unfocused look in his eye that should have warned his mother not to face any more facts just then.

Unfortunately there were one or two more salient facts about Joe that couldn't be omitted. One of them was his girlfriend Vanessa, of Grosse Point and Vassar: a keen horsewoman who had won a championship at Madison Square Garden. They were going to get engaged when Joseph came home and married when he finished law school. Tiger shut his eyes to warn himself not to take the news of all these protracted courtships as criticism of his own rushed affairs. 'Good for Joe.'

Mom was about to postscript his summa cum laude but Dad could not stand the hubris any longer and interrupted to put up a lightning rod of bad fortune. 'Of course he smashed his knee so badly pole vaulting that he failed his physical when they...um...called him up.' He had to use this, as it was the only piece of bad luck Joe had encountered, but before he finished saying it he realized that maybe it was not the most tactful thing he could have said, given the circumstances. Tiger had started to shake.

'So Joe's the real star, huh? He gets to be the hero and I'm the one who brings shame to the family, over and over again. Everything he does is golden and everything I touch turns to shit and –'

'John!' hissed his mother. 'There are people all around us!'

'I wrecked it, didn't I, my big chance to redeem myself, I should have gotten shot and then I could have been at least a picture of a hero on top of the piano and a bunch of posthumous medals.' The hubbub of the ward visiting had faded to staring silence. His parents watched helplessly as he stumbled off the bed and stood against the wall, pressing himself into the corner. 'I'm sorry. I'm sorry I'm a disgusting mess like this and I'm sorry I surrendered and got brainwashed and I'm sorry you can't be proud of me...' He slid down the wall until he was sitting on the floor, pressing his face into his knees, shaking convulsively.

Michael and Virginia looked at one another. 'Call a doctor!' advised someone from the other end of the room. 'I'm going to try to talk to him,' Michael whispered to his wife, with the air of someone undertaking a dangerous rescue. He tiptoed cautiously around the bed and hunkered down a couple of feet in front of the patient. 'Of course we're proud of you. We're so proud of you it just seemed to go without saying, you know?'

A deep choking noise, and the all-out block of shaking suddenly arpeggiated into sobs. Virginia's nerve snapped and she went out to find a medic.

'Come on, Tiger. Pull yourself together before the doctor comes. Come on. Try and stand up.' Michael edged closer and tugged at his shoulder ineffectually. Presently Virginia returned with an intern who observed the patient for a bored half minute. 'Combat reaction,' he shrugged, and walked away writing. A little later, when the sobs were just beginning to space themselves out, a male nurse came in with a hypodermic of chloral hydrate. 'Hold him still for me,' he instructed Michael.

'Come on, Tiger, give me your arm,' he implored, hoping Tiger would spare him the necessity of using force. But Tiger wouldn't even look up, and kept both arms locked tight around his knees.

'Get hold of him,' the nurse insisted. 'He's not gonna calm down until this kicks in.' Michael caught an arm and pulled it free; the nurse pulled the pyjama sleeve up and punched the needle at it as if he was doctoring a horse. 'Let's get him into bed,' the nurse decided next. They each took an elbow and lifted. Tiger shook one arm free to cover his face, took his weight on his own feet and climbed under the covers.

He slept for fourteen hours, not soundly, and not because of the drug, but because every time he approached the surface of consciousness something reminded him he didn't want to wake up in that ward and face what he'd done. Even when he could no longer reclaim sleep, he lay with his eyes shut, ignoring delivered coffee and summons to breakfast.

Oh...shit, he kept thinking. Oh...shit. What had he let himself in for?

It was as if someone – well, no not just someone, *he himself* – had driven in with a dump truck and poured out a huge radiating load of shit in front of his doorstep, and he was going to have to shovel it up and cart it away in honeybuckets before he could go anywhere. All that shit about Korea, everything that had happened; 'shit' or maybe Chang's word 'shame' was the best shorthand for *all of that*. The bargepole of shorthand was all he wanted to touch it with, just then.

And maybe 'all that' about Korea would have been just about manageable, but last night he'd gone and mined seams of shit far deeper, half-fermented dungheaps of stuff about Barbara and Joe...He wished he could have broken down about something other than Joe, at least in front of his parents. It was mean and miserable: instead of being a free man who just happened to have some shit to shovel (on account of having served his country), he was suddenly the failure, a nasty envious little peon who was shovelling grudgingly because shit was his lot and he was never going to be free. What was the point of blaming Joe? What was he supposed to do, drop out of college and sell shoes, just because he had a brother in Korea?

No, it went back a long time before Korea. He had been the troublesome one, the wrong 'un, way back, for ever, before Joe was born, maybe even before he was born there was this energy spinning chaos and destruction, going round and round like a self-respinning flywheel. 'Tiger Sterling' was just a shell, the poor bastard who had landed the job of housing that bad energy in this particular lifetime; Tiger Sterling was disposable (he knew that well enough) but that sparking self-generating electricity was going to go on and on...

If Connelly had been here he'd have stopped him at that point.

Huh. Funny. That thought had stopped him, just as effectively. Maybe wherever he was, on a beach or still in bed, depending on time zones, Connelly had just been saying to himself, 'I wonder how Sterling is, I hope he's not falling into one of those bottomless pits.' Or maybe there was a simulacrum Connelly in his mind; he knew him well enough now to predict what he'd say, and so could Connelly himself, from now on.

If he was here now he'd tell Connelly about that time he was under the big dining-room table, screaming. He'd been maybe five or six, no, younger, because Joe must have been a babe in arms at the time. He was yelling about having to always be the wrong one. Why was it him? What if it was the whole rest of the world that was wrong instead? The two seemed equally weighted to him back then, and they kept going round and around, dizzyingly, growing meaningless, unanswerable, getting scarier and scarier until suddenly, like the tigers chasing each other round the tree in Little Black Sambo, they melted into butter, and his own sense of himself fried up into that energy: he was a spinning stream of golden sparks, like glowing barbed-wire currents of electricity, nothing more. He stopped screaming (electricity didn't have feelings) and crawled over to the nearest socket to test the hypothesis. If he was really only made of electricity, he would be clearing the matter up for once and for all. If he wasn't – well, Mom and Joe and everyone would be better off without him.

Mom must have got suspicious of the sudden silence: she came in just in time, actually dropped the baby on the floor and flew over to pull him away from the plug. He had duly noted the evidence that despite all his wrongness he was wanted, but he also thought he remembered a leftover shred of longing, nostalgia for the pure electric state.

At 9.30 a registrar who looked like he should have been a marine sergeant or a death row screw arrived to bark out Sterling's test results from a wooden clipboard. 'Diabetes, negative. Blood count, negative. Urine, negative. Stool, negative.' And then, throwing the clipboard on the bed, he put his hands on his hips and bawled, 'Your notes arrived from Tripler this morning. Why didn't you just tell us you were a psychiatric patient and save us all this fucking around?'

Sterling stared, but couldn't object: this was what you got for departing from the script. When the harangue was over he picked up his cigarettes and made an escape attempt for the smoking room. Before he reached the door he was intercepted by a porter with a wheelchair arriving to cart him off to Psychiatric for an assessment. He went peacefully. At least a transfer to the looney bin would mean he wouldn't have to face the rubbernecks and the marine sergeant again.

The Psychiatric section was on the ground floor in a back wing of the building. Remembering the mine of information that had pushed the chuck wagon around Tripler, Sterling asked this porter, 'What's Psyche like?' The porter considered, sighed, finally ventured to opine sadly that a lot of folks there didn't seem to be too well in the head. 'Ahh,' said Tiger.

There was a guard on duty at the head of the hall, where a male nurse also sat on a desk and checked Sterling's name off a list. A long corridor of yellow ochre tiles and unclinically pink walls stretched ahead, doorless and uninterrupted. Around a corner you came to the main desk, which faced into two long observation wards. Sterling tried not to look down them, but couldn't avoid taking in the silence, the inescapable fact that this place was not alive with the continual curiosity, banter and verbal roughhousing of the general ward. Maybe there was something to be said for sticking it out with the rubbernecks after all.

As they passed the open rooms and came around another corner to glassed-in private rooms and then the heavily secured doors that led (he suspected) to padded cells or something like that, the silence grew more and more oppressive. Sterling shut his eyes, not wanting to gawp at Pathological Exhibits, well, just not wanting to have to see anything. But the darkness opened up another sense. Maybe it was only memory, recombining as imagination: scenes and pictures and silent shouts: 'Delaney, don't!' at an NCO threatening a runaway private with a revolver – 'Delaney, NO!' – but the sergeant shoots the bug-out right through the head, point-blank. The all-around-him whistle and thud of mortars pounding into foxholes inadequately grubbed out of hard Korean hillsides...

Or maybe it was more than that, telepathy (or sheer fantasy) pictures arriving from other theatres, other wars, other horrors: heavy feet through mud or silt or sand at Inch'on or Normandy or across Passchendaele, burning ships, barbed-wired camps bombarding horrified liberators or repatriators with living corpses, or just being fifteen years old and stumbling into the garage to find your father hanging from the rafters. Sterling opened his eyes to shut it all out, then decided it was worse unexpressed, and shut them, and watched and listened again, and let it all work through him.

'Here y'are; waiting room.' The porter tipped him out of the wheelchair.

This psychiatrist was of the kindly white-haired common-sense school; his assessment consisted of two questions: today's date and the name of the president. Sterling was a little shaky on the date. He knew it was Wednesday, but he had to backtrack a little to arrive at the number. He was careful to show all his calculations, the way you did in a maths exam, so the teacher would see you had the principle right even if you made an arithmetical error. He knew Eisenhower was the president too, but added, 'Don't ask me too many Current Events questions. I've been in a camp for three years and the only news we had was propaganda.'

'Yes, you're the brainwashing case,' murmured the doctor. 'What was the sort of thing they told you?'

'Oh, just rubbish you know, the Russkies have an H-bomb, the communists are taking over Indochina and the State Department, the vice-president has a secret fund for buying votes but nobody minds because he appeared on television with his pet dog and cried.'

The doctor looked at him oddly. 'Welcome home,' he said at last.

When he came out his wheelchair taxi hadn't returned, so he made his way up the corridor, following his nose to the blue-aired den of the Psyche rec room. Every plastic seat was occupied, and he had to stand in the middle of the room to light up. There was no window, no maps or pictures on the wall, nothing to focus on in order to escape the faces of the other patients. They were all motionless silences, huddled around their misery as if defending it against all comers, or flopped back in unnatural apathy. Sterling tried shutting his eyes to tune in to the scenes and sounds that were causing the silence again, but to his surprise and without his consent, he wasn't receiving pictures any more, but being given words which had to be spoken.

'So here you are, back. It's what you've been waiting for. It's what they've all been waiting for. So what went wrong?'

Everyone was looking at him, even the most distantly drugged or catatonic. Someone said, 'Go on.'

From somewhere beyond self-consciousness came the decision: yes, go on. The message wouldn't get through if he didn't, and he was curious to hear it himself 'Nobody ever explained to you that you couldn't go back. Or if they did, you just didn't understand that you had to believe them. All you could remember was the wonderful country you'd left behind, the kind good people, everything clean and warm; you were so hungry to get back into this beautiful world that it never even occurred to you to look at yourself, at the creature you'd become, razor-boned and ugly, explosive with hair-trigger rage, with the crazy race of terror that never stops speeding around and around in your veins and arteries, and the very thin, cracked and cracking line of skin that's keeping your filth from spraying out all over the world. The beautiful perfect world...all those sweet delicate faces, the kind moms and understanding dads and lovely clean wives and all those tiny perfect kids...you can't piss your shit all over them, you can't do that to them, you know you can't and you don't want to and that's why you're here, but where's it going to go? Is it just going to spin around and around inside you, out of control like a twister, destroying everything, flattening everything and everyone for miles around?

'See, I always used to think it was just me, this evil force; I thought all I had to do was unleash it on myself. Then I'd be punished and everyone would be happy, and sooner or later an angel would come down and lift me from the cross. I was hiding from the truth, because the energy just goes on and on, and when it's destroyed you, it's only freed to rage up and down the country and no kind of sacrifice is going to buy it off, and I don't even know if it will ever spin itself out and fade or if it'll keep generating its fury from the stuff of the universe itself. So don't look at me for answers. Maybe all you can do is just keep holding it all in for as long as you can, here in this mental place, be the high priesthood whose sacrifice is keeping the cosmic fall-out away from that beautiful world you can never rejoin.'

Someone started to clap. Sterling came to his senses, to the horrified realization that despite his flop in Homecoming he was a natural as the lead in the drama that was going on in Psyche. He put his cigarette out and ran down the corridor until he met the porter with the wheelchair. 'Jesus! Get me out of here!'

When he was rolled back to the light and noisy world of the normal, he saw Colonel Sedlachek, his once and future commander, at the desk. Barbara was with him, lovely and clean as advertised, and a sudden rush of sensuous hunger jumped him out of the wheelchair, skipping ahead like a kid jumping off a swing at its highest point of flight, ending up in her arms. 'Hey, you can't do that!' objected the porter and the nurse at the desk, simultaneously. 'Just did,' said Tiger, though he stopped himself from adding, 'Nyah nyah.'

'Tiger, you're *awful*,' Barbara giggled.

Sedlachek had been watching this with an air of paternal

resignation. 'Well, where you been, soldier?' was his greeting, when the display of marital harmony had gone on long enough.

'Art's just getting a private room organized for you,' Barbara explained.

It was only when he was getting his stuff together for the move to the new quarters that he rediscovered the brown paper bag Dad had left the night before.

On Friday a doctor came in and discharged him, saying, 'Well, I guess there's nothing wrong with you that home-cooking won't cure.' Sterling pictured Barbara and his Mom wrapping him up in foil and sliding him into the oven.

He was packed up and ready when Barbara came for him just after lunchtime. 'I've been planning today for years,' he told her as they stepped out. 'We're going to spend the whole day in bed.'

'Tiger!' Barbara squeaked, as the iron-haired female nurse at the front desk widened her eyes and inflated her chest pigeon-fashion in affront. Sterling laughed, but made a mental note to himself to remember that things Stateside were starchier than overseas, and if he brought the linguistic habits of Changhung, or even the bantering style of Tripler here, they probably would home-cook him.

They came out into the parking lot. Tiger stood still and breathed in the wonderful air, smelling of minerals and open sky. He shut his eyes as if to keep the euphoria in for a minute, then channelled it all out in a smile at Barbara. 'Freedom!'

'Watch out, there's a car coming.'

He skipped out of the way. Barbara headed across the lot, through all the different colours of cars, reflective as jewels in the cold sunlight, all those cars, big and long and futuristic, like aircraft with their streamlining and the high tailfins. Suddenly he realized that Barbara was making for the one spot of humpy drabness in the next row: his old red Ford. He approached it slowly, almost cautiously, as if he was afraid it would mirage into nothingness; he patted it to convince himself of its solidity. Something was rising up inside him, and he wasn't sure if it was sentiment or fear. He hadn't thought about the car since he'd shipped out to Japan, but here it was. How many other things were waiting to surprise him like that, unchanged and yet different? And what about the things that had been changed? If Barbara had bought a new car, would he even have remembered this old friend? What about all the things that would be lost for ever, even to memory, oh God, and don't even let yourself think about the might-have-beens. Barbara started to climb in the driver's seat automatically, then pulled herself up. 'Want to drive?'

'Uh, no, maybe I better not.'

She piloted it smoothly along the road that followed the perimeter of the base. She had been a timid driver four years ago, but she wasn't any more. He had a sudden realization of her as the unconsciously confident mistress of her world, capable of dealing with things that would have horrified other women because she had to – an image of her tying a bandanna around her hair and donning household gloves to change a flat. A little unsettled, he turned to look out at the passing landscape.

Nothing much had changed here anyway: the dry expanses, the wonderful sagebrush, the sudden greennesses as they came close to the living quarters, watered and mown spaces, the football field, the baseball diamond. Same old jungle gyms and swings and the turning bars where Caroline had cracked her head. Same old rows and drills of houses, and yet not the same, impossibly white, magically rich, charming as gingerbread cottages. People who lived in them led lives of wonderful happiness, decent good people, loving and friendly and neighbourly and Godly. Barbara pulled up in front of the whitest, tidiest, enchantedest house of them all; his heart felt full to overflowing. He went up the porch steps slowly, reverently. Same or different inside? Same, oh, the same, same old furniture – oh, a *television*, Jesus, how had they managed to get one of those? But otherwise, all the same, even the old couch and armchair Mom had passed on to them when they married, and the same dining suite, Barbara's pride and joy. He walked around touching things until Barbara cleared her throat and looked at her watch and remarked that the kids got out of school at three. The look on her face was at once unknowing and significant.

'Consider yourself swept off your feet,' he told her. 'I don't think I could carry you upstairs or even pick you up but...' Coming into the bedroom, the sense of unreality, the fear that it was all a mirage hit him harder than ever. Barbara's mother's patchwork quilt, like a huge candystore of colour, the bed so decadently soft, Barbara like a tiny white china shepherdess, if shepherdesses wore lacy uplift bras and elastic panelled girdles. 'Store-bought cake syndrome,' he warned her. 'Don't worry if I faint.' In fact it saved him from all the things that probably would have gone wrong. The flood of sense data drowned his consciousness so that he couldn't discriminate between the sexual, the purely aesthetic and the simply deliciously comfortable, allowing the body to go about its work unhindered. Then he must have fallen asleep because he was woken up by the sound of many feet on the porch outside, the swinging of the front door, Barbara saying, 'Ssh, don't wake Daddy.'

'I'm awake,' he called down. 'Come on up.'

Barbara shepherdessed the children in. Caroline looked at him critically. 'Every time I see you you're always in bed.'

'I'll be in bed today but tomorrow I'll get up,' he promised. Caroline tossed her head and left the room, followed by Henry. 'I'm a disappointment to them,' he observed.

Barbara looked embarrassed. 'I think it's just the...I don't know...the strangeness...'

'It's OK. They're allowed. Let's make the most of it, hop in.'

'You're *awful*!' she protested, but undressed again and got in. He reached over to touch her hair and her face, and she suddenly noticed the big silver ring on his right forefinger. 'What's that?'

'Huh?' Oh, the class ring. 'Oh yeah, it's from a friend, in the camp.'

Her eye had travelled inexorably to his other hand, to the missing wedding band. 'What...what happened? Did they take it when you were captured?'

'No, it's all right. *He* has it,' indicating the class ring.

'Why?'

He took a deep breath and said, 'The idea was that if I died and he made it he'd bring it back to you and if he died and I made it, I'd take this back to his folks.' This was the truth but not the whole truth.

'So he's dead in Korea wearing your wedding ring.'

'No, no, he's alive, he lives in Arkansas somewhere.'

'Our wedding ring is in Arkansas. Somewhere.'

'You're making it sound awful, as if I'd left it on a bus. Kirby is taking care of it for me. He was my best friend, my only friend for a long time. I was in solitary and this ring was my only human contact, you know, the only proof there was someone out there who cared about me.'

She looked away, and he realized that the wedding ring should have meant the same thing. 'I'm sorry,' he said. 'Maybe it was a mistake. It was just, I don't know, a way of trying to make sure at least *something* made it home. And I wouldn't have made it, except for him.'

She sighed. 'I'd better go see what the children are up to.' She slid out of bed, wrapped herself in her bathrobe, then paused at the door. 'What did you say his name was?'

'Kirby. Kirby Wilson.'

'Oh,' she said, and went out. Twenty minutes later she returned. 'What would you like for dinner?'

'Don't start thinking about supper. It's only four.'

'I wanted to do something special. There's some steak, or chicken...'

'Barbara, I *told* you I didn't want to do anything today except spend as much time as possible with you, in here. And it's only half a day as it is, and you keep jumping up to do things. Now shape up and get in here!'

If she'd been feeling all right she would have replied in kind, salaaming and saying, 'Yes, o mighty master' or doing an impression of Step 'n' Fetchit, 'Yassuh ah's a-comin jes fast as ah kin!' But she didn't and he knew she must still be sore about the ring. But what could he do about it? The more he tried to explain, the closer he got to territory he wasn't ready to show her over. 'Look, Barbara, we can't afford to let the bad stuff get in the way –'

'He phoned, you know.'

'What?'

'Your friend. He phoned here, a couple of days before you came home.'

'Why didn't you tell me? That was nice of him.'

'Was it? He told me you were "troubled in your mind". I finally decided it was a hoax and now he turns out to be this friend of yours who has our wedding ring. So why'd he say that? Huh?'

'Because, Barbara, he was probably trying to find a polite euphemism for "completely raving loony". Because when he last saw me, I was. Have you got that? I went insane. Am I going to be allowed to forget about it now, or do we have to pick over every stinking little thing that happened?'

'I'm sorry.' She bent her head, took off the bathrobe.

'I will tell you everything; I want to,' he said, more gently. 'But not today.'

She nodded, climbing in between the sheets. But as soon as his hands touched her waist she jumped back as if they were electric. 'I'm sorry, I just can't, I'm sorry!' she cried, grabbing the bathrobe and dashing out of the bedroom.

Sterling shut his eyes and howled with frustration. He pounded the bed with his fists and shouted, 'This is just not fair!' Eventually he lectured himself that the imperative of not letting the bad stuff get in the way held for him as well as for Barbara, that he'd better talk to her and do what he could to salvage things. He cinched his trousers around his waist and went down barefoot. She was in the kitchen, ramming stuffing into a chicken's behind with the end of a rolling pin. She looked defensive when he materialized in the doorway, but his voice was peaceable. 'Can you tell me what's wrong?'

'I don't know.'

'Is it... am I... physically disgusting to you?'

'No, it's not that.'

'The ring?'

'Well, sort of... Well, to be totally honest, it's this thing, you know, you've had a bad time, you deserve to call the shots, and I can't argue with it, but it makes me feel like some kind of harem slave and the ring was sort of like rubbing it in.'

'Oh god, I was only joking.'

'No,' looking straight at him. 'You were pretending to be only joking but you also meant it.'

He blinked but couldn't disagree.

'I know this sounds selfish, but I've been through a lot too, so what about what I wanted our first day to be like?'

'You never told me. Tell me now, and we'll do it.'

She wrinkled her face. 'It's artificial if I have to tell you. You'd just be doing it to make up for the ring and everything, and not because you wanted to.'

'So I'm supposed to read your mind and find out what you want and then make myself want it whether I want to or not?'

'I just sort of expected that you'd want to spend the day all of us together, playing with the children and having a nice meal and then as much time as you wanted in bed after they'd gone to sleep. I thought that was what someone would want, but obviously I was wrong.'

'Right, fine, that's what I want too. I just wish you'd told me before and saved us a fight, that's all.' He went to find the kids. They had made houses out of seat cushions and couch cushions and were talking in the wuffly voices of animals. 'Hi, gang. Whatcha playing?'

They fell silent instantly, withdrawing deep into their pillow dens. It was as if he had just walked into an illegal poker game in the enlisted men's quarters. His natural instinct was to turn a blind eye and walk out again, but he couldn't do that now. He had to get invited into the game. Suddenly it wasn't like being in the army, it was like his first day at the private school, realizing that he just didn't know how to make friends with people, because up until then people had always done the work of making friends with him.

Barbara looked out, saw him standing there helplessly. 'Daddy's up now, children.'

This was about as deadly as having the teacher stand you up in front of the whole class telling them to be nice to the new kid. He knelt down by Henry's house and peered in. He was curled up in a little ball, eyes squeezed tight. He leaned over and looked into the other. Caroline's eyes gleamed out at him like the dark fierce eyes of a small wild mammal. 'Watch out,' he warned, reached in and tickled her waist. The cushion house exploded and the air was rent with squeals.

That was better. He reached in and tickled Henry, who squirmed and growled, 'Stop it!' Caroline tapped him on the shoulder and dodged the hand that came after her. He went after Henry again. Henry grabbed the offending hand like a sandwich, and bit it.

'Come and get me, Mr Tickle!' Caroline called, posing in the doorway with a flirtatious smile. She ran around the house screaming with anticipation, shrieking with laughter when caught. A lamp was knocked over. She ran up the stairs. He leaped after her, landing full length on his belly and just catching hold of one ankle. It kicked free and she darted into her room, burrowing under the tautly sheeted bed. He searched in cupboards, closets, emptied toy boxes out all over the floor. He 'knew she was in here somewhere!' He stood very still and silent, waiting for the little lump in the bed to move or make a sound. Presently a giggle escaped, and he pounced, tickling extra hard through the blanket. He crawled in under the sheets, caught a bare foot and scraped its sole across his chin. The other foot kicked him in the face. 'Now

I'm really mad!' he roared, and tore the sheets off the bed, with the little girl still bundled up inside them. He swung the burden from side to side, then all the way around, and around and around until his strength gave out and they fell on the floor together. She wriggled free and stood in the doorway in a sprinter's crouch, the tiny muscles of her legs knotted in readiness. 'Nyah nyah, Mr Tickle!' Gasping for breath he dragged himself up in a mock lunge. She fled across the hall into the grown-ups bedroom.

He staggered after her. She was concealed behind the door and hit him with a pillow. He fell dramatically onto the bed, uttering death rattles. She yanked open a drawer and began flinging Barbara's clothes and underwear at him and everywhere else. Henry appeared at the door, stared at the carnage, then ran back downstairs. 'Mommy! Care and him are making a mess in your bedroom!'

'St – ha ha – stop now, ha ha ha, Mom's coming.' He was rolling around, unable to stop laughing when Barbara came up. 'I don't believe this,' she said.

Caroline froze, her eyes on her mother's face, hoping she was going to smile but not counting on it. Tiger tried to sit up but fell off the bed, still laughing. Barbara folded her arms and refused the invitation to find it funny. 'You'll pick those things up this instant, young lady,' she announced and marched back down again. Caroline stuck her tongue out once her mother was gone, but began putting things away. Barbara obviously ran a tight ship. Sterling sighed and started to help her but found the energy debt he had run up so ruthlessly was now being called home. He had to get his head down between his knees to prevent a blackout. His body had started to shake, as if it knew what to expect from his mind. Here it came, like a dust storm making straight for you across a prairie, the entire weight of shame, the whole three years' worth, and there was nothing you could do but duck your head, drop to the ground, let it pass over you.

It was one home comfort he hadn't been looking forward to, but the delight he experienced on discovering the stationery drawer on Saturday morning was in the sex-and-store-bought-cake league. Tiger found loose-leaf blue-lined and punched paper, a long maize-yellow legal pad, spiral-bound apple-green steno notebooks, five of them, a bulk buy bargain, and a box of top-quality onionskin typing paper, light as silk, dimpled like parchment. Every sheet pure and virginal, square-cut thicknesses of pages, seductive satin smoothness, all speaking the promise of his own voice. Then there were the boxes of Eagle Mirado hard lead pencils, sharpened to perfection, the fine tipped ballpoints in blue and black and red, and look! the old silver fountain pen he'd won from the *Reno Evening Gazette* for his graduation year essay entitled Our Task in the East.

That was the year he'd fallen in love with *bushido*, the Japanese warrior code. Most of his libido and spiritual energy had been invested in the fantasy *alter ego* of a kamikaze pilot. He hadn't admitted that in the essay! But it might be interesting to unearth it; it might throw some light on his susceptibility to Chang, to his embarrassing inner knowledge that if their places had been swapped he would have done the same as Chang had, run away to join the Long March, worshipped Mao as he had in fact worshipped MacArthur. He'd thrown his copy out a couple of years later as an embarrassment, but he suspected Mom had the published version stored away in her archives of Family Achievement. They were going around to his folks later that afternoon, and he'd dig it out if he got the chance.

But for now he didn't touch the silver pen, just slid a pencil out of its box and helped himself to a steno pad (the cheapest and least noticeable indulgences). He slid them inside the billowing excesses of his old jeans and shirt to get past Barbara, who was stitching away at the Singer in the utility room. It did not occur to him to wonder whether this secrecy was something left over from Changhung or a reluctance to involve her in his inner life. He halted on the landing, slunk past the open door of the bathroom, too silent to distract the kids from the splashy tub game they were playing. He sat on the floor of the bedroom, leaning against the wall. The green cardboard cover of the steno pad flew around its spiral binding, the Eagle Mirado swooped.

My Task in the East
The Official Confession and Self-criticism of J. L. Sterling
Commander, First Platoon, Imperial Army of Capitalist Aggression

This part came easily enough, but he wasn't sure quite where to go after that. As a warm-up, he started to reproduce from memory the comments he'd written on the original form as part of his programme of harassing his captors.

1 Pissing in Yalu river (Manchurian side)

2 Murder of brave heroes of the In Min Gun and Chinese Field Army

Both of these were exaggerations: he'd never seen the Yalu and it was probably claiming too much for his marksmanship to imagine he'd actually killed anybody. But he felt he was entitled to the swagger: it had been originally done at considerable personal risk.

He thought a little more, a little more seriously, and came up with what he decided would be his real first line.

It all began with an argument about the MSR with Captain Portland.

He stopped, debated with himself about substituting Main Supply Route for MSR in the interests of a civilian readership, crossed it out, disliked the new rhythm, reinstated the original with a promise to clarify it later in the text. Now what?

I was a 24-year-old First Lieutenant, and the only thing that entitled me to argue with a superior officer was a nightmare memory of the retreat from Naktong, when I'd seen the best part of a company splashed all over the Main Supply Route by two or three snipers hidden in the slope above the road. Portland had seen it too, and no doubt it was factored into his calculations. But I had an ego so big it had to be carried along behind me in an extra jeep, and I was arguing. Hadn't we learned anything from history? It wasn't like you needed to go back to the French and Indian War to realize that marching in constipated columns, tied to the roads by our supply vehicles, was just inviting a fast, light-travelling enemy to hammer us from the high ground. I felt it as a particular insult that two of these trucks were carrying nothing but plucked turkey carcasses: did they think that I was so soft that my courage and morale would fail if I wasn't indulged in a traditional Thanksgiving feast, up here, hundreds of miles from the 38th parallel?

Captain Portland only observed that if we'd travelled across country and had tried to take all the high ground all the way back from Iwon we wouldn't be halfway to where we were now, and speaking for himself he'd thank God for Thanksgiving dinner but he wasn't counting on it; last he'd heard the turkeys were still frozen solid.

It was because of the argument that when we finally left the road to pitch camp, Portland called me over and asked me if I wanted a reconnaissance mission. Ahead of us the road bent around to the left, and the map showed a little road joining it, coming from what was marked as a quarry in the valley behind the next ridge. 'I've been thinking it's mighty suspicious we haven't seen any of these Chinamen.'

'You think they might be camped in there?'

'I'm saying have a look, but don't get too close' was all he would commit himself to. That and, 'If you stay out long enough you might just about manage to miss the turkey.'

Sterling paused. The next section would involve an introduction to the platoon, and he didn't know whether he should use their real names or not. He was just deciding to stick with the originals for the time being, changing them if there was ever a possibility of publication when he heard Barbara calling, 'Tiger? Tiger?' her voice rising with the Doppler effect as she approached up the stairs. He shoved the steno notebook between the bed frame and the mattress and jumped to his feet. 'Up here, hon.'

'I've finished taking these in.' She appeared, bearing his old blue dress uniform. 'Why don't you wear them to your folks?'

'That formal stuff? Aw, come on!'

'Well, just see if it fits. You can't wear what you've got on anyway, you look like an old tramp. – Kids! Are you clean? Time to get out and get dry and dressed!'

If the houses on the base looked charming, his parents' suburb looked like Beverly Hills, all big gates and curving drives and tall trees. The road was full of long gleaming cars with those sinister shark-like tailfins. Barbara had to park about thirty feet down the street and they approached the house on foot. As they came round the bend of the drive they saw a big banner screaming WELCOME HOME TIGER with balloons and flags flapping at the corners. 'It's a party!' cried Caroline.

They could hear the murmur of voices falling raggedly silent as Barbara pressed the doorbell three times (the secret signal). Someone threw the door open and everyone sang For He's a Jolly Good Fellow. And then EVERYBODY threw themselves at him, slapping his back or hugging him or shaking his hand: Mom and Dad and all the neighbours and his tenth-grade English teacher and the minister, Rev. Gammy, every single member of the League of Social Stalwarts and their well-connected husbands, the mayor and his wife, hopeful Howard Goode, a bunch of girls he'd dated in high school and their anxious-looking husbands, the entire anthropology department at the UNR, a bunch of guys from the varsity football team and all their pretty girls, and oh wow, Mr Barson the coach, now in a wheelchair, Arthur and Evie Sedlachek and a bunch of others from the base, Mom's Homebakers' Guild and finally an undulating siren in bobby socks who pressed herself to him so warmly he had to make a face at Barbara to make it clear he was neither consenting to or enjoying her embraces, mouthing 'Who *is* she?' Barbara had only laughed and screamed over the noise, 'Don't you even recognize your own sister?'

'Champagne!' Mom sang out, and corks flew like fireworks. He overheard Evie Sedlachek asking, 'Is it imported?' and one of the social stalwarts informing her that if it wasn't imported it wouldn't be champagne, my dear; he must remember to tell Barbara that one.

'Where did you find all these people?' he asked Dad, when he had recovered from the first shock wave.

'Mom decided to invite everyone who helped Barbara or wrote letters or did anything or asked after you,' he sighed. Then, seeing a round and red-faced figure rumbling towards them, he said, 'This is Congressman Wunsche; you may not be aware that he did a great deal on your behalf...' Michael had to force himself to sound warm. He was an old-style FDR Democrat and the right-wing Republican made his flesh creep.

Wunsche pressed Tiger's hand and told him of his lonely battle with the Inky Pinko and the Chink to get news of him, whether he was alive or dead, where he was being held, how to get letters through to him...

Tiger's face went white. 'Letters?' Wunsche explained that they had organized a letter-writing campaign, flooding the bamboo curtain: personal letters to him and dozens to the authorities. He had discovered that the best way to get personal letters through was via Switzerland and Moscow.

Sterling said yes, that was probably true, and how much it had been appreciated. He didn't have the heart to tell him that not one of them had arrived. It wasn't Wunsche's fault.

'Cake!' Mom trilled, and an honour guard of her baking platoon frogmarched him through the crowd to cut up a yard-long American flag with piped icing and silver stars while cameras flashed in his eyes. 'Speech!' called somebody. Sterling smiled and ducked, bowing his head. 'Speech!' seconded the minister. 'No, please,' said Tiger, then had the inspiration of offering Wunsche the floor.

He took it without reservation and made a five-minute speech about communism. Tiger was just congratulating himself that nobody would want to waste any more time listening after that when Dad sidled up to him and whispered, 'If you don't feel up to saying thanks to everyone I'll ask Mom to do it for you.'

'No, it's OK,' he said quickly; if Mom got up to speak it would only last longer and be more embarrassing. So when Wunsche was finished he swallowed hard and said rapidly, 'Thank you all for coming and making me feel so welcome and this wonderful surprise, and cake, and it's great to see you all. And, um, thank you for the letters you sent, um, I guess this time I had a good excuse for not writing back because I wasn't prepared to write the kind of propaganda you had to produce to get them through.' Mom and Wunsche thought this was hilarious.

He knew that was all he needed to say, but the trouble was, he suddenly was supposed to say more; there was another message to be delivered. He prayed it wasn't from the Muse of the Psyche Ward Smokeroom as he inflated his lungs to receive it. 'I guess the one thing I learned when I was in the camp is that freedom isn't just being able to go where you want and do what you want and say what you want. When you've lost all that there's another kind of freedom that arrives, a psychological freedom that's possible if you're prepared to lose everything else in order to find it. The first kind of freedom is a gift, and the second is a gift you can give back.' He suddenly felt Dad's eyes on him, speculative, curious. Everyone else just looked bewildered, he thought. 'Um, I guess that's all. Thank you for your prayers and everything.' He grabbed the long silver cake slicer and started cutting, to hide his face from the crowd.

Mom's hand stayed him; he looked up and saw that as the clapping was dying out, Colonel Sedlachek was holding up his glass for attention. 'I'd just like to say something.' Everyone fell quiet, though perhaps with a sense of dutiful resignation. 'I won't be long,' he promised. 'But I'd just like to tell you that there's a heroine in this story, too, a little lady who's been keeping pretty quiet today, but who's been holding things together at home and doing a man's job as well as a woman's; Barbara, can I just tell them about the time I sent the GIs around to paint your house? And how they found the job half done already and this young lady lying on the porch roof trying to stretch across and paint the upstairs windows? I think we should all give her a big hand, Barbara Sterling!' Everyone clapped enthusiastically, except Evie Sedlachek, who had already heard the anecdote about the paint about twenty times more than she had ever wanted to.

Cake was finally served, and one of the old teammates produced a football and all draftable males were evacuated to the backyard before anybody else could make a speech. Dad took civilian defence measures, putting on a record of Sousa marches and giving everyone a blast of the *Stars and Stripes Forever*.

Tiger had gone out with the football team, but they were almost as exhausting to play with as Caroline, and after a couple of dud passes he used the excuse of a tackle to hand the command over to his old second stringer, Jerry Meyer. He slipped inside through the kitchen swinging door, stood panting for a minute, then filled a glass of water. American water, clean and strong. He held it up to the light to admire its clarity; stupid tears filled his eyes.

Little Beanie Tibburn, one of Mom's homebakers, came scuttling in to get a tray of rolls and caught him. Tiger was about to explain himself with a comparison between Reno water and the brown rice-paddy runoff that had nearly killed him at Hara Kiri, when she squeaked, 'I know, isn't it awful? We *buy* our water now, Ritchie picks up 50 gallons every time he's up the mountains.'

She scuttled out with the rolls, and he realized he needed a break from people. He sneaked along the walls as he made his way out of the hall, dodged past the open living-room door and ran up the stairs. He went into his old bedroom. It had been redecorated as a Best Guestroom, and today was housing the coats and wraps of a hundred visitors, and one other refugee from social felicity: his father, standing by the window that looked out over the football game. 'Oh, hi.'

'Well, hello,' said Dad, as if he had come up here in expectation of seeing him, and had in fact been waiting for some time.

Tiger sat down on the bed, which was Princess and the Pea-ed up a foot with guests' outer garments, and lowered his head, panting until his heart rate finally slowed. 'Boy, what a mess I am. I sure hope you weren't watching me throwing out there.'

Dad shook his head, astonished: if he had been watching the game it had been as a patterned interplay of human energies, with no interest in whose sons were playing or how badly they were performing. He came over and perched on the other corner of the mattress and remarked, 'I overheard the congressman telling Mom you could have a job as his assistant anytime you cared to leave the army.'

'Ha, ha,' said Tiger, not wanting Dad to see how attractive the offer sounded.

'My guess is he's realized he needs a speechwriter.'

Tiger twisted his shoulders inwards and hunched over a gutful of embarrassment. 'It's this stupid thing that just happens. I open my mouth and something which is either totally insane or sickeningly corny comes out. You should just be thanking your lucky stars you didn't get the crazy version today.'

Dad didn't answer for a long time, which aggravated the gut problem until he had to run out to the bathroom. When he returned, his father verbatimmed the offending psychological freedom line at him, and just looked at him with waiting eyes. 'Yeah, well, I don't know why I said it. It didn't mean anything – well, if it ever did, I reneged on it, so it's not worth shit.' He twitched and twisted, remembered he belonged to the tobacco-bearing classes again and found his pack in his tunic pocket. 'Think Mom'll mind if I smoke upstairs?'

'She doesn't need to know it was you. Go ahead if it helps,' Dad said, but returned with indefatigable patience, to the subject. 'What did you renege on?'

It was a story that had to be told backwards, starting with Connelly, because it was only then that the state of what might have been psychological freedom got put into words you could use to describe it to someone else. But the more he talked, the less sure he was of what it was he was going on about. 'Oh, I don't know. I just don't know how to judge it. Maybe it was crazy. Of course it was crazy; except I was feeling a whole lot crazier before it happened, and I've sure as hell been acting crazier since I came out of it. It was a peaceful, *seeing* state, but if it was really something, you know, like enlightenment, how come I'm back in the mess and fog again? I think Connelly reckoned it was a technique for cutting off pain so that whatever they did to you you could keep on resisting, and now that it's over the pain's come back, like a debt I have to pay.'

'Stop trying to rate it,' Dad advised. 'You know the way Mom always takes the price tag off a present before she wraps it?' Tiger looked bewildered. Michael sighed – he felt uncomfortable spelling things out. 'When something just arrives, like you said this did, then you're not accountable for anything except how you use it.'

He was quiet for a long while. When he spoke again, his memory had made a jump back from Tripler to Changhung, to the underground cell in the guardhouse. 'It wasn't a whole lot bigger than a grave, it was only about five feet high, or deep I should say, and they handed the food down to me through a trapdoor in the ceiling. And I figured the whole thing was intended as an experiment in nothingness, trying to drive me crazy, so I started with a whole bunch of projects like measuring time by the length of my beard instead of by how often they brought food, because they could manipulate that to disorient me. I'd spent enough time in cells already to know that keeping my own control on time was crucial. One trick I was proud of was this thing I invented of going to town on doing push-ups or sit-ups until the muscles went into spasm. You're always stiff for two days after, so that was a definite forty-eight hours I could clock up.

'That was the common-sense phase, only it phased out, so I don't even know how long it lasted after all. Six days, maybe; I went on two of those exercise sprees, but I think even then it was starting to feel unreal. Real and unreal changed places: solid things outside yourself faded into dreams, and the stuff in my head got bigger and brighter and so much more like reality. And once something's real, you lose control of it, huh? So I'd start telling myself a story, some pure wish-fulfilment thing: my girlfriend comes in with a big soft blanket and lies down next to me and . . . and the next thing is she makes some little slip which lets me know she's actually working for the Chinese. And I end up in a pit of despair which I just can't get out of even though I know the whole thing was a fantasy in the first place. And the longer it goes on, the stranger it gets, and the voice of common sense gets fainter and fainter until it just dies. There was a time when I believed they were putting a drug in my food which was turning me Chinese. I would stand up to measure myself against the ceiling, and each time I found I was a few inches shorter. And when Chang came in we would have long and complicated philosophical discussions in Chinese. And not the *Putonghua* that everyone spoke, but Chang's own dialect of Cantonese. I don't know if we were really speaking in English — because Chang and I did use to argue philosophy — and I just hallucinated that I was fluent in Cantonese, or whether the whole thing was a delusion. But I remember him telling me I was much better off Chinese, because I had a jade mind, opposite of bamboo: I'd crack before I bent. Cracking already, obviously.

'The room used to spin round until I was so dizzy I'd vomit, and I'd hear someone screaming and not realize it was me, and it was hell until I learned this trick of bilocating. I couldn't go very far; I couldn't get out, but I could sit beside myself and hold my hand and say encouraging things like "With you all the way", and "As long as we stick together we're OK". That was a pretty good time, but it was ruined when Chang visited next, and told me Kirby — that was my best friend, who was also being held — had lost his nerve and given in. And after hearing that I couldn't bilocate any more, I guess because if I couldn't trust Kirby, how could I trust that other guy?

'So it got bad again, in ways I don't really want to talk about, except I was getting farther and farther away from myself, until one day I realized that I was stretched out as fine as a thread between two poles. One end, down below like an anchor, was a body, and then miles away up at the top was a sort of eye, I mean a register of sensation, and these two were the only real parts. The rest could go.

'Maybe there was a choice made, the rest went. Everything became simple and sane again. There was a body lying there in the dark. It could just lie there for hours looking at the different colours of blackness, or listening to the heart and feeling the blood swirling around, arms going heavy and light as it came and went. It seemed as clean and light as a summer's day down there. Reality was back, solid again, but different. There wasn't a personality there to discriminate whether something was good or bad, nice or painful, and things had their own weight and fullness and isness. A lot of time spent touching things, the cold walls, the tight feeling on the skin of the hand as the clay that stuck to it dried out. Beauty is too subjective a word, but it was something like that: registering things in their full value.'

'Instead of looking at price tags,' his father murmured.

Tiger looked at him suspiciously. 'You've been sitting there not saying a word in case it melted the butter in your mouth and I bet you know more about this than I do,' he accused.

'Me? Nope. Go on. What happened?'

'Well, Chang must have decided his experiment had backfired, and he had the subject brought back into the light, up in one of the ordinary lock-ups, and there was food with vegetables and even meat, twice a day, and he came around a lot, being very sweet, speaking English, wanting to get the personality back. No chance.'

'But in the end you did decide to come back.'

'It was Connelly, he outflanked me.'

Dad snorted disbelievingly. He folded his arms as if he was about to make a pronouncement on it all, then his face suddenly twitched, and he said, 'In about two minutes your Mom's going to realize we're missing. If I were you I'd put that smoke out and get downstairs before she comes looking for us.'

A small package arrived in the mail: a ring wrapped in cotton and an unsigned note saying, 'I guess you'll want this. Please keep mine.' Tiger showed it to Barbara, who shrugged and said, 'Strange man.'

He gave her the ring. 'Put it on for me.'

'What, like getting married again?' she wrinkled her nose.

'Why not?'

She shook her head and stuck the ring on unceremoniously. Symbolic gestures belonged in literature, not life.

There was a return address on the brown paper wrapping, and that afternoon, when Barbara was picking the kids up from school, he got out his steno pad and wrote,

Dear Kirby,

I guess you are home and I hope you had a hero's welcome. Someone who met you in Tripler told me you were doing well and I trust that is still the case.

Kirby, allow me to apologize for the way I was to you after I got out of the cells. I was trying to maintain a state of mind in which nothing more could hurt me, and I knew I would lose it if I got took up with other people again.

Also, I want to explain that towards the end of our stay in Changhung I made a decision that it would be kinder to my family not to return home, as I know you saw. You were gone by the time I changed my mind, on account of the political capital that was being made of it.

Anyway, here I am at last, getting adjusted to having everything too good to be true.

By the way, since getting home I have discovered that a lot of people sent me letters. Have you found anything like that? I'd like to figure out if Chang and co. were keeping them back or if they got lost upstream from the camp. Apparently my folks and friends were trying all different kinds of ways of addressing them, via Peking, Moscow, what have you, so you'd have thunk one or two of them would have made it. The guys who did get letters, how were they addressed?

It's pretty suspicious that it was us who didn't get anything, but on the other hand, if Chang had some he was holding back, why not at least try to use them? 'Some letters for you, comrades, if you improve your attitude?'
With you all the way,
Tser Ling

PS Please accept my frat pin in token. I'd have said keep the ring, except my wife got pretty steamed up about it.

Kirby's letter came back promptly, within the week.

Dear Ster,
Thanks for the pin, I'll keep it. I am happy to hear that everything is too good to be true for you. Unfortunately coming home has been a mixed blessing as my father passed away in March of 1952. So I don't know whether to be angry or grateful the letters did not get thru. But I always knew that Chang or somebody had them. I can't remember him saying anything, just knew it. Don't you remember Eugene and Hutch got them big bunches about a dozen dating way back and all tied together, when they were moved to Uncle Tom's Cabin?

Sterling, I wonder if reading between the lines of your letter you were asking me to explain some things too. My belief is that there is no good dwelling on what you should put behind you. A man comes to the end of his endurance and there is nothing more to be said. For this reason I think also that we should not keep in touch. Please do not take this personally, I just don't think it will do you or me any good to rake over old scars.
Yours,
Kirby

Of course he took it personally. It was a very long time before he could reread it, and realize that maybe the line about a man coming to the end of his endurance referred to the present and not only to the time in the solitary cells. It was longer again before he could admit that Kirby was also entitled to try to maintain a state of mind in which nothing more could hurt him.

From *My Task in the East*.

The First Platoon had been an ill-matched bunch to begin with. They had never looked sharp on the parade ground, with their bodies that jutted and bulged, gangled and gapped, each of them seeming to represent a different physical extreme, pushed near the point of congenital defectiveness. Added to the effect was a determined individualism in dress and personal grooming which was flourishing in the rough living of active service. You wouldn't believe they had all been issued the same winter utilities less than a week ago. Things had been lost, stolen, swapped, scavenged and altered. A bitter divide arose as to whether you wore your parka hood under or over your helmet. Micky Moranha had exchanged his good leather boots for some marine's canvas and rubber waterproof 'shoepacs', which made him look doubly clubfooted. I had a grandiose field officer's overcoat, tailored and wide-skirted, which somebody else had stolen and I had won in a Bean Patch poker game, which I had only dared unpack now that we were a long way from any brass. I thought it made me look like MacArthur. Lt Harry said it made me look like a stormtrooper. Chubby-faced Krajicek had ill-advisedly obtained a padded Chinese Army winter hat, with earflaps which he wore Holden Caulfield style: up until desperate. Even when desperate, Delahunty had an affectation of always leaving something unbuttoned or undone, coat gaping, a strap loose, several extra bandoliers of M1 cartridges slung this way and that. You could tell which way the wind was blowing looking at his slender, cavalier person. Little Kirby Wilson, who wore what he had been issued in the way it was intended, neat and sober, came to look the oddest of all.

The final blow to uniformity came with the addition of two coloured soldiers from the disbanded 62nd regiment. A bad reputation preceded them and bad feeling met them, especially from the two southern boys, Delahunty and Wilson. Hutch Smith was tall with an apologetic stoop and a nervous manner, which you saw as deferential or shifty, depending. The other fellow, Joshua

Eugene, was also quiet to begin with, but it was a quiet with something behind it. He was older than the rest of us, and at this stage the only WW2 vet left in the platoon.

This under-strength, fifteen-man ragbag left the MSR to move up the westward slopes, slanting off so that we would reach the cover of the scrubby twisted evergreen timber that crowned Hill 586 (that was its height in metres) as we came into view of the bend in the road. With real earth – that is, tawny grey gravel – underfoot, breathing in a thin, dusty little wind that came whipping down the valley, so cold it must have come from Siberia, I felt so happy and free I couldn't keep a great big grin off my face. Nobody else wore one. There was a distinct air of sullen reluctance, and I rubbed salt in it with sadistic talk about turkey dinner. Suddenly Delahunty fell sprawling in a patch of scree with a cry of pain. I thought he'd been shot; guys were darting up the hill for cover, until they heard him groaning, 'My ankle!'

I came over to examine it. His boot wasn't even tied properly, and the other one was loose too. This wasn't just Delahuntism, this was deliberate self-sabotage. I laced it up for him, nice and tight, deaf to his screams, and watched while he did the other one up for himself. 'If it hurts too much to walk on, use your wings.' When he was hauled to his feet I made him march along in front of me; he was our best marksman and I didn't want him skulking behind and sneaking home. He limped along, heaving his shoulders unevenly with each step, muttering, between little whimpers and gasps of pain, 'He's just determined to make captain even if it kills us.'

'That's right, Tinkerbell, and the next fairy I catch trying that game I'm personally gonna . . .

He had to stop writing; the deliberate resuming of his old manner was no longer keeping what happened after at bay, it was making the guilt worse. He stashed the notebook under the couch seat, and jumped up, calling to Barbara, 'I'm just going for a walk.'

'What?'

'I'm going out. I'll be back for supper.' He got out the front door before she could come out of the kitchen and ask why and where and so on, and made his way past the playground to the vacant desert stretch that ran all the way to the chainlink of the base perimeter. In the western distance the Sierras were nearly black against the sinking sun.

Delahunty's limp had stuck with them, even when they were scrambling for their lives to the cover of the mine tunnel where they had eventually been besieged. At the beginning of the long march that brought them, three days later, to Hara Kiri, Sterling had fallen in beside him, saying, 'Whatever you do, soldier, don't drop behind.' Delahunty had nodded, with his teeth gritted, and had rejected Sterling's offer of a supporting arm. He kept going, with that strange unexpected tenacity of his, and it was Micky Moranha, with his feet frozen in their own sweat (thanks to those goddamned waterproof shoepacs) whom the Chinese shot for lagging.

A picture of Delahunty from Changhung: frail, red-bearded, a scarf flapping behind him like a windsock. It was after the betrayal that had finished off the platoon; Krajicek was there, too, trying to slink away. But Delahunty raised his head and met Sterling's eye, coolly, greenly. And then one day, maybe a month or two later, his body had turned up among the corpses he and Kirby were throwing into the big pit.

Sterling jerked his mind back to the present and started walking quickly towards the hills, inhaling the scent of the sagebrush again and again, deeply, as if trying to flush something out of his system. If only he could just immerse himself here, in the desert, so completely that his being dissolved in it, and the weight of that death, and all those deaths, just withered in the dry wind to the cleanness of ancient bones. He stared into the reddened sun to blind himself to the perimeter fence and the houses off to his left. The pungency of the desert sage was beginning to affect his brain, speaking into it with a voice more clearheadedly ruthless than anything that could have floated up from his own usual soul. 'You went out there because of guilt and thirteen people are dead.'

He felt cold. He'd come out without a jacket or anything, being used to having only what he stood up in. He breathed out and held his lungs empty, pressed his rib-cage down into his stomach and forced himself to stop shivering, willing his muscles to just relax and stay warm. A fresh breath, a fresh cold voice saying, 'You can't do anything to pay for those deaths.'

This was intolerable. He turned away from the sun, as if this would make him less receptive to whatever was getting into his head. His vision was still impaired by the memory of solar brightness, and he crashed into the chainlink fence. He reached up and put his hands on it, squeezing his fingers into the different angles of the zigzagging wire until they hurt.

OK, he was trapped. He couldn't get out there and die, not without hurting more people. But there had to be another way. He couldn't live with the responsibility for all those deaths, stacked in frozen crazy angles like unburiable corpses.

I'll stop departing from the script. I'll act happy to be home and make my reports in normal English grammar. I won't go out and kill myself, I'll stay alive and be a good husband and a good father and a good soldier, I'll write to Delahunty's relatives and all their relatives and tell them they weren't rats, they were heroes. I'll just keep on living and trying to do good no matter how painful or boring or inglorious it is, and I know it will never be enough, but I'll keep trying.

He turned around, leaning back against the fence as if being held at gunpoint. Please don't say there's nothing I can do.

You can just live.

Wednesday mornings had been Virginia's usual visiting day while Tiger was overseas. She had kept away for the weeks following his release home, as the correct, non-interfering mother-in-law thing to do. But last Sunday after church, which was their day for calling on the Sterlings senior, Barbara said something about how nice it *had been*. It wasn't quite clear whether it had been nice, and she was sorry it wasn't continuing, or whether what made it so specially nice was the tactful way the visits had been discontinued. But then things never were exactly clear between Virginia and Barbara. Their relationship was characterized by a hyperniceness, a tentativeness, a bending over backwards to make sure one appeared to be wanting the same thing that the other wanted. It got so that Virginia, not usually one to suppress her own opinions, had to be careful not to say anything too definite for fear of imposing her wishes on Barbara, and as Barbara seemed to be doing the same thing, it got harder and harder to know what she really wanted. So now it was far from clear whether she was trying to get Virginia to start coming again, or whether she wanted her to think she wanted it, so as not to hurt her feelings. What Virginia said was, 'Oh, hardly nice of me, a pleasure, but of course you don't want your interfering old mom-in-law barging in on you every moment of the day now.'

'Oh no, really, I missed you, it makes such a difference to the week. But I realize you're so busy with the league and Christmas coming and Joseph's visit to think about.'

Stalemate again. Clearly Barbara didn't know whether Virginia would rather be off on her own business, or visiting. Come to think of it, Virginia realized, she didn't know herself. And perhaps Barbara didn't know what she wanted either. Virginia took courage in her hands and said, 'What would you *like*, Barbara dear? Be honest and don't spare my feelings!'

'Oh, of course I want you to come but I don't want you to have to put yourself out, after all you've done for us already.'

Well, of course, it couldn't have ended any other way: Tiger's exasperated suggestion, that Mom came if she felt like it, and they would tell her to go away if they didn't, was just ridiculous. So on Wednesday the next week there they were, sitting at the dining table together, with coffee. 'Tiger's at the optom...optic...the eye specialist,' Barbara explained his absence. 'It's been a fight to get him to go. Because he doesn't have any trouble reading he refuses to believe there's anything wrong. But I honestly don't think he can see two feet beyond his nose. He drove home Sunday and it was terrifying! Then yesterday he backed into the mailbox.'

'I thought it was standing at a rakish angle.'

'Well, at least it wasn't one of the kids, and at least it's forced him to give in and go for an eye test.'

'It sounds,' said his mother, 'as if he hasn't changed at all.'

Barbara sighed heavily, but it was a sigh that had some satisfaction in it, and it told Virginia that this visit had been wanted, and Tiger's absence engineered to coincide with it. Barbara wanted to talk about him, and she discovered that this was what she wanted to do too. 'Has he been talking at all, about what happened?'

'No.' She lit a menthol and exhaled in a thin stream. 'Not really. He says he wants to but he never does. And I don't feel like I can just ask him. I mean, if he is managing to forget it all, it seems cruel to bring it up again.' She did not add that she suspected Tiger had gone back on his decision to tell her because of the way she had reacted to the story of Kirby Wilson.

'How has he been?'

She considered. 'He's been extreme. Things are either extremely wonderful, or... the opposite.'

Virginia played with her gloves, and said carefully, 'The evening we visited him in the hospital he had a... a... I don't know what you'd call it, an incident of despair, which was rather alarming. I don't know if that's happened again since...'

'At least once or twice a day,' she said, in the kind of voice that was usually accompanied by a mirthless laugh. Barbara did not laugh though.

'Oh dear.'

'His temper's better,' she conceded. 'So that's one good thing. I guess.'

'Oh yes,' agreed Virginia warmly. Accentuate the positive!

'Art – Colonel Sedlachek was telling me, um, sort of what to expect, the way they generally react, they can get irrational, you know, hair-trigger reactions, or doing awful things they wouldn't dream of in their right minds.' Barbara's face looked pinched and uncomfortable as she said this.

Virginia braced herself. 'And... has he...?'

'Well, no, not really.'

This was a pleasant surprise: one naturally expected Tiger to explore all the awful possibilities that people in their right minds did not do. 'Perhaps he's escaped lightly after all.'

'Yes,' Barbara agreed, not really sounding like she believed it.

Tiger's new glasses turned out to be the pinnacle and summation of all the things that had changed about him. Suddenly he was in a different category of being: a brain, a skinny, abstract, hunched, twisted, far away person no one in their right mind would have nicknamed 'Tiger'. His hair was growing longer and longer and he was making no attempt to stop it. Barbara found herself walking around him curiously, anxiously. It was as if someone had given her a large, expensive, striking objet d'art, which had to be kept and displayed for fear of giving offence, but which she could not feel certain really belonged in her house.

Only Caroline approved of the glasses. 'They make you look like a regular Dad.' Henry would express no opinion. Something as trivial as glasses could not make him feel better about his father, and nothing could make him feel worse. Apart from looking in the mirror once and shouting with derisive laughter, Tiger seemed oblivious to any difference. And that was part of what was different. The thickness of the lenses, the refraction that displaced the whole gestalt of his face, made him seem even farther away, walled off in a glass prison. And he didn't seem to see any better. Well, he wasn't banging into things any more, you couldn't say it was his eyesight that was wrong, but it still didn't feel like he was seeing and walking around in the same world everyone else was.

It was unfair that having so many other things to get used to, she had to get used to this. It was unnerving that such a small change, and a change that had happened at her own instigation, should have such an unsettling effect. Maybe there were other losses and flaws that had happened in the years he was overseas, and maybe they were all camouflaged by the big impact of his return, a hundred or a thousand little time bombs waiting to go off.

★

Friday afternoons were Sedlachek's day for keeping an eye on Barbara, and this had not been discontinued on Tiger's return. It happened that on this particular Friday she had persuaded her husband to look in at the offices of the *Evening Gazette* just to see if the editor had been serious when he'd mentioned the possibility of commissioning a piece about Korea. 'Tiger's in town,' she informed Art, as they settled into the living-room couch, with glasses of iced tea.

'How is he?' he wanted to know at once; Sedlachek didn't pussyfoot.

'Just so different,' she sighed.

'Is he under control? Has he been violent?'

'No. No...' How could she explain to Art that being out of control or even violent would have been more normal for Tiger than this glassy self-containment? 'He has these sort of storms of emotions, but they're all in his head, and it's all compressed, and I'm sure it would be healthier if he let it out. And then the next thing is he'll go totally ecstatic about something, usually something dumb – I mean, not dumb, you can sort of understand that if you've been deprived for three years that little things we take for granted might mean a lot – but in public, where people don't understand it, it looks, um, crazy.'

Sedlachek narrowed his eyes. 'You ever heard of manic-depressive psychosis?'

'Yes, but it's not that. That happens over a period of weeks and months,' said Barbara, with the precision of someone who has been looking it up in a medical textbook within the last week. 'Tiger can do a round trip from heaven to hell and back again in about twenty minutes.'

He looked just faintly displeased. 'That can't be easy for you or the children.'

'It's best just to ignore him.'

Art nodded and was uncharacteristically silent for more than a minute. Then he took a deep breath and seemed to poise himself as if balancing on a diving board. When he finally jumped in, what he said was, 'Barbara, I want you to know that if Tiger ended up mentally ill, or if you decided to leave him for whatever reason, that... I want you to know that I'm prepared to see you and the kids all right.'

She looked at him, too astonished to be exactly sure of what he meant. Under her eyes he turned his face to the side and muttered, 'I only wish I was free to do more than that.'

For some reason, Barbara's mind had cut away from the present and floated off to the world of Jane Austen. 'What did she say? Just what she ought, of course, a lady always does.' Slowly, from the content of the digression rather than the content of Art's speech, she realized that a proposal, of some sort, was being made to her. And she didn't know what to say at all. There it all was in front of her: everything that was wrong about Tiger, everything that was right about Colonel Sedlachek. 'Th – thank–' she began, then wondered if Jane Austen would think a lady ought to be offended rather than grateful. 'I... I can't...'

'I know. You don't want to be disloyal now, after holding out so many years. But if it was ever a question of your own safety...'

'Please,' she said, probably meaning something like, 'Please don't make me think about this.'

The door swung open and Tiger strode in. 'I've got a job!' he announced. 'On the *Evening Gazette*! Hi, colonel. I'm quitting the army!'

McKenna had been able to get Connelly as far as St Louis. The military planes were badly pressurized, and he was surrounded by briefcase-carrying officers who looked at him suspiciously. Perhaps they could smell civilian, the way animals smell fear: sadistically. It was a relief to get on the Pan Am Stratocruiser, to sink into the soft seat and allow the solicitous blond steward to bring him a continuous supply of Martinis, for the soothing of his bereaved spirit.

The night chill in the air as he staggered out of the plane at Washington Airport felt surreal, man-made, vindictive. His skin was cheated out of the tropical warmth it had apparently decided was its birthright, and an angry protest of unco-ordinated exhausted energy propelled him home (it was crazy to drive but he had left his car at the airport parking lot on the way out) and up the stairs to his little apartment. There everything fell apart. He dropped on the couch, everything spun round until it drowned in a black gap. Sometime later he got up, vomited and found his way to his bed. It was deliciously flat, rising up to meet him like a great roller far out to sea. Dreamless space, a consciousness which was neither wakeful nor asleep, a kind of timeless watching.

It was late in the afternoon when he woke up, and rusty sunset-tinged light was coming in through one of the windows. Feeling very very sorry for his body, he wrapped it up in his warmest winter coat and unscratchiest scarf, and took it out to catch the last rays of the sun. He headed for Capitol Hill on a newcomer's walk, almost a tourist's excursion into the great spaces, the sculpted ocean surrounding the marble archipelago, the idea-islands erupting symmetrical and fully armoured from the human head. So far away from another island, roughed out by the sea and the earth's drive, shaped to speak to the human heart... Stop it, Connelly. You're here now, and you just have to adjust to that. You chose to come here, you loved it once, the scale, the eye-quiet, the serene certainty that man or a nation could create itself great and virtuous, just by building big enough and white enough. You liked it because you were trying a similar project on yourself. So maybe you should just act happy to be home and go and make your report in normal English grammar.

He stood at the back of the Capitol, on the terrace, and looked down the Mall, past Washington's spire to Lincoln's temple, then wrapped his arms around his chest the way Sterling did when he was having trouble keeping things together, and wondered how a small-scale, non-virtuous, but maybe human-hearted person was going to survive on this cold plane of grand ideals.

And then it was Monday and time to drag his poor sulking body and uncertain different self back to work, to the boxy little labs in the basement of an eighteenth-century ambassador's mansion in Georgetown. None of the great men were there; they never arrived before eleven. Only Gloria, the lab assistant was around, fey Gloria with her capezios and leotard under the white coat, dark hair pulled hard back in a ponytail, a sharp passionate little face. She treated Connelly severely, with a sexless manner far beyond her years, as if she distrusted his charm and was clamping down hard on anything in herself that wanted to respond to it. When he came in she barely acknowledged him, as if he hadn't been away at all. 'Percolator's broken, no coffee. You want to see what lysergic acid does to spiders?'

'Yes, Gloria, as a matter of fact I've spent the last five weeks lying on a beach just itching to know how your spiders were doing.'

She ignored both the sarcasm and the invitation to ask him about Hawaii and brought over a sheaf of photographs of spiders' webs, mad, asymmetrical or sagging, the work of arachnid de Koonings and Pollocks. 'Aren't they the gonest things you've ever seen?'

'Pretty far gone,' he agreed. 'What does it do to people?'

'*Well*, Lance and I –' she began, but at this point Oss Pointdexter, the foundation's director appeared. He was a hollow-faced, beau-laid, always already amused character, with a wandering Mittel-Europa accent acquired as a souvenir of his days in the OSS. 'Connelly, my dear boy! What a wonderful time you must hef hed! You look so brown und...exhausted!'

'Wait till you see what the shark did to me!' He undressed to show them the (unfortunately fading) scars. Gloria ran out of the room.

'So how did the research go?'

'Amazing. There was this one amazing guy, a total naïve Bronsky, he just *knew* it, and this other one who...'

'The other project,' grinned Oss. 'Polynesian sexual mores.'

Connelly felt something drop inside him. Then he remembered that before he left, he and Oss had joked about this second unofficial 'research', supposedly the ulterior motive behind his trip. He prayed his face didn't show anything, and launched himself into an animated account of a stormy affair with a flame-haired Hawaiian. 'Was she a hula dancer?' Oss wanted to know.

'No. She was a chicken farmer.' A note of sourness and disgust escaped into his voice, as the realization that this new 'more human-hearted' and honest Connelly had ratted on Hoku, and on himself, at the first, faintest, actually illusory hint of danger. It had been automatic, almost a reflex, like curling up to defend yourself against a blow. Even more indefensibly, it had been a highly polished performance, finely tuned to mesh exactly with Pointdexter's facetious style. Even now, Oss was appreciating the deflationary punch line, rolling it around over his palate like vintage wine. 'A chicken farmer. Ja. I see. Er... tell me about the PoWs.'

Connelly was just beginning, 'There was this NCO...' when Gloria reappeared, so precisely that she must have been listening outside for the subject to change. 'Any of them been given drugs?' she demanded, as if it was too much to hope for, 'LSD?'

'I don't know. They didn't show me their webs.'

'What about brain surgery and stuff?'

'Brain surgery? Are you joking? They didn't even have infirmaries in these camps. The only surgery that happened was when captured corpsmen cut off frostbite necrosis with dirty razor blades.'

In a bargaining tone, 'Electroshock?'

'Sorry. I can give you solitary confinement, sensory deprivation, and a nasty little trick with nooses and wobbly platforms. But that was only for the few. The rest just went along with...' Somehow he couldn't finish the sentence, he felt ashamed to put in words what had happened, ashamed of himself maybe (ratting on Hoku with that stupid chicken farmer!) or maybe of the context, three people sitting on the edges of desks, swinging their legs and *talking* about it.

'Oh well,' Oss shrugged as if it was a disappointment, but only a minor one. 'Never mind. Write it up for the record and we'll get you something more promising.' He sailed out, leaving Connelly feeling quite pulled apart.

Over the next weeks, while Gloria force-fed fruit flies on Sodium Pentathol and mice on hashish brownies, Connelly tried to compress Kirby and Sterling and Eugene and all the others into a report that would cut its way through her single-mindedness and Pointdexter's flippancy. If he couldn't be true to himself he could at least make some stab at fighting back for Sterling. And so, one Monday afternoon he forced himself to look earnest, exposing his flank to the full force of the Pointdexter ironic broadside, and said, 'Look, I think this is important, and I'd like half an hour just to read this case history to everyone.'

'Oh! Ah. Right,' Oss was deeply amused. 'Of course. Bron, Gloria, come over here and sit down. I'm afraid we have something important on our hands.'

Connelly gave him the kind of look Hoku used to call 'the stink eye' and hitched himself up on a lab counter, the moral high ground. He took a deep breath, invoked the muse of psychology and the god of integrity, and launched into *The Case History of the First Platoon*.

Every time Connelly had gone over the story he had been taken one level deeper into it, from the first day he'd heard it from Kirby, and the fragments that Chapman had added, to finding himself understudying all the major roles in Sterling's staging of the drama. It had lodged so deep in him that writing the report had been like digging it out of his own heart. But now, delivering the message, it was lifting and going from him again. He felt light, but bereft, a smaller person. He sighed heavily and forced himself to study the others for their reactions. Gloria looked irritated (this didn't surprise him), Bronsky thoughtful. Oss was staring into a distance that was not in the room, a wide-eyed frown, forehead down, eyelids up, pen pressed hard against his lips. What had happened to him that was like this? Connelly wondered. Who had he been playing? Not Sterling, that was for sure. Chang? Then, abruptly, Oss became aware of his gaze, and his eyes snapped back to the here and now, the mouth stretched into a crooked smile.

Connelly ducked behind his notes and continued, 'OK. When you look at the whole picture, these men are statistically unusual. What has to be stressed is that they aren't unusual in their personal qualities but in their social cohesiveness. The real heroes of resistance aren't the tough guys like the marines in the "KKK" or the patriotic idealists like Lt S. They're the ones who worked to keep people together, like Cpl W. and Pvt E.'

Connelly suddenly became aware of the sweat rolling down his sides. He put his papers, also rather damp, and crumpled, down on the desk and raised his eyes slowly to meet Bronsky's. 'So,' he said, concluding on a deliberately inconclusive note, 'I don't know where it all leaves us on brainwashing and mind control. All it boils down to is that after a certain point of hellishness, most people withdraw cathexis from moral abstracts like integrity and patriotism. The only thing they'll hold out for is other people, the social group they identify with.'

'Ha!' This came, surprisingly, from Gloria. Connelly looked at her rather coldly, and she continued, 'Groups just enforce conformism. That's why the Chinese use them, and that's what this platoon of yours was doing in the opposite direction. And unless a comfortable suburb is your personal idea of hell it doesn't take any point or level of hellishness or torture or anything. It just takes a couple of loudmouths like McCarthy and that drunk Wunsche on the HUAC and suddenly everyone in town's withdrawing their cathexis so fast you could... you couldn't...' Gloria trailed off as she realized a sexual metaphor had loomed up unavoidably in front of her.

Connelly giggled and Pointdexter waved his arms fastidiously, saying, 'Cathexis? Me? Never!' An anarchic interlude followed in which Oss and Connelly explored every possible permutation of the joke (Are you now or have you ever jokes, Nurse, my cathexis is coming loose jokes, cathexes under the bed, in the State Department, with other people's wives...) while Gloria sulked and Bronsky looked sadder and sadder.

Connelly was singing Our boss Oss, Our boss Oss. Well-connected, never cathected, Never at a loss, to the tune of Three Blind Mice, when he suddenly noticed the Professor's face, waking him up like a cock crowing. 'Oh shit,' he said, out loud.

'What?'

'Nothing. I mean... Oh, look, Oss, it's not actually funny.'

'I know,' he said, in a tender voice. 'But I didn't want to hurt your feelings.'

'Stop it! Goddamn irony all the time and it's poisoning my life.'

Oss raised his eyebrows, and looked to Bronsky, with an expression of helpless innocence. Bronsky shook his head and said softly, 'People joke when they're scared.'

'Ha!' exclaimed Pointdexter, looking more profoundly amused than ever.

'Scared!' cried Gloria. 'If you want to know what's the problem, it's nobody's scared enough. When McCarthy gets all the communists and fellow travellers, that's all right with them, and when Wunsche cleans up the homosexuals that's OK, and it's only when there's no one left to pick on but middle-of-the-road playboys who don't go to church, that's when they'll start to get scared, and not a minute before.'

'How come you're always trying to pretend Washington is like Changhung?' Connelly yelled at her. 'It's not, it's just not. And McCarthy is just nothing like Stalin; it's obscene to even compare them. The most that can ever happen to us is words, just words, for God's sake!'

'What happened to the Rosenbergs was just words?'

As if the name Rosenberg was a prearranged signal, or instinctively agreed upon ne plus ultra, both Bronsky and Pointdexter stepped in and separated the combatants, pulling them physically off to separate corners of the room and calming them down with research chemicals and soothing words.

'You were more right than you know,' Bronsky told Connelly. 'It's other people that we need, and not for what they give us, but for what we give them.'

'I wish it was. I mean, in my case. I'm not mad at her, really. I'm mad at myself. Imagining I really cared about what happened to these guys, and the next minute I'm singing a goddamn song!'

'You're telling me no one ever laughed in Korea, or even in Auschwitz?'

'That's different. That's courage. I'm just a spectator, and it's cowardice.'

'So you break off and laugh when it gets too much for you. So what? At least you let it touch you. It was like that for me about Auschwitz, hearing about it at second or third really hand.' He shrugged. 'And if you can't do anything about it except feel always guilty for missing it, well, that's your share, you know, your little piece of twentieth century. When you think of it like that, you can't really want to duck it.'

'Ducking is an irresistible instinct, with me.'

The next blow came three days later. Bronsky came in late, asked Connelly to come into the private office, and told him to sit down in the kind of voice people use to break the news of a death. Oh God, it's happened, Connelly thought. Somebody was watching me in Hawaii. His face went taut with bloodlessness, his knees felt dizzy and his fingers shook, but underneath everything there was a feeling of relief. 'What's wrong?' he asked, in a perfectly even, smiling voice.

'I'm afraid we won't be publishing your report.'

'Ha?' he coughed.

'Nothing to do with the quality, of course. You know that. Pointdexter consulted his angels and he's decided that it's too sensitive. Politically. You know. Just at the moment. Maybe in a year or two.'

'Why? Why is it sensitive?'

'Well, of course, I'm not cleared to know. Just guessing, it might be something like Magnanimity in Victory, or Let's Leave this Thing Behind Us. But of course it might be anything, some little detail that somebody somewhere doesn't want floating loose.'

'Leave this thing behind us. But what about them? Are they and their moms and dads and wives and kids going to leave it behind them as easily as that? Or shall we leave them behind as well, a bunch of pathological exhibits and cowards who ratted on their country?'

Bronsky looked down.

'Oh God, I'm sorry. I know it's not your fault.' Connelly

stood up and walked around the room. 'Would I be allowed to publish it on my own, nothing to do with the foundation? Or something more popular, on the *Time Magazine* level? So people would understand, and not judge them too harshly?'

'You'd have to talk to Oss about that. But you see Connelly, that report — and it's right and it's true — but it's sawing off the branch you're sitting on. If the Chinese can achieve so much with such homespun means, what are our backers doing pouring money into us to study the subtleties?'

'Money!' Connelly looked savage.

'I know.' He turned his palms upwards. 'But that's what this place is, you know, a machine for channelling funds from the CIA to the collection of deserving displaced outdated old academic fossils like me that Oss accumulated on his travels. I'm afraid it falls heavily on you and Gloria to make it all look like the Los Alamos of the Human Brain. But then, you're both displaced people in your own ways, aren't you?'

Connelly wanted to ask, 'What do you mean?' or even, 'How did you know?' but instead said carelessly, 'At second hand, I guess. But why is Oss so... Oss so...?'

'Oss has his own cathexes, which reason cannot know. I think he must have chosen the name Pointdexter so that no one would ever suspect him of knowing what his left hand was doing.'

A letter came from Hoku, a fat letter on quality stationery so many pages it filled a big manila envelope. Connelly had a sudden dropping feeling, as if all the blood had sunk from his brain to boil around in his stomach at the sight of Hoku's big writing, slanting off at a forty-five degree angle. Then there was the reproach: what a horrible thing to feel! But I've only just put it all out of my head, he defended himself. Bad enough having to live with all this moral Sterling angst without being reminded of everything he had left behind in Hoku, Hawaii and the ocean. — Oh shut up and read the damn thing, you think you're the only person in the world with any feelings or something? – I know, but it's not my feelings, is it, it's Hoku's that are going to be rustling out of that envelope at me like a ten-foot wave, so much bigger and nobler, whole-hearted like I could never be, and that's what's going to hurt. – Read it!

Well, it did hurt. Two and a half languages and all the resources they held in prose or poetry weren't enough to express what Hoku wanted to say. Things in Hawaiian, things in English, pidgin tags, translations (Hoku's English grammar was always ultra perfect when he was translating, as if the Hawaiian language deserved a special respect that everyday utterance did not. Connelly was reminded of the way he and Momi stood and spoke when Auntie Lydia was present.) And most of all quotations from songs, so that the whole letter was haunted by music Connelly could only guess at, the swooningly simple melodies, slack key guitars rippling like shallows in sunlight, Hoku's own voice, open and warm in tenor range, or floating like a mountain mist full of sweet condensation in falsetto. And then also, going alongside the basic I-miss-you-sweetheart letter was a standing metaphor, almost a story, which Connelly deduced from little images – a fisherman standing on a beach at a lonely hour of the morning... the feelings of loss and melancholy in the air all around him generate a keening sound in the palms, and the terrible open cry of new grief is pounding in the waves. Are the air and the ocean still aching for that brother lost at sea, so many months ago?

If the fisherman sees a shark's fin in the water, this morning it will be his brother's spirit in a new body, this morning it will be. But the waves throw up many little fins, running before the sunrise, blackness on the water; nobody comes.

And then *holoholo kahakai*, skittering across the golden beach, a sea bird, one of the many that migrate from the north and stop on these shores as winter rolls in. A gregarious, confident little bird, allowing the fisherman to capture it. He feels the speed of its pulse, the intensity of the life inside so frail a body. Joy and fear blend so completely in its being, and sharing these emotions the man knows, briefly, the exhilaration of flight. For a moment they are both creatures of the wind and sea.

Winds and currents part them. In human form again, alone, the fisherman stands on a northern shore, *ho'o hakui nakolo*, the pounding echoing grief redoubles; the rain comes down, a drenching weight on the soul.

Hoku picked his way along the rocky Wailupe shore, the frozen froth of *a'a* lava that bit through the soles of his Japanese slippers. He was prying up tiny *opihi* from the rock with a table knife whose tip he had wrenched to the optimum angle for levering them free. Every so often he looked up at the whale-like dome of Koko Head, the eastern extreme of the island. Every so often it felt like something important was happening far away.

He tested the feeling, bending and twisting it as he manoeuvred the blade of the knife between the brittle bitchiness of the stone and the limpets' salty sucking determination to survive. Bend: a bad feeling? No, you couldn't say that; anyway nothing like the sick weight that had come over his whole body before his brother Alapa'i died. Twist: a good feeling then? No, it was too anxious, too full of upheaval and change, and maybe even sorrow... and yet with something exciting and maybe even beautiful, maybe something he would choose, like choosing to fall in love with someone even if they were going away. He remembered the pure consciousness of blessing and reblessing that had been floating around him like the tingling rainbow spray of a waterfall for one whole week before Connelly had turned up for him on the beach at Waikiki. Well, for sure it wasn't anything like that feeling now. He looked across the flat silver and gold water to the great headland, calm and curved like a monarch, purer and more beautiful to him than craggy Diamond Head. Then he put the last limpets into his melting paper bag, rolled it up and tucked it securely under his arm, began his slapping way back up the peninsula, through the bulldozed acquired-for-prestige-development red dirt.

On the way home he met the mailman; one letter for him, save the buggah the drive all the way up to his valley. Getting home he did not bother to open it, threw it straight into the kitchen garbage. Leimomi caught him, asking sharply, 'What's that?'

'Nothing.'

'You throwing away one letter from Connelly!' she accused, going to pick through the garbage.

'Chee, no! It's just the Bishop Estate, bother me all the time.'

'Try pay the rent,' she advised sarcastically, but checked the return address just the same.

'Dad pays them.'

She looked at him, arrested. 'He pays the rent for this place?'

'Sure, why not? He got the money, I never. Bother you or what?'

'No, no,' she said quickly. 'I never knew, that's all.' A minute later she said cautiously, 'I always used to think he never did enough for you, so I'm glad.'

'Well, I never felt that, Leimomi,' he said, closing the conversation.

Part Three

September 1954

A sizeable chunk of the Rushmore Foundation's time and money was put into what Pointdexter called 'good old-fashioned Vaudeville', big entertainments for contributors, or publicity, or interagency relations, or rather to conceal the fact that there weren't any contributors, that their work never got anywhere near being ready for publication and that the only agency they ever really had anything to do with was the agency with the capital A. Anyway Pointdexter enjoyed parties. At some point in the month he would turn up at the labs with what Connelly called his Judy Garland–Mickey Rooney look on and announce that they'd be putting on a show for a bunch of Texan oilmen, or British diplomats, or Congregational ministers, and he wanted all his best scientific brains there to give it the echt Los Alamos feel – and to set up the gags, take the knocks and work the rubber chicken. He also usually invited all his friends, a large tranche of Chevy Chase and a slice of Georgetown, perhaps because they represented his ideal audience: they knew when, and exactly how, to laugh.

The booking for September of 1954 was the Wild West Show. An assortment of congressmen and moneymakers from points west of Missouri and right of Eisenhower. 'Why?' Connelly demanded. He was on his knees sweeping up the broken glass that had been Gloria's reaction to the guestlist.

'Because there isn't anyone else left to invite,' said Pointdexter simply.

'Don't force Gloria to come. She's permanently on edge at

the moment. She takes more Benzedrine than all the rats put together.'

'Who's forcing her? She'll be the first one there because she won't be able to resist the thrill of seeing just how horrible they all are in the flesh and how right she is to despise them.'

'She'll probably feel duty bound to tell them that to their faces.'

'Well, then let's make it your job to see that she doesn't.'

Saturday evening, the stage was set, Fate was knocking and Pointdexter was enjoying the fine familiar tingle of anticipation. Gloria had arrived at the same time as the caterers, and Connelly, who had been there twenty minutes before, was following her around trying to pick fights about birth control, Leadbelly and the IWW. Professor Dichter arrived early, seized control of the baby grand, and spent the rest of the evening pretending he was a cocktail pianist who couldn't decide whether he was playing *The Golliwog's Cakewalk* or the *Liebestod*. Presently the guest stars began to roll in: a very junior senator, some uranium millionaire, and last of all, Wunsche of the House Un-American Activities Committee, apparently already well-oiled, and escorted, if not actually supported, by one of his underlings, while his wife loped in ahead of him, a long-legged strong-faced woman of the plains, quite a bit younger than her husband. Hm. Ja. But now the audience was arriving, the Randolphs and the Howards and the Pomeroys. 'What an absolutely poisonous social mix!' exclaimed Bunny Wellesly.

'One does one's poor best,' murmured Oss, accepting the tribute with becoming modesty.

'Will they separate out, like salad dressing, or will it just get more and more volatile and then explode?' she wondered.

'No one's ever been injured at one of my parties. Not seriously, anyhow.'

'Maybe not, but no one ever goes home really happy either. – What is that man doing to that poor girl?'

'Ah.' The poor girl was Gloria, hystericking in a corner; Connelly was trying either to restrain her or to conceal her from public view. 'Lab rats. Highly strung,' Oss sighed.

'Shouldn't you do something?'

He shrugged but began a leisurely stroll in their direction, when another potential flash-point caught his attention. Congressman Wunsche was wondering plaintively why these scientists always had to be goddamn Yurpeans, how come you never met any honest Merkin scientists in these places. It might not have mattered, but he was saying it to Bronsky, without any apparent intent to offend. Pointdexter altered his course, arriving in the middle of the red-faced assistant's gallant but hopeless attempt to salvage decency with a quip about the Marshall Plan. 'Ah, Senator Wunsche,' Oss cried (this sort of mistake never hurt), 'there's a friend of mine who's been asking to meet you.' And out of the side of his mouth, 'Bronsky, would you go help with Gloria?' He took the Wunsche party over and deposited it on Bunny Wellesly, who was a Daughter of the Revolution and so, he hoped, uninsultable, then shot back to the casualty in the corner.

'She's hallucinating' said Connelly.

'I'm not! It's the truth but nobody ever says anything!' hissed Gloria.

'For God's sake get her out of here. Lock her in someplace where there's no windows. I know, the fall-out shelter,' Pointdexter directed Bronsky. He dashed over to the piano, whispered in Dichter's ear. Dichter, who had been toying lovingly with one of Fauré's pastel moments, lurched into a mad approximation of the chromatic combat reaction of Wotan's wild hunt. 'Wache, Wala!' The musical sensitives in the room shuddered and spilled their martinis, but it effectively drowned Gloria's screams. Oss turned and found Connelly. 'Come and help me with Wunsche. Oh God, where is he? Bunny, what have you done with him? Where have you put him?'

'Down a peg. Wasn't that what you wanted?'

'No, it was not. I just wanted you to neutralize him for a while.'

'Oh,' said Bunny vaguely. 'Oh well, I don't think he noticed exactly.' She wandered off, declining to be an actor in one of Pointdexter's productions.

'There are so many people here he could offend!' Oss exclaimed, appreciating but a little awed by the scale of the potential disaster. 'There are so many people who could offend him! Where is he? I can't see him anywhere in the room! He's probably looking for security risks in the mens' restroom. Or saying something awful about circumcision scars! Oh, look, there's his wife. You go talk to his wife, Connelly. You know the way you talk to wives. If he turns up again I'll bring him back and you can tell him all about how to catch sex perverts with the lie detector and then everyone will be happy. Ja.'

In fact, Wunsche was in the room, in the corner near the door, muttering about East Coast snobs in their goddamn English suits, and wasn't anything American good enough for them in this place? His assistant, an earnest-looking scarecrow in the most ill-fitting clothes in the room, blinked through his horn-rims and wondered how you could tell whether a suit was English or home-grown. The congressman brooded over his drink for a few minutes more, then told his assistant that he wasn't going to stand for it. No. He was not. Lured into the place and then insulted. Uh-uh. Not him. He went round this several times, growing more sullen with each repetition, but failing to summon the energy to retaliate. Finally his assistant suggested a dignified exit, and guided him out of the room in a manner which, if not exactly dignified, was at least unobtrusive. Out on the street, Wunsche suddenly remembered his wife. 'Oh,' said the assistant.

'You'd better go back for her.'

'Yes, sir.' He started back, then thought better of leaving Wunsche loose on the street and got him secured in the car before returning to the building. He was new to Washington, and paused on the steps to look up at the eighteenth-century façade, as if he could not bring himself to walk in without a brief mental homage to history. As he entered the room, the pianist gave up the attempt to 'halt the turning wheel' and escaped into the jaunty nirvana of I've Got Plenty of Nothin'.

He could not immediately locate Mrs Wunsche and was standing there so obviously at a loss that Pointdexter sailed up and inquired sweetly whether the congressman was indisposed. 'I guess so. Not disposed for this company.'

'I see,' said his host coolly, relieved and disappointed.

'I just have to get Mrs Wunsche but I can't find her.'

Pointdexter indicated the far corner with his glass and walked away. Oh, there she was, talking to one of the Europeans or one of the Easterners.

Crossing the room, the congressman's assistant was suddenly struck by a shaft of illuminating understanding. *That* was English tailoring. He slowed down, daunted by the clean shoulders and tapering back of Mrs Wunsche's companion. Involuntarily, his body tried to make itself unobtrusive, which did not improve the fit of his own clothes. He tried to catch Mrs Wunsche's eye from behind the snob's back, but she was so utterly engaged by his front that she did not, or would not, notice him. He inhaled, marched up, began, 'Excuse me, ma'am,' and then broke off, as if overcome by something.

'What is it, John?'

'The... uh, Mr Wunsche wants to go home. He's in the car.'

'Then he can wait there,' she decided, adding, as the assistant seemed not to understand that he was supposed to leave them alone, 'Thank you, John.' Still he didn't move. Was he planted there? Or spying, or sent to chaperone her? She sighed and introduced him. 'Dr Connelly, this is John Sterling, one of my husband's assistants.'

Dr Connelly extended a hand, saying tentatively, 'It's just possible I may know... do you mind my asking, do you have a brother who was in Korea?'

A big Tiger grin disposed of the brother; for a few minutes it disposed of Mrs Wunsche too. 'My God, I didn't recognize you!' 'What are you *doing* here?' 'What are *you* doing here?' 'You look so well!' But Mrs Wunsche couldn't be disposed of for long. Connelly sensed this before Tiger did and deliberately turned the conversation back to her with the brief explanation, 'We met in Hawaii, on the way back from Korea.' This gave the false impression that he was also a veteran, but at least it concealed the fact that Sterling had been a mental patient. 'But as I was saying, what we really need to do is study the racial and cultural variations. The machine works on Americans because we have this thing with honesty going back to George Washington and the cherry tree. Even our criminals feel a twinge of moral anxiety when they lie. But what about cultures where saving face is more important than the truth?'

'They'd still feel anxious about the thing they were having to lie about,' Tiger pointed out. 'Or they wouldn't bother lying.'

'Just please don't ruin my proposal for a study of the Chinese population of the West Coast and Hawaii.'

At, this point Mrs Wunsche decided she might as well join her husband. Dr Connelly looked terribly significant and said he was sure they would meet again. 'It's a small town.'

'I suppose I'd better say goodbye to Mr Pointdexter.'

'I think you'd better not,' said Sterling. 'I mean, I've sort of ... taken care of that.' He escorted her back to the car; Wunsche had fallen asleep, which was nice. 'Shall I drive you home?'

'No, thank you, I am perfectly capable,' she said, and presently fired the car out of its parking space and down the road with the jerky competence of a perfectly capable young woman who has just had her whole evening ruined by one of her husband's underlings.

Sterling stood on the sidewalk for a minute wondering how he was going to find the neck to go back into the party again. Braving the English tailors was one thing, but offending central Europeans...

Just then somebody slipped out of the foundation building and came alongside him, asking casually, 'Whaddaya say we have a drink at Tony's and catch up?'

'Sure, great,' he said, feeling startled again. 'I just can't get over the surprise of seeing you here. You know, when I left Tripler I wanted to leave my address in case you might write to me, but then I thought, no, got to go forwards, you know? But here you are crossing my path again, and it's... it's great!'

Connelly couldn't bring himself to articulate the reciprocal sentiment: he didn't want to look inside and find out whether it was 'great!' to see Sterling again. He ducked his head, and diverted the conversation. 'Yeah, but I still don't get the whys and hows of what you're doing here. I mean, I gather you're working for Congressman Deadthanred, but...'

'Yeah, well, I had to get off the army conveyor belt, I guess you could have predicted that. I even got an honourable discharge, believe it or not. I got a job on the local paper, but that didn't work out too good... And then Wunsche said if I was willing to move to Washington he'd give me a shot as research assistant. We moved up just last weekend, we're renting in Alexandria for now, but Barbara wants one of these new houses they're building, and it's... well, it's great. Being here is like... it's like...'

'It's like living inside of history and knowing that what you do is making, even if it's only in a small way, a difference to the future of the nation?'

'Yeah, the feeling of making a difference.'

'Don't worry. It wears off.'

Sterling laughed, unoffended. Tony's little joint loomed on the left and Connelly steered him into it, right to the back where there was a table in a corner, a good private place, popular with foundation employees who didn't want to be overheard fellow travelling. Connelly ordered a couple of beers and sat back to watch Sterling as he lit up one of his 'Meiguo yan'. What he saw could have been a healthy, idealistic young man, just embarking on his first job after finishing college. As he let out his first lungful of smoke, Sterling raised his eyes to meet his gaze, returning it with a smile of such innocent happiness that Connelly couldn't help crying out, 'Why are you so different?'

Looking puzzled. 'I'm no different.'

'You are. Happier. Healthier. At peace.'

He smiled again, but this time there was an edge to it. 'You mean I'm not crazy any more.'

'That too.'

'Well, what about you? You're supposed to go around in a Hawaiian shirt and suddenly you're reincarnated as one of these Ivy League snobs! Do you mind my asking, is that an English suit?'

'This? Are you joking? Levin and Son, Brooklyn. Why?'

Quickly, 'Nothing.' There was a little space, and then he said quietly, 'Actually, Connelly, if I was crazy back in Tripler, I'm crazy now. I'm still working on the same project.'

'What do you mean, what project?'

'Oh, come on, I know I told you. It was the thing of finding absolute psychological freedom.'

'Not saying "I", the self is an optical illusion? You're back with *that*?' Connelly looked surprised, and not particularly approving.

Well, he should have realized there was no guarantee that Connelly (this real-life, bizarrely sophisticated Connelly, and not the internalized ideal listener and soup spitter) would have understood this, let alone applauded it. He shrugged convulsively. 'I just know I'm never going to be free, or happy, until I get rid of the apparatus of the ego.'

'Oh, Tiger!' Connelly protested. 'That's self-hatred, not psychological freedom.'

'No, if that was all it was, it would be easier to kill myself.'

Connelly looked into his eyes for a long while, then nodded.

They sat in Tony's until he closed at two. Stepping into the silent street, into the damp autumn air, Connelly realized his head was not quite as clear as it could have been. Tiger seemed to be saying, 'I knew we would have to meet again. I knew there was more.'

'Beg pardon?'

'I'm talking to the Connelly in my head.'

'Oh. I'm supposed to go away or something?'

'No, of course not. You can't just jump into my head for a year and a half like that and expect to walk away like nothing's happened.'

'Tiger, are you drunk? Are you too drunk to go home?'

'No. Yes. Oh, probably. What's it matter?'

'Maybe you should come back and sleep at my place. It's just around the corner from the Library of Congress.'

Tiger nodded. They went back to the foundation building, got in the Ford and he drove along to Capitol Hill. There it all was, the geometrical landscape of Freedom, lit in the dark, stark, essential. Tiger felt fireworks going off in his heart and pulled over to gaze at it. 'What's up?' Connelly wanted to know. Sterling punched his arm hard, jumped out of the car, leaving it in there in the no parking zone right in front of the Capitol, and sprinted off into the sacred space.

He stood for a moment, letting it all come in through his skin, until he noticed Connelly getting out and running after him. Tiger took off up the steps, declaiming, '"Build thee more stately mansions, O my soul."' He stopped halfway up and faced across the open space to the gleaming white pillars of the Supreme Court. Connelly was catching up, slowing to a walk, making his way up the steps. '"Leave thy low vaulted past! Let each new temple nobler than the last,"' he went on, even louder, patchworking over the holes in his memory, '"Shut thee from heaven with a dome more vast..."'

'Sterling, what the hell are you doing?'

At the top of his voice: '"Till thou at length art free, Leaving thine outgrown shell by life's unresting sea!"'

'Sterling!' Connelly shouted, trying to sound stern, trying to conserve his anger. 'Somebody's going to see you! They probably hear you already.'

'So?' he said, laughing, exhilarated.

'So it's a small town. It's... You'll... Everyone will...'

'Narrrrj!' Tiger roared and ran down the steps again, waving his arms. Perhaps it was the light bouncing off a faint mist in the air or the amount he'd had to drink, but Connelly had an impression Sterling was followed by a comet's tail of sparks, as if he was carrying fireworks in each hand. 'Jesus,' he sighed, following at a walk, with his arms folded and his spine stretched as primly taut as it could go, his whole body trying to communicate his disapproval to any distant watching eyes that might recognize him. When he finally caught up again, Tiger was rolling on some grass, trying to get his breath and sabotaging his own efforts with uncontrollable laughing. 'You're nuts! What are you doing? You're crazy!' Tiger sat up, regulated his breath and presently announced, 'It's a free country.' Then he had to laugh again, because the cliché was such a grand complex semantic pun, with meaning piling up on top of one another as high as a monument.

But Connelly stood there looking down at him, not pretending to be angry any more, large-eyed and solemn, and maybe a little sad, or a little scared. 'No, Tiger. It's not.'

Connelly's place was the upstairs of a neat little row of Georgian houses, so appropriate Tiger exclaimed, 'I knew you lived here!' Connelly threw him a censorious look, and he amended it to, 'Well, I know it now.'

'Please don't wake anyone up.'

Silent, obedient and with a certain air of coming to heel, Tiger followed him up the stairs. 'I'll have the couch,' Connelly announced, as soon as they got in. Tiger felt like he still had a lot more to say, and the kind of things that if they weren't said tonight might never float up again, but there was a strange, set look on Connelly's face. He allowed himself to be shown to the bedroom, then burst out, 'Oh, look, I don't wanna kick you out of your own bed. There's room.'

'There's *not*,' said Connelly, getting an afghan blanket from a closet and rushing out of the room, shutting Sterling in.

★

Tiger always woke up at six, and used the time before everyone else was up to think. This morning he was aware that the skies of freedom were overcast by a grey anxiety, an expectation of... of disapproval. Rrr, other people! It shouldn't matter, but there it was: he was in some kind of disgrace with Connelly, probably for being unconventional on the Capitol steps. Not to mention what Barbara would have to say about being out all night without a phone call. The line about the free country probably wouldn't impress her either. Other people! Why did they want to run him all the time? What right did they have? He worked for a while at converting guilt into defiance, and then suddenly it struck him that it was simply funny. The skies cleared, he jumped out of bed and went out in search of the bathroom.

Connelly was curled up on his side with a bent neck. He was straightening up when Sterling came out again. 'Hungover?' he inquired, with malicious sympathy. 'Nope,' said Tiger, beaming health and energy at him. Connelly scowled, wrapped the afghan around himself more securely and told him to help himself to coffee.

'I wasn't drunk at all last night,' Tiger said, trying to find things in the kitchen, then realizing he didn't know how to make coffee. He went back to the living room. Connelly had slid down onto his side again, and was frowning hard with the effort of trying to get back to sleep. 'I just suddenly felt incredibly happy, you know? Ever since I got home I get these times where I feel so happy, or so free, I think it must mean I'm going to die tomorrow.' He had been walking around the room; now he halted in front of the couch and stared at the body on it. 'Like the only thing that could happen next is meeting God.' Connelly twitched, as if in pain. Sterling walked around the room again, less abstractedly this time, looking at things, snooping at the record collection and the bookshelf and the photograph of Waikiki. That was Connelly in the middle, the one with the surfboard. 'You're a lot more regular than I thought you were,' he said. 'Sort of the opposite of meeting God.'

'What?' Connelly sat up again, looking scandalized.

'Oh, you know, how God is bound to be more sort of nonsectarian and strange and just beyond what we can think about... and you're not.'

'Tiger,' he began, then seemed to decide that none of the available protests, not the most scathing of them, did justice to the situation, so utterly strange and beyond what he could think about. He dragged himself up and marched off to the bathroom, still wearing the afghan. Tiger was on the couch when he came out. 'Why haven't you made any coffee?' he demanded, going to the kitchen.

'I thought I'd better get going,' Sterling said. Connelly decided that it would be unforgivably inhospitable to point out that if Tiger was just going to get going it could have been done without waking him up. He rubbed his eyes and filled the percolator.

'I'd like you to meet my family,' said Sterling.

The children were absorbed in the TV and barely noticed him coming in. Tiger went into the kitchen, holding his head very straight. 'Say what you want to say,' he directed Barbara.

She gave a little hybrid between a laugh and a gasp of disbelief, and shook her head, turning her eyes away.

'Oh, come on. Have it out.'

'Why? You aren't going to say you're sorry, so what's the point? – If you would at least phone it would save me having to worry. It's the going back and forth between being scared and being furious that I can't stand. I don't know why. I should be used to it by now.'

'I met this doctor who saved my life or anyway my sanity, back in Hawaii before I got home. He lives in Washington too now, and I ended up staying... Don't look at me like that.'

'This doctor that saved your life that you've never even mentioned until now.'

'Dr Connelly. Oh, come on, Barbara. If it was some woman, I would just tell you, wouldn't I?'

'Yes, and you'd think that just because you were being honest that would be supposed to make it all right somehow.'

Tiger looked at the floor. 'I know I can't make things all right. I know that. And you have every right to be angry.'

'You keep saying that you can't just make things all right, but you never even try. It's beginning to seem like you don't really want things to be all right at all.'

Tiger considered, 'I guess "all right" isn't the pinnacle of my ambition for... for us. I really want something a lot more than that.'

'And what we've really got is something a lot less.'

'No, it isn't. "All right" would be me slinking home with my tail between my legs and washing a lot of dishes until you let me out of the doghouse. We're a whole hell of a lot more honest than that.'

'For your information "all right" would start with you having the consideration not to stay out all night in the first place.'

He laughed loudly. 'You win.'

'Win what?' she said, refusing to smile.

'Hey, anyway, what do you think of this plan? I want you to meet Dr Connelly, and not just to prove he exists, and he had this idea of taking us all for a picnic at this place further up the Potomac where there's a waterfall and stuff.'

'When?'

'Today.' Barbara opened her mouth to protest and he added swiftly, 'I thought we could do a bit of househunting on the way; Connelly knows the place inside out. In fact, I'd like you to see his place, right next door to the Capitol practically, beautiful nineteenth-century but the inside's ultra modern...'

Connelly had gone back to bed to straighten out the kinks in his spine. About two hours later he woke up wondering how much of everything he thought had happened was a dream. The Capitol steps was probably a dream, and so was Tiger asking to see what the shark did to him, but he had an uncomfortable feeling the part where he had invited the Sterling wife and children on a picnic was not. Why had he done it? It was almost as dumb as inviting him to spend the night in the first place. He reheated the coffee and mooched around the kitchen making breakfast with one half of his spirit while the other half looked for picnic food. The phone rang, and Pointdexter's voice demanded, 'Connelly? Are you awake?'

'Just about.'

'Is Mrs Underbed still there? I saw you slipping out after her last night.'

'You did? I'll have to work on my technique.'

'You've got it down to a fine art, my boy; I just knew what to look for. So come on, how did it go?'

'It didn't. I was thwarted at the last minute by Wunsche's gallant lieutenant.'

'Hitler Jugend Quex?' There was a choking noise from Connelly. 'What? What's that?'

'Nothing. How's Gloria?'

'Asleep in my spare bedroom. Bronsky thinks she must have taken some LSD or hashish or something before the party. I don't know why,' Pointdexter sounded aggrieved. 'My parties are usually as surreal as any reasonable person could want them.'

'But she's all right? You're sure it was just the drugs; she's not permanently cracked?'

'Remains to be seen. I'm not in an enormous hurry to wake her up and find out.'

The Sterling family went direct to Connelly's after church, before it had time to get dirty. 'Here it is,' said Tiger.

'Where?' said Barbara, looking around for a palatial residence.

'There. That one.'

She blinked. 'Tiger. That's just a dinky little row house.'

It was maybe a little bit smaller than he remembered from last night. 'Of course it's too small for us, but wouldn't you love to live in something so historic? This house must have been here when Lincoln was president.'

Barbara looked tempted. 'But would we be able to afford it, a bigger one?'

'I don't know. Maybe not right away. Now listen, gang,' he addressed the kids. 'If Dr Connelly invites us into his house it's tip top best behaviour. Get it?'

'Got it,' Caroline giggled; Henry looked to one side, making no promises.

Connelly answered the door, and he was wearing the aloha shirt! Sterling gave a shout, almost a cheer; Connelly wrinkled his nose in a pleased way and said, 'Come on up. I'm still working on the sandwiches. Wow. Is this the family? Hi, kids!'

'And this is my wife Barbara.'

'Pleased to meet you. You have all my sympathy and all my admiration. It must be sheer hell, having that,' he nicked his head in Tiger's direction, 'to contend with every day. Come on up! Make yourselves at home.'

This reception was warmer than Barbara expected for 'back East'; she went up the stairs with an unconscious smile on her face, in the mood to be impressed by the ultra-modern decor Tiger had mentioned. It turned out to consist of a lot of bare flat steel blue space, punctuated by chrome curves and glass table tops, and a big orangey red abstract canvas on the wall. Interesting, but it wouldn't do for their own house: already the shiny surfaces were collecting tiny fingerprints.

'Hey, Tiger kids! Come and tell me what you want on sandwiches. I've run out of bread, so you're going to have sandwiches made out of doughnuts. What do you want inside?' The children went into the kitchen, suspicion mingling with disbelief on their faces. No grown-up was really going to give them doughnut sandwiches, it was beyond possibility.

Barbara was a bookshelf detective. You could tell more about a person from what they read than by any other single method. Now, Connelly was... Oh my goodness, the *Kinsey Report*! She had never seen an actual copy of it before! She caught Tiger's eye, and drew it out to show it to him, rolling her eyes, trying not to giggle. Tiger frowned and came over and whispered that Connelly was a psychologist and had to study it professionally, and took the book out of her hands and slid it back in place before she could look inside. Barbara bit away her smile and blinked the twinkle out of her eyes, and returned to her literary assessment. It had to be noted, however, that none of the other books on view had any very professional slant. On the other hand, he wasn't a fiction reader either: the only novels were a couple of torrid-looking Polynesian romances, *Fire* by Armine von Tempski and *Blood of the Shark* by Beatrice Patton.

'Well, that's cleaned out the fridge,' Connelly announced, coming out with a couple of grocery bags full of food. On the way down to the car Tiger explained, a trifle anxiously, as if he felt trapped between two implacable wills, that he had promised to take Barbara house-hunting, and were there any new developments they could stop at on the way? 'We can take our car so we can stop when we're coming back and you don't have to...'

'We'll go in my car and we'll go on the way,' said Connelly, determined to make everyone happy. His car turned out to be last year's Pontiac. Tiger felt a twinge, a first disloyal twinge of desire to put his old red Ford out to pasture. Barbara sat in the back with the children and periodically warned them against touching anything.

He drove them out to a new subdivision north of Chevy Chase, drove around the bare streets of finished and half-finished permutations on a 'colonial' theme, virtually unpopulated, treeless, lawnless. Gloria's phrase 'unless your personal idea of hell is a comfortable suburb' floated into Connelly's mind, it looked so lonely and desolate. Only the central hive around the model homes was buzzing: parked cars, couples and families consulting, pointing at features, planning.

They all got out to look at the three-bedroom model. The

living room was just about spacious enough, but would the dining room really hold both the table and Virginia's sideboard? The kitchen, with all the latest appliances in place. 'Everything new,' sighed Barbara, 'I don't really like their colour schemes, but it's the feeling of...'

'A fresh start,' said Tiger, giving her a significant look. 'More than all right, huh?' Connelly noticed they were holding hands and decided it would be a good idea if he took charge of the kids. He followed them upstairs and helped them to argue about who was going to have which bedroom. Caroline wanted the bigger room, because she was older. Henry wanted it because it was supposed to be for a boy, the curtains were pink in the other room. But Caroline hated pink. Henry had an inspiration. He and Care could share, and then Dr Connelly could come and live in the other bedroom. Then he wouldn't be lonely. Connelly's mouth fell open at this.

Tiger came racing up the stairs. '"Build thee more stately mansions, O my soul,"' he exclaimed, startling several other house-hunting couples

'Tiger,' implored his wife, from further down, half-cringing, half-giggling.

'Me and Care are going to share so Dr Connelly can move in,' Henry informed his father.

'You're gonna share anyway. Mommy says me and her have to have separate bedrooms,' Tiger informed everyone in the house, roaring with hilarity. Barbara fled back to the kitchen.

Tiger hugged himself, until he had finished laughing. 'Everyone is deciding not to move here if you are,' Connelly informed him.

'But seriously,' Tiger said, 'I think we probably do need another bedroom for me to have nightmares in. You know I still get the most astonishing nightmares; absolutely photographic! And I wake up screaming and sweating.' He shook his head, grinning, as if he was not only amazed at, but rather proud of, how bad they were. 'So it's hell for Barbara. I wonder how much more the four bedrooms cost.' They all went next door, and looked at the four-bedroom model, and frowned over the $1500 price tag and tested their consciences against the just about manageable down payment. Connelly mentioned that there were other developments that might be cheaper; here they were paying extra for location. The Tiger family looked more hopeful. They stood in a little knot in the front yard and stared at the model home. 'What do you think of it?' Tiger asked Connelly.

'You wouldn't be lonely...' he said. 'I mean, the neighbours,' he added, to conceal the fact that he'd really meant something like, 'I wouldn't be lonely, if I had a wife, and cute little kids, and a house like this to put them in...' It was news to him that he wanted these things. It was like bumping into another Connelly, one who could be settled and happy like this, going home every night to cooked food and affection. 'Jesus,' he exclaimed, shaking his head as if to clear it. Tiger looked at him and grinned suddenly, as if reading his mind.

They detoured a bit to look at a subdivision of split-level houses, then made for the Great Falls. Tiger was indignant. 'These aren't falls,' he glared at Connelly as if holding him responsible.

'I didn't say it was going to be Niagara.'

'These are rapids. Just about.'

Barbara said, 'It's just lovely. Could we eat? The children are a bit hungry.'

Connelly unpacked. 'Doughnut and bacon for Miss Sterling. Doughnut and sausage with maple syrup for young Prince Hal. What's next? Oh, pickled herrings and celery. Any takers? Or caviar, well, lumpfish roe, with smetana, on a stale bagel. Salami with lettuce and cream cheese. Sardines.'

'Isn't American food good enough for these people?' complained Congressman Wunsche's assistant.

'Succotash, wild turkey, pemmican,' Connelly pretended to discover in the bag. 'Pop for the kids. Bottle of beer, Tiger? Barbara?'

Barbara whispered in Caroline's ear, 'He's just like the Water Rat, isn't he?'

Tiger, eating salami at an all-American rate, turned back to the irritant of the Great Falls. 'I guess what it is is nature's just smaller here, the way history's so much bigger. Back home in the mountains you feel insignificant in space and here you feel insignificant in time. I have to keep reminding myself that it's the future, the future you have to think of, history's a challenge and you can't hide under it, you've got to overtop it. I keep saying to myself that the thing you have to do with history is be in it, make it.'

'I don't know. When you listen to people who've been right in the middle of history what it mostly seems to have been like is being terribly small and helpless, and the only challenge you can grasp at is just to survive. Does that sound, um, familiar?'

Sterling tilted his head to look diagonally at him, down and sideways. 'That's totally different, that's being at the mercy of history. It's no good harking back to that stuff all the time. You just have to believe that if you survived, you were kept alive for a reason, and that's got to be to do with the future. I don't mean to sound egotistical, it isn't necessarily something big, it might be something nobody ever gets to hear about, but I believe there's something I'm going to do, some contribution to history that nobody else in the world could make.'

'OK. What are you going to do? What's John "Tiger" Sterling's contribution to history?'

He looked wary. 'Well, Wunsche's asked me to help him write his speeches...'

'Tiger can Write,' said his wife, as if the judgment had been forced out of her.

'...and I'm hoping to kinda get to politics...,' he went on, with uncharacteristic tentativeness – then suddenly he grinned and announced 'I cannot tell a lie, I want to be President someday!' and laughed, roared, challenging Connelly to laugh at him. But Connelly looked solemn. It was hard to tell if he was taking him seriously, as a friend he respected, who might really, just possibly, get near the top some day, or if he was looking at him like a patient who was suffering delusions of grandeur. Tiger snorted, shrugged, grabbed another sandwich and lit a cigarette.

Connelly looked off to the distance, and presently said, 'I guess you don't need me to tell you that while you were in Korea all the ambitious ones were scrambling up the tree ahead of you; well, you've seen them all over the Hill, thousands of guys like you... well, not like you, they don't give a damn about making a contribution to history or anything else except their own careers. You're different. And that might be a helpful thing in terms of ambition, but it probably isn't.' He shook his head. 'I don't know. One thing, though. If that's what you want you need to be working for someone a little more well thought of.'

'Why? Whatcha mean, well thought of? What's wrong with Bob Wunsche?' he demanded, and then went on to answer his own question. 'I know he's not exactly a rocket scientist, and it's a shame about his drink problem and his marriage problem. But he's a decent fellow for all that, and anyway, it's the message that matters, not the personality.'

'But that was yesterday's message. The underbed thing is just punctured now; everyone in Washington is sick of it.'

'Everyone — which means you, and your friends and all those Ivy League types, everyone who thinks he's smarter than the other 95 per cent of the American people. You think you're not snobs because you invite Jews to your parties, but...' Connelly's face must have shown how shocked he was, because Tiger said swiftly, 'I'm not an anti-Semite, I'm an anti-snobbite.'

'Oh, Tiger!' Barbara protested. 'Your mother is the worst East Coast snob I ever met. She's from Boston,' she informed Connelly, as if in her eyes this made her mother-in-law a particularly rare and awesome specimen.

Connelly considered confessing to some of the six or seven disqualifications from snobbery he possessed, but before he had picked out the most salient of them, Tiger was saying, 'We're being stupid, turning it into a social argument. It's something spiritual. It's about the real life of America, which is, oh well, it's lots of things, but the essential one is, you know, that kind of what we were talking about last night...' his voice trailed off delicately, as if he wanted the word unspoken, whispering it, '*Freedom* and the way it's being shot at from all sides, not just the left, parts of the right too, and the money men and the admen and the newspapermen.'

Barbara said, 'Oh, you're just still sore about the *Gazette*.'

'No, I'm not still sore, I was right, it's all a goddamn fix,' he flicked his cigarette in the river, 'but that's the way it works, isn't it, that party was exactly the same, a fix, just setting poor old Bob up to make him look like a Nazi. An ignorant badly dressed drunk hillbilly Nazi.'

'Admit that as set-ups go it didn't take a whole lot of work. And it wasn't one, anyway. Oss didn't mean for things to get so far out of hand.'

Tiger looked stubborn, a little sad underneath it. 'He wrote a lot of letters on my behalf when I was in Korea. I'm not going to ditch him just because Mr Oh So Snide Pointdexter, or even Dr Smartass Connelly think he's yesterday's man.'

Tears, howls, interrupted them: Caroline bringing Henry, who'd got stung by a bee and fallen face down in the mud and scratched his knee. He ran up and threw himself at his mother's arms. She dodged him: he was too muddy to comfort. 'Tiger, take him down and wash him off.'

'No,' sobbed Henry, pushing his father away.

'Hey, Hal!' Connelly announced, 'I'm going swimming! Look at that water! Amazing! I'm going swimming right now!' He got rid of his shoes and his Hawaiian shirt and started down the rocks, then looked back. 'Anyone want to come?'

'Me!' cried Caroline, but Hal had already started to follow, and Connelly picked him up and carried him down to the waterside. 'What about me?' Caroline called after him.

'Hush. No. It's just a trick. He's just going to wash him, not really take him swimming,' her father explained.

'You couldn't really swim in that, it's much too dangerous,' said Barbara. But Caroline kept her eye on them with jealous vigilance, feeling that a grown-up who could think of doughnut sandwiches might very well be able to swim in waterfalls.

Tiger laughed, watching Connelly picking his way down the rocks with the child in his arms, obviously chatting to him in a confidential voice drowned out by the roar of the rapids. 'Aw,' he said. 'Something tells me a certain carefree bachelor life is coming to an end.'

There was a sort of pool or backwater, sheltered from the main rush of the river by a stony arm that stretched halfway out to the stream. Connelly set Henry down here, in water which still rushed and swirled, but shallowly. He began an ineffectual splashing and rubbing operation, but it had not been under way long before Hal detected the duplicity. A little dispute took place; Henry won, and his parents saw them walk out to the centre of the backwater. Connelly sat down where it was about eighteen inches or two feet deep, and kept hold of the boy as he paddled around.

'Oh lord, I hope he'll be careful. Tiger, go down and stop them, it's terribly dangerous.'

'No, it's good for him,' Tiger said. He was enthralled: it was the first time he had ever seen Henry do anything daring in his life, the first time he had ever seen anything of himself in his son.

God it was cold! It was the first time he'd been in real water since Hawaii. His body screamed and sang with it. It was so cold it hurt; it was so wonderful to be wet! He chattered at Hal as if he was the little kid. 'Isn't it freezing? Doncha love it?' But he couldn't just crouch there, freezing away. 'Go back and wait by the edge,' he instructed Hal presently, and moved cautiously to the channel that went back to the main body of the river. Here it was nearly a yard deep, enough to stretch out his legs, play a little, edge closer to the real pull of the current, test his strength against it, bang his knee, feel the wonderful pounding of the water, down and through his shoulders, the voice of the river, a scream from the air above and something floundering to him, oh hell, the kid! Trying to get hold of him, get his head above water, losing his footing, a swift plunge backwards, a course hindered only by occasional rocks that struck his shins, his ribs, his hips. He still had hold of the child, kept trying to lift him up, above the water and above the rocks. Then suddenly he was flipped over onto his back, lost Hal, no, got him again, deeper water, hold the boy's head over his chest and swim as hard for the side as he could with one arm, get slammed and stranded up against a long, smooth, oblong boulder, breathe again.

Hal was conscious, unbruised, undrowned and apparently unalarmed. 'Wow!' he said, having scrambled up the boulder. Connelly dragged himself up to his feet and draped himself on it, as if he needed to soak up its warmth and strength. He could feel his heart bouncing against the stone face. Presently he turned and observed that they had come about twenty feet down from the pool where they had been playing. Tiger and Barbara were scrambling down the rocks with terrible faces. 'Henry!' Barbara made straight for the boy and held him tight.

'I'm not Henry any more, I am Hal!' he said, trying to break loose from her embrace and rejoin Connelly in the water. But she kept hold of him tight, and Tiger stood over them, protective and superfluous, patting and checking the bits of Hal that weren't already enveloped. There weren't many, and presently he turned and began moving towards the figure still in the water.

Connelly had a strong momentary impression that neither of them were human beings; he could almost smell the instincts in the air. He was backing up, deeper to the water and saying in a voice he was ashamed to discover he possessed, 'Tiger. Don't. Don't, Tiger, please.' His knees gave out and he lost his footing again, scrambling around the water.

'Get out of there.' Tiger's voice was imperious, and offered no guarantees of safety. Connelly crept up to the land; Tiger turned and walked away. Caroline was up on the grass, crying painfully over all the times she had wished her brother dead. Tiger was cleaning up the picnic, stuffing the remains back into the grocery bags so angrily the paper burst. Hal had broken free of his mother's concern and was running up to his sister crying, 'Did you see me?' Barbara, damp, white and dignified, followed him, ignoring the bedraggled creature that was also making its way up the rocks.

Gloria was back at work on Monday, looking so furious that nobody had the courage to ask if she was all right. This was why it was such a surprise for Connelly when, Bronsky having left the room, she cornered him and said, 'I'm pregnant.'

'What?' he cried, stabbed with what had to be the world's most irrational sense of guilt

'You heard me.'

'Yes... Jesus, I'm... Do you need any help? Do you... shall we get married?' God knew where this came from, but he had an instant picture of himself and Gloria living in a three-bed colonial house next door to the Sterling family.

'Don't be stupid. I'm asking you if you know anyone who can get rid of it for me.'

'Oh, sorry, no, I don't.' But his unexpected reaction continued to disturb him for several days The only explanation anywhere near satisfactory was that it was because work was already his family: he and Gloria a couple of neurotic waifs, Oss an extravagant but hardly reliable father figure, Bronsky the wise old uncle. But it was a little more surprising to discover that work, which had always seemed to be the arena of risk, was in fact a cocoon against a much realer and rougher world, Sterling's 95 per cent of America. The foundation was an artificial environment, a laboratory, a hothouse for the cultivation of bizarre imported species and the odd native freak. All that anxiety, all that deceit, for the meaningless prize of appearing the most hardy, healthy specimen on show. He might as well have been living in Greenwich Village all along.

On Thursday night, a phone call. Tiger's voice, just faintly tentative, suggesting they meet for a drink at Tony's tomorrow after work. 'Great,' said Connelly, carefully editing any surprise or relief out of his voice.

Sterling was already waiting when Connelly got there, and began the proceedings. 'I wanted to consult you as a psychologist, that's why I phoned.'

'No, Tiger. It's not a good idea. I mean, I'd love to help, but you're not a patient any more, we're friends now; it'd be, I don't know, a kind of unfair influence. In fact we probably shouldn't even be friends. It'd be unethical if I was a real shrink.'

Tiger looked confused. 'The whole point about you is that you weren't like a shrink, that's why you were able to call me back. It's not your *job*, but it's the reason you were put here on earth. I mean, what you do doesn't look anything out of the ordinary but there's this kind of, I don't know, magic going on underneath.'

Connelly felt like he'd been given a brief Tiger's-eye view of his own existence: a supernatural being sent by God to heal him, with no past or future or personality other than might enhance his work on Sterling. 'Don't you realize every word you're saying is – '

'It's not just me either. It's Henry, he's noticed it too. He has to be called "Hal" now, you know, because you called him that. He's the one I wanted to consult you about. He told me he wasn't scared last Sunday because he just knew you were holding him and he knew he wouldn't get hurt.'

'Oh, that's just kids, they don't see the danger ahead.'

'Henry does,' said Tiger, grimly. 'Most of the time he sees nothing else. He can't even ride a two-wheeler and he's seven! And not because he's unco-ordinated, he's a bit unco-ordinated but the real reason is that he's...timid.' Tiger pronounced the word as if he was holding it at arm's length between his thumb and forefinger, and pinching his nose closed with his other hand. 'And the thing I worry about is, what if it's more than that? Nobody ticks me off more than these Freudians but I can't help thinking that the time I was away was a terribly formative stage for him. He's never really taken to me, you know, never accepted my coming back.'

'Oh, Tiger,' said Connelly. There was a sad, involuntarily pleading note to his voice.

'That's why I didn't step in and call you back before you went too far out on Sunday. Because he was doing something daring, venturing out beyond his depth, and because I was pleased he'd taken to you; some kind of male role model and not Mommy Mommy all the time.'

I cannot believe this, said Connelly to himself. Male role model! To hide the temptation to dissolve into hysterical laughter, he said, 'Maybe he likes me because I don't give a damn whether he's timid or not. To you it's the end of the world. How come? Feel guilty about being away?'

'No; I couldn't exactly help it, could I? I'm just so worried for him, if he turned out...oh God, he can't be!' His voice was so full of anguish from the gut that Connelly had to cover his face.

Oh God, poor little boy. Or was it, oh God, poor Connelly? Or...several things clicked into place, this evening, last Saturday night. He said, 'Tiger, are you really telling me about yourself?'

There was a frozen transfixed moment made of Sterling's eyes igniting and Connelly thinking, 'He's going to hit me. He's going to hit me.' It lasted maybe a second or a fraction of a second but felt unnaturally prolonged, by the slow graphic consciousness that watches disaster (a shark's fin, a car out of control) approaching. There was a look on Tiger's face that told Connelly he was sadistically prolonging the tension. Then time snapped back, accelerating to an equal opposite superfast action mode: fist slung across table, stool rocking, head cracking back against the wall, body spilling awkwardly onto the floor, a body just too shocked to mobilize itself to retaliate, because events had broken free from the score, because it was Sterling sprawling on the ground and Connelly standing over him, twitching his cuffs primly and saying, 'Pre-emptive strike.'

By the time Sterling had picked himself up and found his broken glasses, Connelly was gone. The barkeeper was just about interested enough to ask, 'You all right?' as he made his way out of the bar. He nodded, though he was beginning to shake, and there was blood on the hand that had mopped his eye. Outside, without his glasses, he felt vulnerable and blind, edging along close to the wall, one arm around his chest holding everything together, the other braced slightly forward to fend off or parry anything that came at him. His left eye was swelling shut and the back of his head felt tight and hot and a dull ache was growing in every part of his brain. His stomach was having flashbacks to Hara Kiri, and his guts were standing by for a depth charge any moment.

Wrongest of all was his vision. He hadn't actually gone blind, he was seeing things, but it was like his brain wasn't doing whatever it was supposed to do to make sense of the signals it received. He was seeing, but in another place, another time.

LOOK. CONCENTRATE. Where the hell are you going? Because at least half of him was in Korea, and that was not a good place to be navigating the streets of an American city.

Something friendly and red loomed up in the fog. Car. He climbed in, sat for a while, explored the swelling around his eye, the bump on the back of his head. Time passed. It became dark. He moved with surprising agility between different darknesses: cool twilight in a narrow street shaded by historic architecture, the cold velvet of the underground cell at Changhung, and the absolute minus of lost consciousness. There was an equality about them all that pleased him perversely.

A hand turns on the ignition, the car bucks backwards and bangs into something and jumps forwards again. Cut the engine. Better not drive. Sterling got out and walked back to the main road, waving at random in case a taxi was going by. Presently one picked him up. The driver commented on his injury. He explained seriously that he'd been jumped on by a bunch of marines. He went inside and made the circuit around the dark places again. Then the driver was helping him out of the car and walking him to the door and explaining things to Barbara.

'Who hit you?' Trust Barbara to get to the root of the problem. Tiger hunched over himself 'Someone. No one.' He went to the bathroom. His face tensed up against an access of tears, waking up the bruising under his eye.

Barbara's voice crying, 'Tiger, what's wrong?'

'Nothing. Nothing,' he said quickly, rubbing his face and standing up. Barbara was blocking his way. More explanation was needed. 'I guess nobody's hit me since Korea and it just took me right back. I'll go to bed now. It'll be gone in the morning.'

'But are you sure you're all right?'

'Yes. Just ignore me.'

Barbara had a fine sense of when not to help, and she vanished again. Sterling carried himself to bed, where night passed neither slow nor fast but in another kind of time measured not by heartbeats or a planet's spinning in space, but by periodic oscillations between Changhung and Tony's.

Planet time resumed in the morning, but 'it' was still not gone. Part of him was there, negotiating the present, getting up, getting a cigarette, staring out of the front-room window, trying to reconstruct the conversation from last night. 'Probably we shouldn't be friends.' 'I don't give a damn whether he's timid or not.' And then... what was it? 'You're really talking about yourself.' Something along those lines. But did it mean what it sounded like? Maybe Connelly was just saying, 'You're not as 100 per cent tough as you pretend to be,' something innocent like that. But Connelly was a psychologist, a *Kinsey Report*-reading psychologist, no innocent.

The other, greater part of him was still fingering around in the silent darkness, in the time before the gift of egolessness had been delivered, bilocating into a second self with a face like Chang, accusing and interrogating, waiting for some final confession and self-criticism.

One Friday later that month, Connelly came home to find a little boy sitting on his front step with a book bag and a lunch box. 'Hello, Hal,' he said, trying to sound friendly while looking around nervously for Tiger or his car. 'Are the others here?'

'I came here on my own,' said Hal, with dignified precision. 'I found it on the map and I walked here from the Office.' He got an impressionistic tourist's map out of his book bag and traced the route from the House Office Building, for Connelly's benefit.

'That's very smart. Will you be able to get back again?'

'I'm not going to go back,' said Hal ominously.

'Does... do your parents know you're here?'

'No,' Hal said. 'And we should go inside in case he comes looking for me. Plus I'm terribly hungry and I'd like a doughnut sandwich please.'

Connelly gazed at him for a minute, sighed and unlocked the front door. 'Come on then. I have a feeling I'm out of doughnuts, but we'll see.' When they got inside he asked, 'So, is this Running Away from Home?'

'Yes.'

'Why?'

'Mommy's in Nebraska cause of Grampa died.'

'Oh, that's too bad. But shouldn't you, um, stay at home and wait for her? Who's taking care you?'

'He is.'

'Daddy?' Hal nodded. Connelly said, 'He'll be awfully worried. I think I should phone him up and tell him you're all right.'

'But then he'll come and get me.'

'Hal, you have to go home sooner or later. You're a smart boy but you're too young to live by yourself.'

'I'll go home when Mommy comes back,' he explained, with an air of patience, 'and you'll take care of me until then.'

And Daddy will come and beat me to a pulp when he finds out, said Connelly to himself. 'No, I can't. I'm going to see my mom and dad in New York this weekend, and – '

'How are you getting there?' Hal demanded.

'By train.' Hal's eyes lit up and Connelly realized this admission was a big tactical mistake. Quickly, 'Let's go see about the doughnuts.' Together they examined the cupboards. There were no doughnuts. 'Tell you what. I'll phone your dad and then we'll go out and buy some.'

The little face looked sweet and compliant. 'No, that's all right, I'll just have baloney.'

'OK,' said Connelly, who could look sweet with the best of them. 'And I'll just phone the office.' He picked up the phone book and flipped through it, congratulating himself that he was rather good with children.

Hal began to cry. Connelly decided that the best, good-with-children thing to do was to ignore this. 'Hello? Is this Congressman Wunsche's office? Is Mr Sterling there?' He was not. 'Well, can I leave a message? Tell him that Dr Connelly phoned and his son is at my apartment and I'll look after him until he gets here.'

Hal continued to sob, even after the deed was done. 'Hey, don't you want your baloney? Aw, Hal, can't you just tell me what's wrong with your Dad?'

This elicited a sniff, a choke, and the information that his father was in a bad mood.

Wonderful, said Connelly to himself. Just what I needed to hear. 'Is he mad at you? Or mad at someone else and taking it out on you?'

'Not mad,' said Hal, and dissolved into tears again, deep hard-fought sobs, crying in a way a child should not cry,

Connelly thought. It wasn't just a case of a sensitive kid mismatched with an overpowering father. Something was really wrong. 'When's Mommy coming home?'

'Monday, if I'm good.'

The phone rang. Tiger's voice, breathless and distraught, 'Connelly! He's there, is he? Is he there?'

'Yes. I told you he was here. He's OK. Don't worry.'

'I'm coming straight over.'

'Wait. Something's happened, hasn't it, Tiger?'

'Whaddaya mean?'

'I mean...', he cupped his hand over the phone, 'the boy's really upset, terrified, and there's got to be a reason, I mean, have you hit him or...'

'Ha!'

'I know. Maybe it's my fault. So I just had this idea, maybe I could take him with me to New York for the weekend. An adventure for him, and it might make it easier for you.'

Silence. After a minute Connelly said, 'And it's my way of saying sorry. OK?'

A little more silence, then, 'OK.'

The 6.10 was hardly a popular family excursion. The compartment was thick with smoke before they even started. There were one or two couples, but mostly it was full of flannel men in ambitious suits, and every single one seemed to glare at them as if to say, 'If that kid puts one toe out of line, one little peep out of that kid and I'm going to darken your daylights, mister.' Hal did not put one toe out of line, but after twenty minutes the first excitement of the train journey began to pall. 'If I get bored I might start to miss Mommy,' he warned his guardian. 'Maybe you better tell me a story.'

'No,' said Connelly firmly. 'I can't do stories. What's in your book bag?' Hal produced a wide-ruled notebook. 'I know. Why don't you draw something on that?'

'It's my spelling book. I'll get into trouble if I draw on it,' said Hal, looking angelic.

'Well,' said Connelly with sweet inexorability, 'I guess that happens to little boys who run away. Getting in trouble is the price of freedom. *Draw* on it.' So Hal drew a map of a city called Capitlle, with Chevrolet Chase and the Pontiac river. 'And that's Connelly Falls.'

'For it every time,' he muttered. But he was charmed despite himself and drew a map of New York that beguiled another half hour. Then the man on the seat behind him had pity and tore out the comic page of his *Post* and passed it over. And then at last the little guy fell asleep and didn't wake up even when carried in and out of taxis.

His parent's little brick house in Queens was dark. Connelly let himself in and carried Hal up to his bedroom. He had already decided he was never spending another night on the couch, not for any member of the Sterling clan. When the boy was settled, he tiptoed downstairs. Sterling's home number was written on a scrap of paper in his wallet. The phone was answered instantly. 'What's happened? Connelly? Is that you?'

'Yes. Nothing. Relax.'

'Then why are you phoning?'

'I don't know. To say he's OK. To say he's a smooth little operator and I fell for it in the worst way and I'm sorry I accused you of scaring him.'

'Oh.' Tiger's voice sounded curiously lifeless. Then, 'Uh, Connelly?'

'Yeah?'

'Can you explain . . . why you . . .'

'Hit you? No, not definitively. Maybe it was because I was scared, or maybe it was to sort of cancel out the fact that I helped you in Hawaii. So we could meet on equal terms.'

An embittered exhalation. 'Yeah. It feels pretty thoroughly cancelled out.'

Hal was nowhere near as comfortable a person to share a bed with as his sweet face promised. He was angular and elbowed and wriggly. He woke up early and started asking questions about New York City, and what they would be doing today, and whether his guardian was aware that he had slept in his clothes and hadn't brushed his teeth at all last night.

Julia Connelly had heard high-pitched tones coming from her son's bedroom and had only come downstairs when she was fully dressed in her most vulnerably thin, floaty clothes, and had drawn stagy lines all the way around her eyes in harsh black. With her frighteningly fine bones and her hollow, noble face, she ought to have been a tragic sight, but she was really too angry, too excited by the scale of the drama that was about to be enacted to remember she was supposed to be frail, injured, betrayed. 'Sasha! How dare – who is that?'

The impact of the small thin dishevelled creature, with its large brown eyes and long dark lashes and its air of ethereal sweetness and vulnerability, entirely cancelled out the lame explanation, 'son of a friend of mine'. 'Oh!' she cried, sweeping the little one into a warm embrace. And then 'Oh!' again, standing up and placing her hands on her son's shoulders and looking deep into his eyes. 'Sasha, I understand.' And then memories overcame her and she fled into the kitchen to burst into tears.

'Well,' said Connelly to Hal. 'That's what my Mom is like. Something tells me you'll get along.'

Hal nodded solemnly, then asked, 'How come she calls you "Sasha"? Isn't that a girl's –'

'She calls me Sasha because she's not very well in the head,' he said ruthlessly.

About an hour later Packy Connelly came downstairs, blinked at the visitors, then looked away swiftly, as one who has learned not to comment on any unusual apparition until someone else has confirmed its reality. 'This is a friend of mine's son who...'

''Allo, la,' he said pleasantly enough, then lost interest until Julia called him into the kitchen and whispered to him earnestly. He came out again and stared assessingly at Hal. 'Your face is your fortune, lad,' he announced. 'Much good it did me.' Packy was badly weathered by years at sea and years on the Liverpool Docks (and Dock Road pubs) but just about recognizable as the source of Connelly's 'movie stah face'.

Presently Julia came out of the kitchen with twenty dollars from one of her hiding places, which she pressed into Connelly's hand. 'Take him to Coney Island!'

This was too much. 'You never took me to Coney Island when I was a kid!'

'Ar, hey, lad. There was a depression on,' Packy laughed.

'Well, I don't need any money,' he said sulkily. Julia would not take it back, and at last he went out with it, just to escape it all.

They took a bus over to Manhattan. 'Is this Coney Island?' Hal asked, as they disembarked.

'This is Greenwich Village.'

Hal looked around. 'Why did we come here?'

'Because this is the place I used to run away to.' Hal looked around again but failed to see the attraction, even when Dr Connelly sang him all the verses of Interesting People on Christopher Street

'But why are we here?' he persisted.

'Because I need to decide if I'm going to come and live here,' Connelly said, and then wondered where the idea had come from. Was it just because of realizing work was also a place of safety? So they walked around, and Connelly bought some cookies as a bribe, and they walked around some more, and Hal couldn't understand what was supposed to be so interesting about it all. 'You would like our new house better.'

'I know. But I can't, it'd not really be allowed for extra grown-ups to move into a family.'

They came into a little square with thin frail birches just starting to yellow, and sat on the cast iron bench in the middle of it all to eat the cookies. Connelly reflected that having a six-year-old telepath around on a permanent basis would keep him honest. Pretending he wanted to be 'friends' with Sterling! How had he managed to fool himself with that one for so long? Stupid stupid stupid.

He called himself stupid until a faint voice from inside squeaked a protest. No, no, it wasn't that, not really. Oh sure, there was plenty of chemistry, *plenty* of chemistry (and Sterling knew about it on some level, and played with it, played not entirely fair with it) going on. But chemistry was nothing. Connelly played with erotic chemistry with all kinds of people: Pointdexter, Hal, people's wives. No, the thing with Sterling was the sense that he could fill the gap, the fault line he himself had opened up back then at Tripler.

Connelly had gone out there, ready to console all these victims of brainwashing: it's not your fault, nobody could have stood all that, you had to survive. He'd gone out to hear narratives of consolation for himself, stories of heroic giving in under duress to inspire prisoners interned in conformist America who have also arrived at the conclusion that survival was more important than integrity.

Instead he had crashed into Sterling, and that was what had been wrong with him ever since. Everything seemed dishonest and crappy compared to that standard and there wasn't even any point in trying to measure up against it; you might as well despise yourself from the start, 'pre-emptive strike'. That's what had filled all those blank months since coming home with miserable grey fog, too cowardly to be what he wanted to be, too honest to be able to partake of life in any other way. And then Sterling had arrived, and lit the mist with fireworks, and it had seemed like a solution, a rescue. But why? Nothing had really changed.

Maybe he had imagined that by worshipping at the temple of integrity he'd earn some kind of merit, take at least some of the pressure off himself. Or that by charming or even seducing the personification of what he couldn't be, an alchemical union of opposites would make it all all right. Somehow. Pretty dumb, because it couldn't happen without Sterling cheating, which would have wrecked the equation. And anyway, Sterling was a human being, and pretty soon he'd start to notice all those little dishonesties and unconciousnesses that, um, he'd started to notice already.

Yes. And here he was in Greenwich Village, thinking of moving here. Which meant – God! – that something inside him had already renounced the Sterling illusion. Or even more than that? He felt his heart speed up. No. Don't get scared. Look around. Remember the shaking car. It's not so impossible.

He took Hal's second to last cookie and looked up and down the street. It was kind of early for any hotstuff kine action. There was a tough-looking kid in jeans hanging around the door of a bar and a Gloria's Gloria staggering psychotropically along the other side of the road with a bag of groceries. And then, oh God, just the last thing he needed to see: a pathetic old fairy in a softly flowing lilac-grey suit mincing arthritically across the square towards them. Connelly felt his stomach twist with disgust and his heart wrench with pity. 'Well, there you are,' said the rat part of his mind. 'There *you* are, in thirty years, or six months' time. That's Integrity for you.'

The old fairy continued inexorably in their direction. Hal gazed at him, understanding the song about Interesting People at last. Connelly looked off to the side, aggressively avoiding his eyes, although it was impossible to screen the orchid-coloured tie and shining white shoulder-length hair out of his peripheral vision. Undoubtedly the old fellow must have read the message, but he continued to approach and then stopped in front of them to say, with a beaming smile, 'I don't get out much these days – such an effort – but what a lovely sight in the sunshine: pretty buildings, pretty trees, pretty boys...'

Hal had been staring, gaping, and now demanded, 'Are you a man or a lady?'

'I'm an angel, my dear, which is neither.' Hal's eyes went wide and literal, and took in the light reflected off or maybe through the pale parchmenty skin, the long thin strands of white hair. 'But you're both looking so sad,' the old man went on, 'and the world is a beautiful place, and you're young...'

Connelly looked up at him and felt his eyes flood up with tears, so suddenly they poured over their banks and down his face. 'Yes, I know, it's like that too, this beautiful world,' the old man said, and drifted off across the square.

On Sunday Packy took Hal out on the Staten Island Ferry so that Julia could corner her son and inform him that if he wanted to marry Hal's mother, they would accept her and love her whoever (whatever!) she was. 'Oh, Mom, don't!' he groaned. 'I can't stand it. He's not mine! I know what it looks like; I know he even looks like me a bit, but it's just not.'

Julia cast her eyes down. 'When I was just...'

'No! No!' Connelly cried, seeing his half-brother looming ahead. Anything was better than that she should start remembering the illegitimate son she left in Russia. As a diversionary tactic he got out every newsworthy fact he possessed and started throwing them at her. 'Hal's mother is married! To my best friend. It was him I thought I was in love with but I'm not. I'm never going to get married or have cute sons or anything! I'm in love with someone but he lives in Hawaii and...'

The last startling fact about Hoku's colour was unnecessary. Julia was sitting bolt upright, looking at him in a peculiarly frozen way. 'What did you say?' she asked him.

'Oh, you heard me.' His energy drained as suddenly as it had arrived. Julia was assimilating the information in poised stillness, with her neck tall and her fingers curved in her lap. 'Don't tell your father.'

'Why not? So you can live carrying a secret like that from him? It's no fun, I can tell you.'

'Well, will you let me tell him when you're gone?'

'Yes, fine, it's not something I'm exactly looking forward to.'

A faint flicker of compassion traversed her face, then mutated into a more theatrical expression of sorrow. 'When did this happen? When you were little you wouldn't even go to ballet lessons!' Connelly covered his face and shook his head at this association of ideas, but she persisted, as if it was a grievance that still rankled, 'You have to admit you would have made a lovely *danseur*. But all I ever got was American boys don't, and American boys aren't called Sasha and American boys this and that and yes, of course I want you to be an all-American boy and now...! And your analyst is telling you it's all my fault.'

'No, it's not your fault.'

Julia looked a little stubborn or a little disappointed, as if she wanted it to be her fault; she had a faint sense that if he was reading the script properly, Sasha would say that his analyst had told him that having such an exotic and desirable mother had spoiled him for all other women. But of course he was going to be awkward and all-American about it. He probably didn't even have an analyst. 'Oh you're worse than your father!' she exclaimed, flinging herself to her feet and retiring to the kitchen.

Well, you've done it, Connelly said to himself, though most of him was not ready to believe that 'it' had even taken place. That's the worst over.

No. There was going to be one person who was a whole lot worse.

They were in the car heading back to the Sterling apartment in Alexandria when Hal started to cry again. 'Uh-uh,' said Connelly in a warning voice. 'I'm not falling for it this time, so you might as well forget it.'

'He's still in a bad mood.'

'You don't know that. He didn't sound mad on the phone. And anyway, so what? As long as he doesn't hit you or shout at you or anything, what does it matter? It's his problem, not yours.' Hal wept more bitterly, hurt by this hard-heartedness. 'I'm the one that should be scared,' Connelly muttered. There was no reason he had to tell Sterling this very night, but a thin, adventurous strand of thought was considering chancing it. Having caught the wave with his mother, he might as well ride it in to the shore.

It was that old fairy in the Village who's done this for me, he thought, deliberately trying to block out the sounds of pain from the back seat. He imagined the old chap getting that old Gatsby-style suit out of mothballs, spending ages painting his face, wondering if all the 'effort' was worth it, but saying to himself, 'No, that nice-looking young fellow will be there today and I've got an important message from the universe to deliver to him.' And as he staggered out into the sunshine his frail body grew transparent, became a vessel of light, and he came straight to where they were sitting on the bench and through and under his words he radiated just the amount of energy to take Connelly to the threshold of... of whatever he was doing now. Then he laughed aloud at this fantasy. The old sweetheart – who probably didn't have the faintest sense of the symbolic impact he had made. That vessel of light quality was probably the last faint flicker of libido in his eyes. He'd probably gone home and died of the exertion. He was in fairy heaven now, laughing in amazement at the way he was being mythologized. God! It's worse than Sterling thinking I was put here on earth to 'call him back'.

And then suddenly the thought that he had been, in a more diffused, unpractised way, something just a little like the transparent old man, *something* like that for Sterling, made his eyes fill up again. Me? He had to pull over to the side of the road and rub the tears away with his sleeves, sabotage the sense of amazement with the ironic memory of his revulsion, back then, just before it happened. 'You'll be like that, in thirty years.'

'Aren't we going?' a tiny, hopeful voice.

'No. No. We're going.' He turned round in his seat to look at him. 'Listen to me, Hal,' he began, feeling that as someone supernaturally empowered to bear light to others, there was something wise and performatively helpful he could say to the boy. Only, just then, there wasn't.

'Yes?' said Hal meekly, waiting.

'Never mind.'

When they got to the Sterling apartment he saw immediately what Hal meant by a 'bad mood' and it wasn't angry. Sterling was hunched and tense to the point of shaking, and his eyes were stiff open and seeing past them in a scary way. 'It's OK, Hal,' Connelly said. 'I'm going to stay here and look after – everyone.'

Hal scooted past his father and disappeared down the hall. 'Hey, Tiger, come on,' Connelly said, taking his arm. Sterling flinched and jerked back from his touch. 'OK, OK, come on, let's go and sit down. Can you hear me, Tiger?'

A brief convulsive nod, and Sterling suffered himself to be led back into the living room. The place was in chaos: Caroline's toys all over the floor, ashtrays overflowing, the foil plates of four TV dinners piled up on the coffee table. Connelly pulled Sterling onto the couch, and eliminated the worst of the squalor before sitting down beside him. 'OK. All right, Tiger? Can you tell me what's happening?'

'I get these things. It doesn't matter.' He spoke quickly, in a low preoccupied voice.

'Hell, Jeez, of course it matters. Come on, tell me.'

Sterling put his hand out blindly and pawed the coffee table until he came across a packet of cigarettes, lighting up in a series of automatic unconscious movements that did not ground him in the physical present but rather accentuated how far away his mind was. Connelly looked at his long, inartistic hands, ugly with tendons and impacted joints, a writer's callous and smoker's stains, dirty fingernails. 'Is it because I hit you?'

'No. Yes. No, it's Korea, Chan –' this was swallowed up by a terrible wounded choking sound. Sterling pressed his hands hard against his face, over his mouth, forcing the noise, the information, the pain back into himself. Connelly tentatively reached his arm out to put it around his shoulders, but Sterling jumped out from under him, and turned to face him, crouched forward defensively.

'Hey, hey, it's OK,' said Connelly. Slowly Sterling seemed to wake up to the present, blinking, straightening up. He exhaled brokenly, and went to sit on a chair.

'I was going to stay there, you know.' He spoke quickly, in an artificially collected voice. 'Because Chang was the only person who could understand. They can't here, it's not their fault. They just weren't there. Chang was the only friend I had.'

'What about Kirby? What about Eugene?' cried Connelly, scandalised, personally hurt, as if he was Kirby himself.

He wiped them out of existence with a sweep of his hand that sent all the ashes wafting out of the ashtray. They were dead, or as good as dead. 'I'm only alive because of Chang. He was taking care of me.' A short little noise related to a laugh. 'Do you understand that? Because I held out, and we needed each other. I needed him to test myself against, and he needed me and oh, I can't explain it.' He lit another cigarette, then returned to hugging his knees and staring sightlessly ahead. After a few minutes his spine uncurved, though he still sat inclined forward; he inhaled through his teeth and said, in a subterranean voice, '"Are you the new person drawn towards me?"'

'What?' Connelly jumped. He wasn't up on Whitman.

'"Do you suppose yourself advancing on real ground toward a real heroic man? Have you no thought, O dreamer, that it may be all Maya, illusion?"' And then Tiger laughed and said, as if picking up the thread of a perfectly normal conversation, 'He made it easy for me, you know? I was useful. I know he could have made it a hell of a lot harder. If I'd been a real threat to him I'd be dead like Eugene. Everyone liked Eugene, but I was a public piece of shit. So Eugene got killed and I was kept alive, and the more I appeared to be keeping the faith, the less anyone else would want to. There's that side to it too.'

'But it wasn't easy,' Connelly protested. 'And whatever bizarre motives Chang had, whatever he made you believe about being your friend, you did hold out.'

He shrugged, as if that achievement was absolutely valueless to him now.

The door from the hall opened a crack and a sliver of Hal's face peeped out. 'It's my bedtime now, Uncle Alex.'

'That's OK, Hal. Stay up a little longer, as a special treat.'

'I have to go to bed at eight or Mommy won't come back.'

Connelly put the children to bed, came out and found Sterling kneeling at the foot of the big black Jacobean sideboard. They used (obviously infrequently) the lower shelf as a liquor cabinet. 'You're right, Connelly. I've got to stop treating you like a shrink. What'll you have?'

'Oh, just a martini or anything.'

'I like martinis but I don't know how to make them.' Tiger stood up and stepped back gesturing that his guest should take charge of the bar.

Connelly genuflected, blinked at the contents of the cabinet, and sent Sterling to the icebox to look for olives in case his face showed what he was thinking. There weren't any martini glasses, just partial sets of hi-balls and old-fashioned tumblers, decorated with brightly coloured pictures of game birds in repose. The vermouth was cheap, and not dry. At least there was a bottle of Beefeater's gin, with its paper seal unbroken. 'We're kind of short of ice,' Sterling called from the kitchen. 'Is that OK?'

'What do you think, Tiger? Or do you want to start a school of thought that believes martinis should be served at room temperature, like red wine?'

'It's just that Caroline puts it in her koolaid, and I keep forgetting to make more. And, um, Connelly?'

'Yeah?'

'I can't find any olives either.'

'Well, if you can't bring me at least one whole lemon, I resign.'

Eventually Tiger came out with four ice cubes and a partially mummified citrus fruit. Connelly mixed a hybrid martini-collins in a pheasant-embossed pitcher, shooing the melted chips of ice into the hi-ball glasses, and parking the remains in the freezer to bring it down to drinkability.

When they were on the second glass, he asked, 'Sterling, how are you feeling?'

'Fine. It works that way. I feel great. I don't mean drunk, either.'

'Because I have to tell you something.'

Tiger raised his sights to gaze at him with that peaceful, utterly sane look Connelly remembered from Tony's, blue eyes crinkling up into a beautiful, innocent smile. 'You're engaged to be married.'

Abort mission. Well, partially abort mission. 'Tiger, I'm leaving Washington,' he said instead, 'I'm selling up and going back to Hawaii.'

The next day at work he told Pointdexter and Bronsky he was moving to Hawaii 'for moral reasons'.

'Moral reasons?'

'Reasons of moral cathexis. I don't really want to go into it more than that.'

'You don't need to, my dear boy,' Oss leered.

'But what will you do?' Bronsky wanted to know.

'There's a university there.'

'Would you really be satisfied, running freshmen round mazes and lecturing to white rats? After all we've given you?' said Oss, with a melodramatic sob. 'Abandoned! for a chicken farmer! – Make sure you find a house with a spare bed, and expect me at Christmas time.'

On this consoling thought he took his leave. Connelly said softly to Bronsky, 'I guess you feel it needs more explanation.'

'No, you don't owe me any. I'm just concerned that when the romance wears off, your desert island might become intellectually unsatisfying.'

'I guess it's a risk. But I wanted to explain to you why, if you haven't figured it out already, I can't live in this town any more. I'm... I'm a security risk. The Wunsche kind, not the McCarthy kind.'

'Really?' said Bronsky, in a wondering, almost an admiring tone. 'No, I hadn't, I would never have guessed. You don't appear to have any of the usual behavioural pathology. What a shame, the times being what they are, you couldn't have told us. Understandable, of course. Your secret is safe with me.'

'It doesn't have to be a secret. I'd tell Oss, except I couldn't bear to sit through his reaction. Tell anyone you want.'

'Don't be silly. You may want to come back here someday.'

Another one down. Connelly told himself it was a relief, but he wasn't quite sure he convinced himself. He knew he couldn't complain: everyone was being perfectly nice about it, none of the catastrophes that might have happened were happening. His mother, after the first shock, was becoming almost complacent about it, which was irritating in its own way. A little more disturbing was Bronsky's tendency to see him as a specimen, well, a subject, albeit an ideal, informed subject, and ask him his opinion of the Freudian etiology, or whether some trauma had made him fixate when he was eleven. It's not Changhung he had to keep reminding himself.

He put his apartment on the market, gave his record collection to Oss, his hi-fi to Gloria and the abstract expressionist to Bronsky. He stuck his skis in the car and drove around to the Sterling household on Thursday evening. Barbara answered the door, looking surprised and not exactly pleased to see him. Connelly explained briefly about leaving.

'Yes, I know.'

'I thought Tiger might be able to use these – or maybe they're a better length for you,' he added, for some reason feeling anxious to ingratiate himself with her. 'I don't know whether the boots'd fit anyone.'

'Tiger's in the hospital,' she interrupted him bleakly. 'He crashed the car last night. Night before.'

'He what? Is he...?'

'Going to live, I guess.' This was just faintly disgusted, as if in her opinion he didn't deserve to.

Connelly didn't dare ask the questions that were flying around inside him. Only one was necessary. 'Can I go see him?'

She shrugged and obviously wished he wouldn't, then mentioned that she wouldn't be able to go tomorrow in the morning because of a school meeting. Connelly nodded, and left, with the skis.

Sterling's face was cut and bruised, and his leg was in traction. Connelly shook his head and asked directly, 'On purpose?'

'Depends what you mean. I didn't intend to end up here,' said Tiger, resentfully.

'What was it about?'

He rolled his face away, declining to answer.

'Oh, come on, don't spare my feelings. Was it because I said I was going away?'

'You must think you're mighty important.'

'Well, what was it then?'

After a long pause he admitted, 'The truth is, I was just plain drunk. And you didn't have any right to go and leave before I was a 100 per cent stable. So I was coming over to tell you that. But yeah, maybe you're right. Maybe the accident was a way of telling you that. I don't know.'

Connelly looked at him sadly. 'The crazy thing is, Tiger, the whole reason I'm going is because of your thing of freedom. The old Escape Plan, remember?'

He managed a smile. 'Yeah, I remember. And you're free to go. I can't ask you to stay on my account. As a matter of fact they've got me lined up to start seeing an analyst, from next week.'

The sale of the apartment was going through, the bank account had been emptied and turned into traveller's cheques; it was the day before his flight and he drove to the Sterling place for the last time. Tiger was home, parked on the couch behind a big cast. 'Just wanted to say goodbye,' said Connelly.

'It's a shame you had to go,' said Barbara hypocritically.

'Yeah, I . . . oh, look.' He extracted a small box from his pocket. It was maybe just big enough for a watch, and gift wrapped in red paper. 'Here. Don't open it until I'm gone.'

'Thanks,' said Tiger, rather helplessly, not sure how grateful to be.

'And I wanted to let you know....,' he stalled a bit, wishing Barbara would walk out of the room, but she didn't, 'you mean a lot to me, and you've influenced me probably more than anything I've done for you. Anyway...'

'Wait!' Sterling said. 'Let's keep in touch this time. I guess we won't be moving for awhile,' he slapped the cast on his leg. 'But make sure you write with your new address before we do.'

He promised he would, laughing rather weakly. 'Anyway!' he said again, making for the door. 'My love to Hal, and Caroline. Aloha, everyone.' And he went out.

'He was kind of emotional,' Barbara remarked. 'Do you think he'd been drinking?'

Sterling looked down, keeping his eyes focused on the little package. Too small for a watch really. He wished Barbara would go away so he could open it alone. It had the aura of being something significant, like a class ring.

'Well, come on, open it.'

So he did and it was a set of keys. Tiger looked at them uncomprehending; Barbara figured it out first and ran to the door. 'Oh! Why, he's given us his car!' She dashed out. Tiger hoisted himself on his crutches and followed swingingly. White, newly polished, with swaggering tailfins almost a foot high, last year's Pontiac.

Part Four

The scent of plumeria and the embrace of warm wet air was like the shallows of Kahala beach after the pressurized smoke chamber of the Stratocruiser: a soft invitation to relax, to soak in love and beauty, to lean on Hoku's chest and just rest for ever in the sunlight and sweetness. But Leimomi was anxious to pry him loose and give him a pale orange-gold lei with the damp livingness of real *ilima*. It had been ordered specially from a little florist downtown as soon as they had heard of his return.

There were so many things to say that none of them got expressed very efficiently. They led Connelly down to a jeep parked in a no waiting zone, with the sharp nose of the blue board jutting out of the back at a lethal angle. 'My car from work,' Leimomi introduced it proudly. She had got a job as housekeeper–caretaker at an estate in the mountains. 'You got to sit in the back, Hoku too fat and you getting skinnier than ever.'

'Eh, watch the remarks,' Hoku protested.

'Where you like go?' Leimomi demanded. 'I thought you like surf, Hoku say you like rest – lazy too, that's how come he so fat. They coming in big on the south shore today; we go First Break, eh?' With this example of democracy in action, she started the jeep and barrelled out of the airport.

Connelly would have liked to rest, he probably would have fallen asleep in the car, if he hadn't been sitting sideways, getting flung in all directions. But the first touch of the water, warm, alive water, changed everything. He was where he belonged, his whole body was singing, he was surfing with the kind of nervy ragged energy made of long hours sitting still, transmuted into something that felt like the sea sparkle running through his arms, a don't-care passion and commitment, flinging himself in front of the waves, spectacular rides, spectacular wipeouts. Leimomi was a connoisseur of a good wipeout. 'You been practising on the mainland?' she demanded, having caught the board after a particularly dramatic roundhouse and backwards somersault. 'How you get so much better?'

'By missing it, I guess.'

'Because you gave up everything to come here,' said Hoku, but neither Connelly nor Leimomi could hear him. Connelly was surfing with his whole spirit together again, and it was fast, and slashing and dangerous as a mako shark. It was expressive surfing that you could watch and feel at the same time: just seeing him Hoku understood more about why he had come back than the letter had ever explained. The letter had been all full of ideas like integrity and authenticity, that sounded big but could have signified anything or nothing. Now, seeing, Hoku knew exactly what it all meant: Connelly was going to do whatever he wanted to do from now on, no matter how crazy or stupid-looking or dangerous, and if you got in the way, watch out. Leimomi approved; Leimomi loved anything or anyone that went for broke.

But for Hoku the ripening of a thing, something coming into itself, being for itself, touched straightaway into a bereavement. The wave arches, circles into itself and rolls towards the shore for a few seconds, a few seconds of energy and light and foam between the sun and the sea, and then a warm, sobbing death on the sand, a few last minutes in the sun, before the dark current pulls the last of what is left out to the cold sea. That's what you were made for, to ride a few waves like that, and maybe you shouldn't mind, maybe if you lived like Connelly was living now, you wouldn't mind when your time in the sun was up. Maybe you would feel only gratitude. Maybe it only feels like a loss when you haven't had enough yet, and you should not think about this kind of thing when you are still young. 'Eh, Momi, try let me, these waves too big for you!'

'Outa my way, you fat mahu!' she screamed, determined to match Connelly, angling for the third wave of the incoming set. He watched the horrible scowl of determination on her face change to slack-mouthed shock as she slid down the face of the wave and found herself speeding along out in front of a six-foot mountain. Then Connelly swam over to where Hoku was treading water and kept arching himself around the small of his back, like the shark. Momi cruised up to them, dropping to her knees on the wave's dying breath. 'That's how you're supposed to do it,' she explained, with an arrogance that was partly self-parody, but quite unapologetic. 'You supposed to stay on top of the board, that what it's for.' As she turned back out to sea, Hoku seized the board, turned it over, depositing her and made off down the rip as fast as he could paddle, to catch a few minutes of life in the light.

Leimomi drove them back to the old house, where Hoku still lived. It was quieter and lonelier than ever: Leimomi had taken the dogs and horses, and he had got rid of the chickens in a series of stews, so that what you heard in the mornings was the voice of the wind or the rain, or even, if these were still, the sound of the little stream that came down from the uninhabitable valley behind. Quietness and loneliness were no problem when you were tucked in to the last little corner of land before the slopes stabbed upwards in vertical blades, covered in green tangly scrub, always cool and damp feeling, even in the worst Kona weather. Six months of peace was what you needed, after two years in close quarters with Leimomi. But what would happen now? Was Connelly going to move in? He wouldn't be able to get a military house any more, and Hoku had assumed that he would come and live with him. He'd been practically staying there the last few weeks before he went away. But maybe he wouldn't like it, for permanent. Maybe the place was too falling down. *Haoles* had a low tolerance for that sort of thing. Or maybe he would want a house of his own: Connelly had a streak of touchiness about always looking like a man, and he might be scared of living off Hoku, like some kind of wife. So when he held the door open and said, 'Please think of this as your home from now on, for as long as you want to stay,' it was up to Connelly to decide whether he wanted to hear this as a genuine invitation, or a cliché of Hawaiian hospitality. Connelly gave him the old sweet smile and carried his suitcases in. That was enough of an answer for now, Hoku decided.

Leimomi had stayed for an early supper of teriyaki chicken and beetled off in the jeep as the sun was setting. 'Wasn't that nice of her,' said Connelly, feeling the velvet coolness of the lei between his fingers, and marvelling at the warmth of Leimomi's welcome. 'I know she doesn't like me all that much.'

'No, she like you, she told me,' said Hoku, rather anxiously.

'Well, you could have fooled me. Until today, anyhow.' He suddenly laughed. 'Today I thought she'd never go. Oh, God, I've missed you, Hoku.' He bounced down on the big square bed in the corner. 'I'm only just beginning to realize how much I missed you! While I was away I couldn't even bear to think about... it all. Not until I knew I was coming back. Hey, come on, come over here.' He extended an arm straight out to the side.

Hoku walked quietly over to the arm and put himself under it. He felt tears were very close, and not of joy like they should have been. Something about sadness, maybe about the brief time you have of happiness in the light. Or maybe it was all those months apart, months when, unlike Connelly, he had thought about 'it all' a lot. The time of loss was coming to an end, and that was a loss in itself. Missing someone, wanting him, writing songs about it, that was a kind of having, and it seemed a more permanent possessible thing to Hoku than the brief crest of perfection that was approaching, about to swell up under them, and race out its course, and return to the sea.

They spent the whole next day surfing, and now Connelly was going to have to spend the whole next week peeling and getting some new skin together before he could go out in the sun again. But there were other things he had to do. Open a bank account! Put down some money and get a car! Look for a job! He had to get all these business things going at once! Why go out and look for problems, when enough of them arrived in the mail? Hoku was not sure if worrying about all these bothers was a compulsion or an actual pleasure for him. In Hoku's experience, if you ignored business, even the kind that attacked you through the mail, for long enough, at least half of it went away of its own accord. Or, to put it more accurately, the bills could be rerouted to his father, who had the same first name and anyway was the official holder of the property, and everything else could be thrown away. It was all about having a sense of proportion, he explained to Connelly, of what was important in life and not letting people intimidate you with official letters and so on. He would understand when he had lived a little longer in the islands, when his skin was the right colour, and he had learned to eat sashimi, and cook rice so that it stuck together in perfect snowballs, not all falling all over the place in separate, individualistic crunchy grains.

Then one day they came home to find a black Oldsmobile parked in front of the house, and a man in a tie waiting at the door. 'Abraham Manono?' he asked as they approached.

Hoku eyed him carefully, trying to decide if it was a good idea to be Abraham Manono or not. 'Try go inside while I *kokua* this guy,' he whispered to Connelly. 'I'm Abraham Leleiohoku Manono,' he ventured to say to the visitor. 'If you want just plain Abraham Manono, that's my father. He lives Cleghorn Street.' And then dismissingly, with one of his father's stage smiles, 'Tha-enk you.'

'I'm looking for the Abraham Manono who is the leaseholder of this property,' said the man sternly. 'I'm from the Bishop Estate.'

'Oh,' said Hoku, a little alarmed. The Bishop Estate was the big royal legacy; it held most of the land on the island 'in trust for the children of Hawaii' and he probably owed it some sort of loyalty because it paid for Kamehameha school. But at this stage in his life it was more of an annoyance, responsible for a lot of unpleasant-looking mail, and if they were going to start sending people on top of letters, things might even get worse. He said, with some firmness, 'That's my father you want. Cleghorn Street, the white house, old style, with the fancy lanai. You might just catch him if you hurry.'

'But you are the tenant, the one who lives here?'

Hoku's head went back, and he stood a little straighter. 'Is there a problem?'

'And you're aware of our decision not to renew the lease?'

He turned his face away, up towards the mountains. 'Yes, I read the letters,' he lied.

'So you'll have vacated the property by January the first at the latest?'

'Please discuss this with my father,' said Hoku, walking away from him swiftly, then turning again to add, 'and his lawyer.'

When the man was gone, Hoku went up towards the shed at the top corner of the property, as if he wanted to stagger around crazily under the weight of this blow for a few minutes before Connelly saw him. He was aware of it only as weight, impact; he was conscious that it was not yet pain, but that it soon would be. He went right up to the shed, and leaned into the soft weathered wood as if he wanted to embrace it. He walked blindly to the stream, where the tingle in the air and the sound of the water rinsing over the black rock tapped the current of pain inside. What would happen to the little stream after he had 'vacated the property'? They would make it into a cement canal like down at the beach park. Or maybe force it into pipes underground like a sewer. No, No, this was too much pain for all at once. He ran back down to the house and practically fell on top of Connelly. 'They evicting us.'

Of course Connelly had to have it explained. He didn't even know what the Bishop Estate was, he'd assumed the letters he'd seen in the wastepaper basket were from some sort of church fundraising drive. He found the most recent of these unopened, and began slitting the envelope with his thumbnail, directing a wide-eyed solemn look of disbelief beyond censure at Hoku. 'You need a lawyer.' Then, having read the letter, 'You needed a lawyer.'

'It would not make a difference,' said Hoku, finding his dignity. 'The lease expires, you cannot force them to renew.'

'Tenants have rights.'

'Look all around.' He gestured at the world spilling out from his valley. 'Kahala. Wailupe. All the new subdivisions. And it's all Bishop Estate land, and it all used to be little homesteads like us, and now it's going for the big executive houses for the rich folks. I knew in my heart this was going happen from a long time ago, and not because of reading letters. That's why I never read the letters!' he said emphatically, realizing it for the first time himself.

Connelly seemed to agree that there was not much they could do beyond visiting Abraham Manono Senior, getting his advice and allowing him to get them drunk at the bar of the Pikake Terrace. He didn't have much advice (You cannot win against the Bishop Estate) but Connelly extracted from him the names of a couple of the best law firms in town.

The next morning, or anyway the next day, Hoku watched him unpack his mainland suit. 'You going bake,' he warned. 'No wind this morning, Kona weather coming in. You got one job interview?'

Connelly frowned at him, as if he was screwy. 'We're going downtown to find you a lawyer, remember?'

'Ho, chee, not today. Only thing you can do today is run for the beach.'

'There isn't time.' He had the grace not to point out that Hoku should have got a lawyer months ago, but it was clear enough he was thinking it.

'It's too late already. And there never was a chance anyway.'

'You've got to fight it, on principle, even if you don't have a chance.'

Hoku looked up at the higher reaches of the valley and

sighed. 'You think I'm not fighting because I'm a stupid lazy kanaka, but it's not that.'

Connelly laughed. 'Of course it isn't, but what is it?'

'I don't know. It hurts too much already, and the fight is only going keep opening up that hurt. Better to just decide it's *pau* already, and then it cannot get any worse than this.'

He looked concerned. 'That's fatalism.'

'Well, then, I'm a fatalistic kanaka. Better than stupid and lazy, I guess,' he muttered.

Connelly stood there, trying to digest the attitude for a few minutes before rejecting it. 'Oh look, I just can't let it happen. Will you let me at least try – you don't have to do anything. You just forget about it, and if it doesn't work, well, nothing's lost, and if it does, well, that's great. OK?'

Hoku looked at his face, leaning one way then the other to get a couple of different angles, and finally concluded that the guy really wanted to go downtown in a woollen suit today. And he really wanted to pick a fight with the Bishop Estate. Probably he thought it was just the same thing as any other big company, like Amfac or A&B; he wouldn't have any reverence for the memory of Bernice Pauahi Bishop or Kam school or anything. But if he tried to explain these complicated feelings Connelly would think he was only making more excuses. And anyway, just imagine if he did win, some magical way, just say it happened... The Bishop Estate wasn't going to go bankrupt from not developing this little corner of the valley; you could probably only fit two or three of those big houses on his whole farm. So that was only one or two extra rents they were losing out on. 'OK, go try,' he told Connelly at last. Connelly grinned and jumped into the car and shot off down the track, like a white knight galloping off on a charger. Hoku went inside to lie down. It was too late and too hot already to escape to the beach.

Every day after that for more than a week, Connelly rode off into town, and every evening he came home, all hot, but full of excitement and news. How the first law firm had turned him down, how he later learned they did work for the Bishop Estate. Whoops! How he had walked the streets up and down, searching for an attorney that would take the case 'pro bono', how he had finally met and made friends with a young New York expatriate at 'Smith Wild'. He was unfortunately a tax specialist, but he introduced Connelly to a friend... who was too busy to help. And then there was some other lawyer... it all got confusing but they had lots of lunches together, Connelly and his growing collection of pals. Hoku had this picture of them, sitting in the Hob Nob Restaurant eating club sandwiches, Connelly smiling away like anything. Hoku met a couple of them one day, when he was dragged downtown to an Italianate brown building where he had to sign some papers in front of a notary public. Connelly had introduced him as 'my surfing buddy', a phrase which grew to be the standard explanation of their togetherness. 'You got a lot in common with those people,' he remarked, when they were driving home.

'Not really,' Connelly said. But he sounded a little embarrassed, even evasive.

Each morning during this time while the trade winds were not blowing, Hoku woke up telling himself he was going to go to the beach. Walk down to Kahala. Get the bus to Waikiki. Make Connelly take the bus, and drive himself all around to the leeward side, surf Makaha. But he never did these things. It was the stream he chose to cool off in, slipping and stumbling on the smooth black stone. Wading in the stream you could get higher up the valley, because although small trees and saplings spread over it to make a roof, underneath it was the only interruption in the tangled undergrowth. In the water there were freshwater gobies, little sucker-finned fish guys who fought their way upstream by kissing upwards from rock to rock. So he made his stooping way up to where it came down from the steepness of the mountain as a needle-thin waterfall. As the Kona weather continued, the fall and the stream grew more and more enervated, draining to a trickle.

Maybe it wasn't only the weather. Maybe the stream also knew about the Bishop Estate, and was fatalistic.

And then came the afternoon when he heard the thunder breaking on the other side of the Ko'olau mountains. He came out and looked up at the ridge, and the black clouds around it, big excited-looking clouds, barraging each other this way and that, like a football game was going on up there, the big heavy defensive line determined to keep the storm on the windward side of the island, but getting poked back here and there by the dodging runs of blacker clouds forcing in. Hoku rubbed his skin. 'You should just rain and get it over with,' he told the weather, but the weather was determined to resist, to fight to the last gasp of heat and pressure.

And then Connelly came skidding up in the new car, and came bouncing out, crowing, '"You can't win against the Bishop Estate!"' but sarcastically, triumphantly.

'What happen?' Hoku stood there, just taking in the victory radiating from Connelly's body. Suddenly he laughed and shouted up at the cloud defenders, '*Imua!* Geev um!'

'You'll never believe this,' Connelly was spilling the story out, 'apparently the attorneys from the Bishop Estate heard this rumour that your father had got this shark lawyer from New York, and was going to make a public stink about it, "much loved Island entertainer kicked out of his ancestral home" or something like that. They got scared! Look!' He held up a thin scrap of paper. Hoku came over and squinted at it. A cheque for $4500. 'What's that for?'

'Goodwill. Like compensation, but I guess they don't want to call it that. You know, for the buildings and having to move and everything.'

'Having to . . .' Hoku echoed.

So he had to move.

His father had been fatalistic, Leimomi had been fatalistic, and Hoku had believed that he himself had been culpably fatalistic about the eviction. Now he realized the secret hope, secret even from himself, that he had been pinning on

Connelly's championship. Oh God. And Connelly thought he had won something. 'That's great,' he forced himself to say, and threw his arms around him, because it was the only way of making sure Connelly couldn't see the expression on his face. Above their heads, the offensive clouds fought their way over the razor peaks, and the valley was burdened with drenching rain.

'You could use the money for a down payment on a mortgage,' Connelly said. 'And if I get this teaching job, I'll take care of the weekly payments.'

And it all had to be done double quick when what you really should be doing was saying goodbye to the valley, and not just the personal goodbye of someone who was leaving a place that would remain unchanged in his absence, but the complete and final goodbye you have to say when someone was about to die. Instead they went house-hunting: new houses, old houses, apartments, say hello to the new! Off to the savings and loan to open an account in the name of Abraham Leleiohoku Manono! What next? Life insurance? Then Connelly put on the suit one more time and galloped off to joust for a job at Chaminade College, a big Spanish-looking building a couple of valleys closer to town. It was a Catholic college and the bishop was there for the interview. In addition to teaching psychology and animal behaviour, the post included giving Marital Advice to the students, and the bishop wanted to make sure that whoever got the job wouldn't. Connelly came home looking green and shaky. 'I know I didn't get it. These people always make me feel like I've been caught smoking.'

'Never mind, sweetheart. No big thing,' Hoku consoled him automatically.

'But what are we going to do? We've only got a month!'

'It's OK. We can stay with my Dad, or Auntie Lydia, plus my cousins in Waimanalo, Nanakuli . . . ,' Hoku enumerated his relatives. And it was true, he could command a place to stay with any of them especially his cousins, who valued his skills with children. What wasn't so certain was that they would welcome Connelly. Well, they would want to welcome Connelly, but... It wasn't as if his lover was someone who would just quietly fit in with people's ways. 'Or we could rent or just find someplace cheap out in the country, just a shack, a roof over our heads. Nothing to worry about, sweetheart.' He took Connelly in his arms, but it was his own heart that needed the comfort.

But anyway, he got the job: the bishop trusted him more than the married candidate. And then a little house was found, not far away from the college. A little place way high up in the mountains, a miniature plantation house with a latticed veranda and a wicker swing hanging on chains that broke as soon as Hoku tried it out. This was what told him he had to buy the house; not guilt like when you had to pay for a bottle you broke in Long's, more a feeling that the house had reached out and pulled him into its history, that they were already involved together. And Connelly went bug-eyed when they walked around and saw all the different kinds of fruit that was dropping off the trees: mangoes (hanging over from next door), papayas, bananas ripening suggestively upwards, pomegranates and two different species of avocado. It was practically a farm in its own right, and it just happened for you, and the spaces were either gravel or fine mossy McCoy grass so you didn't even have to mow the lawn. It was not that he felt anything disloyal about Waialae valley, but this new place at least meant he could say, 'Now my new life begins here in this place I share with Connelly: a smaller life maybe but prettier, neater, better controlled, and... finally grown up.' They would pay all their bills themselves. Connelly would get up on time every morning. They would walk outside together and just pick their breakfast. Hoku would drop him off at work, then take the car and go fish anywhere on the island he felt like.

Leimomi came up to view and approved, Dad came up and approved; Auntie Lydia came up and leered approvingly at this 'charming romantic retreat for you two' – and moreover, she was able to teach him the names of all the ferns that grew on the slope up from the house: *'ama'u, uluhe,* lacy *pala'a* which is used for decorating the tables at luaus and great occasions. 'What's that one?' Connelly pointed at the largest of them, dominating the others like a great palm tree.

Auntie Lydia seemed to blink for a moment. 'Which one?' she asked coldly.

Hoku realized she had forgotten the name, but Connelly thought it was her eyesight that was fading. 'This one!' He clambered up the slope and stood beside it as if posing for a photograph with Duke Kahanamoku.

Auntie Lydia narrowed her eyes. 'Oh, that. That is not a true fern. It's a bromeliad,' she dismissed it.

Connelly's mouth fell open: he was there, touching the tree fern's delicate leaf, there were uncoiling fuzzy fronds all round him, looking up he could see the spores on the undersides, silhouetted by the sunlight against the translucence. It was a fern! Hoku stepped behind his aunt's back, gesturing violently at him not to argue, and saying quickly, 'You know what I love most about ferns? The way you can only smell them once. Have you ever noticed? You're out hiking in the mountains, and then suddenly that very sweet smell just fills your head, maybe you just brushed against them without noticing... and oh! so beautiful! And you empty your lungs, and fill them up again, thinking the scent is going to make you faint – only there's suddenly nothing. You can't make it happen. Then you walk along a little farther, and it takes you by surprise again.'

'It's probably to do with the scent receptors in your nose,' said Connelly, crunching down the slope to join them.

Hoku gave him the stink eye. 'Thank you, professor. I thought it was to do with the wisdom about life receptors in the brain, but I was wrong.'

Auntie Lydia could just grace conflict out of existence. She said, 'I'll bring you some root cuttings of ginger and stephanotis to plant around the lanai, so you can sit outside on cool evenings and enjoy.'

'And argue,' said Connelly softly, laughing.

'*Hapu'u!*' said Auntie Lydia, suddenly remembering. '*Hapu'u* is the name of that ... bromeliad.'

Some days Connelly came home from work early enough and they could go surfing in the afternoon. The only trouble was that at that time the waves were already overcrowded with high school kids, and you had to be kind of mean and aggressive to get in on any good wave that showed its head above the south shore winter slush. 'Like driving in New York,' Connelly complained. He had a couple of brushes with trouble, and Hoku had to move in and save him. Usually inflating his shoulders and intoning, 'You like beef?' was enough to scare people off, but he didn't like doing it. It was against his nature, and bad for the sea. So on weekends they went to farther away places, up the Leeward Coast where big swells steamed in from Siberia, or exploring the scalloped deserted bays of the windward side north of Kane'ohe, looking for uncharted breaks off points or reefs. One day Hoku took his friend up to the North Shore to watch (only watch) the huge mountains of water rolling in majestically at Waimea Bay. Their slopes were the purest kind of blue, the blue you can't really believe is an ordinary earthly colour, and the waves themselves had never been violated by a human being on a surfboard. The area around had been sacred ground, and an ancient heiau stood up on the slopes behind them.

'Wow, that's got to be twenty feet!'

'Fifteen-eighteen,' Hoku agreed calmly.

'It's incredible!' They got out of the car and walked down to the shore. Connelly was hopping from one foot to the other, swinging his arms, fizzling with excitement, and then Hoku saw that look on his face. Whoa, big mistake to come here with the boards strapped on top of the car. He seized Connelly by both arms, restraining him from behind, and hissing in his ear, 'That temple up there is a luakini, a human sacrifice heiau. OK, the missionaries closed it down, but this is still that kind of place, and you are not going in that water.' A tour bus came lumbering around the bend and headed up the valley for the waterfalls.

'Hey, ouch, let go! What's got into you?'

'Number one: you are not a good enough surfer. That last Sunday at Makaha wasn't even eight feet and you were just lunch!'

'I know, I know!'

'Number two: that ocean is pure power. It would just crunch your bones – powder *your* bones.' He squeezed Connelly's tiny wrists until he yelped, to demonstrate how easily they could be broken.

'Uncle! I know I can't!'

'Well, then, just calm your insides. Just step outside yourself and see how arrogant you look. "Fresh from his single-handed triumph against the Bishop Estate, Connelly takes on the ancient sacred kapu power of Waimea Bay."'

'It hurts!'

'Oh, sorry.' He picked up the wrist again and apologized to it.

'I mean them.' Connelly threw his eyes out at the waves. 'So beautiful and I can't and it's just not fair!'

Hoku walked away from him and sat down in the sand. He felt disharmonious. Not fair? The ocean wasn't supposed to be fair, and you were just a fool if you expected it to be so. And it was worse than foolish to want to be out there, it was what? greedy? ugly? to want to scramble up and down those unpolluted peaks. Couldn't anything be left alone? Then he felt guilty. Connelly probably couldn't help it. 'Try come here,' he summoned him, and put an arm around his shoulders, and explained, 'If man could surf that break this place would just turn into Waikiki, eh? You should be thanking God some things are unconquerable, not jumping up and down bitching about it.'

'What's got into you, Hoku?' Connelly said again, looking half-worried about him, and half-scared for himself. Hoku breathed in and out a couple of times, then said, 'Too much power in this place and neither of us can handle it right. Better to go.'

But Waimea kept staying with both of them. What a big mistake, going to a place like that, which just opened up everything that was wrong with you, everything that was disharmonious. Everything, Hoku thought, that was too big about him and too small about Connelly. Every night, lying on his back in bed, when Connelly had fallen asleep, he felt these great slow swells of physical heaviness rumbling up his spine, like a dark, resentful ancient power of the earth and under the earth. It wasn't anger, it was less human than that, less merciful, a cold thing.

As for Connelly, well, the crazy thing came home the next Monday night with a set of graduated barbells lifted from the college gym. Suddenly body building was the big thing and surfing 'three finger poi' at Waikiki was a waste of time. If you did manage to get him down to the beach on a weekday it was only for roughwater swimming to build endurance: from the Natatorium at Queen's Surf to increasingly distant marks on the other side of Waikiki. And you could not really complain about it, because Connelly's eyes were always saying, 'If I was six foot three and two hundred pounds...!' As if Waimea cared about six inches or sixty pounds!

'Why don't you just relax?' he finally cried. 'You know, if a miracle happened and you woke up one morning as big as me, within forty-eight hours you'd have burnt yourself back down to your own size again!'

Connelly just laughed and quoted, 'A man's reach must exceed his grasp, or what's heaven for?'

'Yeah. That's right. Ambition makes you small.'

But no, 'If something matters, you have to put your whole heart into it!' He said this at least once a day, or that's what it seemed like, in that flat, dogmatic, 'don't argue with me I'm from New York' voice. And you couldn't argue with it, not really, especially if you suspected you had told him the same thing yourself not much more than a year ago. But what if you had been wrong? Could you really give your whole heart to anything, or anyone? Oh, maybe for a time, but for ever? And what did you mean by 'giving' anyway?

I must stop being disloyal. I must think about the good things instead of the things that are wrong all the time. If I don't stop being critical I'll drive him away; he's smarter and cuter than I am even if he's older, and he could find anyone... what if one of those lawyers was a mahu...? Chee, you'd think I wanted him to go away, the way I keep noticing all the things that bother me... everything's been wrong ever since he came back, maybe he should not have come back. People can be perfect more easily in your thoughts. It's not his fault I lost the farm. But it feels like his fault, and I know it isn't but I cannot get the feeling away.

I never said he had to be perfect, I'm not perfect. I guess he's noticed that too, maybe that's what I don't like.

Imagine the ancient Hawaiians greeting Captain Cook: 'Yes, aloha, we love you, now please go away!' As in, go away before we discover you are not a god, or even, go away before we lose all our land.

They moved in two days before Christmas, and on Christmas Eve a flash-flooding stream of relatives arrived with presents of all kinds of house things: Leimomi brought a television, and Dad brought a huge antique mirror with a golden koa wood frame, ornately carved and only a little termitey, Auntie Lydia turned up with a red and white quilt, handsewn in a classic breadfruit pattern, and the Waimanalo cousins brought a special machine for making popcorn, and the Nanakuli cousins came in a pickup truck with a big round dining table in the back, plus chairs. 'This is incredible!' Connelly exclaimed.

'I guess they realized they were never going to get me wedding presents.'

'God, that's nice!' said Connelly, looking like he wanted to cry.

Even Mama turned up late in the evening, with the old Lapinha, the nativity figurines and things wrapped up in tissue paper, and the stage thing you put them on, tiered like a wedding cake. 'It gives me no joy any more so you might as well have 'em,' was the way she discounted this generosity. She wouldn't stay: Esposito was waiting outside in the car. Hoku set the Lapinha up on a card table against the wall. Some of the figures had come from Portugal more than fifty years ago; and the ones that had been replaced he had broken himself. The Lapinha was just about the only memory of his very early days in his mother's house, before Auntie Lydia had taken charge.

On New Year's Eve, when not just the oriental peoples but the whole neighbourhood was going crazy with firecrackers, and the gutters were lined with tiny scraps of red paper from them, Hoku dug up one of the *pala'a* ferns. He went alone to the Waialae farm and crept up the stream bed, and planted the fern at the highest, most inaccessible point that had any depth of soil. 'Grow here for me,' he told it, and never came back to that place again as a living man.

Sterling sat at the secretary's desk in Wunsche's little corner of the House Office Building, typing a letter to Connelly. He always used the office typewriter for personal correspondence, at least to people like Connelly and Mom, who would know that the bright blue ink was congressional.

The analyst's verdict, believe it or not, is that I've got a 'weak Ego'!!?!!? Of course that's speaking technically. Apparently it explains why I'm unable to contain my impulses the way normal people do. Barbara's pretty disgusted with this; she says it's like having a medical excuse for bad behaviour! I wish I'd been sent to this man when I was in the 3rd Grade! (Dear Miss Baker, please do not punish John for misbehaving in class. The doctor says he has a weak ego and is unable to contain his impulses. Yours, Mrs V. Sterling.)

Actually, once the 1st shock wore off I was pleasantly surprised. I mean, if the ego's weak, it must mean I'm well on my way toward eliminating it altogether. Of course, Dr Varady is 100 per cent against this project! As far as I understand it, what he wants to do is get the ego built back up to Normal Strength. I can't even be analysed in the proper sense of the term until then, because the interpretations and stuff would overbalance me on the side of the unconscious. So I'm only going once a week for now, and he gives me a little pep talk.

Tiger paused. He wanted to make it clear that Dr Varady had also acquitted him of latent homosexuality, without making it clear that he had been worried enough to ask him about it. He took a deep breath, sighed it all out and started a new paragraph.

> It seems the only other problem with me is I've got a case of unresolved transference which I guess is what you were picking up on in Tony's.

Thumps and clatters from Wunsche's private office behind him. Tiger ripped the sheet from the cylinder, folded it swiftly and stuck it in a pocket. When the congressman emerged, his assistant was standing to attention, proffering a manila folder. It contained such information as he had been able to gather on Connelly's old foundation, and the origins and alignments of its current employees. Not a lot; the organization was well protected. 'The files you wanted, sir.'

Wunsche's head circled like a courting albatross's as he endeavoured to focus on Sterling's face. Oh hell, he must have had a bottle hidden in there. Today of all days – the HUAC was in session this afternoon. 'Uh, would you like me to drive you home, sir?'

'Home? Shee-it no. Committee meeting.'

Well, at least he was stringing words together. Sterling tested his motor control by moving the folder off to one side and then the other as he extended it. Wunsche's ineffectual lunges at it decided him. You couldn't entrust the security of the nation and the civil liberties of Connelly's ex-colleagues to a man in that state. 'I'm sorry, sir. No. It's for your own good.'

He had tried to manage things quietly, offering his boss black coffee and suggesting a little nap, but Wunsche, intent on his revenge against Pointdexter, had made a dash for the door, and Tiger ended up having to tackle him to the floor to get his office keys out of his pocket so he could lock the place from the inside. Wunsche fired him four times before he finally fell asleep. Sterling was not particularly concerned. He'd been dismissed like this before, and it was always forgotten in the morning. He phoned Mrs Wunsche, explaining that her husband wasn't well, but not explaining his part in it. When he got home he didn't even mention the incident to Barbara. It was all in a day's work, and ever since Connelly's remarks on the banks of the Potomac, he'd felt a bit protective of poor old Bob.

When he turned up at the HOB the next morning, he discovered that not only did Wunsche remember enough of what had happened to resent it, he also remembered at least one of the firings. 'Get your things and go. Go back to Nevada. You won't find another job in this town.'

It was like a bolt from the blue for poor Barbara, of course. She'd been just settling down with a cup of coffee and the latest *New Yorker*, and had jumped up suddenly with the guilty start of someone who is leafing from cartoon to cartoon before they've even read The Talk of the Town when he came in.

The story had to be told from the beginning. 'But, Tiger,' she wailed, 'the doctor told you to count backwards from one hundred before you did anything impulsive!'

'It wasn't impulsive. It was an act of responsible citizenship.'

She looked at him, shaking her head, then broke down into tears.

Whether or not Wunsche had anything to do with it, there didn't seem to be any other work for him in the Capitol. When the rent they'd already paid on the apartment ran out, Tiger loaded his family into the Pontiac and drove them back across 95 per cent of continental America. The sideboard and other big stuff was freighted ahead of them. They came back to stay at his parents' house, with nothing to show for his adventures back East except the flashier car.

There wasn't any work for him in Reno either, or rather, the kind of career that ought to have been his wasn't easy to embark on at the age of 28, without a college degree. Of course there were always jobs in the casinos, but he was reluctant to go down that road until he was certain that every other path was closed off. He told Barbara it was because he didn't want to embarrass Mom, who was a prominent anti-vice campaigner, by working in the gambling industry while he was living under her roof, but there was more than a little of his own pride in there too.

Then one morning, about a month after they had returned, Barbara insisted he came along with her to drive the kids to school. They had put them back in their little old school by the base, though it was a long way from the senior Sterlings' place: it was important that the children had some kind of continuity, especially Henry. 'At least they're happy to be home,' Sterling observed, watching Caroline racing off with her hair and book bag flying, and Henry making his more sedate way to join a little group in the playground.

Barbara set her shoulders and said, 'Tiger, there isn't any way to say this except bluntly. Colonel Sedlachek and I are in love. I don't want to cheat on you, but I want a divorce.'

It was like playing chicken on your bike versus adults in cars. You know you've been heading for trouble, but when the accident finally happens it is a world-upending shock. Probably pretty soon he would pass out from screaming pain and wake up immobilized alone in a bed, but now all he could feel was a protest at the impossibility of it all. 'You can't be in love with Sedlachek.'

She blushed. 'If you mean because he's just a desk officer and not some kind of dashing lunatic, well, that's what I need right now, steadiness and depen—'

'No, I mean, if you've known someone for six years you don't fall in love with them on the seventh.'

She took a deep breath. 'No. That's true. You see, there was something, just in the air, never acted upon, I don't think we even exactly admitted it to each other — how could we, when you were away? I was glad when we went to Washington because it meant I would be able to put him out of my mind and concentrate on us. And I did, but when we came back and there he was, and there it all was again, only more so. And I — I just can't force myself past my heart any longer.'

For some reason it was easier to feel the romance of her story: the quiet renunciation, the reblossoming after such a distance in time and space. It was as if he had been through all that, and the sunset outcome was something that belonged to him, that he deserved some day. But why? Quiet renunciation, duty before inclination, that wasn't something he had ever been good at. And with whom? You couldn't exactly put Fumiko in that class of things.

Maybe it was just one of those floaters, little pictures of himself as a hermit in Korea, or a kamikaze pilot, things that felt like they came from other lives, previous incarnations or novels he'd never got around to writing. Or maybe it was that the rings of personality were larger, more inclusive than people realized when they talked about being an individual. The things that happened to people around you were shadows you cast: projections, responsibilities, resonances of your story; he kind of knew that anyway. Perhaps all it took was a bit of expansiveness to be able to feel them too. Expand, he instructed the surface membrane of his soul.

'Tiger, what's wrong?'

'Nothing. Just dissociating.' Quickly, with instinctive guilt, he attempted to seize hold of his own perspective on all this. Dr Varady would be saying that thinking about philosophy when Barbara was talking about a divorce was the worst kind of bad faith.

But she heard the shrink-speak as an accusation. 'Tiger, I know it's going to hurt and I'd stop it if I could, but I can't and it's just one of those situations where you'd say that to apologize would just be an insult.'

This put him back in touch with his own perspective, effectively enough. The impossible was happening. Impact registered before pain, that was something he remembered from his childhood career in self-destruction. But this impact just kept going on and on, as if his body was being slammed, repeatedly, into a wall. He tried pulling back into disbelief again. There had to be something he could do or say to make Barbara change her mind. She kept telling him there wasn't. The only explanation she could give was that it was about 'security', but she got angry when he interpreted this as economic.

Tiger suddenly couldn't stand looking at the school

playground for another minute. 'Let's get outa here,' he said, but Barbara jumped out of the car as soon as he touched the key in the ignition.

'Please,' she said. 'Let me drive.'

Sedlachek was going to rent an apartment for her and the children to live in until the divorces were through and the new ceremony had taken place. They would be moving on Saturday. She said, 'I'll tell the children, but I don't think I could face your parents.'

'Mom'll behave,' he said. 'If she says anything, she'll probably take your side.'

'It's not what your Mom will say, it's what your Dad won't. Please don't tell them until after I'm gone.'

Neither of them wanted to have to go back to his parents' and act normal before they had to. Barbara decided to go shopping, and Tiger went for a blind walk around the centre of town.

Three days after she moved in to what still felt very much like Evie's house, Barbara was startled to receive a visit from Tiger's father. 'Oh! Come in!' She managed to make her voice sound cordial but was conscious that she had gone very pale and probably looked almost as frightened as she felt.

'Only if it's no trouble.'

'Of course not. Please.' She stepped back. Michael removed his straw Stetson and entered. He took a seat in the ugly old rocking chair, his long legs folding up at an acute angle with every creak forward. Barbara got him a cup of coffee. Just stay calm, she instructed herself. Be calm and pleasant and don't say anything about Tiger.

'Thank you,' he said, when she joined him. And then, 'Well . . .' in a tone that claimed the floor and saved her having to make conversation. But it was a long time, more than a minute, before he spoke again. 'What happened?'

She found herself replying, 'I bumped into Arthur one day

and when he heard about what happened, why we were back, he wasn't going to take no for an answer. He's...he's very attached to the children, you know, and...' But this train of thought led to a criticism of Tiger, so she abandoned it. 'And he went straight back and asked Evie for the divorce, and he's taken a lot of stick —'

'Yes, I can imagine she didn't go quietly.'

'And with him having made that sacrifice, I couldn't really...'

'No, you couldn't really do anything else,' he agreed.

She looked up at him. He smiled. 'Virginia wouldn't have gone quietly either.'

This was pretty shocking, but as he was looking off into the distance and not talking directly to her, it was easy enough to pretend she hadn't heard it.

Coming back to the present, he asked her how the children were settling, and how her mother was coping on her own. Then, just as he was getting up to go out, he observed that 'the Tiger' had been known to throw a punch when frustrated.

By the time she was able to answer it was too late to deny anything. 'Not — since Korea.'

'I was just wondering if I should stick around when the children were visiting him.'

'Oh no, never the children!'

'Har-hum. Oh well, I guess that's something.'

One morning, after two months in which he had been powerless to do anything, productive or destructive, Sterling got out of bed in a different mood, and by the end of the day he had a job dealing blackjack at the Silverlode and an informal assurance from an old colleague of his father's that there would be a place for him at the University of Nevada, Reno, next semester. He had already decided to major in history. English was too saturated with images of Barbara. They would carry over his credits from his freshman year at Stanford; he could graduate in three years' time. 'Eleven years late,' he told mom, to save her making the calculation herself.

The Years of No Sleep (Dad's name for them) passed with all the speed time can, when you live without ever having the time to wake up to yourself and wonder how you are and what you're feeling about it all. Sometimes, on his Sundays with the kids, dragging them on a Long March in the Sierras, the beginnings of a protest would float up: what was he doing? The hills and the high skies and the sagey desert were real life, and he was shutting them out, locking himself into prisons of unreality, dark red casino glare or lecture hall fluorescence. Then the kids would start to complain, and the moment would be lost. The children (Hal, especially, of course) did not like the great outdoors. Tiger bullied them up hills and through gullies to see the place where Grandma Sterling shot the wildcat or the haunted cabin of Boss-Eyed Mike, because that was what good fathers did, but it didn't work for him the way it had for Dad.

What Hal and Caroline liked was being driven through the neon to the casino restaurant for dinner, and the glamour of knowing he worked there in one of those fancy suits with a bow tie, like someone in a movie. They had to learn every fancy shuffling trick and dealer's mannerism going. They liked stocking up on complimentary decks of cards and ashtrays and matchbooks with the flamboyant Silverlode logo on them. Tiger had no doubt that Sedlachek sneered when they came home with these treasures. Let him. Seeing the casino from the kids' point of view as a cave of wonders was better for his ego than seeing it as a boring and degrading if not immoral employment.

It even had its moral side. One summer evening, as Sterling was stepping out the casino back door after an early shift, inflating his lungs and stretching his eyes to take in the last intense gentian blue in the sky, somebody grabbed his shoulder from behind, instructing him to 'Come here, you'.

He spun around to deliver a straight punch from his shoulder, and then there were more people – about eight, it seemed. All he could feel as he fought was an enormous exhilaration, pride and pleasure even as he was being knocked to the ground. It was such a relief that his instincts had led him to fight back. Ever since Connelly had floored him at Tony's, he'd been haunted by a fear that events had turned him into a physical coward.

He was expecting to be robbed but his assailants (there were only four of them in fact) strong-armed him back into the casino and down a flight of stairs to a room he'd never seen before. He guessed it must be near the vault where they counted the take every night. There was a big wooden table in the middle of the room, with two strange men sitting behind it, one bald and dark-suited, the other younger and more bohemian-looking, though perhaps the turtleneck sweater and long hair were worn to conceal an extensive ugly yellow and pink burn scar that rose from his neck to cover the lower left side of his face.

Sterling was invited to stand in front of them, and when he had finished wiping the blood from under his nose, the older man introduced himself as Jimmy Plischke. He was the new casino manager, he said, in a Midwest twang. He was here to clean the place up. 'Turn out your pockets.'

Sterling placed his car keys, his wallet, and a loose forty-five dollars on the table. 'That's from tips,' he indicated the cash, hoping he didn't sound nervous.

Plischke shrugged; a dealer was entitled to his tips, and forty-five dollars was hardly excessive. 'Take off your shoes.' There weren't any Silverlode chips in his shoes. Nor were there any concealed pockets in his jacket, shirt or trousers. Sterling stood there, half-dressed but vindicated. Plischke demanded, 'What'd you fight back for if you were clean?'

'Combat reaction, I guess.'

The dark man beside Plischke spoke for the first time. 'Looks like you've found one, Diogenes.'

The next night he turned up to find he was just about the only survivor of the inspection, and that he'd been promoted two jumps up the ladder, to floor manager. Apart from a few waitresses, the casino was being run by new faces, most of them from out of town, by the sound of things. Frank Gandy, the casino owner, must have decided he needed to take drastic measures to clean the place up. It shouldn't been have surprising: skimming was an accepted practice among his fellow employees, and the higher they got, the more they stood to make.

Tiger turned the episode into a moral fable for the kids. 'Everyone at work used to make fun of me for being a square, but I had the last laugh.'

'So the good guy is finally allowed to come out on top?' asked Dad, who had been listening. He wore a significant, but kind of amused look. 'I'd been wondering how long it would take you to decide to write yourself a happy ending.'

Tiger snorted. 'I just think it's kind of ironic that someone who's probably just one step up from a gangster by the look of things cares about honesty, while someone like Wunsche fires you for it.'

★

In January 1959 Mom had a stroke. She recovered enough to discover she was half-paralysed and unable to speak, then, with her usual forthright decisiveness, had another and died. Dad stayed in the flatlands long enough to hear the will and put the big house on the market, then went up to spend the rest of his life as a hermit in the cabin by the lake. Tiger chose to treat the business of giving away her possessions, sorting out furniture and finding an apartment of his own as complications that only made conscious reflection more impossible than ever.

By the time three years was over, when he had his BA and his feet back on the bottom rung of the Carson City ladder, in the Enforcement Division of the State Gaming Control Board, he was so used to living at this speed that he figured there was no reason to stop. It wasn't worth commuting from Reno, so he moved to an apartment near his new office. There weren't a whole lot of casino jobs in Carson City, but Plischke had warmly recommended him for some evening work in a two-building ghost town out in the country. The Flying D Saloon, his new employer, was a decaying ranch house with a bar, a few slots, a blackjack table, and a back room for private poker. It was a small place, further dwarfed by Annie Oakley's, the cathouse next door, with its ornate, Carpenter's Gothic façade painted intense lavender.

Apart from the occasional single-drink patrons stopping by on the way in or out of Annie Oakley's, the Flying D was so quiet that Sterling began to wonder whether he had simply been hired to keep the proprietor, a German immigrant called Manfred Vogel, company through the long winter evenings. The first three nights he worked there nobody dropped a bet, or placed so much as a quarter in a slot. On the fourth day a party of three arrived, going straight into the poker room at the back. Vogel made up a tray of drinks swiftly, and carried replacements back at anxious fifteen-minute intervals. At eleven the players emerged, two going straight out, the third stopping in front of Sterling's table, asking Vogel, 'Who's your new man?'

'He is from the Silverlode. Cousin Jimmy recommends him.'

Tiger, reacting badly to being discussed in the third person, raised his chin to stare the patron in the eye. He was slightly thrown by seeing a face he remembered, but couldn't place immediately. Dark complexioned, fairly young, disfigured by a burn scar – where would he have known someone like that? The camp? The army? The Los Alamos of the Human Brain? It was the not-quite stranger who made the identification. 'Oh, that's right. Operation Diogenes. That's fine, Manny.' Then he threw a wad of bills on the table. 'Three hundred.'

Sterling passed him the chips; he staked it all on a single hand, played perfunctorily and lost. A thirty-dollar tip slipped to Sterling, a 'Wiedersehen' to Manny, and he was gone.

'Who was that?' he demanded of his boss.

'We will just call him der Stammgast, I think.'

Sterling obediently called him der Stammgast, imitating Vogel's thickened 'shtam' sound. The Stammgast came to the Flying D once or twice a week, sometimes with Jimmy Plischke, sometimes with other people, always with the tough little fireplug of a bodyguard, one of Tiger's Operation Diogenes assailants. At the end of every evening he always made a three- or four-hundred-dollar lay-down bet. Initially Tiger thought it was an extravagant way of paying Manny for the complimentary drinks. Later he decided that the Stammgast was keeping him in business, for his own purposes. God knows, the joint wouldn't have survived without him.

The Flying D was not the kind of place you could bring your kids to dinner. The one time he had driven them out to the little ghost town, Caroline had fallen in love with the lavender curlicues of Annie Oakley's exterior, and sulked when he refused to take her inside. 'When I grow up I'm going to live in a house like that.' 'Over your father's dead body.'

It was in some ways just as well that he couldn't see as much of them. The divide between the two halves of his life was growing, and with it an uneasy sense that the two extremes would not sit very happily next to each other if anything brought them forcibly together. From nine to five on weekdays he typed up dossiers on prospective casino owners and key employees, hunting for felonies and undesirable associates. The entire transcript of the Kefauver Committee Hearings on Organized Crime was hammered into his memory. From eight to midnight most evenings he sat keeping Manny company, very actively not knowing anything about the Stammgast and Plischke apart from the fact that they were generous people who valued honesty in their key employees. It was best not to see the two jobs stereoscopically, as separate activities connected by a shared actor. It was sensible not to let Manny know he was daylighting in 'Enforcement' and probably not a good idea to admit that he was moonlighting as a dealer at the office. Keeping himself busy and tired, he was able to cease to be a subject again, fading into a perpetually moving verb. As a state of mind it shared many advantages of the way of things Before Connelly, and the added one that nobody seemed to find it pathological.

Then a couple of things happened together. A job on the second rung of the Carson City ladder came up; he applied for it and failed. He was shrugging it off, telling himself he was used to knocks by now, but when he met the guy who got it, a 23-year-old straight out of college, he was ready to quit in disgust. Luckily the boss wasn't there to be resigned at, but he walked out of the office in a very public temper, scattering or destroying anything that got in his way. At home he phoned Manny to say he was sick, got drunk until he nearly was, and wrote a long letter to Connelly.

This last was a *really* desperate measure, as he hadn't sent anything other than Christmas cards and change of address notes since he'd come back to Nevada, not wanting to admit to the divorce to the Great Seducer. Now he had to, and the backlog of failure generated a stunningly self-pitying letter. He mailed it while he was still drunk, regretted it when he was sober, and was astonished when it produced a result.

Two weeks later a letter came from Connelly, saying he was

heading back East in the spring, and maybe he could break his journey and they could meet up. His own 'approximation to domestic bliss' (Tiger took this to mean that he had not actually gotten married and wondered if this was for reasons of colour) had also failed. As for the job, well, he was sorry, but was career success, getting ahead just for the sake of it, what Tiger really wanted? And anyway, Tiger should face the fact that he was never going to rise through the ranks of anything, because he was an insubordinate cuss and sooner or later there would always be a McKenna or a Wunsche above him, mediocrities who didn't appreciate too much talent or passion in their underlings. He hoped he didn't sound ruthless. He was trying to be dispassionate about things in his own life, trying to keep a hold on what really mattered. Integrity, not success. Love? Maybe, but probably in ways that were more to do with pain than happiness. He was sorry this was such a depressing letter; he was to tell the truth probably rather drunk, but what the hell, he was yours truly Connelly.

The effect of the letter was actually far from depressing. It wasn't that he was glad Connelly's old lady had left him, it was just the way it confirmed that kind of thing could happen to anyone. And of course it was much pleasanter to see yourself as talented and insubordinate than a has-been at 34. A sense that he was going to start putting his life to work for him, that he was going to take control of his own destiny, had started to grow inside him. Connelly was right. He had to be his own boss.

Everyone at the office was fixated on the Giancana–Sinatra affair, but the fact remained that the Cal–Neva Lodge on the stateline up at the Lake was doing good business, and Frank Gandy's new Silverlode Tahoe was reputedly booming. Why not start his own little venture up there? He could live at the Lake all year round, and keep an eye on Dad, who wasn't getting any younger.

It was a Thursday in the middle of February: snow was forecast, and no one was taking the risk of driving the desolate miles for twenty minutes of simulated human warmth at Annie Oakley's. Manny didn't expect the regular guests, and had initiated a 'spring clean' and stocktake. Tiger was balancing on a stool to dust the upper shelves behind the bar, occasionally fortifying his fantasies, no, his *plans* of starting his own operation with a little sniff or taste of the strange and colourful liqueurs that were kept so far out of reach.

Mom had left him a little money. Joe was investing it for him at the moment, but there was nothing to stop him asking for it back. Most of his share of her legacy was tied up in trust for the children, and there were a lot of ferocious trustees (including Barbara) patrolling it to make sure he didn't get hold of it and do something Impulsive. But it was just possible that he could get Dad to talk them into investing in his project. And if he could put together a really professional prospectus, maybe Joe and Vanessa would stake him. Who knew? Maybe Connelly had some funds, and would want to come in as a partner, now that he also seemed to be at a loose end in life.

Twenty minutes later than usual, headlights swung round the room through the front window, announcing the arrival of the Stammgast's party. 'Get down!' Vogel ordered, hurrying to the door to welcome them. Tiger, mindful of his character as an insubordinate cuss, obeyed slowly, with an unwitnessed show of languid disdain.

What came through the door woke him up instantly. First of all, Frank Gandy, and that was surprising enough: Tiger had never seen him with the Stammgast before, though the connection, via Plischke, was implicit. Gandy was noisy and good-natured, a big fat fellow, with a body like a balloon on little dancing feet, the life and soul even when there wasn't much of a party, and as he squeezed past the door and into the space of the room he threw his arm around the shoulder of a pallid-looking steel spectacled man, whom Sterling recognized instantly as William Naylor.

Naylor was not his actual boss in 'Enforcement', but the man who should have been, the one who had turned him down for the senior case clerk's job. Instinctively, Tiger spun round making very busy at polishing the mirror behind the shelves. Through it he could see Naylor, too involved with Gandy to notice Sterling as he walked past. Manny was dancing attendance and creating something of a screen. The Stammgast followed, with a faint air of indolent irritation, his head tipped back, eyes straying heavenwards. Tiger imagined Gandy was getting on his nerves.

When they were all safely closed in the back room with their first tray of drinks, Sterling turned to Manny. 'I quit,' he said, and drove back to Carson City through the snow.

Connelly's visit was in April, and a lot had happened by then. Sterling had come to pick him up at the airport in Reno, and as he strode out to the arrival gate he felt as if he was giving off little electric sparks of excitement. It was only with difficulty that he restrained himself from running up and down the broad bright corridors as he had once run up and down the Capitol steps. It had been such a long time since anything good had happened to him, and even longer since he'd had anything to boast about, but now he had plenty, and topping it all off beautifully, here was his ideal audience arriving just in time to hear all about it!

Through the panoramic window at the gate he could see Connelly disembarking: a self-contained, casually dressed figure that caught the eye before all the weekend gamblers and suited business travellers. As he came closer Sterling observed that he now wore a quiff in his hair, and he laughed out loud: still the kid among grown-ups! As the passengers filed through into the building Sterling was there to launch himself at Connelly, seizing his hand, grabbing his whole arm and hugging it, nearly knocking him over and causing a domino effect all the way back down the line.

'Oh God, Tiger, you haven't changed a bit!' exclaimed the victim.

He only had his carry-on baggage, so they were able to go

straight out to the parking lot. 'Ho! Chee! Da old car!' His New York accent had gone native.

Tiger laughed some more. He hadn't really stopped laughing since the plane had come in. 'I'm sentimental about cars. I drive them till they die and I'd bury them in the back yard if I could. But there's a lot of years left in you, ain't there, old girl?'

Connelly hadn't eaten on the plane; the trip from San Francisco was just about long enough for complimentary peanuts, but no more. 'I'll take you to the Goldrush,' Sterling decided, with a magnanimous wave of his hand. It was obviously the best place in town.

'Am I all right like this?' Connelly asked. The things he was wearing came somewhere on a spectrum between low budget and beatnik. 'I didn't bring a tie or anything. All my big cases are in a locker at SFO.'

'The way it works is, we pay them to eat there, so they don't get to tell us how to dress.'

'That's a way of looking at it.'

'Reno's not too big on dress codes. Why should you put on a tie to throw your money down the slots?' With a flush of pleasure, Sterling savoured the way the wheel of fortune had turned since Washington. They had changed places. Now he was the smart aleck, the one who knew the score and even, despite his remarks, the one with the hipster dress sense, unconsciously copied from *Ocean's Eleven* and the Stammgast.

As they entered the high-vaulted dining room – it was a kind of mix of the Winter Palace and some mining town bordello – the head waiter greeted him by name and showed them to what was probably one of the best tables, beside the great gilt fountain in the centre of the room. It seemed incongruous when Tiger insisted they have the ribs; all this gold and crystal and damask and they were going to eat with their fingers? But most disturbing of all to Connelly was the cognitive dissonance induced by seeing Sterling so glad and at home in it all. He thought of that first morning in Tripler, that first evening in Tony's, and wondered what had happened.

When the waiter left them alone, Tiger felt Connelly's eyes on him: they were smiling but puzzled, and maybe, behind that, there was a touch of wistfulness. 'Well, you'll never guess what's been happening!' he said.

'Something has been, obviously.'

'Uh-huh.' He leaned forward and lowered his voice to a level that would be drowned by the plash of the fountain to all but Connelly, and said, 'For the past four years I've been working for a gangster!'

'What?' – and this was loud enough for everyone in the restaurant to hear. There was an edge of fear in it, and perhaps he was as frightened for Tiger's ideals as for his personal safety.

In the undertone: 'You heard me. Enrico Calise. He's the point man for the Kansas City syndicate, and he's the hidden owner of three of the biggest casinos in Nevada.'

'Oh, Tiger,' Connelly laughed with relief. 'There isn't a syndicate in Kansas City.'

'There is so. It's a branch of the Chicago outfit.'

He was interrupted as Connelly insisted on singing as much of Everything's Up To Date in Kansas City as he could remember. And then conversation was further delayed by the arrival of a high-piled bust-and-blonde hairdo, mounted on legs just two inches too short for the evening's show, bearing a misty bottle of champagne and the house's compliments. 'Enjoy your evening. Mr Sterling,' she giggled. 'Lola and I finish at six if you and your friend are looking for company.'

Connelly held onto the table and kept the room steady while Sterling fluted away half of the house's compliments. When he looked up for air he said, 'Say Uncle, and admit that Kansas City is the Fourth Rome.'

'Uncle and Kansas City is the Fourth Rome. But...how? Why?'

Well, he had to go back to the beginning, and all that about the Silverlode, and what he had seen that snowy evening at Manny's – 'at which point I couldn't ignore things any longer.

When I was back at the office on Monday morning I started looking into Frank Gandy.

'Gandy is the kind of guy the gaming regulators like. He's an old-time Nevadan – his dad was a drinking buddy of Grandma Sterling's, I believe, and Louisa Gandy was in one of my mother's clubs. Popular fellow, a Jack Mormon, you know, best of both worlds, he's a bit of a lush, but the Elders still have a soft spot for him as one of their own. And he built the original Silverlode, which used to be the grande dame of the Reno casinos, until this place got built (what was it? year after I came home from Washington?... fifty-five, that's right). The poor old Silverlode was looking her age by then, and the entire staff was on the take, like I said, until out of the blue this guy Plischke came in and plugged the leaks. Within a year, Gandy had opened a grand new Silverlode up at Lake Tahoe, and had bought another big casino, the Jack of Diamonds, in Vegas. And I guess, if anyone thought anything of it, they assumed, like I had, that it was the upped profits after Operation Diogenes that funded the expansion.

'Only it wasn't. Not on the paper that was filed in Carson City. The take from the Silverlode the twelve months after the night I got searched in the basement room was up four and a half thousand dollars.' This was accompanied with a loftily dismissive sweep of the arm that let Connelly know this was peanuts to the new Sterling. 'Gandy's income for that year was $57,000, same as his tax return said. And when I looked a little deeper into the Silverlode Group accounts, it turned out the Tahoe and Vegas ventures were entirely funded by an unsecured loan of two and a quarter million, from something called "Cachet Capital Partners". The loan had been made in June of fifty-seven, the same month Plischke took over management of the casino, and nowhere in the books for the three years following was there anything that could possibly have been a payment on that debt. If you're following me, you'll be arriving at the conclusion that Plischke was repaying it with interest, from the proceeds of a skim, or rather, that the

Cachet partners were the hidden owners of the place.

'It was important to me to play fair, so at this point I went to my boss and Naylor, and just laid this out to them: "Isn't this suspicious?" Their line was, "We're here to keep the real mobsters out, not to pick on indigenous Nevadans. Gandy's a respected, humanitarian guy; he's done a lot for charity, that new children's hospital wouldn't have been built except for him." You know – ' with a despairing little laugh, 'Are we talking about the same guy? Frank, not his brother Mahatma?

'So I went away and did some research on my own. Chased up this "Cachet Capital Partners". It turned out to be a division of another company, UPF Holdings, which was shelled up in something else. There was a bad moment when I thought I'd lost the trail in the Dominican Republic, but that was a red herring and eventually I traced it all to a little investment house based in Kansas City. The fund manager was Henry Calise.

'Well, of course I had heard of Rico Calise. In fifty-five the Gaming Control Board turned him down for a licence to redevelop the old Moose Lodge as a casino – the site Gandy had turned into the Tahoe Silverlode. When I first started at the office I personally spent a lot of time typing stuff up against his appeal. I knew a lot about this guy: he was an Annapolis graduate, he'd served on the USS *Mount McKinley* at Inch'on, and had been decorated for his part in fighting an explosion on the *Midway*. But then I also knew that when he came home from the China Sea he and his brother-in-law had shot up a restaurantful of rival gang members, and ran the city between them after that. The FBI had been keeping close track on him, and I'd seen some transcripts. I had this very disconnected, very intimate knowledge of parts of his life; the bedroom stuff, the suicide attempt, but I didn't know his face... didn't know that I knew his face. He was the Stammgast.

'Once I had the paper connection that matched up to what I'd seen the last night I worked at the Flying D, I went directly to Grover Gibson, the head of the Enforcement Division, and showed him what I'd found, and told him what I'd seen. He promised to look into it. I waited three weeks. Nothing happened. I went back and got the line about indigenous Nevadans again. I mean, what is this Gandy? A Washoe Indian? So I quit, but I took home copies of all the files on the Silverlode group, and I wrote up the whole story, and took it to an old high school pal of mine who's just made editor of the *Morning Post*.' Tiger sighed, arriving at the fulfilment of the story, 'and he's been serializing it.'

'Well,' Connelly had to admit. 'I'm impressed. I don't think I understood more than 50 per cent of it, but I'm impressed. You'll have to let me see a copy of your article when we get home.'

'Hm,' Tiger grunted, and extracted a wad of clippings from an inner pocket. He had brought them for the occasion, but he couldn't help going red as Connelly unfolded them, especially when he discovered the third piece, which was decorated with an exaggeration of the Sterling profile, imbedded in the figure of Don Quixote, by the house political cartoonist. The inevitable windmill was labeled THE MOB for the benefit of *Post* readers who needed things spelled out, and Sancho Panza, saying 'Giant? What Giant?' was STATE REGULATORS.

'Cute,' said Connelly.

'That's what Barbara said.'

Quickly, 'I just meant the idea. In real life your nose isn't anywhere near that... small.'

'They're giving me a weekly column, to chase up other cases like this.'

'But that's brilliant, Tiger! No, I'm not being sarcastic. You've found your niche, the only job where people will pay you to be a stubborn and insubordinate cuss – a muck-raking journalist.'

'Yeah, well... The only problem is what I'm going to do for material when this seam plays out. I'm not an insider any more, I've alienated everyone back at Carson City, they've been making it hard for me to even get hold of records I'm perfectly entitled to as a member of the public.'

'I think I'd be even more worried about the guys from the other side of things.'

'Oh, yeah, I expect Calise wants me dead,' he said, waving his hand as if it was hardly worth mentioning. 'I have to keep one step ahead of his goons, but... I don't know, it's the kind of thing I enjoy.'

Their plates of ribs arrived, with all kinds of extras they hadn't ordered, and more champagne, until Connelly began to find it all oppressive. 'This is ridiculous. We couldn't finish all this in a week. What are they doing it for? Is it to bribe you not to start looking into their finances when you run out of stuff on the Silverlode?'

Sterling shook his head, looking displeased. 'It's just the way it works, it's just a sign of respect. I'll take care of them before we go, I won't be in their debt.' Connelly was looking at him with his chin twisted up combatively. Why was he blowing so hot and cold, one minute impressed, the next critical? Tiger didn't mind the sarcasm, he recognized that as a little gentle jealousy, a tribute in a way. But he didn't like the feeling that he was having to defend himself. 'It's a different way of thinking, Connelly, and it's not corrupt in its own terms, it has its own kind of honesty. There was one week when Calise didn't come into the Flying D at all, he just sent Vella, the little bodyguard, with the usual money. The next week the two of them came, and Vella was white and shaking. "Did he place a bet last Wednesday?" Calise asks me. "Yes, sir, I believe so." "How much?"

'It was obviously one of his Diogenes things. I got out the count book and showed him where it said $440. Vella was so relieved he wet his pants. Really. I guess he'd been scared that I might have pocketed it, and he would have taken the blame. But Calise was frowning. "What's the forty? Why'd you bank the forty? That was supposed to be your end." He was shouting at me – for not taking my cut. And I was apologizing and making excuses: it was all there in a single roll, it had been put down as one bet. He turned back on Vella again. "What are you, some kind of motherfucking cave man? You grow up in one of those houses with pictures of fucking deer on the walls? You put this guy on the spot because you don't know how to lay down a civilized bet and treat people the way they're entitled to be treated. *Everybody has to get their end.*"

Connelly smiled. 'I suspect you've actually got a sneaking admiration for Calise.'

'Nothing sneaking about it. I've got a whole lot more respect for him than I've got for Naylor.' He looked directly at Connelly. 'But it's nothing to do with my "end" of his operation. Which must have amounted to a couple of thousand dollars, but it didn't stop me from writing the article.'

The ruins of the feast were cleared away to make space for a Baked Alaska they hadn't ordered and couldn't eat. Tiger lit up a cigarette over it, shook his head and said, 'Connelly. The fact that I've got an ego that's been starved from 1949 until about four weeks ago isn't really an excuse for the way I've been hogging the floor. Tell me about yourself and kick me under the table if I open my trap again.'

Connelly blinked and sighed his way through a fog bank of reluctance that made it impossible to find anything to tell, and finally blurted, 'I'm going to join a Carmelite monastery in upstate New York.'

Tiger stared and stammered, 'A – what?'

'A monastery. The Carmelites.'

'They the ones who don't speak?'

Connelly folded his arms into imaginary robe sleeves, put his eyes into the custody of the middle distance, and finally shook his head.

'But why?' Tiger cried. 'You of all people! And anyway, I had you figured for an agnostic.'

'That's right, I was and probably still am.' The wistful look that had been haunting his admiration and suspicion of

Sterling's adventures was now in undisputed possession of his face. He sighed and pushed his plate away. Tiger said gently, 'Is this because the escape plan went wrong?'

'Maybe. I'm trying to be more dispassionate than that, but yeah, probably.' The total bleakness that can swamp you if you start thinking about the wrong kinds of things on top of a large meal in the middle of the day threatened him; he made an effort to lean forward and be brave and admit to Sterling that it was more than that.

He tried to explain it in terms of the waves, the things that fifteen-foot surf can do to your soul, and not just by forcing you to think about your own insignificance and your own death, but the power and the caressing softness of that warm ocean, the aliveness in it or behind it, and how it made you want nothing more than to lie listening to the pulse in its breast, and just cause yourself to dissolve into it. He tried to explain about Gloria's visit out there to him, and her Salinger-induced religious crisis; how she'd brought back a copy of the old brainwashing report that she'd filched from work, and had latched onto certain evocative phrases, attributed to one of the prisoners. Was he a real person? Could Connelly direct her in his direction? Or was he, as she really suspected, just a 'Seymour Glass', a fictional vehicle for some of Connelly's own mystical discoveries? In which case would he please initiate her into his spiritual discipline?

She wouldn't listen to his denials, but luckily actions spoke louder than words and she hadn't spent long there before realizing Connelly was no closer to enlightenment than she was. 'And the upshot of it all was that she introduced me to St John of the Cross. Here. Look at the cartoon I keep in my pocket.' He fished out his billfold and extracted a strange little diagram, drawn in pencil on lined paper. It was a picture of something like a thick-stalked mushroom or maybe a stumpy phallus, with illegible scribblings all over and around it. Sterling squinted at the uncouth thing for a minute, then turned bewildered, pleading eyes on Connelly.

'Oh, *listen* to it,' he said, embarrassed and feigning irritation. 'Do you understand Spanish? Never mind.' He flipped it over and read from the translation on the back, 'To reach satisfaction in all, desire satisfaction in nothing. To come to the knowledge of all, desire the knowledge of nothing. To come to possess all, desire the possession of nothing. To arrive at being all, desire to be nothing.' He breathed in deeply, rolling his head around to look at the fountain spray glittering in the spotlights, at the chandeliers and the gold *trompe l'œil* mouldings, at the soggy baked floating in the melted puddle of Alaska, then intoned, 'Nada, nada, nada, nada, nada, nada, e aun en el monte nada.'

Although he knew, or felt that he ought to know, why Connelly was reading him this, Sterling chose to say, 'But... what's it all about?'

'Don't you even remember what you used to call your project?' Connelly wailed. 'Finding complete psychological freedom? Well, this is it. "In this nakedness the spirit finds its quietude and rest, for in coveting nothing, nothing tires it and pulls it up, and nothing oppresses it by pulling it down, for it is in the centre of its humility."' He spread the paper out on the table, turning it around for Sterling to see, saying urgently, 'This is the map. These are complete instructions, for those to use who can. This, Tiger, is the only real Escape Plan.'

Sterling looked at him with conflicted pity. Connelly, having broken past his embarrassment, raced on. 'I know it probably sounds baroque and Catholic to you. But can't you see what it's saying? Get rid of the cravings – without being a puritan. Get rid of the guilt, without being a libertine. Don't allow yourself to get trapped in being any one thing. It's the *subtractive process*! Don't you even remember the person who said, "I just know I'm never going to be free or happy until I get rid of the apparatus of the ego"?'

Tiger bowed his head and lit a cigarette. When he found his voice, all he could say was, 'Connelly. That was a long time ago.'

★

There wasn't anything to be gained from staring into the distance they had travelled from each other. Sterling paid the bill and all the tips, and on the way out paused at the first card table he saw to lay down a civilized bet, with a stylized spoiling of a good hand that Connelly strongly suspected was copied from the mobster Calise.

Coming from the air-conditioned semi-darkness of the casino into the heat and glare of a desert city downtown was kind of hard. Sterling asked half-heartedly if his guest wanted to see any sights: The Silverlode, or the 'Big Top'? Or maybe the Catholic Cathedral? Connelly said he just wanted to go home and sleep off the jet lag and the champagne. So Sterling drove him to his 'home' of the past thirty-six hours, a red-roofed motel of the inexpensive but clean variety, located miles away, in the outskirts of a neighbouring town, a drab settlement badly misnamed Sparks. 'I keep moving,' he explained. 'No point in making it easy for Vella to come and find me.'

He let Connelly into what had been a plain clean double bedroom before he had moved in. Now the floor was littered with discarded clothing, every available surface was covered in papers and files, and on the bureau was a shiny new Olivetti portable typewriter. Connelly couldn't rest until he had gone around emptying ashtrays and filling a laundry bag. 'Here you are, muck-raker. Go case out the nearest Laundromat. It's one of those operations where the slot machines are very large and white. And if you find a clean, inexpensive woman anywhere, marry her and bring her back.'

The champagne, or the jet lag, must have hit him harder than he thought, for he slept for a solid four hours, until Sterling shook him awake. 'Hey, come on! I've got us reservations for a dinner show and it's six already!' Even after Sterling had shoved him into the shower and dressed him up in a borrowed shirt and tie, his eyelids kept falling, and his mind kept trying to check out. He definitely fell asleep again in the car, and was only jolted awake when Sterling was entrusting the Pontiac to a valet parking boy, outside the unbearably garish façade of a casino. 'I felt like trying something exciting,' Sterling was saying with an explanatory air, as they entered the building.

'Ah,' said Connelly vaguely. Sterling led him swiftly past a huge pulsing clanging hall of slots, to the Edwardian velvet of the show room. It was maybe a bit more tasteful than the Goldrush; the colour scheme was limited to purply red and old gold. Sterling said to the host, 'Table for two? I phoned earlier.'

'Mr Connelly? This way please.'

When they were seated the real Mr Connelly wanted to know, 'Why did he call you that?'

'Because I booked the table in your name.'

'Oh. For one bad moment I thought we were married.'

Tiger snickered, then suddenly looked at him sideways. 'You do know where we are, don't you? This is the Silverlode.'

Connelly digested the information slowly. 'I want to go home,' he whimpered.

'Don't worry. Nobody's going to recognize me, this side. We'll be alright as long as we keep out of the pit. '

They had simple steak dinners, unmolested by comps. The show was excruciating, an endless procession of feather-clad women wobbling around on shoes like stilts. Connelly was surprised to discover that despite his resistance to ballet lessons, he had inherited something of the Theatre Street aesthetic, and he regarded this as an insult. Even more annoying was the way Sterling was enjoying it all, with such a lavish display of venal heterosexuality that Connelly would have called it over-compensation for their second meeting at Tony's, if only it weren't so clear that Sterling was suffering amnesia for everything pre-1955.

'Great, isn't it!'

'No, it's not great. My mother understudied Karsavina, so take it from me, it's not great.'

'Hey, whaddaya say I see if the waiter can introduce us to a couple of girls after the show?' Sterling was already folding a twenty into his palm.

'No! No. It's not a good idea, Tiger.'

'Yeah, you're probably right. These dancers drag things along and clean you out. You end up saving a lot of time and money heading straight for an out-of-town cathouse.'

'You go ahead. I'll get a taxi back to the motel.'

'You can't do that! You've got to do something to mark your last night of freedom!'

'I know, but really, Tiger, I can't.'

Sterling looked at him with sudden understanding. 'She's really burnt you bad, that hula girl of yours.'

To make up for this disappointment, Tiger decided to flirt with danger on the outskirts of his old workplace. Beyond the ranks of the slots, the card tables were up a couple of steps, a gold-painted balustrade hinting that only high rollers were welcome. There was a concentrated coolness in the light bouncing off green baize, there was a faint winding thread of bossa nova subliminal; there was, Tiger thought, something different in the light, in the mood. He couldn't place it until he realized that the giant chandelier was gone, replaced by something that looked like a sputnik, an argos-eyed metal contraption suspended from the ceiling. Rico Calise monitoring the honesty of his guests as well as of his employees. Time to go.

He was just edging along the balustrade, out of range of the sputnik's lenses, he hoped, with Connelly in tow, when Jimmy Plischke came running, hunched and ducking, to warn him, 'Are you crazy? The boss is here! Get out now; I'm going to have to call him.'

'OK, OK, just showing a friend around town, I'm going now.' As he made for the door, intuition told him he'd better run. Dignity vetoed this, and by the time he neared the entrance he saw four Calise cave men arriving to intercept him.

He hadn't seen what happened to Connelly. He'd been dragged directly downstairs to the interrogation cell where he'd first been introduced to the hidden ownership of the

Silverlode. It was a low-ceilinged, windowless room with a steel door, unfurnished except for the same big wooden table his pockets had been emptied onto, and a single black leather chair, presumably not there for his comfort. After a few minutes alone, he decided he was being kept waiting on purpose and looked at his watch. Three minutes to eleven. Important to keep his own register of the time.

Calise came in at eight minutes past the hour, standing just inside the door to observe his prisoner for several minutes without saying a word. Sterling looked directly into his dark-eyed face, trying to read it. All he could sense was a faint air of weary melancholy, but that was probably a pose. And he's not taller than I remember him, he had to tell himself. That's just my fear. He opened the proceedings himself, saying, 'My friend's from out of town and he's got nothing to do with this business. I just wanted to show him a good time before he goes to join the Catholic priesthood.'

Calise opened his eyes, then opened the door and called to someone down the hall, 'Tell Sal to get the other jerk down here.' Damn, thought Tiger. I should have realized the truth would sound too good to be true.

'Why'd you come here?' Calise stepped around the table and stood by the chair.

'Like I said. A night on the town. Plus this dumb thing I have of taking risks for the hell of it.'

There was a suggestion of a pained shudder. Tiger, standing opposite him, wished he'd sit down and get things moving, but Calise just stood there, with his long, ringed fingers resting on the chair back. Presently, noises off suggested Connelly was being escorted ungently into an adjacent room.

Oh God, Sterling mourned inwardly. What had he done? What was wrong with him? *Why was he making it all happen again?*

He tried to force himself to calm down with the reflection that whatever happened tonight, it couldn't last three years. Calise would have a civilized feline game with him for an hour or two, and then the end would be swift.

Calise sat down at last. 'Relax. If I'd wanted you dead, it would have happened. Like maybe the night you ran away from Manny's, you know?' He leaned forwards and set his hands on the table, twisted a diamond ring up past the first knuckle of his forefinger, wiggled it back and forth over the bone. 'I'm saying to myself right now, what's he doing here, and is there something interesting I can do with that? Was there something interesting you wanted to do with me?'

Sterling shook his head. He didn't understand what was going on, but he strongly suspected his hopes of a swift ending had been optimistic. Calise sighed and leaned back in the chair, and rested his hands in his lap and regarded him from under heavy-lidded eyes for minutes and minutes.

Was there something sad in those eyes? Or was the sadness coming from inside, memories of wasted hours, wasted lives and unburiable corpses, Kirby screaming for him from some other cell, Delahunty limping; was it coming from a part of him that just didn't want it to circle round and happen all again? But what was he supposed to do to stop it?

'I hate waste,' said Calise. Sterling jumped as if electrified, generating a faint ghost of a smile from his interrogator.

He wondered if he should draw attention to their shattered past in Korea, then decided it would sound transparently manipulative, like Connelly joining the Catholic priesthood.

Calise suddenly yawned and stood up. 'I'm going to talk to your friend with the vocation now.' Sterling stared, and pressed his hands against his forehead as if this would make his skull less permeable, defending him against this apparent telepathy. 'Give me your room key, in case I decide to send him home. It's the Pinyon Motel, isn't it?'

When it had stopped being all too unnerving, Sterling decided he should see it as hopeful. Calise had known where he was staying, and he wasn't dead.

He was left alone in the low room for an hour and twenty-three minutes, more than long enough for a reprise of all the worst states of mind he'd discovered in the cells of Changhung and the wards of military hospitals. He was sitting under the table when voices outside recalled him to the present; he just had time to scramble out and get to his feet before Calise came in again. He must have been outside the casino while he was gone, he was wearing a light overcoat, and his second-string bodyguard, the one with the fearsome sideburns, was lurking in the hall outside. This time, Calise came directly to sit on the table, and moved as swiftly to the point. 'Who are you, Sterling? Who are you working for?' he wondered, then stated, as if he had his ways of being certain of this one fact, 'You're not a fed.'

'No. You know what I am. I'm a nobody who stumbled onto something and tried to turn it to my own account.'

He shook his head. 'That doesn't figure. You sat there like a dumb square watching everything for what must have been years. You had me – me, who should have known better than to trust a guy who banks his own cut. Then, out of the blue, fireworks and headlines. But what have you made out of it? What have you earned? I can't see the logic behind it.'

'Maybe that's because you've never been in a position to want to take revenge on the world for your own failure.' There was no reason to say this, but a building pressure of self-directed bitterness forced it out of him.

Calise took out a cigarette, bounced it against his upper lip a couple of times, then abruptly jumped up and left the room without lighting it. Tiger checked his watch – it was nearly one. He went over and occupied the chair, stretching forwards to rest his head on the table. If the conductor was going to keep playing at such a slow tempo it was going to be a long night.

He was too sleepy to think to check the time when he was woken again, with the news that 'his friend the altar boy' had been seen home safely and tucked in bed. When he was alert enough to have put his defences back in place, Sterling decided to treat this as a tactical manœuvre and not information. *He wants me soft.*

An upstairs waiter knocked and brought in coffee – for two.

Calise pushed a pack of cigarettes across the table. He really wants me soft. But why?

'You know the Control Board has started Black Book proceedings against me?'

'I know.' Tiger lit up and felt softened enough to say, 'I'm sorry.'

'Sorry? Oh, you're sorry? Why, fuck.'

He shrugged. 'I'm sorry they're only picking on you and not on Naylor and Gandy.'

'Of course they're picking on me! I'm the wop.'

This first evidence of some emotion other than amused sadism ignited a faint pilot light of hope in Sterling. He leaned across the table and threw his heart into saying, 'Then you do know what it feels like? To want revenge?'

Calise looked just slightly wrong-footed. He sank back in the chair, flicked his ash on the floor, and allowed his face a transparent (or maybe only pseudo-transparent) interlude of weighing things up.

Sterling pursued his (maybe illusory) advantage. 'I know you've got to know enough to bring those people down – and maybe people upstream from them? Grover Gibson? Governor Crocker? Bob Wunsche?'

At eight in the morning he bumped into the plain clean motel room. Connelly sat up with a yelp. 'It's OK. Go back to sleep.'

'Sterling! Is it you?'

'Of course it's me. Go back to sleep.'

But Connelly couldn't go back to sleep. 'I've spent all night wondering if I'd have the guts to go to the police about you this morning, or if I'd better just get the first flight out to anywhere and thank my stars I'm alive.'

'I know. You don't know how sorry I am I put you through that.'

Connelly sighed and burrowed back into the covers. Then something else struck him. 'Tiger, listen. They took all your papers.'

'Huh?'

'Three of them came in and took all your papers and stuff. I'm sorry. There wasn't anything I could do about it.'

Tiger looked around the room and realized that its unaccustomed cleanliness wasn't only due to Connelly's work with the ashtrays and laundry bag yesterday afternoon. The files he'd stolen from work and the draft of his next article were gone.

He was already beginning to lose his grip on last night, but it now seemed clear that Calise must have been reading them in at least one of those sadistic gaps between interrogations. And what he read must have convinced him that Sterling was on some level trustworthy. It was disorienting; he began to wonder who had gone soft on whom first. 'Don't worry. It's probably saved my life.'

Connelly relaxed again and dozed off. Sterling washed his face and went out unshaven to the coffee house across the road. Best not to sleep. Connelly had a plane to catch and he had a whole new article to write before tonight's deadline.

Driving through the flat suburbs of Sparks and Reno, under a disorientingly innocent sky, Sterling explained last night's outcome. 'I can't figure out now if I've somehow managed to convince him, or if it's what he's been keeping me alive for all along, but what the heck, I'm alive. Even if it's only like Scheherazade, for as long as I can keep the stories coming.'

There was no immediate answer from Connelly. Sterling glanced at him, but couldn't keep his eyes off the road for long enough to read his face. 'I guess you think I shouldn't be working with a gangster.'

'No, it's not that. Presumably that's what muck-rakers have to do. But shouldn't you be making your escape *now*? Before this guy decides you've served his purpose and crumples you up and throws you in the wastepaper basket?' A wild desire to add, 'Escape to Hawaii, and I'll come with you,' had to be censored.

'Aw, I can't do that. Not now I'm onto something big. This

is my chance of making a difference, and I might never get another one.'

'I know, and I'd love to just sit back and admire you for having the guts I could never have. But there's a phrase that goes back to Korea, and it keeps kicking a can around in my mind. "Bucking for a hero" – you remember what that meant?'

'In the first place, that was rat vocabulary, and in the second it doesn't matter whether I'm a hero or not. There's actually a principle of justice involved here. They're making Calise the scapegoat because he's got an Italian last name. If he'd been born into the Mormon Mob, none of this would have happened.'

'Maybe I'd care more about his civil rights if he'd paid a bit more attention to mine,' Connelly muttered. 'But can you really put your hand on your heart and say it's your sense of justice and not your ego that's the prime mover here?'

Sterling stared at the empty road ahead for a while. 'With my hand on my heart, I'd have to say it was none of the above.'

'I know it's none of my business, but – '

'That's right, padre. None of your business.'

'Just let me make one more point. Please?' Sterling laughed despairingly, but he went on, 'Do you remember what *happens* to heroes? Remember the six-foot guy with the certain kind of chin who ends up getting kicked to shit by both sides?'

'Yes, doctor. I've been locked up all night staring the parallels with Changhung in the eye. And maybe there's a reason for it. Maybe this is my chance to rewrite the ending.'

His natural instinct was just to throw everything he had heard into one huge rocket of an article, an explosion that might be big and noisy enough to be heard across the nation (he imagined Joe coming across it, syndicated in the *Wall Street Journal*). He restrained himself: the Scheherazade aspect of his situation called for a leisurely approach, one that would ironically reflect something of the Calise style, the subtle playfulness of power withheld. This week he would only repeat what Rico had said about certain established figures in the gaming industry, all the dubious pasts and unsavoury associations that had nevertheless been acceptable to the Gaming Control Board. Not that they were indigenous Nevadans either: they came from New York and Chicago, and their antecedents from Danzig and Mullingar, they were veterans of the Kefauver Hearings and federal penitentiaries, but they weren't Italian, and that made them honest investors and square businessmen once they crossed the stateline.

Tiger wrote it as a spoof nightmare: what a relief it was to wake up in the last paragraph and discover it 'wasn't true'! But the paper's legal advisors insisted he use pseudonyms for all the people and casinos, so he had to badger his exhausted brain for ethnic surnames and go through phone books to make sure he wasn't accidentally maligning an out-of-town cathouse when he renamed the Goldrush 'the Golddigger'.

It raised a storm anyway, particularly the threat that next week he might start dreaming about regulators and maybe politicians after that. The governor's office demanded advance copies of all future articles, and Bob Wunsche phoned personally from Washington to yell at anyone who would listen. A member of the Gaming Commission quietly resigned in mid-week and retired to Florida for his health.

The Flying D had folded, and Manny had used the proceeds of Calise's parting handshake to retire back to Franconia. Tiger and Rico had to meet in a stretch of the central desert so lonely no one had ever even tested nukes on it. They left their cars a couple of miles off the road and walked. Tiger, dressed for the outdoors in jeans and mountain boots, kept having to hold up and wait while Calise, in a silk suit and handmade shoes, charted a cautious, wandering course through the gaps in the sagebrush. He was worse than Delahunty and Hal put together!

'The editor says he's not going to run anything on any elected politician unless "my source" is willing to testify if (or when) they stick us for libel.'

Rico cursed. 'Slow down, Tiger, slow down. Literally and metaphorically, you gotta slow down.'

This was kind of surprising. 'I am going slow, and these lawyers are keeping me slower. Jesus, they castrated my piece on the regulators so bad I had to go to Annie Oakley's just to make sure everything was still there and working.'

Apparently this was not very funny. Rico had halted altogether. He looked around at the sky and across at the distant blue and grey skeins of hills, then said, 'There's a vast potential for disaster in this stuff. We don't want to push it to the brink. We have to move forward carefully, because it's not revenge if you sink your own fleet with everything else.'

'I don't have a fleet, and yours is on the rocks already,' Sterling reminded him.

Calise winced and walked a little further, his arms folded around each other. The pained expression was still on his face when he said, 'You've got a destructive mentality, Sterling.'

In other circumstances he might have been prepared to acknowledge that there was some truth in this diagnosis, but he felt it was a bit much from the author of the Severino Luncheonette Massacre. 'It's not destruction I'm after, it's *cleanness*. When you start cleaning the trash out of your backyard it seems like destruction – ' he broke off, deciding not to go on to say 'to the rats'. Vella was back there reclining against the hood of the black Cadillac picking his nose; there was nothing in this wilderness to stop Calise getting out his lupara if he felt offended.

He hadn't been listening, he was drawing breath to go on, 'I've seen people like you in my own family. When they get angry they don't care who they hurt, they don't care if they bring the whole edifice down on top of their own heads.

'I'm a sensitive person and I can't take that. I want to build and not destroy. You know, Sterling, I don't think we can work together.'

There was something so sad and fine and scarred in his eyes as he said this that a tidal wave of feeling rose from Tiger's gut and engulfed his fears and defences. They *had* to be able to work together! And not just because he'd be killed if he was no use! 'Rico, please,' he found himself saying desperately, 'I'll slow down. You set the pace.'

'I don't know,' he said, and repeated it several times, picking his way around scrub with his head bowed. Tiger stood where he was, with his eyes fixed on the boss, like a hound that had been ordered to sit and stay. At last Rico turned around – he had only progressed a waltzing five yards or so – and said, 'I need for you to think in terms of what you can achieve in all this, instead of what you can ruin.'

Released, Tiger bounded forward. 'Whaddaya mean? Whaddaya think I can achieve?'

Rico shrugged, smiling a little. 'Why, I don't know. A man's ambitions are in his own heart. If you're asking me, I'd call it a successful revenge for you when "Honest John" Sterling opens the biggest gambling palace on the Strip. But maybe that's not what you want.'

'I used to dream about starting my own business in Tahoe,' he admitted. 'But a big Vegas casino is way over my head. I'd never get the capital.'

Calise stopped and rocked backwards in his tracks, dramatizing shock. 'Do you seriously think... you'd have... trouble... finding capital?'

It took a long long time for this – the full import of this – to sink in. 'Oh,' said Tiger at last, in a voice that shook unhappily. 'Oh, I don't know. I don't know, Rico.'

'OK, OK. I thought it was beautiful myself. You're the guy on the white horse and I'm the ugly villain and no one in the world would imagine we were working together. But we're talking about your ambitions, not mine.'

'See, the job I've got now is already a hundred times more prestigious and exciting than anything I've expected for a long time.'

Calise flexed a nostril in derision. 'You drive around in that rustheap of a car and you live in those shitheap motels and you say you've reached the summit of your ambition?'

'Well, I uh... did used to – I've always sort of wanted to get into politics.'

'Yeah. That's what I thought you were aiming for, before you started going crazy with the machine-gun. I just hope you haven't made too many enemies already.'

'I probably have,' he felt obliged to admit. 'Wunsche already hated me and Governor Crocker – '

Calise burst out laughing. 'He's worried about Wunsche!' He laughed some more, then said, 'You're cute, you know that? But you're going to have to grow up fast. It's a good thing you've got Uncle Rico to hold your hand.'

Tiger listened with widening eyes as Calise took his hand and led him through a game plan for the next ten years. It was almost an hour before they turned around again and started walking back toward the black Caddy glinting and shimmering in the zenith sun, and the tarnished white of the rusting Pontiac.

But even Rico would have been a bit wide-eyed, wrong-footed by the speed of events, Sterling reflected, if he had seen the letter from the governor that arrived two days later. 'Jesus!' he kept exclaiming. He was jumping around the place, shouting at hallucinatory printers to hold copy he hadn't even written yet. He had headline news and he needed to share it, but the editor was out at a brunch, he'd been forbidden to contact Calise, and he didn't have a phone number for Connelly's monastery. In desperation he jumped in the rustheap and charged out to Fort Wynkoop.

Barbara answered the door. She had her hair tied up in a bandanna in a way that accidentally mimicked a showgirl's bouffant pile, and her thin, sleeveless blouse was tied over her ribs for coolness; she had been doing heavy housework on a hot day. Tiger exclaimed, 'Wow! You look wonderful!' and gave way to the impulse to throw his arms around her then and there on the doorstep, without any nonsense about counting backwards from a hundred.

'I've come to ask your advice,' he said, more soberly, when Barbara had brought him into the kitchen and cooled his ardour with a glass of iced tea. 'Governor Crocker's asked me if I'd accept an appointment to the State Gaming Commission.' This was the five-man panel the Control Board reported to: he saw himself patronizing Grover Gibson from a great height, and casting Naylor into the outer darkness. He would be taking the place of the fellow who had fled on the wings of his revelations to Florida.

If he accepted it. There were moral problems he wanted her opinion about. At the very least, his reputation as a clean-up campaigner was being used. Possibly the governor imagined the offer would buy him off.

'But you don't have to consider yourself bought!' Barbara exclaimed. 'Once you're there, you'd have so much more power to change things than you do with the paper.'

He wasn't sure this was a given. Once he was there, he was one of five, outnumbered by the Mormon Mob. And Rico's game plan called for him to spend another year or so at the paper, building his reputation for honesty and his popularity with the voters, firing a few carefully calibrated shots across the bows of the regulators, sending up a few flares to make the people who counted in the party machines aware of his presence. He didn't put this to Barbara.

'You've got to be a pragmatist at some point or you'll never put your ideals into practice,' she was telling him. 'You've worked so hard all these years, you can't let minor scruples get in the way now there's some chance of claiming your reward.' She looked at him rather directly, and some unspoken meanings began to rise from behind her words and to float in the air between them. Then she lost her nerve and jumped up. 'I've got some coffee cake in the fridge, would you like some?'

But Tiger had jumped up too, and he was right there standing close behind her.

The trouble was, they knew each other too well, they knew each other's erotic shortcuts. He knew the exact degree of strength he needed to seize her with, so that she was 'forced' but not hurt, she knew That Expression, the shaky euphoric tension of half-closed eyelids, all it took to knock his 'weak ego' out of action. There wasn't any chance of regaining coolness or conscience; there wasn't any need to rush to finish things before anyone thought better of it. He took her all over the house, necking in the kitchen up against the icebox, carrying her out into the living room (and nearly breaking both their goddamn necks tripping over the vacuum cleaner) and getting into her shirt on Mom's old sofa, under the swagged display of Caroline's horse show ribbons. The front room curtains were open, so they went upstairs to what he could only think of as Sedlachek's bedroom. Revenge. Then they lay in silence; words would have meant the return of consciousness and conscience, and neither had any eagerness to face them.

The pool was only forty feet long – all that could be squeezed onto the lower terrace that had been scraped out of the side of the mountain. The redwood deck overlooked the lake but tall pines screened it from the resorts on either side. Lying naked like a lizard on a rock, Calise was resting after the thirty-four laps that made his morning's quarter mile. Except for occasional breezes speaking through the trees, it was totally silent, and he was as close to alone as he ever got. Vella was in the house in one of the rooms upstairs, improving his mind with daytime TV.

Every once in a while Calise opened an eye and peered through the gap in the slats of the sunlounger to look at the paper lying on the deck beneath. It was the *Reno Morning Post*, and he had it folded open around the John Sterling column. Tiger, following his instructions, had persuaded the subeditor not to keep using the miniature of that stupid Quixote cartoon at the head: now there was a little photograph of him, looking very blond and fearlessly honest.

The content however was displeasing: for some reason he had taken it into his head to start reminiscing about the Inch'on Landings. Maybe he was just hanging fire while he waited for advice from his uncle about accepting the place on the panel. Or maybe it was directed at Uncle Rico, some kind of claim to fraternity. He couldn't have picked a worse patch of shared territory. The memory of those years invoked nothing but bitterness in Calise. It wasn't about pain or disfigurement (he didn't care what he looked like, and there are areas of life in which it is an advantage to be inhumanly ugly) nor even about being forced out of the navy and into some of those areas. It wasn't directed at the enemy or his own commanders or even at the careless fool who had caused the explosion. It was just a well of bitterness inside him, something it was not good to get near.

But it wasn't that (his thoughts hurried away from the wellhead). It was *Sterling* who was angering him. Those stupid heroics during the Landings. The even stupider tone of humorous self-deprecation. Any marine behaving like he claimed he had on the launch Calise commanded on that day would have been given one warning and then shot. Of course Sterling was not even a marine, he was apparently some kind of cavalryman. That probably explained a lot: the anxiety to do, lack of anxiety about dying, and the inability to reason – not only why, but about the likely consequences of his actions. Calise was a sailor by instinct as well as by training. If he had been taught that knowledge, control and discipline were his only allies against the great natural forces, he had grown up already knowing that they were the only way of surviving the even more dangerous human forces of violence, stupidity and greed.

His body twitched; he stood up, put on his bathrobe and went over to the terrace railings to look through the pines towards the lake. He could just make out the sharp white prow of his new boat, moored down there at the Silverlode Marina. Above and beyond, on the opposite shore, was Michael Sterling's cottage, had he cared to know it. His mind settled a little, and he reflected that it was that cavalry quality, the ability to project himself as braver and brighter white than he really was, that was so potentially useful about Sterling.

He turned around and looked up at his house, three storeys

of Frank Lloyd Wright, slow curves, big blank spaces, domed by two gradually rising asymmetrical conic sections. The sun rebounded down at him from the smoked living-room windows. He thought: Sterling is my opposite, but also my front, my *alter ego*. He has to be different, because he's going to do the things I can't.

He went inside to make himself a chicken sandwich. Vella heard him and came downstairs with the news that Vinny, the brother-in-law and business partner, had phoned, wanting to check that everything was all right. 'What's wrong with him? I already told him I found a way of laying all this off,' he complained. 'So what am I supposed to do now? Fly all the way home to pat him on the hand and tell him everything's all going to be OK?'

'I guess that's what he wants you to do,' said Vella.

Rico shook his head and passed him the chicken carcase. 'Might as well feed that to the Dobermen.'

'It's bad for them, the bones snap in their guts.'

He took the sandwich outside. Now there was another thing to consider. How much should he tell Vinny? He'd have to give him enough to allay his anxieties, but he felt reluctant to be very specific about Sterling and his plans for him. Whenever Rico discovered something good, Vinny had a way of muscling in on it. He thought about this for a while, then felt chilly after eating. Economical as a cold-blooded animal, he went to bed and slept for an hour, until the savage roaring that announced the guard dogs' lunchtime woke him up.

The anger at Sterling had returned, was stronger than ever. He didn't understand why; he felt like he didn't understand what was hitting him. He had no reason to be angry with the poor fuck. Sterling had not sunk his fleet, far from it – though it was perhaps typical of him that he believed he had. The regulators and the feds could run up and down Rico's paper trail wasting taxpayers' money for years and not find anything illegal. As long as the mechanics of the casino skim were secure the profits would keep coming in, and as long as Vinny kept the 'small investors' who had involuntarily financed the venture quiet, no one would find anything illegal. He got dressed for the day, gave the wooden frame of his icon of Garibaldi a devotional pat, and went downstairs, passing the TV den where Vella was indulging in nostalgia for his family home in front of *The Flintstones*.

Rico wandered around the upstairs rooms. Spilling into each other on an open plan, demarcated by steps up or down as often as by walls, some of them still unfurnished, they were conducive to wandering. He went along slowly, visualizing the paintings and sculptures he'd fill them with some day. He considered the possibility that he was envious of Sterling, but rejected it. Eventually he found his way down the stairs to the kitchen, and poured himself a glass of V8 juice, shaking Worcestershire sauce and salt over the ice cubes, and then moved meditatively to the glassed-in balcony. When he looked across the view of the lake, he imagined taking Sterling out in the white boat, shooting him somewhere just a little less than vital, then pitching him into the water to see how far he could swim.

Whoa. He was going to have to watch this! His own words came back to him. 'It's not revenge if you sink your own fleet.' 'I want to build and not destroy.' What was wrong with him today?

An unsigned typed letter that said only 'Play it your own way' had arrived for him at the office and Sterling had decided to accept the post. He went to Carson City for an informal meeting with the white-haired, crinkly-eyed governor, rented a new apartment and made a down payment on a new car. Some day when he had time he would take the Pontiac up to the cabin at the lake and put it out to pasture with Dad. He called Barbara to give her his new address and phone number.

'He knows,' she said flatly.

'What? Oh God. What happened?'

'Nothing. He just figured it out. I'm no good at acting.' Her words were stiff and muttered, and he could tell she was talking through the side of her mouth and preparing to light a cigarette at the same time. After a hissing intake of air and a gusty exhalation, 'So I guess it's not a good idea for you to show your face around here for a while.'

'Jesus, Barbara, I . . .'

'Way it goes. We'll weather it, I guess.' He recognized the same bleak self-sufficiency she'd shown when first breaking the news she was 'in trouble', more heart-breaking than any pathos could have been. This time there wasn't anything he could do to help.

Two days before he was due to be sworn in, the editor called and asked him to come to the journal's offices as soon as possible, no, not tomorrow, *today*, and before the paper's bedtime. He didn't understand it; he'd done his farewell piece last week, there wasn't anything he had to do there, there wasn't anything he owed them. But the man's voice was urgent, and he went. Driving past the decaying bones of the Flying D, it occurred to him that maybe something awful had surfaced about Governor Crocker, something that would make it impossible for him to accept the appointment after all. Oh please, please, no!

The girl at the front desk routed him straight to the editor's inner sanctum. Dread made him walk slowly, and take the stairs instead of the elevator, but nothing arose to stop him getting there. The boss, notified of his arrival, was pacing nervously around his reception room. 'Oh, there you are, Tiger. Come in where we can talk privately.' His secretary wasn't even there as he said this. Oh boy, were things bad.

Tiger followed him into the carpeted peace of his office. They sat across his walnut desk from each other, and eventually the editor sighed. 'This morning a gentleman named Smith brought me a file of documents he claimed were your medical records.'

Tiger didn't see what his medical records had to do with anything, and framed his face into the polite blankness that invites further explanation.

'I have to say they... *looked*... genuine. He wouldn't let me keep them, but he gave me a copy of some of the more salient entries. Which I only kept,' he added, with an air of conscience, 'so that you would have a chance to see what was being said about you.' He pushed a paper-clipped stack of sheets across the desk with one fingernail, as if its touch soiled.

Sterling picked it up. 'This is a carbon copy,' he observed. Details were all he could take in.

'Yes. I'm afraid it's almost certain Mr Smith is distributing them to other papers, and maybe further afield.'

'But why? What's so interesting about my records?'

'You don't know? They might be fakes?' he demanded pushing the phone towards him. 'Get onto your lawyer fast You might be able to block anyone running with it.'

★

He had phoned, not very coherently, run all the way to the other side of town where Addison, Murray and Fronk had their offices, and it was only as he was sitting down with Fronk, still panting for breath, that he began to understand what he was supposed to be panicking about. The lawyer was talking about court injunctions and the legal difficulties of subpoena-ing his real notes, which would be army property. Sterling quietly reached forwards and slipped the carbon copy off his desk, forced himself to scan its headlines.

Brainwashing subject...depersonalization with paranoid features...violent and hysterical combat reaction...threatened psychotic breakdown...egoic structures failing, analysis counterindicated.

He shut his eyes and forced himself to choke out the words, 'But what if these are my real notes?'

Fronk stared. 'Are they?'

'They could be,' he admitted. 'Or else they were falsified by someone who was looking at the real ones. The dates of the times I was in hospital are accurate, and I remember some of the doctors' names. Don't worry,' he added, with a brittle laugh. 'I'm not crazy, I just have a gift for alienating shrinks.'

Maybe it was a paranoid feature, but Fronk looked scared, as if he was expecting a violent and hysterical combat reaction. 'So you have been in a mental hospital?'

'I've been in ordinary hospitals, and one or two psychiatrists have dropped in to have a look at me. It's not unusual. Most vets nowadays see a talking doctor on the way home. And as for being in analysis, that was just *de rigueur*, back East. Everyone with a college degree gets on the couch at some time.' He said this with a loud confidence, but his heart was racing. Something told him this was a speech he'd be reeling off again and again over the next week or so.

Fronk had put his bald head in his hands, submerging himself to think. When he came up again he said quietly, 'Are you sure you want to fight this?'

'Of course I want to fight this! Who's leaked it, and how did they get hold of it? Even if it wasn't my reputation at stake I'd want to fight it on principle.'

'I understand, Mr Sterling. But you need to consider whether there is anything potentially embarrassing in your past, because the harder you fight the more likely it is to come out. You need to ask yourself whether it wouldn't be better to go quietly now.'

'You mean – quit my new job?' his voice broke. 'No, sir. There is nothing in my past that I'm ashamed of.'

A phone call that night instructed him to wait on the jetty at the Silverlode Tahoe marina at ten the next morning. He was there on the hour, and a huge streamlined forty feet of shark-like white cabin cruiser roared into life and came to pick him up, Calise himself at the helm. Sterling sighed heavily as he moved to step aboard. Only one of the papers he had been able to get hold of had printed anything, but such a public meeting could only mean it was all over.

Calise powered him out into the centre of the lake, then cut the engine, and just stood there looking at him.

Tiger said, 'Was it you?'

'What? Hey, I'm the one who's running along behind you trying to salvage things, and every time I get one explosion under control something else is fucking up. It's crazy! How do you do it?' Calise suddenly realized he was shouting and waving his arms. He pulled himself back, took a deep breath, then said, through his teeth, 'I'm never going to forgive myself for getting involved with you.'

'You think there's nothing we can do?'

'There's nothing more I'm going to do.'

For a long time he just stood there, looking past him toward the distant California shore, with that expression Tiger kept imagining was rather sad, though perhaps it was only bitter. Then he took a deep breath and said privately, 'I hate waste.' He powered the cabin cruiser up again and took Sterling back to the marina.

★

Tiger phoned his resignation to the governor's office from a payphone at the Silverlode, then drove around the north end of the lake to hole up with Dad.

Someone was knocking at the door of the cabin, a thing that very rarely happened. Answering it Michael saw a large fair-haired young man, looking wild and windblown. He wasn't sure who it was, but he was standing there expecting to be recognized. Maybe it was a neighbour, maybe it was a relative – but they were all relatives, all the young men and trees and wildcats. Michael sensed that there was something wounded about this one, and he let it in.

The young man sat at his fire and told his story. It was a very strong story, the kind that had to be enacted with many tears and much shouting, danced with violent movements across the room. To tell the truth, Michael did not take in many of its details, but he listened with his head bowed. Stories like this deserved the respect accorded to the great forces of nature. Almost certainly he would wake up tomorrow and find his guest gone, and the things blown about his room the only indication that he had entertained a personification of the North Wind.

Tiger walked to the nearest store the next morning to buy all the papers and phone Fronk. From the various vantage points on the road he saw the white cabin cruiser buzzing furiously around the lake, destroying the peace of so many little bays and beaches.

When he came home and let himself in, Dad nearly jumped out of his skin. 'Tiger! What are you doing here?'

It was a question he found himself having to answer four or five times a day. There were times he almost wondered if Dad even knew who he was. He might have been more patient if this forgetfulness hadn't meant he had to keep ripping open scabs, again and again and again. It was only half way through the week that he realized the answer, 'I'm just here, Dad,' explained things as well, or better, to his father's frame of mind. A little further along, he recognized it as a blessing. Dad allowed him to be without a past. He could spend the days walking in the hills or quietly helping out with all the little chores that weren't getting done as well as they could have been. In the evenings they sat in front of the old woodburning stove. All Dad's old books and Indian artifacts were still in their same places on the shelves. They looked slightly shrunken and grey with dust, as if they were aging in gentle concert with his father. Tiger invented a game he called 'Dad Roulette' in which he used the dementia as a form of divination. Sometimes the answers to his questions were just surreal ('Should I forget about suing the *Review Journal*?' 'Ask your senator friend why they're bombing us,' – apparently an allusion to the nuclear tests going on in the south of the state), and sometimes they were more than that. When he took courage to ask the one that was really troubling him, 'How come I keep falling in love with my enemies?', what came back was 'Well, she's your Mom, son, and sooner or later you're going to have to make your peace with her.' He doubted even Varady could have made such an interpretation.

He let his beard grow and his lawsuits drop, he stayed up there living like a backwoodsman, making Dad's frailty his excuse when anybody bothered to ask why. It was easy enough to forget about the past, but he couldn't get rid of the knowledge that his motivations were seriously flawed, and the only safe course was to *do nothing* until he got himself untangled.

It was almost a year later before he came down from his mountain. Caroline was riding in a Stock Seat Equitation championship at the State Fair and wanted him there, and Barbara had written a note which communicated that Sedlachek was prepared to tolerate his presence.

He met them at the fairground. The horse business seemed to have grown from Caroline's hobby into a whole family project: Arthur had bought a powerful Chevy pick-up to tow the trailer – Tiger had laughed at the idea of a horse travelling in state, and they had all stared at him like he was crazy when he pointed out that a horse was supposed to be a form of transport in itself. But apparently the chunky golden creature that emerged, wrapped up like a boxer in bathrobes and bandages, was no mere horse, but a $3000 investment. Leaving Barbara to unwrap and polish the animal, they left the competitors' area for the main stand, to buy ice creams for the kids, watch the show, gaze at the trophies and prizes on display. Sedlachek instantly homed in on the hand-tooled, silver-plated saddle that went to the over-all champion in the Equitation Division. If Caroline won her class she'd be eligible to compete for it, against all the other winners of all the other age groups (most of them older than her). 'Pretty, huh?' Art said. 'Ride to win.'

Tiger saw her face go pale under a forced smile. She threw her ice cream away half eaten. On an impulse to come to her rescue, he sneered at the saddle; it was flashy and trashy, the silver would rust in the first rainstorm. 'Ride to lose, sport!'

'There's the Tiger Sterling philosophy in a nutshell,' muttered Sedlachek.

'There's no honest silver left in this state,' he flashed. He wasn't sure why this applied to Sedlachek, whose worst enemy couldn't accuse him of corruption, but it did. Then he controlled himself: a public fight wouldn't make Caroline's ordeal any easier.

His eye fell on the sign advertising that the prize had been donated by Slim's Tack and Western Wear. They had a tent at the show today. Inspiration seized him, he grabbed his daughter's hand and pulled her along, running, to Slim's display. 'Whaddaya want? Anything you want?'

She stared at him, looking confused, then concerned. Perhaps she followed current events enough to know her father was a maniac. 'Daddy, you don't have to!'

'I just want you to know that it doesn't matter if you win or lose. To one person anyway, for what it's worth.'

She looked down. 'I know that.'

'How much is that saddle?' he demanded of the buxom saleslady (Mrs Slim?), pointing to what seemed to him to be an identical model.

'$350.'

He worked fast to conceal his shock from Caroline. 'Can you take a check?'

'Daddy you can't buy a saddle just like that!' Caroline cried desperately. 'We don't know if it fits me or Stardust, and if I just went in the ring with it today without getting used to it, it will change my seat and wreck my chances!'

'Well, look around, and pick what you want.'

She looked at him with a wistful look that by rights belonged to Barbara: torn between desire and duty. It just so happened that he knew exactly how to take that particular look by storm, by plunging with all his heart into the sensuous imperative. So he ran around the temporary store, exploring the velvety solidity of Stetsons, the dangerous sophistication of snakeskin boots; the expensive naïvety of Navajo blankets, silver-ferruled bridles, shotgun chaps of buckstitched suede, rhinestone hatbands, and everywhere, haunting them, the smell and feel of brand new leather. But as he rushed around he couldn't help noticing the price tags, most of them in three figures, and almost nothing under the fifteen dollars he had in his wallet. It was for big players, this horse game! How did Sedlachek afford it on an army salary?

Caroline kept coming back to the ferruled bridle, rich chocolaty leather, rolled cylindrical, and alternating with inch-long ingots on the cheekpieces. She'd look at it for a few seconds, then jerk herself away and try to focus on utilitarian kits of liniments and fly sprays or dandy brushes and curry combs. He picked up the headstall and asked, 'Is using this going to affect your performance today?'

She swallowed, stared, finally shook her head. She couldn't even thank him as he paid for it, something deeply feeling was constraining her, and she had to fight her way past it to say to him, as they walked back to the truck, 'You know what you said about winning and losing not mattering?'

'Yeah, sport.'

'Well, I think the same about what people say about you.'

When they got back to the Sedlachek war camp it was time for Caroline to disappear into the trailer to change into her show clothes. Hal was being permitted to warm Stardust up, riding him bareback up and down the rows of trucks and station wagons and trailers. 'Is he safe like that, Indian-style?' Tiger demanded.

'Oh, he's fine, he's only walking,' said Barbara.

'He's shaping up to make another fine rider,' Art said. 'He'll be competing here himself next year.'

Over my dead body, Tiger would have liked to have said. But his muck-raker's nose was twitching, there was an investigation to pursue, and he needed to keep his marks reasonably sweet.

Sedlachek looked at his watch, and shouted towards the trailer, 'What's going on in there! Half an hour till your class is called! Hal, git back here!'

'I'm too fat for my shotguns!' a miserable wail answered. Barbara ran in and helped her zip up the legs of her chaps. Sedlachek saddled the horse. Presently Caroline came out, walking John Wayneishly with unbending knees. Barbara whipped her long braid into a hairnetted coil at the back of her neck, and settled her hat on her head. Art pinned the number on her back and boosted her straightleggedly into the saddle. She was just about to ride off when she remembered 'My new bridle!'

Sedlachek had followed the horse and rider to the ring to shout 'Heels down!' and 'Chin up!' at her, and Hal had joined up with a feral gang of horse children to leave Tiger and Barbara alone. She was looking nervous, as if she thought at any minute he might lose control and they'd end up making love on the floor of the horse trailer, in the straw and manure. But Tiger only said blandly, 'Well, this is some family enterprise. It must take up all your cash and most of your time.'

'Oh, well, it's such an opportunity for the children, and something all the family can do together. It's nice for them to have *something* after all the trouble at school.'

'What do you mean, trouble at school?' he demanded sharply. 'They're bright kids, they shouldn't be having trouble. And if they are having trouble, maybe they shouldn't be spending so much time at the stables.'

She looked sorrowful. 'Not that kind of trouble. Just other kids. You know.'

He did not; he looked blank until Barbara took a deep breath and said, 'The newspapers. You know. Your records.'

Oh. He looked at the ground. The muck he'd been smelling was his own. Holed up with Dad, avoiding things, he hadn't realized how much of a splash he'd made. 'We'd better go to the grandstand and get some good seats saved,' said Barbara, as if this would take him away from his reflections.

As they walked through the heat and dust and toward the noise of the fairground he recovered enough to say, 'Do you think you could rein Art in a bit? The pressure he's putting on them, you know?'

'I know. I know, but . . .'

'But?'

'It's just his way of trying to make it up to them.'

It was bad enough, the way Sedlachek took over all the good parts of fatherhood, but this usurping of his guilt was a real insult. 'Jesus! What's it got to do with him? It wasn't his fault their dad ended up in all the papers.'

Barbara reached up and gave the top of his arm a small hard squeeze, an appeal for restraint. 'What if it was?'

He stopped, and stared at her.

'What if he was the one who got hold of your records and gave them to the papers? Because of us, that morning?'

Caroline came loping out of the showring, too busy trying to manage the yard-long ribbon and the two-foot trophy to control Stardust. Art grabbed the flapping reins and dragged him to a halt, Mom took the prizes, Hal was hugging the horse's neck and kissing his nose, there was so much happy commotion that it was only when they were back at the trailer, and she turned around to thank Dad for her Good Luck bridle that she realized he was gone. 'He had to rush back to the lake,' said Mom anxiously. 'He was so sorry to miss your class but he was really worried about Grandpa.'

Caroline understood. It was his way of demonstrating winning wasn't everything. And it wasn't, she knew that.

But it was nice.

Halfway through the mountains to the lake, Sterling left the main road for the track that went into the Forest Reserve at Galena. He walked a quarter of a mile up the slopes, then caught the sound of the fast running creek and angled towards it. Nature wasn't big here, it was in fact considerably smaller than at the falls of the Potomac, but it was lonely and sweet and quiet, an antidote to the heat and dust and noise of the State Fair, if not to what he had learned there. He found a long flat boulder that jutted into the stream like a pier, speckled with damp from the spray but not too wet to sit on. It sheltered a little depth of comparative stillness, a round well, floored with red and brown and grey pebbles, gently flickering in the play of light on circling ripples. The 'well' was maybe only two feet deep, but it had the trick that certain patches or small bodies of water learn of suggesting an enclosed world, alien and seductive.

Sterling looked into its small profundity for a while. When he looked up into the sky there was a hawk circling on the updrafts, looking down at him. Maybe if you were up there, the whole treeless stretch along the creek had the clarity and depth of another microcosm.

Maybe what he'd been lacking all along was the right perspective for examining things. What if his major faults had only been faults of vision? Connelly and even Rico had sensed the disaster coming even before he'd assembled all its com-

•

ponents. He, even when he had all the data together, had not.

He tried to regather what he *had* seen. He remembered telling Connelly that he was aware of 'the parallels with Changhung'. Ha! But what had he thought they were, back then? Something about the stupid risk he had taken in bringing Connelly to the Silverlode, and how it repeated his arrogance about the MSR, and Delahunty and all that. But had there not been more, even then? Like for example the similarities between Calise and Chang? Whether or not the paternal oracle was right in connecting them with Mom, they were essentially the same person, that enemy who had the power of life or death over him.

Suddenly he saw very clearly that it was because Chang had been the one conducting the siege against his spirit, with all the resources of starvation, pain and isolation at his disposal, that he had believed that Chang was the only one in the universe who could validate him as a man of courage and integrity. If Chang had been smart enough or cold enough, he could have just stepped back and allowed Sterling to do his best to astound him with the gallant totality of his will to self-destruction, always reserving his seal of approval. Instead, because of his principles, or his horror of total humiliation (everybody, even the lowest, had to keep some face) – and maybe Chang also had a dash of that susceptibility that Sterling had blamed himself so bitterly for, alone in the pit, and alone in the darkness after he'd been hit in Tony's – he'd got caught up in the drama, and been forced to admire the mind of jade that broke before it bent.

Yes, certainly from that hawk angle things looked different. He was no longer cringing in shame over his susceptibility, he was staring in a kind of shock that was almost admiration at the stupidity that granted Chang the role of judge in the highest court in his conscience.

He thought of Dad, and how he had been wise in refusing that bench, way back when. What was it he had done wrong? Oh yeah, Grandma Sterling's shotgun. So why hadn't he learned the lesson? Maybe it was too scary, when you were ten or twelve, to accept that you were the only power you had to answer to. It was kind of scary now. If there was no one to reward or punish, was there anyone to keep you safe? He remembered his sense that Chang had 'kept him alive'.

On the other hand, if Dad had just beaten him, like Mrs Shaw had said, would he have needed Chang? Would he even have needed Korea?

He felt like things were clicking into place, like a tool, no, like an M1, cleaned, reassembled, properly loaded. There. That was better. Now all he had to do was apply the same logic to his latest disaster.

But could he? Suddenly everything that had seemed so clear in parallel was going unfocused again. What had made him imagine that Chang and Calise were 'the same person'? They weren't even remotely alike. Beneath the cool overlay of Chineseness, Chang Wo was a warm and even romantic character. Calise had ruthlessly stomped down everything in himself that might evoke the stereotype of the emotional Italian. Even his temper tantrums, Sterling suspected, were calculated for their intimidating effect, not an overflow of genuine anger. Chang was an idealist who had thrown away a promising academic career to join Mao's cadres at the most doubtful point of the Long March. Calise saw ideals as purely destructive, and perhaps they were. Maybe if you wanted to build anything that was substantial and lasting you had to subordinate means to ends.

He was tempted to stray along this abstract thoughtway: was all 'building', all creativity essentially unprincipled? But no, that was conveniently dodging the real and uncomfortable issue: his problem with vision. He dragged himself back to the most painful kernel of fact, that he had accepted Rico's patronage of his prospective political career without seeing that he was sacrificing his principles. It wasn't a question of hypocrisy, or not admitting things to himself: he simply *had not seen it at the time*, though it was staring him in the face.

Only it wasn't, of course. He hadn't been looking at himself but at Rico. He recalled the way he'd seemed to him: lit from within, noble, embattled, and if not exactly honest, at least seeming to be allied more closely to integrity than anyone else in that unpleasant world, a sort of Milton's Satan figure. Then he remembered how they had first come face to face, as a result of Operation Diogenes, Calise sitting there in judgement, like Satan in the Book of Job. Sterling had been hooked, without knowing it, from that evening on. So it was the same as Chang after all. *The Adversary.*

Only the ending was different: Rico had refused to play. He wasn't Satan, he was a second-generation type who wanted to get rich quick. He wasn't too fussy about the means, and he was sure as hell not going to waste his valuable time in moral dramas, not even if you offered him the role of the most glamorous villain possible.

And what had sunk Sterling was friendly fire: the US Army, as personified by Colonel Sedlachek. And maybe that was actually part of the pattern come to think of it. The betrayals of Delahunty, Krajicek and eventually Kirby were what had really hurt him, not the game he played with Chang. But he had brought those on his own head, by multiple acts of arrogance...just like he had with Art. He laughed aloud at himself, stood up, and stretched. When he looked at the sky the hawk was no longer in sight.

A couple of nights later, Sterling had what he later decided to treat as a dream and not a vision. He was alone in what he instantly recognized as a prison camp, though it was in the middle of a plain, not the North Korean hills, and it was strangely clean. Prisoners in grey clothes were working in a field. Something cold in the air made him think Siberia, but as he turned his attention to the buildings he knew it was China, perhaps Manchuria somewhere. Then he was inside one of the blocks, going along until he came to a small, single-windowed room. A man in baggy black was sitting kneeling – a thin tired man, hair sprinkled grey, eyes shut in meditation, but instantly recognizable to him as – 'Chang!'

The eyes opened and stared, and he was on his feet in shock. 'Tser? Tser Ling?' And then, starting up the rusty machine of Yinghua, 'You here how come?'

'It's a dream, Chang. One of us is dreaming.'

'Ah,' he nodded, sat down again. 'You are like the picture of reactionary thought, there is Tser Ling in my own mind. I have much still to reform.'

With a dizzying swell in his heartrate, Sterling realized that Chang was a prisoner. He couldn't give a name to the feeling this invoked, but it was very powerful. 'What happened?' he cried.

Chang told him patiently that he had translated, printed and distributed Kruschev's speech denouncing Stalin. 'But that was years ago!' Tiger cried, and for a long space he found himself denouncing Mao for the bitter hypocrisy of the Hundred Flowers period, in pictographic images and personified abstractions that were not his own.

He had talked about and to the 'Connelly in his own head' carelessly for years now, but it was not pleasant to find himself representing a trend of somebody else's thought. At last he pulled himself out of the tirade. Chang regarded him sadly and repeated, 'Much still to reform.'

And then with a crushing weight of bleakness he saw Chang's years stretching ahead in this cold plain: hunger, cruel labour and self-reproach; repetitive days expanding into years, but perhaps only a few; then sickness; then death. 'No!' he yelled, and ran around punching out the windows and kicking the walls, trying to unmake the cell. This could not go on! It had to stop here! The world had had too much of this evil already!

In the dream the prison did indeed begin to disintegrate, but Chang sat where he was, stubbornly, with his head bowed.

Part Five

September 1967

Honolulu Airport was crowded. The last of the summer tourists jostled with the families of college kids being shipped off on tides of flowers and tears; military wives who had come out to meet their husbands for a week's R & R sighed stoically as yet another DC8 left with no standby places. Pearly twanging chords came through the canned music system. Connelly shuddered and skipped through a line of sunburned Texans to find the escalator to arrivals.

He was kind of late and the plane was already at the gate, the passengers already streaming in as he reached it. How to recognize someone you haven't seen for thirteen years, someone who was six years old when you last saw him? Oh. Oh! Not at all difficult, if he has inherited his father's height, if the face rising above the grey heads of a hundred retired Iowans like the peak of a mountain rising over a lei of cloud, reproduced so closely the long lines and high planes of a face you have studied more closely than any other. 'Oh my God,' said Connelly aloud.

Of course Hal was different too, but those differences didn't do anything to forestall the sense of beautiful doom that was shaking Connelly's stomach and knees. His eyes were brown, but so huge and long lashed, still full of that 'Are you an angel?' wondering innocence. His hair was honey blond, rather conservatively cut – it touched his collar, but not his shoulders. The only 'good' point was that he had not inherited his father's physical presence: his shoulders were rather narrow and rounded, and there was a slight pigeoning of his chest. I have got to be *so* careful, Connelly addressed himself, not aloud this time. Then he raised his hand and called, 'Hal!'

The boy spotted him; the processes of surprise, of confused comparing with memory were visible through the innocence of those eyes. 'Uncle Alex?' What did he see? Someone so much smaller than he remembered probably, with salt-leathered skin and hair as long as a Greenwich Village angel's. Maybe it was kind of shocking to see someone of your parents' generation dressed in a T-shirt with a picture of Snoopy thinking 'Surf's up!' and ragged denim cut-offs.

He had brought a lei, home-made double plumeria, yellow and pale pink, spicy smelling, and he placed it around Hal's neck, but chickened out of giving him the traditional kiss on the cheek that was supposed to go with it. He led him along the open air walkway through the hot wind and the warm wet air, asking politely about the flight. It was the first time Hal had ever flown alone, ever travelled out of state on his own, and he was full of excitement over every detail. The stewardess had given him a beer without even asking to see his ID! He was going to have three extra hours today, because of the time zones! Weird, huh? 'It works that way,' Connelly smiled. By the time they reached the car he was talking as confidingly as a six-year-old, all strangeness apparently forgotten. Hal was going to stay with him for the three days before the university semester started.

'This is yours? Wow!' Hal exclaimed as Connelly opened the unlocked door of the VW van that waited for them in the no waiting zone outside the baggage claim. Perhaps it was the fat psychedelic lettering 'Kalani Surfari' on the side that impressed him. 'Little business I run,' Connelly apologized.

'Cool!' Eyes the opposite of cool turned on him, warm and golden and glowing.

Connelly dodged them. 'Cool to the point of bankruptcy.' He slid the suitcases into the back, jumped in and started off. As they came out of the airport onto the main highway to central Honolulu, he gestured for Hal to look past him. 'See that big pink building on the hill up there? That's Tripler Hospital, where I first met your dad.'

'Oh,' he said, just about politely. Then, with an air of having to gather courage, 'Do you teach people how to surf?'

'Do you want to learn?'

'Do I!'

'Then I will teach you.'

He pointed out the high-rise buildings of the city, but evaded them, sweeping onto a road that climbed a long slope that cut deep into the mountain range. The VW chugged and strained under vertical ridges, richly forested in greens that caught emerald fire under the darkening sky, the clouds gathering around the needle peaks, stormy grey-blue, in places condensing directly into long spindling waterfalls. Thick impassible jungles, fragile unclimbable heights, beauty set safely for ever out of human reach. They went through two short tunnels, along the edge of a cliff that overlooked green plains, and the blue line of sheer ridges as the mountains stretched northwards. They kept their cloud cover, but there was a silvery haze where the sun broke free on the sea beyond the flatlands.

Uncle Alex questioned him gently about his plans and dreams and ambitions. Hal explained seriously that he had chosen the UH not for the sun and surf but for the new East-West Center: he wanted to study Asian culture because he was convinced that the Pacific Rim was where the future of international relations lay. He wasn't exactly sure what he wanted to do or even to major in, but he knew he wanted to work for world peace, in some way that made a difference. 'Making a difference,' Connelly echoed, nodding.

They drove through grasslands and swamps, through a few tracts of wooden houses, great shady mango trees, plantations of bananas with their tattered fronds, until they came to a coast road, the water flat and silver, or coming into turquoise bays, little shacks and farms and homesteads tucked into jungly valleys, or dried-out headlands where the mountains jumped out to the sea, ranches with red cattle and elegant white egrets resting on their backs.

And then, 'Here's the pad,' and Uncle Alex turned onto a track that took them under a grove of tall shaggy ironwood pines. They came to a clearing and he parked on a pair of sandy scars in a dry lawn that surrounded a square white shack. Three tall palms slouched languidly in one corner, a spreading breadfruit shaded another. Under the whispering of the pines they could hear another sound, the pulsing cough of the sea. The sun baked down hot on them until Connelly kicked the screen door open and held it back with his foot for Hal to enter the pad.

The whole house was just one big room: kitchen fittings ran along the wall on the left, a king-size bed dominated the opposite corner. Woven native mats covered the floor and a collection of green glass fishnet floats was stowed on a shelf that ran like a picture rail around the wall. And that was pretty much it, bare and neat, seamanlike. 'Sit down, relax,' said Uncle Alex, going out for the cases. But there wasn't really anywhere to sit. Hal perched on the bed experimentally, then decided it might be bad manners and got down crosslegged on the floor.

Maybe it was the beer on the plane, maybe the three hours' time difference, but he felt a little disoriented. Uncle Alex was so much more counter-cultural than he had remembered or expected. And while he had chosen an out-of-state college on purpose to get away from his parents' reactionary mindset, things now seemed to be accelerating in the opposite direction rather faster than he wished. His rebellion so far had been confined to the realm of ideas: arguing with Mom and Dad about civil rights and Vietnam left little moral energy for smoking pot and making out. But it looked like that was going to change.

And it was funny about Uncle Alex. He'd been trying to talk himself out of the childish memory of the mysterious doughnut libertine, moving in a separate reality where everything was allowed, where dangerous things were safe, a reality peopled by extravagant eccentrics. He'd been lecturing himself that he mustn't be disappointed to find Connelly was just an ordinary adult. Instead he'd found that though some of the props had changed, the spirit of that separate reality was stronger than ever. He was relieved rather than disappointed when Uncle Alex came back and offered him a coffee to clear his head and not a joint (or worse) to expand it. Then it was time to go surfing.

Two or three disastrous 'surfaris' had taught Connelly to take nothing for granted when introducing people to the waves. He always started with a body surfing lesson, just to make sure that his clients could swim.

Hal could swim, that is, he knew you were supposed to rotate your arms, kick your legs and breathe every once in a while, but you could see from his tensed muscles that he was expecting the icy water of a dead lake and just didn't know what to expect from a rowdy ocean that ran up and roughhoused you and threw you over like a judo expert, a nubile tease of an ocean that swallowed you up in warmth and then dumped you in a soup of sand and then ran away laughing with your pants. Connelly watched him for a while, wondering how anyone with such soft eyes could make such a fight of swimming. Then he gave him the half-sized 'paipo' board and taught him to launch himself into already broken waves and cruise on his stomach right up onto the sand. 'Wow!'

'Better than the Potomac, or what?' Connelly laughed.

Hal swam and semi-surfed until he felt dizzy and sick, then went up to lie in the sand and start work on a tan. Connelly kept catching one more wave and then just one more. He should have been ashamed of himself, playing like a kid in the shore break, but he was such a sucker for the slow erotic *lomilomi* of body surfing. The sun was disappearing behind the mountains to do its evening show for all the beachfront hotels at Waikiki when he finally dragged himself out of the water.

He woke Hal and they trudged up the coarse pale ochre sand and rinsed off in the hose by the house. The water was warm, heated up in the shallow laid pipes, and tasted sweet after so many mouthfuls of salt water.

He was just cracking the evening's first six-pack when Hal let out a yelp of conscience. 'Mom!'

Connelly looked at him. 'You want me to stand in for her?'

'I just remembered I promised to call her as soon as I landed to let her know I was alright. Can I use your phone? I'll call collect of course.'

'I have two phones. Which one would you like to use, the one a couple of miles up the road in Kahuku, or the one a couple of miles down the road in Laie?'

Hal looked like a three-footer had just dumped him on the sand. 'Oh.' Connelly took pity, re-fridged the beer, and drove him up to the little country store in Kahuku. Leaving Hal at the payphone, he went inside and chose Plantation Burgers for their supper. Hal was just signing off when he came out again. 'Bye, Mom. – Gee, thanks, Connelly.'

'It's OK. Shall we phone your Dad, now we're here?'

'I just talked to him. Oh, you mean...'

'...the other one. Shall we?'

'I don't think I've got his number on me.'

They followed the road back through the plain of abandoned cane fields, with little islands of farmed land and banana groves. There were no other cars on the road, no visible houses or farm buildings, a place you might have called lonely, empty, but for the presence of the green ridge inland, very alive, very still, giving its fullness to the air all around. 'How is he, the other one?' Connelly finally had to say.

'Huh? Oh. OKish, I guess.' Hal gazed out of the window. Presently he added, in a careful voice, 'You would probably find him very changed, you know, since Washington.'

'We've all changed.'

'Well, you have and you haven't. But he...I don't know if you ever realized he's, um, mentally ill.'

Connelly couldn't answer. A deep sadness filled the darkening country air. 'Is...is he in a hospital?' he finally forced himself to ask.

'Oh, no. He manages, you know, it's kind of...I guess it comes and goes, and he's kind of OK for a while, and then just locks himself away in between.'

'I see.' Connelly told himself that perhaps things were no worse than they had ever been: perhaps what had changed was Hal's perspective. In an effort to dispel the sadness he said, 'Is he still working for the paper?'

'Huh? Oh yeah...' as if remembering something from the distant past. 'No, he works in a casino. I don't even know which one, at the moment; he's in and out of work, depending on his state of mind.'

'Oh,' said Connelly and let the topic drop. The sadness remained. Information wasn't going to shift it, he realized, because it wasn't actually about Sterling. It was about Hal, and the way he spoke of his father, the mixture of caution and matter-of-factness with which he talked about mental illness, like someone who had grown up used to having this particular skeleton in the family cupboard, and the very very faint regret or pity diluted by a much greater volume of distance, dissociation perhaps, or lack of interest. Not that you could blame Hal, it was understandable from his perspective, but when Connelly remembered the way Tiger had agonized about him, in Tony's for example, it seemed very sad.

They had another body-surfing lesson the next morning. Hal actually caught one wave, instead of letting it catch him, and Connelly announced that tomorrow they'd hit Waikiki. The rest of today they could spend on the official Kalani Surfari tour of the island. Treating Hal as a sort of VIP client was the easiest way of not having to treat him as anything else.

Connelly took him past Sunset Beach and around the curve of Waimea. Everything was flat and silent, and little kiddies splashed in the shallows of beaches that would be red flagged in four months' time. They stopped for lunch at Haleiwa, a one-time plantation town, now in the process of being colonized by stoned blond people, a few of them distantly connected with the waves. The van was parked outside a rackety old ranch building, a distant relative of the Flying D. It was approaching old age with a desperate lunge at youth, like Connelly himself, Hal thought. It had painted itself submarine yellow, and put up blacklight posters on its interior walls, and its name was the Pakalolo Cafe. *Paka* meant 'weed' in Hawaiian, and *lolo* meant 'crazy', Connelly told him.

In the Crazy Weed Cafe the High Priesthood of the winter surf had assembled to read the latest *Sports Illustrated*, in which one of their number, Freddie van Dyke, was interviewed. Connelly introduced Hal to Allen Atherton, the Zen oceanographer and Waimea pioneer, his old lady Star, a tie-dyed Galadriel with eyes like a constellation reflected in a deep pool, to massive Robby Keala and mean Mark Gonsalves, to a freckled Californian who called himself Thor, and several others. But nobody was paying attention to Hal; everyone wanted to tell Connelly something; finally it was Robby Keala who pounded on the table and read out the information that had everyone so worked up. All big wave surfers, according to Freddie van Dyke, were *latent homosexuals*.

Mark Gonsalves was muttering something that sounded like 'All on account of you, fucking bastard mahu.' Perhaps Star picked it up, for she smiled astrally into Connelly's eyes and said, 'Isn't it a beautiful paradox? You're the only one who can absolutely say, "It can't be true of me."'

'It's a *koan*,' said Allen. 'Has a big-wave surfer Buddha Nature? Connelly answered "mu".'

Connelly took Hal up to the greasy counter to order. 'Try the kim chee.'

'What did they mean?' Hal asked.

Connelly started to explain that a koan was a Zen meditation paradox, then sighed and pulled himself back to answer, 'What it means, Hal, is there's nothing latent about me. I'm a fag.' Then he added, 'If it bothers you I'll take you straight to the UH campus.'

'No... no... it's alright,' Hal managed to say, but so dizzily that Connelly cancelled the kim chee order, substituting bland nourishing saimin.

Poor boy. He was taking it so bravely. Connelly wondered (wistfully) whether he could use this reaction as an index of what Tiger might have been like – if Connelly had been a braver boy, way back when. Well no, of course he couldn't. But it was so tempting, with such a resemblance...

'Could we just... go home?' Hal said faintly.

'Sure.' Connelly cancelled the saimin and took him out, pausing only to inform the High Priesthood, 'What he was trying to say was, "The bigger the waves, the queerer the surfer."'

'Banzai!' smiled Star.

Hal was very quiet for the next two days. He was perfectly polite, excessively gentle indeed, the way you might be with someone who has a secretly brewing cancer – or a mental illness. He had obviously decided Connelly was more to be pitied than censured.

Maybe if his self-respect had been more demanding, Connelly would have been irritated, but mostly he felt relieved of a pressure that had been weighing heavily: the responsibility for making sure nothing happened between them. Hal picked that burden up and ran with it, locking himself in the bathroom to change, just quietly severing that confiding channel of communication they had opened up straightaway, those first few minutes at the airport. On the first day of the term, Connelly drove him down to the rainy Manoa campus, helped him find his dorm and settle in. Then he did not see him until the next semester.

Allen and Star Atherton celebrated the New Year with a pilgrimage around the coast of Oahu, making ceremonial stops at each Significant Break, where the surf was propitiated, and gifts floated out to the distant winds and currents that generated the waves, to the different *akua* and *aumakua* that generated the weather and looked after the surfers. They started before dawn at their home break of Haleiwa, House of the Iwa bird, with gifts of Maui Wowie to that dark, high-coasting flyer, and vodka poured into the outrunning current to bear good thoughts in the direction of the Siberian blizzards that would pulse the North Pacific swells into life. As they travelled, others joined the procession. At 'Three Tables', Keala gave three sweet leis for the three sisters whose bodies were the coral formations that gave the place its name, and for the Pipeline, Thor threw his second best bong out into the sea. There were more than half a dozen gathered by the time they were standing silent at the human sacrifice heiau that overlooked Waimea Bay.

Significant breaks were a dime a dozen on the North Shore, but as you came around to the windward side of the island you had to stretch the definition a little to include *wahi pana*, storied places, places of spiritual or personal significance. 'Like finding a sincere pumpkin patch,' was the way Star explained the mental process of choosing them, though indeed the only excuse for stopping at Malaekahana was to pick up Connelly.

Kahana Bay had no waves, but it was high on sincerity, and the convoy of woodies, pick-ups, vans and beetles paused here to send offerings and ambivalent thoughts to the waves and surfers of California. Makapuu, famed for body-surfing and broken necks was propitiated energetically. Sandy Beach was not sincere, and they passed it without stopping. Then there was a long drive around to Honolulu, to Kaluhuwele, First Break under Diamond Head. Here a descendent of the priestly clan who once manned the heiau was there to show them how to do it: Hoku Manono, the singer.

He had started his career as the son of the better known Abraham Manono, but since his father's death he had grown to be more famous in his own right, establishing his own style of contemporary Hawaiian music, and attracting an audience of younger, local people. He had inherited his father's *mana* and his father's belly but had respectfully allowed the 'tourist thing' to float out to sea with the older man's ashes. He did not call 'You and me in the Spray' the 'Hawaiian War Chant'. Auntie Lydia had died, but Leimomi had inherited her *mana*, and as often as not she was in the audience, keeping a ferocious eye on Hoku's cultural integrity.

The surf pilgrims found him standing barefoot in the midst of many fans on 'Dog Beach', in a flowing white shirt, a rosebud haku lei on his head, *maile* fragrant around his neck. He spoke to them about Makahiki, the ancient Hawaiian New Year, in which the Akua Lono made his way around the islands, receiving the gifts of the children of the land; he chanted, long and sonorously, and he took over the office of presenting the gifts for the rest of the day. Pale orange *ilima* leis sent out here at the foot of Leahi, and again later at Pearl Harbor, for the royal house of the sharks. Roses and pikake jasmine for various human royalties at Waikiki, a whole yellowfin tuna thrown from the lethal rocks of Panic Point, meant for the necromantic *akua* Ku-waha-ilo, devoured by the sharks that hung out there. Then, nearly twenty carloads strong, the procession continued around to the Ewa side of the island, many sacrifices at Makaha, and from Yokohama, *sake* poured out to flow to the earthquake zone around Japan, where the great tsunamis come from.

It was at Queen's Surf, the only stretch of Waikiki that was anything like sincere enough for them, that Connelly noticed Hal in the midst of a crowd of young people who had wandered over to see what the action was. He looked away, not wanting to push himself, but Hal had seen him, and came over, and greeted him warmly, and apologized for not having visited him lately. When Connelly explained the Atherton Makahiki, he thought it was really cool, and he and as many of his friends as could fit in the Kalani Surfari van joined the pilgrimage.

Most of them dropped out around Pearl Harbor, after which it was going to be heavy finding their ways back to Manoa by bus or lift, and by the time they got to fearsome Nanakuli, Moke City, Hal was Connelly's only passenger. He had so much to tell his mentor, about his roommates and his classes, his professors and his new friends. He was taking Japanese language, and Professor Sugimoto had told him he had a genuine gift for calligraphy; she had never known a haole to learn it so well in just one semester. But most of all he was getting involved in politics. He was on five committees! 'Wow,' said Connelly. 'That's a lot for a freshman. In just one semester, too. It must be a gift, like the calligraphy.' He noted that Hal was talking to him again in the old way, and wondered whether it was just a case of time easing the shock.

After the prolonged ceremonies at Makaha, stage-managed by Hoku to time with the drop of the *ilima*-coloured sun, everyone sat on the sand for an evening meal. Star had spent the previous day making picnic food, and Keala had accessed the leftovers of an unsuccessful huli-huli chicken sale (and many who partook of them vomited that night), and Hoku and Leimomi contributed several grocery bags of pupus; there were two ice chests of beer in the back of the Kalani Surfari van, and Thor supplied the drugs. It was only at this time that Hoku's attention was freed to wander over the company; Connelly he knew was there of course, but for the first time he noticed the boy in his company. 'Ho!' he exclaimed, in melting tones, 'da sweet!' He went over and obliged Connelly to present him. Connelly was predictably reluctant, but the 'son of a friend' had heard of him, and was very sweet indeed. Their talk was curtailed by the fading of the twilight. Hoku was far too culturally authentic to stay near the coast, so near to ... that Place, after dark. Keala gave him a lift back to town.

At last the pilgrims dragged themselves up, and the convoy made weaving process up the last stretch of the road that led to Kaena Point. VWs were soon abandoned to the terrain, people got out and walked, big cars bounced a bit further, Mark Gonsalves' Toyota pick-up got the farthest, but was stranded irretrievably when Thor's big Chevy truck avalanched a piece of the road behind it, and only escaped disaster by fast backtracking. Hal, a little drunk and a little stoned, walked by Connelly in the falling darkness and told him confidingly about his adventures exploring inner space. 'It was really *important* for me to drop acid,' he explained. 'Because I had this polarity, you know, craziness on one side and sanity on the other, and you had to keep as far as you could on the right side, you know? But it's like, you know, looking at the world, what could be crazier than the sanity side, you know, nukes and napalm and all that, but still being too scared to kind of take the step that would turn them inside out.'

'Because of your father?'

'Yeah! That's right!' he exclaimed, obviously making the connection for the first time, but then letting it go to race ahead with the story. Connelly would have liked to bring him back: it was a good interpretation, he thought, it deserved chewing over, and anyway, he would have liked to know more about Hal's perception of Tiger's craziness, and less about what happened when Hal finally screwed himself up to swallow the microdot. But Allen overheard him describing the discovery that crazy and sane were the same thing, and that he contained them both in himself, and he joined them with the opinion that dualities always resolved into the One in the end.

This kind of talk always brought out a grumpy Thomism in Connelly. Hal was unable to compete, or even to follow the short hand of the two old sparring partners; he found himself falling into step with Star, and it was to her that he confided the furthest reaches of his inner explorations. There were other psychological polarities, like 'male' and 'female' – or maybe, more accurately, heterosexual and um . . .

There was a magic about Star, and she radiated it at Allen and Alex, and the (ridiculously *male*) philosophical argument faded and died as they approached the spiritual extreme of the island. They walked as a foursome in silence, feeling the division of the wind on their faces, listening for the breaking apart of the two voices of the surf: sonorous North Shore singing from his belly, stealing in to harmonize with the haunting leeward waves, who sang with the sobbing rasp of Hoku Manono at the top of his tenor range. Foam shone blue in the moonlight, and without conscious decision the foursome divided into unifiable opposites: the Athertons, male and female; Connelly and Hal. Hal's shoulder kept bumping disingenuously into Connelly's; their arms kept brushing. Allen and Star settled down to nest in the sand, whispering and laughing, but at the jumping-off place Connelly halted. He took Hal's face in his two hands and pulled it forward to kiss him angrily. Then he dropped his hands to the boy's shoulders, set him firmly an arm's length away, turned, and walked swiftly down the Ewa coast, alone.

On one of his shopping trips to Laie, Connelly looked in to say hello to his PO Box and discovered that it contained a telegram. Oh my.

ARRIVING 1600 UA175 FEB 17 TIGER

The seventeenth...that was tomorrow! No, that was today!! Panic took hold of him, he forgot his shopping, raced home, realized he had no food in the icebox, went back and bought two steaks, raced home again, ran around looking for a decent shirt, remembered he'd given them all to Goodwill two years ago, ran around looking for a *clean* shirt, finding a pair of jeans whose narrow lower leg showed how long it had been since he'd worn them. No point in even looking for shoes, he knew they weren't there. It was only when he was urging his van through the central plain of the island that he emerged from the frantic state of mind to wonder what he was so afraid of, or rather, to wonder what on earth had induced Sterling to come out here, out of the blue like this.

He had not seen or spoken to Tiger on the phone since he'd left Reno to go to Carmel, and although he'd written a long and honest letter since, explaining why he had left the monastery and so on, Sterling's reply had been brief: 'Dear Connelly, My father died a couple of weeks ago, and there's not much I feel I can say at the moment. Yours, Tiger.' After that, nothing but the usual Christmas cards and change of address notes. Connelly eventually concluded that this wasn't just sulking about the moral lecture that had concluded their last meeting. After seven years of silence from someone, you just had to accept that he didn't strongly want to be friends any more. So why was he coming now, without so much as a letter of explanation, only a telegram? Obviously it had been a sudden decision, 'something impulsive' as Tiger himself would describe it.

Suddenly the likely reason for the impulse presented itself to his mind. Hal must have written and told him... everything. He braked automatically – the car behind swerved around him, horn blasting – no way was he going to meet him at the airport if that was the case! He pulled over onto the dirt roadside, waiting for his heart to stop beating so fast before he turned around and made for home.

He could almost picture the letter, three long paragraphs about taking acid, and realizing craziness and sanity were equal, too breathlessly enthusiastic to sound patronizing or give offence even to a certified lunatic, and then the final killer about resolving the polarity of sexuality and kissing Connelly on the beach at night. He only wondered whether Hal would assume that his father already knew about him. No, he was more likely to *inform* him about it, in exactly the way he had informed Connelly that Tiger was mentally ill.

Connelly covered his face with his palms, and gave a little whimpering laugh of despair. 'He'll *kill* me!' he bleated. It made no sense at all that when he started driving again he did not turn around, but went all the way to the airport. The sense of doom did not leave him, but he was propelled by a motive force of curiosity, as one who in the slow motion moments of early shock sees instant death approaching, and thinks, Well, at least I'm going to find out what it's like, and what comes after.

As he walked out to the gate, the contingency plan of denying everything and blaming Hal kept presenting itself to his mind, though time and again he rejected it as ignoble. Say the kiss was intended as a fatherly thing (Hal's always been the son I never had) and he misinterpreted it! That wasn't so far from the truth. And truthfully, nothing *had* happened!

No. No, he had to do this right, and defending himself like that was giving away territory unnecessarily. In the first place, it was best to avoid scenes in public, so he would refuse to discuss anything until they were in the car. Then he would say... what? 'This is the way I am. You don't like it? Tough shit. I did not seduce your son, but even if I did, he's an adult and it's none of your business.' There it was, simple. Absolutely perfect, except that there was no chance he'd be able to carry it off, barring supernatural intervention by an angel in a Gatsby suit. The old sweetheart better come quick, though; here were the first class passengers coming through the gate.

The old man from Greenwich Village did not arrive. For the longest time, Tiger did not appear either, and then, after a space in which no one was coming out of the tunnel, and just as Connelly was about to wilt with disappointed relief, an old lady was wheeled out in a wheelchair, and a last half dozen passengers who had been blocked behind her followed, and one of them was Sterling.

Sterling had shaved the beard he'd been growing since he'd been laid off from his Christmas job at the Desert Inn, but he was otherwise embedded in his usual unemployed 'backwoodsman' persona: the Levis, the Pendleton shirt, carrying Dad's patched sailing oilskin as protection against that tropical rain. The first sight of Connelly's shocked face pleased him perversely. No doubt he was expecting the snazzy, rat-packish muck-raker of seven years ago. Well, things were kind of different now.

As he got closer, and his eyes focused a little better, he was put through a similar sense of dislocation. Connelly's hair was almost as long as Hal's! Maybe this should have been predictable – always the kid among grown-ups – only, he just wasn't a kid any more. His skin was like creased leather, brown, thick and wrinkled, the pinpoint freckles puddling into liver spots over his brows and cheekbones, and something terribly sad was written into his eyes. Tiger was struck with pity, and postponed his plan of going directly onto the warpath. He would make his point, but later, and more gently. For now he squeezed one hand and grabbed the opposite shoulder. 'Connelly! How are you?'

'Uh – fine!' Connelly exclaimed, suddenly breaking past that sadness to smile and say, 'Good to see you, Sterling.' And then there was a long spell where neither could think of anything interesting or important to talk about.

At the baggage claim Sterling suddenly remembered to say, 'I've got a room reserved at the Holiday Inn.'

'Well, you shouldn't have. Stay with me.'

'That's good of you,' he said seriously. Then, 'Here come my cases, those grey ones.'

Sterling travelled heavy, and Connelly re-wrenched the chronically inflamed rotator cuff of his right shoulder swinging his third suitcase off the carousel. 'Jesus! How long are you staying?' he cried, stung by pain into rudeness.

'As long as it takes.'

Warily, 'As long as what takes?'

'We'll talk about it later,' Tiger said, with a kind of quiet firmness Connelly had never seen in him before. Maybe he didn't want a public scene either. He picked up the suitcase with his good arm and led him out to the van.

Meeting before, in Reno and in Washington, there hadn't been enough time for all the things they had to say to each other – Tiger saying most of it, of course. Now they drove in silence through the grimy stretch of warehouses, pineapple canneries and car sale lots between Pearl Harbor and Honolulu. An overhanging road sign announced the turnoff for Fort Shafter in large white letters, but Sterling said nothing. At the last minute, Connelly swerved lanes to take it, and drove up the hill, stopping just before the sentry box. The guard inside cracked his knuckles in anticipation of a beef: long-haired beach bums in sandblasted vans did not get onto army territory easily. Connelly said, 'There it is. Historic site.'

'That's not... Tripler?' Tiger gasped at the desecration. 'They've painted it pink!'

'It was always pink.'

Sterling shook his head. 'It can't have been.'

'Believe me, it was.'

'I may have been out for the count when they brought me in, but...' Then, abruptly, looking at Connelly, 'Are you really telling me about yourself?'

His solar plexus dropped about six inches with shock, and his guts writhed in protest. Here it came. Repressing an instinct to duck, he unlocked his throat to allow a rush of air into the vacuum of his chest, sucked in his stomach muscles and braced himself back against the driver's seat. 'What on earth are you talking about?'

'You've been a fellow traveller all along, haven't you?'

He choked. The air rushed out of him again, and he flopped forwards, deflated. 'What?'

'It's why you had to leave Washington, wasn't it? That Pollack at the Los Alamos Place, I met him at a committee hearing after you'd gone and he told me.'

'He said I was a fellow traveller?'

'Oh, nothing so clear-cut, but I read between the lines. I should have cottoned on earlier, you making your getaway just a month before the HUAC subpoena-ed the foundation.' He smiled, as if the memory amused him, then folded it up tenderly and put it in a drawer, to say, with that strange new authority, 'That's why I'm here now. You're a bad influence on Hal. I'm asking you as a friend to stop seeing him for a while, till he settles down a little.'

'I don't see him. I've seen him once since he first came.'

'That's not the impression that you'd get from his letters.

Politics, protest marches – and Connelly and co. Barbara and Art have been concerned for a while. The last straw was this Japanese girlfriend. They were going to come out here themselves, but I persuaded them that I could do it more diplomatically. They paid my airfare.'

'You hear the funny noise I'm making? It's what I call my hysterical laugh of despair. Why is the Japanese girlfriend my fault? I didn't even know about her. And what's wrong with having a Japanese girlfriend anyway?'

'I know,' Sterling admitted. 'I'm kind of in a bind with that. I had a girl in Japan myself. But I hadn't told Barbara at the time, and it's late for confessions now. Anyway, I know what you mean, but I can also see how Sedlachek feels. He fought in the Pacific theatre.'

'But the girl didn't.'

'I hope not, or we'd be having to worry about Hal's eyesight on top of everything else.'

As they laughed (the deflation of Connelly's anxieties made him find it funnier than it was) a first faint glow of the old electricity began to warm the air. 'I know you probably think we're getting overexcited about nothing, and Hal's just doing what every normal American kid does nowadays. But don't underrate your influence. You've got everything that's cool in his eyes, not just you but your whole crowd, these famous surfers and singers, just that much older for him to look up to, just dangerous enough to be glamorous. I know exactly how he feels, I'm a fool that way myself, it's the same as the fascination I used to have with the Mob scene.'

'Gee thanks. Who've you just compared me to?' Connelly tried to sound offended. He should have been offended about the whole thing, but he wasn't. Was it because he was secretly flattered by this tribute to his influence with Hal? Maybe, but there was something else deeper and harder to get hold of. He felt... what? grateful? to Sterling for ordering him off, backing him up in his resolve. Hm. He started the car up and hauled it through a U-turn, to the bitter disappointment of the sentry.

'As a matter of fact, I have been keeping away from Hal. I haven't seen him since New Year's Day. I don't mind promising to keep away from him for as long as you like. Is that enough for you?'

'Thank you. It's nothing personal. You know that.'

'So whaddaya want? You were going to stay as long as it took, and it hasn't taken very long. You want to catch the next flight back, or you want to string it along and make the most of the free holiday?'

'If it's all right with you. I wanted to talk to Hal too.'

So this... this was where he lived. The escape plan, after all. Tiger imagined a *Coral Island* existence, fishing and living on the coconuts and breadfruit that grew in the front yard, scavenging the beach for supplies. He stood in the bare windblown room, gazing out of the window to the sea.

There was a ledge around the walls a foot down from the ceiling, but Connelly's manitous were green and blue glass globes that had floated to his feet from across half an ocean. 'I'll... go stretch my legs,' he said. Connelly heard that he wanted to be alone and did not follow him out onto the beach.

After his father had died, Joe and Mary had insisted the Tahoe place be sold: it was too valuable as real estate to be wasted on an indigent brother. He had moved to Las Vegas, where his face was not known and casinos would still hire him. Dad's old cabin had been knocked down for a California millionaire's redwood A-frame, and maybe it was easier to accept it was just gone for ever than to think of somebody else living there, or to live with the impossible dream of some day making enough money to buy it back.

He was surprised to see that the beach curved for a mile, and was utterly deserted. Other houses dotted its length, but they were set back in vegetation, long needled singing pines, a shrub that looked like it belonged in a desert, with its scrubby, desiccated branches and round succulent leaves. There was quite a wind whipping in from the sea, carrying a smell of salt that was almost the smell of blood. The sand was thick grained and a very warm yellow colour. Tiger walked until sand forced him out of his shoes. At the water's edge he automatically stooped for a round, flat pebble, then realized you couldn't skim stones on water that was so ungraspable, so alive.

Acceptance of loss. The last defeat had sobered him to the stillness of a Tahoe cove, sheltered even from the wakes of power yachts. Here a fat, mouthy breaker hijacked its retreating forerunner and surged up the steep berm, soaking his ankles and jeans in warm foam before he could skip backwards. Impossible dreams? But hope hurt so much, and he didn't know what he was hoping for.

There was a sense of great heaviness, a premonition of hard work and difficulty, as he picked up his shoes and trudged back up to the house.

'Wash 'em!'

'What?'

'The *sand*. It's why I keep a hose by the door.'

Sterling ducked guiltily and backed out, rinsed the sand very carefully from between every toe, then hung around, shifting from foot to foot, shaking the drips off and wishing the wind would hurry up and dry them. Age was not softening the waspish edge of Connelly's temper.

He called, semi-apologetically, 'I don't mind if you come in wet, it's just the sand. I go barefoot all the time, and it's horrible.'

'Sorry.' He came in, leaving wet footprints, studded with grass clippings and segments of ironwood pine needles, but no sand. Connelly was at the kitchen counter, stabbing meat tenderizer into a couple of supermarket steaks. The only place to sit was the big square bed in the corner, and he took cautious possession of it, experimenting with different positions and different arrangements of the pillows and bolsters. The only really comfortable way to take it was to recline with your shoulders only slightly raised, like a Victorian invalid on a *chaise longue*.

He shut his eyes and tried to relax into it, unsuccessfully. Maybe the problem wasn't the bedding but the unspokenness that was going on. What was eating Connelly? If he was sore about being asked to back off from Hal, why didn't he just say so, and they could fight it out, like they used to fight things out in the old days, no holds barred. Or was it something else? He jumped up and joined Connelly in the kitchen. 'You haven't told me what went wrong, why you left the monastery.'

'I did tell you. I *wrote* you.'

'You did not. Or it got lost in the mail. So which was it, missing the sex or deciding you didn't believe in God after all?'

'Neither. Jesus! I missed not being able to have a beer whenever I felt like it more than sex. I still believe in God, it's just that after six months of trying I wasn't any closer to losing my ego, let alone meeting Him, and finally a very wise person called Sister Anne made me realize it's no good trying to do things St John's way, or even Tiger Sterling's way, if your way is different. And that my real mistake had been abandoning the one way God really had communicated with me: the waves.'

He could still remember the moment, and it wasn't something he could tell Sterling. Sister Anne had accused him of working backwards, trying to start from the goal. No wonder he wasn't getting anywhere! He had defended himself with the image of a maze in a kid's puzzle book. 'Tom, Dick, and Harry are at the zoo. They all want to see the tiger. Which one gets there?' If you want, Connelly had said, you can trace each of their paths until you find the right one, but if you're smart, you just work backwards from the tiger. It was out of his mouth before he realized what he was saying, and he had to face that his whole 'vocation' had been a piece of self-delusion. He didn't want Jesus, he wanted somebody else.

The funny thing was, after admitting that, even before he had completed the Descent of Mount Carmel and picked up the pieces with the Pacific Ocean – no, he couldn't go into that with Sterling either, and anyway, he still cried whenever he thought about it.

He had been standing there staring past Tiger into the middle distance. Now he shook himself, washed the raw meat slime off his hands, and got a couple of cans of the local beer Primo from the icebox. They went out to sit in the front yard, where it was sheltered from the wind. The sun was just notching down behind the ridge of the inland mountain, and a last orange ray stretched like an arm, brushing the upper leaves of the breadfruit tree and resting a golden hand on the roof of the little house. 'That's it, really,' Connelly told him, sitting in the grass. 'I came back. I couldn't go back to teaching, but this new oceanological research station opened – the Los Alamos of the Cetacean Brain, to you – and I got a job giving psychometric tests to *Tursiops truncatus* and *Steno bredanensis*. Which was interesting, but they weren't very understanding employers. I mean, my bosses, not the dolphins. You see, most Island companies understand the trade-off: if you want all the benefits and kudos of having a big wave surfer on your books, you accept that he's going to phone in sick now and then in the winter, and you turn a blind eye to the newspaper photographs that prove he was wiping out at Makaha instead of lying in bed with double pneumonia. But the project manager was from California, they had a real work ethic problem there.

'So I started my own little thing, taking people on surf tours. I don't make much, but hell, I'm 42, time's worth more than money.'

'I'm with you all the way on that one.'

Connelly looked at him cautiously. It was so unlike Tiger to have given him the floor for so long. Even now, with the story finished, he seemed in no hurry to grab the mike. Something painful or embarrassing there, he guessed: Hal's words about mental illness came back to him. Only it was funny, whatever it was that was different about Sterling now, he could swear it had to do with strength, not weakness. The way he'd been in the car: quiet authority was the only way you could describe it. Connelly stole a look at him now. He was tracing the outline of the Primo Hawaiian warrior in the condensation on the beer can, and thinking. Suddenly Connelly exclaimed, 'You're not treating me like a shrink any more!'

He grinned, semi-privately. 'That's right.'

Sterling wanted to see what meeting God looked like, and so, despite an unpromising surf report on KPOI, Connelly loaded the beer chest and the longest board in the back of the van and made Sterling smear Tanya on every exposed inch of winter white skin. 'You're going to be hot in those woollens,' he warned him. But Sterling refused to borrow any of the clothes he offered. He had observed Connelly shirtless, and had noticed that the line he had once credited to English tailoring, curving outwards from his shoulders, then twisting inwards again to the small of the back, was still there. His body preserved what his face had lost, the unself-conscious genial swagger, that 'let's have fun' look that had troubled Sterling so much that first morning in Tripler. Tiger had instantly promised himself he would not take off his own shirt in Connelly's presence, and that when he got home he'd start a religious programme of sit-ups and push-ups.

They went to Sunset Beach. The Athertons and Thor were there, but they were sitting in the sand, staring out to sea in resigned melancholy. 'Mush' and 'crap' they characterized what seemed to Sterling to be beautiful and impressive mountains of water. Connelly nodded and sat down.

Sterling followed suit, asking, 'Aren't you going to surf?'

'Can't. See how the top of the wave, where it's breaking, it just sort of... splutches over? Ideally, it makes an arc, and then travels along the length of the wave in a circular plunge. This is the surf equivalent of premature ejaculation.'

Thor squinted at the obvious mainlander. 'You work for *Sports Illustrated*?' he demanded suspiciously. 'Don't quote him on that. We got enough bad press already.'

Before Sterling could ask for an explanation to this koan, Connelly re-directed the conversation, asking Allen, 'You looked anywhere else?'

'Haleiwa, nada. Waimea hasn't even gotten out of bed yet. Pipe's closed out.'

'*Impotence*,' Thor translated to Sterling. 'But that's strictly off the record.'

'Low water's in 45 minutes,' Allen said. 'I'm just hanging on to see if that helps.'

Connelly weighed that slim possibility against the likelihood that Thor would mention homosexuality, latent or otherwise, if they waited long enough. 'Nah. Tiger, let's go. I'll show you around the island.'

'Whoo!' yelped Thor. Connelly ran for the van.

'Wait,' said Star, getting up and walking with Sterling. 'You're Hal's dad, aren't you?'

'That's right.' Her perceptiveness was maybe a little surprising, but not nearly as confusing as the behaviour of the others.

She gifted him with her astral smile. 'Connelly's a special case, you know. Things that would be immoral for other people would be OK for him, because at a deep level he's for others, not himself.'

He was wrong. She was the most confusing of them all. 'How do you mean?'

'It's like the way he's got no right to be a big-wave surfer. He's too old, he's too little, he started too late, he didn't grow up in the islands or even in California. But the waves like him and he gets away with it. I like that. It makes me feel the ocean is deciding who surfs and who doesn't. Don't worry about Hal.'

Sterling was too unnerved to say anything to Connelly about this. All he managed was, 'Those the people Hal was writing about?'

'Probably.'

'Is it drugs that makes them like that?'

'*Thor is permanently on mescaline*,' Connelly said savagely.

They drove to Honolulu down the central plain. Connelly

showed him the pineapple, the sugar cane, the chainlink fence around Fort Shafter ('*From Here to Eternity*,' Tiger nodded, remembering). They were allowed into Pearl Harbor, but the lines to get on the launch that took you to see the Arizona memorial were too long. It was a hot and frustrating day, glary and headaching even in the green valley of Manoa where the university was sited. Predictably, Hal was not in his dorm: his roommate told them that he was at a meeting.

The old HUAC cold warrior snooped around his son's bookshelves, looking for *The Communist Manifesto* and the little red *Sayings* of the chairman but not finding them (Hal had taken them to the committee meeting). Connelly gazed at the long strip of soft paper, covered in elegantly brushed characters, and indicated it to Sterling. 'Yeah, he made that,' said the roommate.

Tiger helped himself to a piece of Hal's typing paper and left the message that he was staying with Connelly and hoped to see him. As they trooped out and down the dormitory stair, Connelly said, 'You don't need to worry about him, you know.'

Sterling repressed a desire to ask why everyone on the Island was saying this to him today. 'Hey, I screwed up my life at his age without half the resources he has at his disposal, you know?'

'Maybe. But then Hal wouldn't exist, and we'd never have met, if you hadn't, so was it really such a fuck up? And Hal... Hal's gonna be fine. The thing with politics is just his way of making a difference. Even if he tries drugs, they're not going to do him any harm. He's already got a good bridge to the unconscious, a bad trip's not going to throw him into something he can't cope with; he's so mentally healthy it's sickening, believe me. And as for the Japanese girlfriend, well, if it was my son, I'd be proud about that.'

'On an ideal plane I agree, but really speaking... I mean, no offence, but what happened to you with the hula dancer...'

'That kind of thing can happen to anyone. And Hal's much

more, how would you say it?, *culturally sensitive* than I was.'

Tiger smiled. 'Those calligraphy things were good, weren't they? I'm going to ask him to do one for me.'

By the time they got home Sterling was so hot, and so oppressed by the smell of his own sweat that he reneged on his promise not to undress and stepped into the warm water of Malaekahana Bay for the first time. Alternately bouncing over and ducking under the surges until he felt dizzy and intoxicated, he called over to Connelly, 'What would that red-headed man say about these waves?'

'These aren't waves, they're jailbait.'

In the earliest shallows, the breaking waves churned up golden clouds of sand. Other patches were dark with seaweed. Tiger fought his way through to a space of clear water, blue and comparatively calm. A school of thin silver fish hovered there, but darted away at his presence. He launched himself after them as hopelessly as a twelve-year-old going after an imaginary trout. He felt the weight and length of his own arms as they stretched and fought forwards, the water spoke to him of his own strength. An approaching wave called him forwards, he accelerated effortlessly, got hit in the face by a splutch of cum-coloured foam, and for all his adult power was shunted back to where he had started. He stood up, laughing and choking. The silver fish zigzagged up, observed him, shot away again.

The next morning he discovered Connelly's old fishing rod in the utility room that housed the surfboards, and he went casting up and down along the shore, until he had caught half a dozen of his silvery acquaintances. Connelly called them *papi'o* (he didn't know their English name) and said they were edible.

Sterling realized he was enacting the escape plan, and something inside bid him follow it through, though his host was inclined to laugh at him. So he cut out a circular turf from the front lawn for a firepit, and scavenged driftwood from the beach and leftover charcoal from the neighbours' barbecues. He scrambled up the *ulu* tree and knocked the largest and ripest-looking breadfruit to the ground with an old broom handle, wrapping it in foil to roast it. Then he got to work on a fallen coconut with a clawfoot hammer and screwdriver, while Connelly made ethnological observations to an imaginary audience. Then a rogue wave of jet lag caught him and he fell asleep under the palm tree.

Connelly woke him half an hour later. 'The breadfruit's burning and so are you.'

There was indeed a tight hot feeling on his face, and over the skin of his shins and ankles. He sat up and pincered the blackened foil bundle out of the embers with a couple of green sticks. Then he beachcombed the neighbours' barbecue grill and cooked the *papi'o*. He hadn't made much progress unwrapping the coconut; that would have to wait for supper. He welcomed Connelly to his feast, and couldn't resist moralizing a little about the decadence of living out of supermarkets, when with hard work and a little patience you could live off the land. But he had to admit that the breadfruit was only really edible with the butter and sour cream that the tide had washed into Connelly's icebox.

He decided that the Hawaiian Warrior Beer was also allowed, and brought it out. 'Now,' he said, giving a bottle to Connelly, 'we're going to drink this, and you're going to tell me what's eating you.'

'What do you mean?'

'You've been holding me at arm's length since I came. And something's different, I can't put my finger on it. You've changed.'

'*I've* changed? What about you? And I would actually like to know what happened about your job on the paper and your friends in the Mob. Are you afraid I'm going to laugh at you or say I told you so or something? Don't you know me better than that?'

'No, it's just the thing about turning you into a shrink.'

'OK. But what about a friend?'

Sterling rolled the cool sides of the beer bottle against the tight burnt skin over the top of his foot. 'See, I've put a lot of work into clearing things up, and I feel like I've finally got my soul to a quiet place. I really don't want to lose that. I don't have any objection to telling you, but I was hoping to keep the focus off myself, for a change, this time. And, you know, Connelly, I feel like I know you, but I don't actually know much about you. You're quite a self-contained little character.'

The crazy possibility of saying something about himself crossed Connelly's mind fleetingly. After all, if Sterling really had cleared up that transference or whatever it was... To give himself time to consider, he asked Sterling to 'get the casino story out of the way.' But when the narrative was drawing to a close, he had come to the decision that it wasn't fair to knock Sterling's soul out of its quiet place. I'll tell him more about the spiritual stuff instead, he decided.

Sterling was postscripting the story. 'Last year, Rico's house burnt down, and they found his body chained up to a pillar inside it. The paper actually got in touch with me and asked me if I'd like to do an investigative number on it. They obviously thought I was the only person crazy enough to do it.'

'You didn't, did you?'

'I was very tempted,' he admitted. 'I thought maybe he'd staged his own death; the body was the kind of mess that it could have been anyone. But then they got a definite identification from the dental records, and I knew there was someone unpleasant out there who wasn't likely to have any Man of Honor inhibitions about killing an honest journalist. I mean, imagine doing that to poor Rico, after what he'd been through on the *Midway*. That took some kind of sadism.'

Connelly was just about to congratulate him on having cured himself of his Death Wish, when the crunch of tyres onto sand warned him of approaching visitors. It was a white Mustang convertible, piloted one-handedly by a big relaxed Hawaiian with long, windblown curls: Hoku in all his glory.

Next to him was Hal. It was over. Connelly looked at Sterling and said goodbye to him in his heart.

Hoku looked at them, and saw, or sensed, something which made his back stiffen. He got out of the car with slow dignity, and crossed the yard with all of Oscar Wilde and a twist of Auntie Lydia in his bearing. Sterling's eyes were going back and forth between the grand figure and his son. 'Oh, *no*,' he said in a whisper that was almost a sob. 'Oh, *poor Hal*.'

Hal looked, on the contrary, rather pleased with himself. Wasn't it nice of Hoku to give him a lift all the way up here? He greeted his father casually, Connelly with more warmth, and, oblivious to the shock on one face and the distress on the other, he bounced into the house to get changed for the body-surfing.

Auntie Lydia was still standing there, waiting for a proper introduction to be made, eyeing Sterling with an expression of politely suspended dislike. Connelly presented the 'old friend of mine' to the 'singer you've obviously heard about' then said, rather desperately, 'Hoku, would you excuse us for a moment? I need to... explain something here.'

He curled a lip. 'Perhaps I should go.'

'No, no, please. Let's go inside, I'll get you a drink...'

He sounded so desperate that Hoku's heart had to relent. 'I'll go check out the beach,' he announced and departed, with appalling dignity. Connelly sat down again, next to Sterling.

'Why didn't you tell me?' he asked, in some anguish. 'Why run round with all this pretext of the Japanese girlfriend?'

'It's not Hal. At least, I don't think so. It's me. Hoku is the person you used to think of as "my hula dancer".'

It had taken him a long time to process this information, or at least it seemed long to Connelly. Events, remarks – *Tony's!* – and what Bronsky had said, all had to be shifted around in his head, an entire history re-mapped. And even when he understood, there was a spell of some five minutes in which he could only sit there in a paralysis of fury, which the words he finally found did little to express. 'How could you?'

'It's not something you can help.'

Tiger stood up, delivered a barefooted placekick to the coconut, driving it over the hedges into next door's yard. Hal and Hoku, watching through the screen door, jumped back and scattered as he headed into the house. He did not speak to them, just went around the room getting his things together and shoving them into the suitcases.

He was packed by the time Connelly crept in, looking puffy-faced, as if he had been punched out. 'You're going?'

Sterling nodded.

Hal, finally catching on to what had happened, tried to tell his father that people had to be accepted for what they were, that we all have these polarities inside us...

'This is about dishonesty, Hal. About lies, and worse than lies, going back over years.'

Connelly bent his head. It couldn't be denied. It couldn't even be apologized for. All he could do was offer, 'Do you want me to go up to the phone in Kahuku and see if there's any free flights out tonight?'

'Take me straight to the airport. I'll wait there until I get something.'

Connelly drove in silence until they came to the plain of sun-baked red dirt, ugly with the sharp foliage of pineapples. Suddenly he pulled over, turning down a plantation track next to an irrigation ditch. He rolled down his window to let in some air. 'Tiger, at least allow me to explain it from my side, why it was so impossible to tell you.'

He kept his eyes straight ahead, fixed on the blue distance of the Ko'olaus. 'It can't have been impossible, but you might as well have your say.'

'It was impossible in Tripler — you'll grant me that? I mean, you were a patient, you had no right to that information, I didn't know I was going to see you again. And you were very fragile mentally.'

'Fine. I'll give you Tripler,' he said, with an air of astonishment that so small a concession could matter.

'And Washington. You know what it was like, in those days –'

'No! Not Washington. Not after Tony's. I can forgive cowardice, Connelly, but not what you did there. You stuck the blame on me, and hit me for it, and just left it there for fifteen years, all the time knowing it was really you.'

'Christ.' Connelly could feel his face growing hot. 'But . . . I didn't realize you'd taken it to heart like that. There wasn't anything to show that you'd taken any notice of what I'd said.'

'Not the nervous breakdown I had immediately afterwards?'

Connelly was silent for a long time, then said, 'Sorry.'

Sterling gestured at the ignition. 'Get going. I'll miss the plane.'

He reached for it obediently, then pulled his hand back. 'No, wait. If I had told you about myself, say that night I brought Hal home from New York, when I was going to, but chickened out, what would have happened?'

'I don't know. Maybe I'd have felt entitled to hit you back. But at least I wouldn't have been the one carrying the can for . . .'

Connelly leaned forward as if he was poised to jump on something. 'Yes. *That's* what I want to know. Carrying the can for *what*?' There was a new, fierce note in his voice.

'I don't know what you mean.'

'You do so. You damn well do.'

'OK, but I don't know how to describe it, what words to use.'

'Chemistry between us.'

A sharp intake of breath. Then, 'You want to hear me admit that, huh?'

'Only if it's true,' Connelly shrugged. 'You're as free as the next man (just like you were in that bar in Washington) to say, "No, sorry, that doesn't apply to me."'

'I don't know what difference it makes. It's not something I'd ever act on.'

Connelly leaned back in his seat. A faint breeze, whistling through the pineapple spikes and rattling the sheets of black plastic ground cover, came through the window to breathe in his ear. 'This something you'd never act on, this thing you've been carrying for fifteen years... we've had some pretty long and intense conversations in our time, but somehow I just don't recall you've ever mentioned anything like that, even in the middle of the nervous breakdown.'

Sterling turned to look at him for the first time. 'What are you getting at?'

'Just that it's not always easy to tell the truth, you know?'

Back at the beachhouse Hoku's car was gone, but when Connelly kicked open the door he saw Hal on the bed, reading *The Teachings of Don Juan*. 'Hoku said I better stay in case you were upset – oh...' his voice fell as he saw his father step in.

'Hah,' said Tiger, dropping the luggage and going straight out to the beach.

'What's happening?' cried Hal, jumping up. 'Why's he back?'

'Beats me,' said Connelly, shelling open a bottle of Primo. 'But let's give him credit for it, OK?' He put his arm around Hal's shoulder and drew him out the sliding doors to the shore. Tiger was below them, ankle deep in the water, whipping small stones and pieces of coral into the breakers, one after another. They stood at the crown of the sand and waited quietly until he turned and started making his way back with a sigh that could be heard over the breathing of the waves.

Sterling's glow-in-the-dark watch said 12.30. 'I can't sleep, can you?' It was an unnecessary question; the other body in the bed had been restless, with the particular cover-stealing twist of someone being extra careful to keep at arm's length while tossing and turning.

'No.'

'I'm going for a walk, want to come?'

'Yeah, OK.'

Sterling pulled on his jeans and windbreaker, while Connelly just wrapped up in the fluffier of the two blankets. They stepped over Hal's body on the camp bed, tried to push the sliding doors open silently. Outside, they were far from city lights and the sky was pulsing with packed stars. You could count six and sometimes seven of the Pleiades.

They walked heavyfooted through the sliding dry sand near the berm: in the dark it was the only place you could be sure of avoiding the stinging blue jellyfish stranded by the tide. After a while Tiger said, 'I've been thinking. I should never have let that word "chemistry" pass.'

Connelly made a shrugging noise. 'Whatever. Don't run away with the idea that I'm trying to score points by making you admit you're a pansy or something. You're not, and I am, and maybe that's just the end of it.'

'The end of what?' Sterling demanded, turning Connelly's earlier tactics on him.

'Chemistry's the only word I know for it.'

'What's wrong with "friendship"?' Tiger wanted to know.

'Nothing, but I meant that extra spark, the electricity which for my part anyway was erotic,' he spoke this fast, and low, 'but it's not going to be acted on, so that's the end of it.'

Sterling frowned, pressing his hands down hard into his jacket pockets as he paced along. 'The end of the friendship?' he asked at last.

'No! But the end of the dishonest thing, the kicks you get when you're pretending there's nothing going on.'

The breeze-bent pines and singing palms stood out as jagged black silhouettes on the point. Sterling felt terribly sad, one of those ancient bleaknesses, so sudden it stopped him physically and pushed him back several steps. It arrived with pictures: a nuke-tested Nevada landscape, scrapped cars, Bakelite ashtrays. His voice would come out shaky with tears he knew, but the prophetic spirit of the Psyche Ward smoke room was rising and wanted to speak through him. 'You used to spend all day with me in that room in Tripler. It didn't matter if I was treating you like shit or crying like a baby. If you're going to tell me now that was just smut then yes I am getting the next plane home if I have to carry my suitcases on foot to the airport. I told you the craziest most sacredest things that happened to me and instead of pathologically exhibiting them in my medical records like everyone else you took them away and tried to put them into practice in a goddamn monastery, just in time to keep them alive when I was forgetting them in the grandest and fatheadedest fuck-up of my life. So if you're saying *that* was just erotic chemistry then allow me to punch your stupid head in until you learn some self-respect. And then there were those times I still hate you for when you knew just where to find the lies I was telling myself and spat in the soup: "Is it yourself you're telling me about?" or "If the ego is the prime mover in all this..." (my god were you ever right about that one!) And – ' Oh hell, he was really crying now, but he forced himself to go on, 'If that was... some kind of... dishonest kick...' The imperatives of a sobbing rib cage finally exorcised the smoke room rhetoric, and he dropped onto the sand, hugging his knees. Connelly was right there beside him. 'What *was* it?' he cried. ''Cause I don't know.' He reached up, finding Connelly's face, which was also wet. 'Hey, you're as bad as I am!'

'Of course, stupid,' – but he was laughing too.

'So what *is* it?'

'I don't know, Sterling. Just our own particular brand of honest dishonesty, I guess.'

A couple of weeks after his Dad's return flight, Hal came up to the beach house again, this time with Sherri Yano, who had secured the use of her parents' car. Connelly was at the front of the house half-reclining against the slump of the palm trunk, agonizing over his monthly report to Sister Anne (what a lot there was to tell her!). He jumped up to greet the guests. Sherri had a flat, fox-shaped face, and the simple beauty favoured by Christmas card illustrators when they want to make a point by showing the Madonna and Child as oriental. She did her best to subvert this effect by chewing gum and smoking at the same time; everything in her manner and pidgin speech warned you not to take her for a Cherry Blossom bride. She wore a tiny crocheted bikini top and low-waisted cut-off jeans. 'Howzit,' she just brought herself to say to Connelly, with a disdainful flick of her head and a saliva-amplified click of the tongue.

'Come through, I've got something to show you,' Connelly told them. Stepping into the house they saw it, through the glass doors on the beach side: a twenty-foot wooden boat in a state of disrepair, mounted on a metal trailer.

'Wow!' Hal exclaimed. Then, in dismay, 'You're not retiring from surfing or anything?'

'Nope. She's not mine.' He shoved the sliding doors open, and Hal saw his Dad, crouched on the opposite side, scraping the old paint off her prow.

'Hi, son.'

'Hi. You didn't go?'

'I went and I came back.' He unbent, caught sight of Sherri, and stood up, obviously struck. 'My God, Hal, I was wrong to worry about you,' he said under his breath.

When the introductions were over and the swimsuits changed into they all wandered down to the water. 'So what's happening?' Hal asked.

'I realized this place was as close as I was ever going to get to finding something like Grandpa's old cabin up at the lake,' his father told him. 'And since the landlord is too nice or too dumb to kick me out, I'm here.'

Connelly snorted. Hal looked at him; a crazy possibility flitted across his mind. He looked at his father, and dismissed it. Impossible.